THE STORY OF AN IMMIGRANT IN NOVA SCOTIA AND MANITOBA

THE YOUNG ICELANDER

JÓHANN MAGNÚS BJARNASON

TRANSLATION OF *EIRÍKUR HANSSON* FROM THE ICELANDIC

BY BORGA JAKOBSON

FORMAC PUBLISHING COMPANY LIMITED

Copyright 2009 © Formac Publishing Company Limited

Formac Publishing Company Limited recognizes the support of the Province of Nova Scotia through the Department of Tourism, Culture and Heritage. We acknowledge the financial support of the Government of Canada through the Book Publishing Industry Development Program (BPIDP) for our publishing activities. Formac Publishing Company Limited acknowledges the support of the Canada Council for the Arts for our publishing program.

NOVA SCOTIA
NOUVELLE-ÉCOSSE
Tourism, Culture and Heritage
Tourisme, Culture et Patrimoine

The Canada Council | Le Conseil des Arts
for the Arts | du Canada

FSC

Recycled
Supporting responsible use
of forest resources
www.fsc.org Cert no. SGS-COC-003153
© 1996 Forest Stewardship Council

Library and Archives Canada Cataloguing in Publication

Bjarnason, Jóhann Magnús, 1866-1945
The young Icelander : the story of an immigrant in Nova Scotia and Manitoba / Jóhann Magnús Bjarnason; translated by Borga Jakobson; introduction by Birna Bjarnadóttir.
Translation of: Eiríkur Hansson.
ISBN 978-0-88780-869-2
1. Icelanders—Nova Scotia—Fiction. 2. Immigrants—Nova Scotia—Fiction. 3. Icelanders—Manitoba—Fiction. 4. Immigrants—Manitoba—Fiction. I. Jacobson, Borga II. Title. III.
PS8453.J37E3713 2009   C839'.6934   C2009-904000-X

Formac Publishing Company Limited
5502 Atlantic Street
Halifax, Nova Scotia
B3H 1G4
www.formac.ca

Printed and bound in Canada

Publishing history of the original work in Icelandic

First Edition
Book I, Copenhagen, 1899
Book II, Akureyri, Iceland, 1902
Book III, Akureyri, Iceland, 1903

Second Edition
Books I-III, Reykjavik, 1949-1950

Third Edition
Books I-III, Akureyri, 1973
Edited by Jakob O. Petursson
Publisher Björn Jonsson

Fourth Edition
Books I-III, 2009

CONTENTS

In memory of Jóhann Magnús Bjarnason and
the pioneers who were his friends and neighbors

— B.J.

TRANSLATOR'S ACKNOWLEDGEMENTS

I thank members of my family for help with this undertaking and for their patience overall.

I thank David Gislason for his translation of Eiríkur's poem.

I thank Dr. Birna Bjarnadóttir, Chair, Icelandic Department, University of Manitoba for her advice, insight, and kindness.

— B.J.

PRONUNCIATION GUIDE

á as ow in owl
é as ye in yet
í as ee in seen
ý as ee in seen
ó as o in hole
ú as oo in wood
æ as i in high
ö similar to u in under
þ as th in breathe
ð as th in breath
ei (and ey) as ey in they
au similar to the vowel in her or in purr

TRANSLATOR'S NOTES

Eiríkur Hansson: A Novel from Nova Scotia, by Jóhann Magnús Bjarnason, was published in three parts in 1899, 1902 and 1903, in Icelandic.

In an epilogue in the 1902 edition of *Eiríkur Hansson, Book II,* Magnús mentions that the narrative was already laid out in the winter of 1895. That would have been twenty years after he left Iceland and he would have been about the same age as Eiríkur is when that character writes his story. The epilogue was reprinted in the 1973 edition of Ritsafn.

In the epilogue Magnús makes it clear that he has not intended to disparage any man or woman and that he had no particular person in mind when he described the appearance or the personality of Mrs. Patrick, Dr. Braddon, Mrs. Flanagan, Mr. Sprat or any other character in the story.

In a letter to his friend Eyjólfur S. Guðmundsson (dated March 28, 1930) Magnús says, "I have never thought that my stories were great literature . . . I have hoped that people would realize why they were written and that they are fiction rather than actual events."

In the original, each chapter is enhanced at the beginning with a couplet or a few lines of verse. To the Icelandic reader of that time these lines would call to mind a familiar longer poem. Any attempted translation of these verses would not produce the same effect, so they are not included here except for a couple of lines by the well-known Stephan G. Stephansson, at the beginning of Chapter I.

Readers may wonder when Amma says that they set sail in the eighteenth week of summer. According to the Old Icelandic Calendar *Sumardagurinn fyrsti* (the first day of summer) is celebrated on the first Thursday after April 18th (the 19th to 25th), so the eighteenth week would fall in the middle of August. Iceland is an Arctic country, and by June 21st people are enjoying almost twenty-four hours of daylight.

The Markland Icelanders moved from Nova Scotia in 1882, as mentioned in the novel. Some moved to Manitoba, some to North Dakota. About five years later Eiríkur moved further west, to the North West Territories, probably to present-day Saskatchewan. By this time the railway had been built, land was readily available and grain was already being shipped from that area. Saskatchewan and Alberta did not become provinces until 1905, some years after the novel was written.

PREFACE
Birna Bjarnadóttir

A young man stands in front of what seems to be a settler's house, surrounded by children. There is a look of determination on his face, and his gaze is full of anticipation. The sense of belonging is inescapable: this is his place, these are his children.

The young man in the photograph is the son of Icelandic immigrants who left Iceland for Canada in 1875. The white painted building is a small Icelandic school in the Geysir district of Manitoba, and the children are his pupils. It must be around the end of the nineteenth century or the beginning of the twentieth, and he has already established himself as a teacher to these children, whom he may understand better than most others in this vast country. He is, like them, a child of immigrants, carrying the wound of departure kept fresh by the rift that separates him from others. At the same time, he believes in the children and their future, knowing in his heart that life must be taken as it comes; that they, as they become adults in this land of plenty, have everything to win, and nothing to lose. Those who speak his language are already familiar with his rich perception of their condition, for by the time the photograph was taken he was not only an exceptional teacher but also a writer of poems, plays, short stories, fairy tales and articles. He was soon to become known as a novelist and, eventually, as a writer like no other in Icelandic literature.

The young man is Jóhann Magnús Bjarnason (1866–1945). Given his place in the history of Icelandic literature on both sides of the Atlantic Ocean, the publication of Borga Jakobson´s English translation of his novel *Eiríkur Hansson* is nothing short of a cultural event. As Borga Jakobson notes, Magnús was not someone to promote his stories as "great literature." In his humble and sincere manner, though, he did express his hope that "people would realize why they were written and that they are fiction rather than actual events." This is an important point, particularly in *Eiríkur Hansson*. Its realistic style seduced (and still seduces) some readers to view the subject matter as being closer to lived experiences than to fictional reality, prompting them to read the novel as a story of Magnús's life, as autobiography rather than fiction. However, like some of the masterpieces of realism and neo-romanticism, Magnús's novel is a *Bildungsroman*. Set in Nova Scotia at the end of the nineteenth century, *Eiríkur Hansson* is a story of one character's life that becomes a timeless reflection of specific historical, cultural and personal circumstances. What sets this novel apart from all others in the genre is the protagonist's cultural roots: an Icelandic boy, motherless, landed with his grandparents in the oceanic vastness of North America. While the novel evokes the artful style of Dickens, Kafka's *Amerika* also comes to mind. In addition to Magnús's careful evocation of the vulnerabilities of the ever-hopeful human heart in seemingly heartless circumstances, the novel brims with the poetics of immigration, striking a creative balance between the trials and the wonders of an immigrant's life.

The novel is divided into three parts: "Childhood," "The Struggle," and "Aspirations." The first part takes the reader back to Iceland and the first years of Eiríkur Hansson's life. The reader follows his departure from his country, seven years old, with his grandparents. The year is 1875 and the emigrants' destination is "Nova Scotia, in a country called Canada, which was a part of America." (*Book I, p. 22*) If it were not for the Icelandic–English dictionary Eiríkur's grandfather brings with him, the journey into the land of a foreign language, of a different kind of people and of far from familiar circumstances would have been even rougher than the stormy weather on the Atlantic Ocean. The sailing vessel *Maria* takes them safely to England, where they board the steamship *Columbus* for New York. The trip from England to New York takes nineteen days, introducing the young Icelandic boy to things he would never forget, one of them being a death of a sailor and a sea burial:

"We watched as his body was lowered ever so slowly down to the deep, dark ocean. The waves closed over the body and the wind smoothed the eddy that formed where it sank, smoothed all so there was nothing left to mark the place where he disappeared. Rán, the mighty goddess of the sea, took him into her keep." (*Book I, p. 27*)

From New York they travel onward, first on a ship and then on a steam carriage, the latter being something they had never seen and could not have imagined:

"There were rows of benches along the entire length of the hall. We sat down there and waited to see what would happen next. All of a sudden we heard a loud horn like the horn of a steamship. At the same moment we realized that the hall we were sitting in was moving. We moved slowly at first and then faster and faster." (*Book I, p. 28*)

They finally arrive in Halifax, "cold and hungry, without funds or words, in a strange country," (*Book I, p. 32*) but soon join their fellow countrymen in the Mooseland hills, an Icelandic settlement about fifty miles east from the city of Halifax, with the ocean only twelve miles to the southeast, and the beautiful Musquodoboit Valley to the west. The Icelanders name their home Markland.

The part of Magnús's novel describing the Icelandic settlement in Markland is based on historical facts. This provides the reader with a singular opportunity to explore in some detail a chapter in Canadian history, from the soil under the feet of the late nineteenth-century Icelandic immigrants to their high hopes in a new country. Simultaneously, the author's depiction of life-sized characters and circumstances capture the reader's attention. While many of the novel's characters are of a beautifully generous nature, others appear as signs of either bad luck or ill fate. Those cherished and loved provide the young boy with the strength to persevere, whereas others are a reminder of life's less pleasant elements. One mark of a profound writer, however, is that his characters are not too clear cut. In fact, when it comes to someone like Cracknell, the boy's teacher in the Icelandic settlement's schoolhouse provided by the government of Nova Scotia, the reader needs to pause. Despite the obvious shortcomings of this somewhat eccentric mentor (due in part to his teaching methods, which will later be questioned), there is more to the man. When reflecting many years later on his first teacher, Eiríkur not only admires the teacher's ability to teach the children much more than he was expected to, but also realizes: "He was not gentle but he was not a bad person. His flaws were many but they were outnumbered by his good qualities." (*Book I, p. 46*) Another character from the novel's first part is, if anything, more adventurous. In Mrs. Patrick, the wealthy widow, the author has a character of even greater scope in the spectacle of human nature.

When our protagonist finds himself moved into the spacious house of Mrs. Patrick, in a village close by the sea about twenty miles from Markland, Eiríkur is eleven years old and is experiencing the hardship of pioneer life. After the death of his grandfather, his aging grandmother has not been able to manage the farm and he has been torn away from her. While feeling and understanding the boy's grief, the reader clings to the hope of a good life for him in his new surroundings. However, true to the uncertainty that underlies the young, vulnerable protagonist, the author introduces what seems like a watershed moment: arriving from painful and heartbreaking poverty and entering, we think, a life of plenty, Eiríkur finds himself faced with the insensitive, almost theatrical behavior of an unstable character. How to reconcile the old with the new — a former life that was full of sorrow, yet blessed with good-hearted people — with this seemingly flawed and unpredictable bounty? This much is certain: Mrs. Patrick is no trivial matter. But those words, "no trivial matter," could well describe the story of Eiríkur Hansson, the boy who arrives from an unindustrialized country and crosses the threshold of modernity. From the introduction of Mrs. Patrick onward, the reader sees intensely how the winds blow from one chapter in Eiríkur's life to another; from Mrs. Patrick to other colourful characters, from rural Markland to the city of Halifax, from sad acquaintances to life-savers, from the end of Eiríkur's childhood into further struggle and challenges, and eventually, out into the open, gleaming field of deeply felt aspirations.

Who was Jóhann Magnús Bjarnason, this gifted young man in the photograph, surrounded by children?

Although Magnús's reputation as a writer grew steadily in his lifetime, as he was widely read and published in Winnipeg, Iceland and Copenhagen, there is only one other book by Magnús available in English: *Errand Boy in the Mooseland Hills*, a collection of short stories, also translated by Borga Jakobson. This may seem a strange fate for a writer of this quality, someone who at the beginning of the twentieth century was being written about in literary journals in places like Leibniz and Weimar, places that had long been at the cultural heart of Europe. But even if a man writes from a language region that no roadmap recognizes, a region bereft of highways, the literary seeds find soil. Halldór Laxness (1902–98), the recipient of the Nobel Prize for literature in 1955, was still a boy when he had read everything available by Magnús. He acknowledged decades later the profound effect these readings had had, and how he viewed Magnús as one of the best writers of Icelandic literature. Stephan G. Stephansson, too, was impressed by the writer in question, and more explicitly, by *Eiríkur Hansson*. In a letter to the author dated April 13, 1902, Stephansson foresees a prosperous future for the novel, and feels that it will serve as a definitive reflection of settlements in North America, expanding the boundaries of Icelandic literature.

Jóhann Magnús Bjarnason might indeed be the writer *par excellence* for expanding the boundaries of Icelandic literature, and that for several reasons. Unlike his fellow writers back home, he was immersed in two literary traditions: the Saga heritage (from the German-Scandinavian tradition), and the Anglo-Saxon heritage. He was nine years old when he left Iceland with his parents and migrated to Canada in 1875, thus spending part of his childhood and his formative years absorbing a "foreign" literature that gradually became his own. Like most of the Icelandic children arriving with their parents in the wave of the great emigration from Europe in the latter part of the nineteenth century, Magnús was not showered with educational opportunities. Despite a discontinuous education, he did attend a public school in Nova Scotia, and later a high school in Winnipeg (from 1886 to 1887 only), and then he not only graduated as a teacher from the Collegiate Institute in Winnipeg, but he taught himself to travel in those parts of world literature that were out of the reach of most Icelandic writers. Charles Dickens became a favorite of his, not to mention Thackeray, Irving and, in particular, Robert Louis Stevenson.

The result of these two literary traditions' coming together is important. As the following lines indicate, quoted from a letter Magnús wrote to his friend Eyjólfur S. Guðmundsson, dated October 7–9, 1930, here discussing the special fondness he has for Dickens's *David Copperfield*, the writer himself is fully aware of the challenge:

"[Dickens] is such a sincere and kindhearted spokesman for the underdogs and paupers that one has to forgive him for the abundance of words. In this sense, he is far from being Nordic in style, which expresses much in only a few words. In fact, the Nordic style is not mastered by many. Other than Snorri Sturluson and the authors of Njal's saga and Egil's saga, we have only the other authors of the Icelandic Sagas." One might well attend closely to these words. When writers reflect upon other writers, particularly those close to their hearts, they may be revealing things about themselves that some of the most qualified critics of literature tend to overlook. When interpreting the unique literary style of Magnús's novels, some have indeed accused him of using too many words, and of expressing too openly the softer side of the emotional spectrum, as if he were not Nordic enough. Again, the writer himself may be the best one to explain what he is up to (also quoted from a letter to the same friend Guðmundsson, dated January 24, 1931): "I do not care much for the literary movement now prevailing in novel writing in the Nordic countries. In order for me to feel otherwise, I would have to shake off the influence I experienced in my formative years, from the English 'Victorian' novelists."

Jóhann Magnús Bjarnason was a native speaker of Icelandic, a child of Iceland, and he wrote in Icelandic. Still, unlike most other Icelandic writers at the time, he left his native shore and became a citizen of a much bigger country in a faraway continent, acquiring thereby an opportunity not only to combine, as a writer, the two literary traditions mentioned, but to grow and mature differently.

As might be expected, his views on literature, and his preferences in world literature, cannot be separated from his personal circumstances. A passionate reader of Icelandic literature, well versed in the majestically compressed and emotionally enigmatic saga style, he also admired other kinds of books — books like *Alhambra* by Irving, and that for its open display of "pureness, kindness and beauty." His outlook and view of life are no less significant, for in this extraordinary writer we encounter a rare human being, characterized by a profound belief in the possibilities of kindness and beauty. Nowhere, some say, does the reader get closer to the essence of this man's fiction than in his fairy tales. According to Richard Beck, who was no stranger to Magnús's life and literature, the fairy tales are more original and their style more refined than anything else he wrote, resulting in no other Icelandic writer of fairy tales being able to compete with him on that front.

The fairy tale, indeed, was beloved by romantic writers and poets in the eighteenth and the nineteenth centuries. Is Magnús perhaps a romantic writer at heart, even at times one in the style that has been referred to as *new romanticism*? In this context, another farm boy from Iceland comes to mind, who like Magnús sailed from home in the nineteenth century and dived deep into urban culture. Like Magnús, he could not shake off his belief in the possibilities of kindness and beauty — so much so, that shortly before his premature death in Copenhagen, ridden by exile, poverty, broken dreams and haunting memories of unfulfilled loves, he composed what many think is the most beautiful poem ever written in Icelandic, *Ferðalok*, or "Journey's End." This is the poet Jónas Hallgrímsson (1807–45), who, along with a few of his friends, introduced romanticism into Icelandic literature. He also wrote spellbinding fairy tales and fragments. The reader of *Eiríkur Hansson* will notice the pervading presence of this romantic poet. Of all the books the young protagonist would never dream of departing from, we have the New Testament and a book of poems by Jónas Hallgrímsson. In the novel, at a watershed moment in the matters of love and belonging, there is a subtle homage to the exiled poet Hallgrímsson and to the singular depth of romantic literature — a reminder of how far from simple is this novel's narrative style.

In his lifetime, Magnús did enjoy both blessings and good fortune. He was happily married to Guðrún Hjörleifsdóttir, and much loved as a teacher. As a writer, he experienced significant recognition in his lifetime on both sides of the water. His health was never good, though, and he and his wife may not have experienced too many days without financial worries. They could never afford a trip back home. The young man in the photograph thus shares a thing or two with his protagonist, one of them being an unquenchable longing for the country they left in childhood. There is a word for this longing in Icelandic that no translator has been able to convey in English. It is *heimþrá*, and its meaning rests on a powerful amalgamation of the words "home" and "desire." The Germans have *Heimweh*, a word that is somewhat related to the Icelandic *heimþrá*, but the German involves a twist of explicit pain. When severe, *heimþrá* can in fact cause considerable pain, a condition well known among the Icelandic settlers in North America and their children; in some cases it is incurable.

This is how Eiríkur Hansson, the protagonist, describes his *heimþrá* at the very beginning of his story, revealing its vicious and illogical effect on the fragile and the vulnerable, yet also the sense of singular beauty it creates:

"For some reason I do not remember storms or blizzards or earthquakes. I do not remember ice floes, or lava fields or barren hills or stretches of hard-frozen snow or tracts of land strewn with large boulders or anything that suggests the harshness of nature. I can think of Iceland only as a land of beauty and happiness, because I saw it with the eyes of a child. I saw only the bright side of Iceland, the beauty of summer, the majesty of the mountains. And now, after twenty-two years, that picture, with all its beauty, is as bright and clear in my mind as if I had sailed away from Iceland's shores just yesterday. When I view the boundless prairie of the Northwest Territories there is nothing that holds my eye. I am filled with an unquenchable longing to be at home, at home in the place of my childhood, in that land that all Icelanders should be proud to call their homeland, to be at home, yes, to be home to see Iceland again, even for a moment, and to die! I know that my circumstances would not be as comfortable there as they can be here. The yearning to return to my birthplace is quite apart from the desire to earn a reasonable living." (*Book I, p. 9*)

The drama of the novel unfolds in the eyes and the heart of a child; in the *simplicity of vision,* to borrow a title from another book, written about the ancient Plotinus, who was another master of perception. Jóhann Magnús Bjarnason introduced a new style to Icelandic literature by allowing himself to express a child's perspective on the most subtle and dramatic subjects, introducing thereby the spirit of the fairy tale into a story full of life's hard facts. The reader of this novel will connect to this style all way through, this bridge connecting the land of dreams with the sometimes harsh realities of the life of a young immigrant on his way to manhood.

A little more than a century ago, Stephan G. Stephansson may have been right in predicting a prosperous future for this novel. On his journey, in becoming a man, protagonist Eiríkur Hansson cannot but carry a few cultural seeds with him from Iceland to Nova Scotia and beyond, thus naturally enriching the soil of his new country. Simultaneously, his story inspires the reader to reflect upon the eternal question of belonging, and to realize that the immigrant might be the most accurate vehicle there is for such a reflection.

BOOK I
CHILDHOOD

CHAPTER 1

Svo ertu, Ísland, í eðli mitt fest,
að einungis gröfin oss skilur.
[Iceland, it is only the grave that can set us apart.]

— Stephan G. Stephansson

Since I am going to tell a story about my life, this story begins in
Iceland. Actually, I can't tell you very much about Iceland because
I was only seven years old when I left my country. Most people
agree that we remember only a few incidents from the first seven
years of our lives. Still, our recollections from those years remain the
clearest of all our memories — whether the incidents themselves
were happy or otherwise. My memories from those early years seem
now so pleasant and bright, so strangely pleasant and bright, and
there is nothing distasteful or ugly. When I think about the place
where I spent my first years (Fljótsdal district) it seems to me that
it must be the most beautiful place under the sun and Iceland must
be the most fascinating country on earth. I see the river we called
Lagarfljót flow gently through a broad and impressive valley, its
waters sparkling like silver in the sunshine. I see rows of farmsteads
on either side of the valley. I see bright-green homefields and pas-
tures full of spring flowers. I see flocks of sheep on the slopes. All
around there is grandeur, beauty and wonderful light. I carry with

me clear and pleasant memories of crags and fells, moors and marshes, stony hills and ridges. I can almost hear the sound of rippling water, of birdsong and summer breeze. From high up in the mountain comes the shepherd's call.

For some reason I do not remember storms or blizzards or earthquakes. I do not remember ice floes, or lava fields or barren hills or stretches of hard-frozen snow or tracts of land strewn with large boulders or anything that suggests the harshness of nature. I can think of Iceland only as a land of beauty and happiness, because I saw it with the eyes of a child. I saw only the bright side of Iceland, the beauty of summer, the majesty of the mountains. And now, after twenty-two years, that picture, with all its beauty, is as bright and clear in my mind as if I had sailed away from Iceland's shores just yesterday. When I view the boundless prairie of the Northwest Territories there is nothing that holds my eye. I am filled with an unquenchable longing to be at home, at home in the place of my childhood, in that land that all Icelanders should be proud to call their homeland, to be at home, yes, to be home, to see Iceland again, even for a moment, and to die there!

I know that my circumstances would not be as comfortable there as they can be here. The yearning to return to my birthplace is quite apart from the desire to earn a reasonable living.

Now I will review what I can remember of my life in Iceland.

It is all like a disjointed dream. Some of the incidents are clear, but others are so vague that I am almost afraid that they are my own ideas. The only things that are really clear in my mind are the places where the incidents happened.

From my earliest memories I was with Amma and Afi, my mother's parents. I was told that my mother died when I was barely two years old. Whether I spent some time with my father after she died or whether he gave up their home and left me right away I do not know. I never asked about it. I do not remember my father at all. I was told that he was a big man. He had a black beard that reached down to his chest, and black eyebrows that lowered in a scowl when he was displeased. He had dark eyes that could take on a piercing look under certain circumstances. I was also told that my father had gone to America two years before I left and that he had settled first in Wisconsin in the United States of America but that he had later been seen in California, in the same United States. He had remarried. His wife, a woman of Danish descent, spent more than he could earn. It was rumoured that he was going to sail to Australia. Whether these reports about my father are true or not true, I can't say because he has never inquired about me — or, at least, I have never received any word from him.

My Amma's face is the first face that I remember, and hers is the dearest of all the faces I have known, with the exception of one. Amma was a woman of medium height and she was rather stout. She had strong features, rather plain, but her expression showed unyielding steadfastness which immediately called for respect. Her blue eyes and her arched eyebrows showed sensitivity and kindness. She always held her head high. She had definite ideas about right and wrong and she was strict in that regard. She looked straight into people's eyes when she talked to them. It was always hard to look into her eyes whenever I had done anything that I was not supposed to do. I felt that Amma could read my thoughts if I ever tried to hide anything from her. I always had to tell her the truth. Whenever I was troubled or unhappy her eyes were full of sympathy and encouragement. When I look back as far as memory can take me, Amma was always a guardian angel hovering over me. What I first remember about her are her blue eyes and the cap she wore with its decorated tassel. I wanted to play with that tassel whenever I could reach it. When I was little I cried if Amma was out of sight. I felt that it was my right to have her always with me. When I saw her return I stopped crying and I was laughing while the tears were still running down my cheeks.

In memory time passes quickly. Now I am much bigger. I am

running in and out of the house and out in the front yard. The farm-
stead consists of three buildings connected to each other, with
timbered gables facing the river. The middle section has a high gable
with a weather vane up at the top. On windy days that weather vane
makes a loud noise. We enter the house through a door in the middle section and a long narrow hallway takes us into the kitchen. In
the kitchen there is a hearth; over the hearth there is a wide chimney. From an overhead beam hangs a heavy chain with a hook,
which holds the cooking pot. There is smoke in the kitchen and
that makes my eyes smart. From the roof hang pieces of meat. In
one corner is the quern or hand mill that the hired girl uses to grind
the rye.

From the kitchen I can go into the pantry, or *búr*[1]: in the pantry
there are large casks and troughs and tubs and shelves that hold various containers for cheese and butter, sausage and *skyr*[2] and other
supplies. And in the pantry Amma dishes up the food at mealtime.

Another door opens off the hallway. This is the door to the guest
room. I rarely have a chance to enter there. I am aware of a table
and a big chair and a made-up bed. Sometimes there are men in
that room and then I can't go in there. Then I cover my head and
run down the hall and fall and hurt myself. I don't dare to make a
sound. Just across from the door to the guest room there is a long
narrow and dark hallway that leads to the *baðstofa*[3], but the
baðstofa is up in the loft. Under the loft there is a space that is in
total darkness. I am afraid of that darkness and even more afraid of
the cows that are sometimes kept in there. A stairway leads up onto
the baðstofa platform. I often fall when I am going up those stairs.
I hurry too much because I always think that someone will grab my
feet. I am sure that this someone is always under the stairs when I
am climbing by myself. I am always safe when Amma or another
person is with me.

The baðstofa is a big room. There are several beds, end to end,
on either side of the room. There are windows on one side of the

room, but my bed is not under a window. I am sorry that my bed is not under a window because I think it would be fun to stand up in the bed and look out to see the homefield and the sheep sheds. The others will not allow me to stand upon their beds to look out their windows. Things are not always the same in the baðstofa. Sometimes this room is empty and at other times there is someone sitting on every bed. Sometimes there is a lighted lamp hanging in the middle of the room. This lamp seems to require a great deal of attention. Often, during the winter months, there are several spinning wheels whirring away at once. I like the sound of spinning in the evenings. That sound helps me to go to sleep. I lean back on Amma's bed and look at the light. After a while I see rays streaming from the light in all directions. One ray comes right into my eyes. The sound of the spinning wheels seems to move farther and farther away, becomes softer and easier to listen to, and soon it disappears into distance and I have gone to sleep.

On other nights there is no spinning. All the people are working with wool. Some people are teasing the wool, some are carding the wool, and some are twisting two threads together to make a stronger yarn. Many people are knitting. On these evenings someone will entertain by telling stories or chanting rhymes. On other evenings they sing, then read, and then sing again. I have to be very quiet during the reading and soon I fall asleep. I wake up when I am being undressed and I realize that all reading and singing is over for that evening.

As I recall these things time passes by quickly, so surprisingly quickly. Suddenly I am running out on the homefield that we call the "*tún*." A little brook runs beside the homefield. I love to play beside that little brook. On long summer nights I am often interrupted from my play and carried, much against my will, into the baðstofa. There I am undressed and put to bed. I soon get out of bed and run around the floor again. I can't see why I am undressed and kept indoors when the sun is still shining. Another time I go out to the homefield and I find that everywhere there are poppies and dandelions. I love the dandelions. I want to call them my own and I pick them. I am more likely to spare the poppies.

I go out to the corrals with Amma. I love the little lambs. I get some vague idea that they are bleating because they can't be with their mothers and I cry in sympathy with them. I don't want Amma to know why I am crying.

Another time I am running around in the hayfield and suddenly I am aware of my grandfather, Afi. He grabs me by the shoulder and orders me to go into the house. I have been tramping down the grass, he says, and spoiling the hay. I have never really paid much attention to Afi before. He is very tall but not heavy. He has a big hat on his head and the brim hangs down. His voice is not gentle. I am afraid of him and I run to Amma.

Things become clearer to me. My field of vision becomes wider. I become aware of other farms in our neighbourhood and many mountains. Soon I begin to notice more and more peaks on those mountains. I think that I would like to climb up a certain peak to hug the beautiful sun. Then all of a sudden the sun disappears behind the peak. The sun's disappearance is beyond my understanding. I tell Amma about this and she smiles kindly and she tells me many things about this glorious sun. I have many toys made from bones, and many ships made from folded paper. Time slips by. I am told that I am six years old. I feel very big now. I stand on tip-toe so I will seem even taller than I really am. People laugh at my antics.

Now I recall my last year in Iceland and that is the year that I remember best. I have reached the age when children have to learn the alphabet and they have to learn to read and spell. I am rather slow to learn, according to the woman who has been asked to teach me. She is old and her face is wrinkled and creased. She is always chewing something. Her name is Jórunn and folks call her Madam Jórunn. I do not like to learn from her. I always feel uncomfortable around her. She always sits on her bed when she is teaching me. She always sits on her bed anyway except of course when she is sleeping. Then she lies on her bed.

She has me stand at attention beside her bed while she puts on her glasses and takes snuff from a tin can with a silver design on the lid. Then she takes a book of sermons for home devotion and she points with a knitting needle to the first letter on the first page that she opens. It is a different page each day. I know that because every page that we have studied before has little brown marks on it from being held under Madam Jórunn's venerable nose. The more time it takes for me to read the more drops fall on each page. While I am sounding the words the old woman has her left arm around my neck and she holds the book in her left hand. The longer it takes me to read the heavier is the yoke around my neck. Otherwise she is not strict with me. Each lesson begins with the words "Spell, child, spell." (This means she wants me to read slowly, sounding letter by letter.) If I do well she says, "Dó, dó, ná, ná." If I am having a difficult time she says, "*Nú, nú*. Remember, little wretch, that the old witch, Grýla, waits to snatch kids who are slow readers." I am relieved when the lesson is over. But that is not all. Madam Jórunn also has the task of combing my hair each day, and while she does that she tells me ghost stories.

I remember well the agony I endured while this was going on. I thought that every hair on my head would be pulled out. I didn't dare complain because I was sure that old Grýla would be hiding under the stairs ready to snatch me and put me into her sack. There were countless stories about Grýla's husband and her children. Madam Jórunn also told me stories about ghosts and apparitions, about the hidden people, about outlaws, giantesses, imps, changelings and sorcerers, all of which had their eyes on naughty children, especially little children with uncombed and tousled hair. I believed all this stuff and was prepared to endure any torments so that I would not be at risk from these unseen creatures. All these stories had a bad effect on me because I became very afraid of the dark and I was afraid of ghosts for years after that. I also remember that Madam Jórunn had little hope for me as far as intelligence was concerned. I overheard her once telling one of the hired girls that it would be impossible to teach me because so far I had not learned the evening prayers and hadn't really memorized anything except the Lord's Prayer and one short set of rhymes. For years I was sure that I was indeed a very poor learner and I worried about that.

There were many people living at the farm besides my grandmother and my grandfather. I do not remember any of them very clearly except Madam Jórunn. I do remember that one of the women who worked there was lame. Another woman was very tall and she smoked a pipe. She slapped me across the face once, with my socks! And then there was the shepherd boy who enjoyed scaring me by telling me ghost stories, and he was always claiming that he could see "hidden folks" in the *fells*[4] behind the farmhouse.

I remember that I was the only child living at the farm. However, there was a woman who often came to visit and she brought with her a boy who was about my age, a boy that I was afraid of because he always wanted to hurt me in one way or another. He would give me a *fillip*[5] on the cheek, on the mouth, on the nose. Once he nearly choked me under a heavy quilt. He threw me into a mud puddle. And he found other ways to torment me.

I remember Christmas Eve, 1874. This turned out to be my last Christmas at home. I always say "at home" when I talk about Iceland. That was a wonderful Christmas Eve.

I am wearing new clothes and I am very proud. I have been given a big candle and a handkerchief. I have raisins and a cookie and a waffle and doughnuts and rice pudding served with white sugar and cinnamon. I laugh and sing as I go around to all the people to show them my new clothes and my candle.

A poor couple and their daughter have come to our house that Christmas Eve. The little girl is probably about six years old, like me. I remember clearly, just as if it happened yesterday, that the little girl starts crying when I am showing the people my new clothes and my candle. She cries because she does not have a candle and she has no new clothes. I understand her feelings. I cry too. I want to give her my candle but her father will not allow her to take it. Then all of a sudden he takes off his vest, turns it inside out and gives it to his little girl to wear. He tells her that she looks very nice when she is dressed up because the vest is really very pretty when it is worn like that. Pretty! Well, the vest was lined with a patchwork of small pieces, yellow and green and red and blue and black and white. That is very pretty, he says. The poor man! He tries his best to make things better in the eyes of his little daughter. The child stops crying and with tears in her eyes she begins to examine the vest which is so pretty when it is turned inside out. Just then Amma comes into the baðstofa. She gives the little girl a candle and a dress which is a little too big for her. Otherwise it suits her well. The girl is happy as she tries on the dress and lights her candle. Her face glows with pleasure. Her mother kisses Amma over and over and says that God will remember her for her kindness. The father also kisses Amma. I see a few big tears roll down his cheeks. I do not understand why he is crying just because my grandmother gives his daughter a candle and a dress. At that time I thought that he should laugh, hop around and dance. But I was a child and I thought that others would have the same feelings as I had myself.

Soon it is Easter time. After this my memories become clearer and more connected.

On the day after Easter the farm was in total darkness until noon. I heard strange sounds coming from far off, and ash fell from the sky. I remember that Afi read the morning prayers by lamplight. All the people were sad and silent. I heard Madam Jórunn say something about Doomsday. I had the feeling that something even more awful than the strange sounds that I heard and the falling ash[6] might be close at hand.

Soon, I realized that my grandparents were preparing for a long journey and I was going to travel with them. The journey would take us to a wonderful place where there was never any falling ash, and no frost or snow. There was always summer there, with birds and beautiful trees, with raisins and figs, coffee and sugar. There would be gold and riches, milk and honey on either hand. There people felt well and had everything that they needed till the end of their days. This wonderland was called America.

Then spring came, the spring after the falling ash, and the poppies and the dandelions began to appear in the homefield. Some plovers were singing, the little lambs were bleating, and the murmur of running water could be heard, the shepherd was calling up in the slopes but everything that Afi owned was being sold so that he would have money to take Amma and me to America. I got a set of clothes done in a new pattern. Amma got new skirts and sweaters and for Afi they sewed trousers and a jacket made from woven cloth. Trunks called *kofforts* were built. The kofforts were painted green and they were fitted with new hinges. Afi's name was painted on each koffort in large black letters. Next they began to pack things into the trunks. They packed clothes and blankets, hymnals and bibles, rusty chisels, saws, knives, drills, planes and various small utensils. Afi and Amma planned to start farming again as soon as they found a place in America.

A few weeks went by while Amma said goodbye to friends and relatives. She had to visit many farms and I was always with her. We spent a few days at some of the farms and we only stopped briefly at some of the other places. I learned the names of many farms at this time and I also learned the names of many fells and hills and peninsulas, rivers and lakes. Ever since then I remember names like Birnufell, Hafrafell, Meðalnes, Miðnes and Mjóanes, and names of rivers like Rangá, Jökulsá, and many other names. Amma had friends or relatives at all these places and all of them tried to deter her from going off to an uncivilized country. I could not understand how this uncivilized land and the wonderland could be one and the same. When we left each one of these homes the lady of the house would see us off. She would embrace Amma and kiss her again and again and she would cry and Amma cried too. Of course I cried with them. Then the lady would help Amma into her saddle and lift me up in front of her. And so it went until Amma had visited all the people that she needed to see before she left her birthplace for the last time.

One day in late summer we left the valley of the Lagarfljót[7] for the last time to begin our journey to America. Two horses carried the kofforts. I rode behind Afi, and Amma rode on a grey horse that seemed to be very nervous. We were accompanied by a man who had been hired to get us to Seyðisfjörð[8], for that was where our ship lay waiting. We travelled over a low mountain which Afi called Vestdalsheið (the west valley heath). I remember that we followed a long valley and crossed many rivers. I remember riding down many steep hills and I well remember the sudden fog that met us at the bottom of one of these hills. We dismounted and I was wrapped in warm blankets. I quickly fell asleep. When I awoke the sun was rising.

We loaded the horses and continued on our way. After a short ride I saw the fjörd. The weather was calm and the water was like a mirror. In the distance I saw the ship as it lay at anchor. I had never seen a ship with masts before. I was intrigued by the sight. The view changed as we followed bends and turns in the path. At one point the ship seemed quite small, and then all of a sudden it seemed so very big. Gradually I got a clearer picture. Finally we rode into the village that was nestled around the head of the fjord. It was exciting to see the marketplace that I had so often heard about. I had associated it mainly with figs and raisins and other unusual treats.

The marketplace at Seyðisfjörð has doubled in size, I have been told, since I was there. However, at that time I found it very impressive. We spent eight or nine days at the home of a man who was called "Vertinn" by everyone in the marketplace. He was a cousin to Afi. This man was very good to me and he said he was sure I would become a wealthy businessman in America. At that time I was ready to believe that.

I enjoyed those days. I ran from place to place and made friends with all the young boys that I met. There were many interesting shops there. One shop was called "Liverpól," another was called "Glasgow," and I think a third was called "Edinborg." There was an interesting pier in front of Liverpól. On the beach were piles of dried fish, which were held in place with big stones. There I saw men who were probably Norwegian and also men who came from the Faroe Islands. These Faroese men wore unusual clothes and because of that I was afraid of them. I got the idea that they were somehow related to the sons of Grýla. Nowadays, of course, I have read about these people and hold them in high regard.

The man in charge of one of the shops gave me a large candy. One of the stores was called "Vertshús" and there the manager's wife kissed me and said that I was a fine-looking boy. I was glad to hear that, and that made me try to look after my appearance. I saw the sheriff, and the sheriff's secretary and the sheriff's dog. And in the village there I saw for the first time a man who was drunk.

Then I saw the little girl who had visited us at Christmastime. I found that her name was Elin. She recognized me right away and she was eager to show me her large collection of seashells. She lived with her parents in a small hut beside the ocean. I saw her father often in the stores. He was often drinking something from a glass. I think now that her father was a chronic drinker although I did not think anything like that at the time. I had no idea what that meant and I had no idea that there might be a connection between drinking and poverty. I remember that I often saw this man in the stores, especially in Liverpól, and I saw him often drinking something from a glass. I heard him say, more than once, to one of the storekeepers, "I am so dry! One more, one more." I thought at the time that he was sick, that his chest was really dry and that the drink was a nourishing drink that he urgently needed.

Once when I was playing outside I noticed a plank that was used as a bridge over a little brook in front of one of the houses. I thought that it would be fun to run across this little bridge. I tried to do that but I soon fell off the plank. Next I sat down in the middle of the bridge and bounced up and down on it. Suddenly it broke. I was very worried because I knew that I had caused serious damage to some man's property and I knew that man would be annoyed. I might be accused and asked to pay the costs. I hurried back to the house where Amma was staying and I did not care to go out any more that day. The next day I heard some kids saying that a bad boy had broken a board that belonged to old Jón and that this old Jón was going to try to find the bad boy to bring him before the sheriff. I was conscience-stricken beyond words. I was sure that old Jón would soon find out that I was the bad boy and then the sheriff would come to get me. More than likely the result would be that I would not be allowed to travel with Afi and Amma when they left to go to America. In that place they would not want anyone who damaged public property. How I hoped that the ship would leave before anyone found out the truth. Old Jón and the sheriff never came but I was in a panic over this until we were well out to sea and I felt sure that no boat could catch up to the ship.

CHAPTER 2

It was in August, in the eighteenth week of summer, so Amma told me later, that we set sail from Seyðisfjörð and left the shores of Iceland. Our ship was a Danish merchant ship called *Maria*. She was a sailing vessel, and she had brought a variety of goods to the Liverpól market in Seyðisfjörð.

Maria was bound for Hull, England, with a cargo of wool and salt fish. We (Afi, Amma and I) were to be dropped off in Hull. We were the only passengers, aside from a young woman named Matthild, who was friendly with the Captain and was travelling with him to Copenhagen.

As I look back I am amazed at my grandfather's courage. He set out on a sea voyage in late summer, in uncertain weather. Both he and Amma were approaching sixty years of age and I was just a little boy. We had no Icelandic companions and no interpreter. Our destination was Nova Scotia, in a country called Canada, which was a part of America.

Afi knew of several Icelandic families who had travelled to Ontario, Canada, in the previous year. He had learned that some of these families were going to move to Nova Scotia in the fall of 1875. He knew that the capital city of Nova Scotia was called Halifax. He thought that all that was necessary was to be able to say the name Halifax, and to have on hand five hundred Danish dollars for travel costs. The fact that he could not manage one word in any language except Icelandic was no big problem because after all he had a copy of the first edition of the Icelandic-English dictionary, which had been prepared by Halldor Briem. Furthermore the sheriff at Seyðisfjörð had given him a letter for the Danish Consul in Hull. And, indeed, both of these things would serve him well. More important than anything that he carried with him, besides his Danish dollars, was his courage.

We went on board ship in the evening. We were immediately sent down into the prow of the ship and there we made ourselves as comfortable as possible in amongst the bags of wool that were to be delivered to England. I will never forget the dampness down there or the stench that was so noticeable as soon as we came down from the deck.

The following morning the anchor was raised. Progress down the fjord was slow because the wind was not in our favour. It was sunset by the time we emerged from the fjord. Amma was already seasick in the morning and I became nauseated as the day went on. Then I asked Afi to take me back to land and give up the idea of going to America. He did not think much of that suggestion. He was never seasick and he never wavered in his resolve. I was sick all night and all the next day and the night after that. Finally I started to feel better. Afi often took me up on the deck and into the captain's cabin. Matthild stayed in the captain's cabin. She never got up from the time we sailed from Iceland until we arrived in England. She stayed in a locked bed-closet beside the cabin door. Whenever I went there Matthild was eating and when she finished eating she brought up what she had eaten and then she drank some water, which was always close at hand, then she laughed; and after that she ate some more, brought up again, drank some more water, and laughed again. But she always stayed in the bed-chamber with the curtain half-drawn. Matthild was probably about eighteen years old, quite pretty, and obviously good-natured. Amma said that Matthild was engaged to the captain but perhaps she only thought that because Matthild was lucky enough to be allowed to stay in the captain's cabin.

We had a crew of four men: the captain, the mate, the deckhand and the cook. The captain was a tall man with a big beard. He was good to us and tried to make us as comfortable as he could during the crossing. The mate was a small man with a black beard, quick in his movements but rather severe in manner. The deckhand was a big man, round-faced, and always smiling. The cook was special to me. He was about seventeen years old, a sturdy fellow, with fair hair and rosy cheeks. He seemed to be a genuinely happy person and he was always very good to me. He gave me treats to eat whenever I was with him in the kitchen. He showed me many drawings of ships and boats. I think these were drawings he had done himself with red and yellow and blue crayons. I felt that I understood what he was telling me and he seemed to understand me completely. It did not seem to matter that I spoke Icelandic and he spoke Danish. I learned that his name was Markus, and since then I have always liked that name. One time I found Markus crying and I thought that the mate must have beaten him. I was always wary of the mate after that. One time I noticed that Markus was limping and one foot was bandaged. I felt sure that he had burned himself when he was boiling beans. No one said anything about that to me, yet I was certain that it was so. From this experience I know that children get ideas about things that happen around them and often they regard these ideas as fact. Children may be unaware of it but these perceptions are based on close attention to life around them. Children are more likely to look for reasons for things that happen than adults are, but less likely to think about the results. But on with the story!

Our ship *Maria* brought us safely to Hull. To be sure, the journey took a full three weeks, but this was partly because the weather was not favourable, partly because the ship was not designed to go very fast.

Hull is a big city, famous for its harbour and for its markets. Of course I knew nothing about that at the time. I stared in disbelief at the huge buildings and the multitude of ships that were gathered there. Some of the ships were so large that *Maria* looked like a little rowboat in comparison. On some of the ships I saw women and children. Some of these children were barefoot, the boys in short pants and the girls in sleeveless dresses. Amma thought that these people were so poor that the parents could not dress their children properly. Here and there on the piers were piles of boxes and bags of every description. People were milling back and forth and horses and wagons came and went. There was screeching and noise all around us. The whole atmosphere of the place was upsetting. At first I felt utterly confused by all the sounds around me and by all the commotion. Gradually all this noise faded into the background somehow and I stopped paying attention to it.

An important-looking man came on board soon after the ship was tied to the pier. He spoke to Afi in Icelandic. His duty was to examine the cargo that the ship had brought from Iceland. Several times I heard him ask Afi whether the wool was fine and whether the salt fish was still in good condition. Then this man helped Afi to find the Danish Consul. It was decided that we would travel to New York on the American steamship *Columbus*. The ship was in harbour and was due to leave for the United States. The Consul helped Afi to make arrangements for this trip. The Consul also wrote a letter which Afi was to present to the Danish Consul resident in New York. Then we were taken to a boarding house, which was located near the pier where the *Columbus* was being fitted for the return journey. As it turned out, the ship would not be ready to leave for another week.

The couple who owned the boarding house were from Norway. All the other guests were Norwegians. Some of them had been to America and were on their way home again. They gave Afi a few glasses of wine which he said was the best wine he had ever tasted. He was sure that they had brought it with them from Vinland the Good. He tried to ask the men about America and he understood them to say that there was much gold to be found over there.

While we waited at the boarding house Afi explored the city and he always took me with him. We saw many interesting sights out on the streets and in the shop windows. Afi often bought apples or pears from barefoot boys or old ladies. There seemed to be innumerable street people and nowhere else have I seen so many fruit sellers. There were times when people thought that we were a little too curious or intrusive. That happened especially when we were looking at flower gardens or workshops. Sometimes we had trouble finding our way back after our travels. As it happened there was a huge statue of a man on horseback on a street corner not far from the boarding house. The statue was so tall that we could see it from far off and it helped us to get our bearings. Afi said that the statue was the largest toy that he had ever seen.

On the day that *Columbus* was ready to leave, our host from the boarding house helped us to get on the ship with our belongings. He ushered us into a grand hall and he solemnly said farewell to us all. The *Columbus* was an impressive steamship. It had two huge smokestacks. There were spacious rooms on the deck, and there were many white boats hanging on the gunwale. I thought these boats were there as a decoration or just as items of interest. The large room we had first entered was actually the dining room. There were rows of tables with benches on either side. Cabins, or bedrooms, were ranged around the outside of this room and we were assigned to one of these. Our cabin contained four small beds, actually two bunk beds. There was one round window, which let in light although the glass was so heavy that one could not see through it. For our meals we sat at table with the other passengers. As far as Afi could determine all of them spoke English. Here our Icelandic-English dictionary was very helpful. Afi kept consulting the dictionary for words that we needed. Ever after Afi treasured that book and said that it had brought us unscathed to Halifax.

We had poor weather and hence a rough crossing over the Atlantic Ocean. The journey from Hull to New York took nineteen days. I remember that for a few days everything was topsy-turvy. Dishes and cutlery were flying around when we were trying to eat. We could hardly keep in our seats. One day our window blew into our room and seawater poured in. The problem was soon fixed but stormy weather continued. One evening one of the mates was brought down into the dining room. He had been hit by something that came loose on the deck while he was working. I remember how shaken we were when we heard his cries. He died soon afterwards. The next day the storm abated. All who were well enough were asked to come up on deck to take part in a service. The body was wrapped in a large flag and placed on boards. We all gathered for a solemn ceremony conducted by the captain. All were very sad and some wept. I remember an old man who cried bitterly. Some thought that he was the father of the dead sailor, who was evidently a young man. We watched as his body was lowered ever so slowly down to the deep, dark ocean. The waves closed over the body and the wind smoothed the eddy that formed where it sank, smoothed all so there was nothing left to mark the place where he disappeared. Rán, the mighty goddess of the sea, took him into her keep. The ship hurried on its way with flags at half-mast.

Finally we saw America, at first just a blue rim on the horizon. Afi looked at this blue rim for a long time and he shouted over and over again, "*Vínland hið Góða. Leifur heppni.*" This is the Icelandic for "Vinland the Good. Leif the Lucky." The passengers who stood nearby laughed out loud and tried to repeat his words.

At last we docked in New York and we were immediately taken to a boarding house operated by a portly Danish gentleman. This man helped Afi to find the Danish Consul. He arranged for tickets that would take us to Halifax, but that purchase cost all the money that Afi had left. The last five dollars were spent on a bag lunch to take with us for the rest of our travels. As it turned out, that was not quite sufficient.

We spent only one night in New York and nothing special happened to us there except that one of the guests who sat down to dinner with us that evening pushed me away from the table. I had taken sugar from the sugar bowl with the spoon that was in my cup. Therefore I had wet the sugar in the bowl. No one else seemed to notice. But if I broke table manners in so doing, then he also broke them by pulling my chair away from the table. At least that is the way I see it now.

We boarded yet another ship in New York, travelled for twenty-four hours, and then we were brought ashore again. I have no idea what that place was called. We were roused from a sound sleep in the middle of the night and taken a short distance in the dark. We were led up two or three steps and into a long narrow hall. There were rows of benches along the entire length of the hall. We sat down there and waited to see what would happen next. All of a sudden we heard a loud horn like the horn of a steamship. At the same moment we realized that the hall we were sitting in was moving. We moved slowly at first and then faster and faster. Soon we were hurtling along at high speed. The light that hung from the ceiling swayed back and forth.

"This is a steam carriage," said Afi. "As I live and breathe, we are travelling in a steam carriage." Amma agreed.

I remember that I found this trip quite interesting and I wondered what kind of animal could pull this wagon so fast. Then all of a sudden we stopped. We were taken on board ship again and we

sailed along the shoreline until evening. Then the ship docked and
we got off with other passengers. We were later told that we were at
that time in Portland, Maine. As it was, we had no idea where we
were. It was getting dark and there was a chill in the air. The lunch
we had brought with us was all eaten by this time and Afi did not
have one coin left. People went back and forth but no one paid any
attention to us. "Have we come all the way? Is this Halifax?" wondered Afi.

Amma said nothing. She pressed her lips together. She was getting a bit worried about the situation. She wrapped her shawl
around me. We waited yet a little while.

"This will never do," said Afi. "I will have to think of something." He went over to a man who was walking by just then.
"Halifax?" said Afi.

"Halifax?" repeated the man.

"Já, Halifax," said Afi, "*til Halifax, íslenzk, sprogum ekki engelsku*[9]
(Icelandic, don't speak English) . . . *til* Halifax."

"Halifax, Halifax," said the man.

"Já, Halifax. Halifax?" said Afi in a questioning tone, as he indicated the houses in the neighbourhood.

Now the man understood what Afi needed. "Hotel. Hotel," he said.

"*Enga peninga,*" said Afi, "*getum ekki borgað.*" (No money, cannot pay.)

The man said something that we did not understand. Then he
motioned to us to follow him, which we did without delay
although we could not see him well in the gloom of the evening.
This man took us to a big house not far from the pier. Afi knew
right away that this was a guest house. We were received by a fat
woman and she showed us into a room with two beds and a small
table. This fat woman smiled sweetly at Amma and talked and
talked to her although Amma did not understand one word of what
she said.

"Halifax, *til* Halifax," said Afi. "*Enga peninga, kunnum ekki engell-*

sk sprog."[9] (Halifax, to Halifax. No money, cannot speak English.)

The fat woman smiled more and more and her face lit up encouragingly. Afi understood her to say that she would like to give Islandsman milk and bread. Soon she brought all kinds of food that Afi and I enjoyed. Amma hardly touched the food. The next morning we were served a generous breakfast. When the meal was over we were shown into a sitting room where several guests had gathered. Many of them were reading newspapers. A man with a badge on his cap was there and he gave us to understand that we were to come with him.

"Ship," he said, "Halifax".

"*Gott, gott,*" said Afi, "*til* Halifax, *til* Halifax."

"Thank you, thank you," said Afi to the fat woman in Icelandic. "Islandsman thanks you for the food and for your hospitality," said Afi. And Afi and Amma both shook hands with the woman to thank her and say goodbye to her.

But the woman wanted more than thanks for her food. "Money, money," she demanded. All her smiles had disappeared. "Money, money," she shouted.

"No money, no money," said poor Afi, who now understood what is meant by hospitality in hotels, and why this woman had seemed so generous. "I cannot pay. I have no money."

"Money, money," she shouted, nearly beside herself with rage. She grabbed at Afi's jacket and searched his pockets. But all she found was Halldor Briem's dictionary, a red handkerchief and a few scraps of paper. Next she indicated that he was to turn out his pants pockets, which he did at once. She found a holder with some keys, and a wallet. The wallet contained only his travel ticket. Then she searched his vest pockets, but they had no money either.

"Money, money!" she shouted, and she grabbed the front of Afi's shirt. He kept trying to make her understand that he had no money but she could not be convinced of that. The dictionary was of no use now. The woman would not look at it, even though she had looked at it the night before. Many people had gathered around us and, judging from their expressions, many seemed to sympathize with us but no one offered to pay the bill for us. The man with the badge on his cap was trying to talk to the woman and to indicate to us that we had to come with him. The woman would not let go of Afi's shirt.

Amma stood aside while all this was taking place. Now she stepped forward. She pulled her wedding ring off her finger and handed it to the woman. The woman let go of Afi's shirt and examined the ring. "Gold! gold!" she whispered to herself, "gold, gold!" She flung herself into a chair and turned the ring around in her hand. "Gold, gold."

Amma never looked more dignified than she did at that moment. Her blue eyes flashed and her voice was full and clear. "Keep it," she said in Icelandic. She was never one for many words, but in this instance it was sufficient to say "Keep it." Her blue eyes said much more, said it in a language that only women fully understand, a language that only women can truly employ.

The man with the badge on his cap led us back to the pier and we got on board ship exactly where we got off the evening before. We spent less than twenty-four hours on this ship. Twice a woman on the ship gave Amma and me tea and some bread. Afi took nothing but water for one and a half days. When we got off the boat we were told to get on a train. This train rushed along at high speed, or so it seemed to me. We hurried along all day and into the night. Finally we heard the name "Halifax" and soon after that the train came to a stop.

"Thanks be to God!" said Afi, "We have come to Halifax." We got off the train. The night was dark. The people who had been travelling with us disappeared immediately and soon the three of us stood alone at the railway station. Once again we found ourselves cold and hungry, without funds or words, in a strange country.

"This will never do," said Afi. "I will go to talk to somebody. You two wait here."

With that he disappeared into the darkness, just as if he knew his way around the city. Amma sat down on the sidewalk with me on her lap, and she wrapped her shawl carefully around me. We sat there quietly and waited for Afi. Soon a man approached us and spoke to us but we did not understand what he said. Then he disappeared. We waited for a long, long time. It must have been hard for Amma but of course she did not say that to me. Finally Afi came back and he had two men with him. These men took us to a house which was near the railway station. We knew that this was not a guest house because it was very small. A woman and two children were there. Right away the woman brought out some food and Afi was made to understand that the food was given to us. We sat down at the table. Afi said that he had never been more in need of food than at that moment. Beds were prepared for us on the floor. One of the two men who brought us to this home disappeared but the other, probably the owner of the house, remained. I fell asleep quickly and woke up to find that three well-dressed men had come into the room and were talking to the man of the house. They were taking notes. Then they tried to talk to Afi, who turned quickly to his dictionary. The three men looked at the book carefully. Next they were checking Afi thoroughly. They checked his height, took his measurement across the shoulders, they checked the muscles in his arms. They looked at his shoes, and his clothes. They made notes. They did not pay as much attention to Amma although they certainly looked her over. Then they noticed me and they checked me as well. One of them patted me on the head and gave me a large apple. Afi was getting concerned over this strange behaviour. In the end they gave Afi a few silver coins. They bowed politely to Amma, shook hands with Afi and prepared to leave. I noticed that one of them was still writing something in his book as they went out the door.

"Those were strange men," said Afi. "What do you suppose this means?"

"I don't know about that," said Amma.

"Do you think they were just having fun?"

"I don't know," said Amma.

"Do you think these men were crazy?" asked Afi.

"I don't know," said Amma.

The next morning we were taken in a covered wagon to a boarding house in the city. Afi was surprised that the owner never approached him for payment while we were there. We learned later that the government of Nova Scotia had paid all costs on our behalf.

We were given a room to ourselves up on the third floor. Our window faced the street and Amma sat at that window, day after day, waiting to see someone in Icelandic dress. Afi was wondering why we were left there without any further word, and why no Icelandic person came to meet us. Before he left Iceland he had understood that there was an Icelandic agent in Halifax and he would be on hand to meet with newcomers when they arrived. With the help of the dictionary he was able to explain to the owner of the boarding house that he needed to see the Icelandic agent or some other man from the Icelandic community. With the help of the dictionary the owner managed to explain to Afi that he would have to wait for seven days. Seven days went by and still there was no message from the agent or any other Icelander. The eighth day arrived and then the ninth. And every day the owner of the house, through the help of the dictionary, said to Afi, "You have to wait." Afi waited. What else could he do?

On the tenth day of the wait Amma, who was always watching out the window, exclaimed, "There is definitely an Icelander crossing the street and he is coming this way." Afi looked out the window but said he could not see any Icelander on the street. A few minutes later a man was brought to our door, and as soon as he entered he said, "*Komið þið blessuð og sæl.*" (This was the traditional Icelandic greeting which means, "Come ye blessed and happy.") I cannot describe our joy when we saw an Icelander and were greeted in our own tongue. What happiness and relief!

This man was one of about twenty farmers who had taken land in the Mooseland settlement that autumn. He said that he had been asked to take us to the settlement and he said that the agent would be coming to see Afi shortly. Sure enough, the agent came later that day. He had not been in the city when we arrived, he said. He had just returned from a long journey. He took us to his house that evening and played the organ for us. He said that he played for all who settled in Mooseland and he always played the music of Mozart.[10]

We set out for the settlement, which was about fifty miles from Halifax. Ten weeks had gone by since we left Seyðisfjörð.

CHAPTER 3

The Icelandic settlement in Nova Scotia was on a range of hills about fifty miles east of the city of Halifax. These hills were heavily forested and difficult to clear. The soil was poor and very rocky. Scattered here and there in the forest were openings covered with coarse grasses, and there were bogs covered with moss. There were also rivers, brooks and ponds with clear, cool, beautiful water. The air was fresh and there were pleasant breezes off the ocean. There it was never very cold in winter and never very hot in summer. The ocean was only twelve miles southeast of the settlement. The shore-line was very jagged and there seemed to be a village in every cove and inlet.

To the west of the hills was the Musquodoboit valley. There were long-established homes there and the most beautiful farms that I have seen anywhere. When you came out of the forest and towards the edge of the hills you saw before you a beautiful valley and, at the bottom, the Musquodoboit River wending its way to the ocean.

The banks of the river on both sides were cultivated, smooth and green. At the top of the valley stretched rows of farms as far as the eye could see. The houses were all painted white, and near them were large barns. These homes were sheltered by trees that yielded the best apples that could be found anywhere on this earth. The farms were all well-kept and obviously prosperous.

It was only natural that the new farmers who lived upon the rough Mooseland heights soon felt that their lands were poor and difficult when compared with the beautiful district that lay so close to them. It was understandable that they would pull up stakes and look for better properties elsewhere. They must have realized right away that neither they nor their children could prosper on these hills where no one had wanted to settle before. It was their duty to their children to seek new homes again, even though they would be criticized for that. They were there for seven years, but they should not have stayed longer than six months. That was how it was with the Icelandic settlement. But that place was still called Markland after they left.

All agreed that the Icelanders worked hard to support themselves and their families. They worked "like vikings" from the time they came and until they left. Signs of their work can still be seen; the hills will long show that they were there. They all worked like vikings. There was no exception. I have never seen a finer group of my countrymen. I have never seen more energetic or courageous men. In my mind's eye I still see them all as one group attacking the heavy forest, carrying huge logs into piles, struggling to get rocks out of the ground, uprooting seedlings and shoots. I see them carrying or hauling necessities for their families. I see them harnessing themselves to pull harrows between the stumps and the rocks. Yes, the Icelanders in Nova Scotia were, all of them, men of strength and endurance. Even so, they realized that their hard work paid only for bare survival.

In many ways the government of Nova Scotia treated the Icelandic settlers very well. They gave each family a hundred acres of land, built a good log cabin, cleared one acre of land, provided a cookstove and the most necessary furnishings, and food for about one year. Although this was originally offered as a loan, repayment was never called for.

The settlers felt satisfied during their first year in Nova Scotia. They had enough food. To be sure, there was little coffee to be had but there was plenty of tea and syrup. Syrup was an important ingredient because there was a shortage of milk. Syrup was used in bread, in porridge or pudding, and in all beverages. The Icelandic men deserved good food because they showed right away that they were productive workers and they were held in high esteem by local employers.

Afi chose a lot in the middle of the settlement. He called his home Egilsstaд (Egil's Place) since his name was Egill, Egill Þorsteinsson[11] (pronounced Aye-ill Thorsteinsson).

Our house was built on a hill. On one side there was a fast-flowing river and on the other side of the hill there was a little pond. We had a pleasant view after Afi had cleared some of the brush off the hillside. Like the other settlers we enjoyed the first year, but after that provisions were often low. Afi liked his new home but Amma never spoke about her feelings. For my part, I was pleased enough with everything while I could be with Afi and Amma. I did not feel homesickness for Iceland until much later.

The first man that I got to know after we moved into our house on the hill was a bachelor, or so it seemed. Indeed he was the most unusual man I ever encountered. He gave no information about himself even when people inquired about his name and where he had come from. One of the Markland[12] farmers claimed to have seen him when he was leaving from Sauдárkrók in northern Iceland. People knew that he had come to Nova Scotia from Ontario that fall. Some thought that his name was Eiríkur, some thought it was Helgi. When folks talked about him behind his back they often called him Eiríkur Gisli Helgi (the names of three silly brothers in an Icelandic story). When people addressed him they usually called him Eiríkur, and I do think that was his correct name because he called me his namesake.

He might have been close to thirty years of age. He was tall and broad-shouldered. He had a fair complexion and fair hair. He was an exceptionally fine-looking young man. He never spoke unless he was spoken to, and then he responded with only a few words. He came to our home just a few days after we moved in. On his back he carried a big trunk, which was securely wrapped and tied with a rope made from horsehair. He walked into the house uninvited, set the trunk down in a corner, said hello, sat down beside the cook-stove and began to think. Some time later he asked Afi whether he could stay in our house for a few days. Soon he would go into the English district to look for work. A few weeks went by.

He did not pick up a pail to get water for Amma, he did not look at a book, he did not write a note, he did not recite a verse, he did not talk to a neighbour, and he did not open the big trunk. He sat beside the stove and thought. Once in a while I got him to talk to me. He tried to be good to me. Often when I was sleepy in the evening he would take me on his knee and I would lean against him and fall asleep. I felt comfortable near him and wished that he would stay on with us.

One morning, after the New Year, Afi asked him what his plans were. "When are you going to look for work, Eiríkur, my friend?" he asked.

"Soon," said Eiríkur Gisli Helgi.

"If I were in your shoes I would not sit idle, day after day," said Afi.

"You wouldn't?" said Eiríkur.

"No," said Afi. "I would look for work in the English district."

"Is that so?"

"Yes, definitely. Healthy young men should be able to succeed in this country if they are willing to work."

"I guess so."

"When are you going to look for work then?"

"Soon."

"It is not good enough to say 'soon,' Eiríkur. You should have gone to look for work long before this. You should go right away," said Afi, raising his voice a little bit.

Eiríkur Gisli Helgi made no reply. He lowered his head and thought. After a short while he stood up, took the trunk from the corner, and called out "*Verið sæl,*" which means "farewell" or "be blessed."

Afi called to him and asked him to come and eat with us because Amma was just setting food on the table. Eiríkur Gisli Helgi made no reply. We watched as he strode down the hill with his trunk on his back.

"He is in God's hands," said Afi. "He is in God's hands. Eiríkur will prove himself when he gets started."

We heard later that Eiríkur had not stopped anywhere in the settlement. He walked without a break, westward, along the road that lay through the heights, and then down into the Mosquodoboit valley. Many people noticed this big man who carried such a large and unusual trunk.

Late in the evening he stopped beside a house, walked in uninvited, set his trunk down in a corner, and sat down beside the stove. This house belonged to a newly married couple. They had heard of the Icelanders and guessed that this strange man was one of them. They served him food and drink and offered him a bed on the second floor. They were a little surprised when he picked up his big trunk and set it down beside his bed. The next morning they expected that the man would continue on his way but he stayed on and left his trunk upstairs. The man of the house went out to the barn and began to thresh some grain with a flail. Eiríkur Gisli Helgi went out to the barn as well and for a while he watched the farmer at his work. Then he grabbed the flail and started threshing. He worked without stopping until noon. He walked into the house at noon and took lunch with the young couple. Then he returned to the barn and went back to the job. He accomplished as much as two men would be expected to do in one day. He continued to work like that day after day until all the grain had been threshed. He did not leave that home. He was like a member of the family there. The young man and his wife became fond of him. He seemed to do whatever he thought needed to be done as if he himself were the farmer there. He never asked for pay but he was provided with clothes as needed without asking for them. He never read a book, never wrote a letter and never received a letter. He wore much the same clothes in summer or winter. Eiríkur Gisli Helgi was loved and appreciated by all who came in contact with him. Years went by.

The government of Nova Scotia built a schoolhouse during the first spring that we lived in Markland. Furthermore, the government provided a teacher for the children of the Icelandic settlers. The teacher's name was Cracknell.[13] This man was probably close to fifty years of age. He had been a teacher in a senior school in Scotland but for some reason he had decided to move to Halifax. He did not hesitate to apply when he heard that the government wanted to hire a teacher for the Icelandic children. His application was quickly accepted and the government built a house for him. He moved in with his family. There were twelve people in all.

Old Cracknell, who was often called Professor Cracknell, was a big man, with a big face and a long beard. He always wore a long black gown over his clothes, and on his feet he wore high boots. He always walked with his hands behind his back and he held his head very high. As we soon discovered, he was either in a very good humour or in a very bad mood. If he left the house in a good frame of mind he wore a wide-brimmed felt hat, but on other days, when he was not happy, he wore a dark Scottish cap that seemed to match his grim expression.

I well remember the first day that the Icelandic children went to school. It was a foggy day with a light drizzle. There were twenty-five children, all anxious because we did not know any English. Most of us had learned to read Icelandic and we had been taught to write the letters of the alphabet. That first morning we had gathered at the school before the teacher arrived. We soon saw him on his way. We stood in a group, the boys in front, just inside the door, and the girls behind them. When the teacher came in he greeted us with a small bow, his hands still behind his back. "Good morning," he said as he took off his wide-brimmed hat. We stood quite still and said nothing. He led us to our desks, two boys to one seat and, in turn, two girls to one seat.

Next came the first lesson. He started by telling us the names of various things. We were very quiet and polite and we tried to understand what he was telling us. Many weeks went by before we understood what we were trying to read for him. He had us recite many poems from memory even though we did not understand the meaning at all.

One cloudy day he wrote the word "sun" on the blackboard. Then he pointed outside and said, "Sun, sun!"

We looked at each other and we did not know what he was talking about.

"Sun," he said again, and he pointed at one of the boys, and then he pointed to the outside. "Maybe he means 'son'" said my seatmate, Jón. "Maybe," said I.

"Jón's son," said Jón, and pointed at another boy who was Jónsson.

"No," said the teacher, shaking his head.

"Hansson," said I, pointing to myself as I said that.

"No," said the teacher, louder than before. I shook in my seat.

"I know what he means," said the oldest girl in our class in a whisper. "He means 'God's son,'?" she said in Icelandic. Then she spoke up: "God's son," she said and she pointed up into the rafters.

"Yes," said the teacher in a pleasant voice "Good girl, smart little girl." We were all very happy that at least one of us understood the word. We all smiled at her in appreciation. The next day brought sunshine. Then we came to realize that the smart little girl had been mistaken after all.

Little by little we came to understand more, but the more we learned the more the teacher expected and the stricter he became. It came to the point where one or another of the class was beaten every day even though we tried to be very well-behaved and very conscientious with our homework. We had to bring him a supply of willow twigs. He used these to whip us if we did not read well or if our pronunciation was poor. He whipped us if we came in late. For every spelling mistake we received a slap across the fingertips. We always worried when the black Scottish cap appeared because we knew that did not bode well. It was always a relief when we saw the felt hat with the wide brim.

Whenever we made a mistake of some kind, Professor Cracknell would say, "Blunder." Then he took up one of the willow twigs. "Fiddlesticks!" he would say, just before he hit us, and always as he hit he would say, *"Palman qui meruit ferat!"* (Each gets what he deserves.) He always followed the same pattern so we always knew what to expect. Mr. Cracknell was very insistent about regular attendance. If it happened that one of us missed a day, then we would have extra homework assigned the next day. So we quickly saw that it would not do to take days off. Once it happened that I was kept home for a day. The next day I was called up to the teacher's desk. I was very anxious and hesitant because I knew that I had offended the teacher by not attending class.

"Why were you not in school yesterday?" he asked. "I was sick, sir," I answered.

"Sick! Can you spell your words?" he said.

"I think so," I replied.

"Let's see. Without looking at your book can you spell the word 'eight'?"

"A-g-t," I said, half crying.

"Blunder!" said the teacher crossly.

"A-h-g-t," I tried, although I was shaking as I stood there.

"Fiddlesticks!" said the teacher, as he picked up a big willow twig that lay on the desk.

"A-t-t-t," I stammered.

"Palman qui meruit ferat!" said the teacher solemnly, and he hit the palm of one of my hands. I started to cry.

"Why are you crying?" asked the teacher. I did not answer, but kept on crying. "Why are you crying?" asked the teacher again as he took my other hand. I did not answer but cried all the more. "Why are you crying?" asked the teacher for the third time and he shook me roughly. Once again I did not answer because I could not speak. I cried louder than before. Then Jón stood up.

"We come here to learn, not to be beaten, sir," said Jón with tears in his eyes. A bombshell would not have created such a stir as did Jón's action. There was dead silence in the schoolroom. The children's faces were pale and their gaze moved from Jón to Mr. Cracknell and back again. We all knew what results this would bring. The teacher relaxed his hold on me and for a moment he seemed shocked.

"Take your seat," he said to me. I hesitated for a moment because I knew this meant that Jón would have to take my place. "Take your seat!" yelled the teacher. I went.

"You come here, Jón," said the teacher in a resounding voice. He pointed at Jón. Jón was always brave. He walked slowly up to the desk and looked directly into the teacher's eyes.

"Why do you come to school?" asked the teacher.

"I come to learn," said Jón.

"No, you come to school to be beaten, not to learn," said the teacher.

"I come to learn," said Jón.

"Blunder," said the teacher and he picked up a big twig.

"I come here to learn," said Jón, and the tears ran down his cheeks.

"Fiddlesticks! That is not true!" said the teacher, *"Palman qui meruit ferat!"* and the blows came down on Jón's shoulders but he bore the assault as best he could.

"You come to be beaten," said the teacher. "Isn't that right? You love the whip. *Palman qui meruit ferat!"* Along with each word came another blow on Jón's back and shoulders. Finally the teacher got the boy to admit that he came to school to be beaten, not to learn.

When at last he came back to our seat I quickly wiped at his tears and then we picked up our slates and started to write. We attended this school regularly for three years. Then Mr. Cracknell resigned because the government would not raise his salary. No other teacher came to take his place and so the school was closed from that time on.

During those three years when we were under his rule, he did work hard for us. He was determined that we should learn as much as possible and that we should learn as quickly as possible. I must say that what we did learn from him stood us in good stead later on in our lives. His position as our teacher was in many respects very demanding. Few teachers would have wanted to walk in his shoes during that first year and few would have accomplished so much. We, the students of his first year, have long since forgiven him for being strict and harsh. We now understand that he did not know any other method of teaching. He was not gentle but he was not a bad person. His flaws were many but they were outnumbered by his good qualities.

When I look back to those years, the years when I was a schoolboy in Nova Scotia, I remember many children who were of similar age and I see their faces in memory. They all seem so honest and brave. Above all, I remember my seat-mate, Jón. During school holidays we two delivered eggs and butter to a mining town near the Icelandic community. Often we were met by boys from the town and we had many a skirmish with them. Sometimes we had difficulty protecting our butter and eggs from damage. Yet those were happy days. We were tested and we proved ourselves. Jón and I were the same age but he was always much braver than I and stronger, and he always had a ready answer in any situation. When he saw the town boys coming towards us, he'd say, "Now we'll have to fight, Eiki,[14] to show them that Icelanders don't run away from trouble." I might say, "There are five of them against the two of us." Jón would say, "Even if there were ten of them, we must show them that Icelanders would rather fall than flee." His words always gave me courage. In the end we often left with a few broken eggs and a few scratches on our faces but they had a few marks on their faces too! We were really just testing our skill and our strength like warriors in Valhalla. Those were happy days.

But those happy days were soon to come to an end. I was not quite eleven years old when Afi suddenly died. The hardships of pioneer life became too much for this hard-working, enterprising man. All the farmers from the settlement followed him to the grave to pay their respects. I remember them all standing there, grief-stricken because one of their own was gone.

CHAPTER 4

After Afi died Amma knew that we could no longer manage the farm. She was about sixty years old and I was barely eleven. She rented the land to a couple who had just arrived from Iceland and she stayed on at the house with them. She tried to look after herself by knitting and sewing for the women in the neighbourhood. Amma felt that I would have little to gain from staying with her because now the local school had been closed and she wanted above all to allow me the opportunity to get an education. After a few weeks had gone by Amma was told that a lady called Mrs. Meynard had been making enquiries about an Icelandic boy who might be looking for a good home. Mrs. Meynard lived in a village down by the sea, about twenty miles from our place.

As it turned out she was not interested in a young boy for herself. She was acting on behalf of a woman known as Mrs. Patrick. This Mrs. Patrick was a wealthy widow. Her husband had been a judge. She was said to be a most respectable person and she had no children of her own. Friends advised Amma to let me explore the opportunity of staying with Mrs. Patrick. At least I would have a chance to go to school. Amma was convinced that there would be some benefits at any rate so word was sent to Mrs. Meynard that there was an eleven-year-old boy who would be interested in her offer. Then Mrs. Meynard arranged that I should come to her home on a certain day and Mrs. Patrick would meet me there.

Soon the day came and I had to go. One of the men from our district was prepared to walk with me to the village where Mrs. Meynard lived. I cried as I bade farewell to Amma. I asked her to inquire about me as often as possible. She tried to encourage me and she asked me to try to be a good boy at Mrs. Patrick's home. Maybe in just a few years' time I would be in a position to look after my old Amma, she said. I kissed Amma over and over again. Never have I experienced such a sad parting. This was not any easier for her. She tried to smile as I left but her blue eyes were full of tears.

The man who was accompanying me was named Ingvar. He carried a small package for me. It contained a set of underwear, one patched shirt and two books, the New Testament and the book of poems by Jónas Hallgrímsson[15], first edition. These things were all that I owned aside from the clothes I was wearing, a set of ordinary blue denims.

Ingvar and I started off early in the morning and we reached the ocean by noon. By that time we had walked twelve miles. I paid careful attention to the route that we took because I was thinking that it could happen that I might have to travel this way by myself some day. Several times I asked Ingvar whether he thought it would be dangerous for a boy like me to travel this way alone. He said that he did not think that would be a good idea because he knew that there were sometimes bears in the Mooseland hills. I knew that he said that so I would not be thinking about of running away from my new place if I was homesick. Nevertheless, his reply did bother me because I had always worried about bears. In the afternoon we followed the shoreline through two small villages and then we took a ferry over the fjord to Ship Harbour. Before long we found ourselves in front of an attractive-looking house that stood above a slope near the fjord. "This is Mrs. Meynard's house," said Ingvar. We approached the house and Ingvar knocked. Immediately a small middle-aged woman opened the door.

"What would you like?" asked the little woman.

"I have brought the Icelandic boy who is to meet Mrs. Patrick," said Ingvar and he bowed to the woman when she introduced herself as Mrs. Meynard.

"Oh, of course! This is Mrs. Patrick's little boy! Of course this is the little boy!" said Mrs. Meynard.

"Yes," said Ingvar.

"Oh, wait there for one minute! Just wait half a minute," said Mrs. Meynard. "Of course this is the boy!"

Then she went into another room. "Oh, Mrs. Patrick! Your little boy has come," we heard her say. "Your little boy is here. Of course! This is wonderful!"

"Well, well, well," said a deep voice. "He is here so early in the day. He is here, my blessed little infant! Oh, my dear Mrs. Meynard, let him come right in so I can hold him in my arms."

Mrs. Meynard returned to the doorway and invited us to please come into the parlour to meet Mrs. Patrick. When we came into the room we saw a woman sitting in an easy chair in the middle of the floor. She was by far the heaviest woman I had ever seen. Her face was rather dignified, her forehead high, her nose big and slightly hooked, her mouth well-shaped. My first impression was that here was an arrogant woman who had never had to deny herself anything that she wanted. This was Mrs. Patrick.

When we entered the doorway she shouted, "Well, well! Come into my arms, my little sweet! Come into your mother's arms, my dear little bird of paradise. And you, man, take a seat there beside the door." Ingvar sat down on a chair beside the door and I walked hesitantly towards the woman who sat with her arms open, waiting to embrace me. She put her fat arms around me and pressed me towards her bosom until I felt like screaming. She kissed my cheeks, my nose, my mouth, my chin. Her kisses, combined with a strong smell of alcohol, were almost suffocating.

"Oh, how sweet you are, my little treasure. You are my son! You are flesh of my flesh and bone of my bone! Isn't he now, Mrs. Meynard?"

"Of course. That is so," said Mrs. Meynard.

"Oh, I will never get tired of kissing you, my little skylark! Isn't his face just the face of an angel, Mrs. Meynard?"

"Yes, of course, that is right," said Mrs. Meynard.

"Oh, I will enjoy your sweet kisses, my wonderful nightingale," said Mrs. Patrick. "Aren't his eyes beautiful and intelligent, Mrs. Meynard?"

"Yes, of course," said Mrs. Meynard.

"Oh, my wonderful little one," said Mrs. Patrick, and she held my head between her hands and kissed me on the forehead. "You will love me very much. Isn't that right?"

"Yes," I said, but I knew full well that I would never be able to love this woman.

"Well, well! My dear little honey pot says 'yes.' Did you hear that, Mrs. Meynard? Did you hear how nicely he said 'yes' just like an English boy of good family? Yes, he is just like an English boy, Mrs. Meynard!"

"Of course," said Mrs. Meynard.

"Dear Mrs. Meynard! Please get some cookies and applesauce for my dear little bird and bring it in here for him."

"Of course, Mrs. Patrick," said Mrs. Meynard as she left the room.

"How far did you ride today?" asked Mrs. Patrick and she pointed at Ingvar who sat by the door with his hat in his hands.

"We walked twenty miles today," said Ingvar hesitantly, in English.

"Well, well!" shouted Mrs. Patrick. "Well, well! Disgraceful!

Disgraceful to let my dear little infant walk twenty miles in one day! Well, well! You Icelanders don't know how to care for children. You have no mercy! You should never have children! You let the child walk twenty miles in less than one day! Well, well!" Ingvar had no answer. "You must be exhausted, my little angel?" she said.

"No," said I.

"Well, well!" said Mrs. Patrick with a serious expression on her face. "You must never tell a lie, my little hero. You are tired. Say 'yes'."

I said, "Yes."

"God bless me and my little parrot," said Mrs. Patrick excitedly, "bless us both. He says 'yes' in English. My dear little child says 'yes'. Did you hear that, man? Did you hear what the child said?"

"Yes," said Ingvar, looking down at the floor.

Mrs. Meynard came into the room with a dish piled high with cookies and a bowlful of applesauce. "May the Lord save us, dear Mrs. Meynard! Lord save us! The dear child has walked twenty miles today! Did you hear me, he walked twenty miles — he didn't ride, he walked! Isn't that awful?"

"Yes, of course, Mrs. Patrick," said Mrs. Meynard shaking her head.

"Yes, Mrs. Meynard," said Mrs. Patrick with a sigh, "they let my little chick walk. Please give the man something to eat. I think he might be hungry."

"Yes, of course, Mrs. Patrick," said Mrs. Meynard. "Come with me, man. I had forgotten. Of course!" She left the room and Ingvar went with her.

Mrs. Patrick took the dish with the cookies and the bowl of applesauce. She set the dish in her lap and held the bowl in her left hand. She told me to kneel down beside her. She broke a cookie with her right hand and she fed it to me. Then she took a teaspoon of applesauce and put that in my mouth. She gave me another piece of cookie and followed that quickly with some more applesauce. She continued so fast that I hardly had time to swallow between servings. I tried to tell her that I had had enough but she would not stop till I had eaten all the cookies and all the applesauce.

"That will do for now, my little swan," she said, as she wiped my mouth with her silk handkerchief. "You'll have more to eat after a while. Dinner will be served soon. You will have to eat well so you will put on some weight." I could not bear the thought of eating anything more.

Then Mrs. Meynard and Ingvar came back into the room. Mrs. Patrick looked at Ingvar. "You are leaving now?" she asked.

"Yes," said Ingvar, but I could see that he would have liked to spend the night there before walking home again.

"Tell my boy's grandmother that she need not worry about him. He will be better off with me than with her. If she wants to know how he is doing she can get information here from Mrs. Meynard."

"Of course, Mrs. Patrick," said Mrs. Meynard.

Mrs. Patrick spoke to Ingvar. "Please give my boy's grandmother this money. Here are five dollars. Don't lose the bill and don't forget to give it to her."

Ingvar said goodbye to me with the traditional "*Vertu nú sæll, Eiki minn!*" meaning "May everything work out for you, Eiki, my friend," and he added, still in Icelandic, "Don't worry too much."

I answered, in Icelandic, "Goodbye now. Please give my love to Amma." I wanted to ask him to take me back with him but I knew that would not happen. It was hard to see him leave. I watched him hurry down the slope towards the shore.

In the evening, I forced down some dinner, which included some ten or twelve courses. Then I was asked all kinds of questions which no eleven-year-old boy could answer properly. Then Mrs. Patrick kissed me again and again. Finally I was taken into a small bedroom on the second floor and I was allowed to get ready for the night. Mrs. Patrick came into the room and examined the clothes that I had taken off. She wrapped them into a bundle and took them out of the room. She took the lamp and carefully closed the bedroom door as she left. Now the room was in complete darkness. I had never been left alone in a dark room before and all my old night fears came back. I pulled the covers over my head. I said the prayers that Amma had taught me years before and that helped to calm my nerves. At last I cried and cried until my pillow was wet. I fell asleep but woke up with a start. The lamp was back in the room. Mrs. Patrick was leaning over me with a glass in her hand.

"Well, well," said Mrs. Patrick. "What is the matter with my little treasure? You have been crying, my little canary! You are hungry, my dear little chick."

"Oh, no, no," I said. I shuddered at the thought of being forced to eat more cookies and applesauce.

"You are exhausted, my poor little pet," said Mrs. Patrick, and she kissed my chin. "You are ill from weariness, just at death's door, my dear little Lazarus."

"No," I said.

"Yes, I say," said Mrs. Patrick, "Say 'yes,' my little crow."

"Yes," I said.

"God bless us both," said Mrs. Patrick, "God bless us. 'Yes' says my blessed child. Blessed child! Drink from the glass, my dearest. This is Dutch wine, and it will give you strength." I drank what was left in the glass, I dared not protest. I gulped it down, trying not to let it touch tooth or tongue. "You are a lovely boy," said Mrs. Patrick. "Now go to sleep, and dream about new clothes, and fast horses. We will go to my home tomorrow, my little jewel. Good night. You do not have to be afraid of ghosts, because they do not exist."

With those words she picked up the lamp and left the room, closing the door behind her. Again I was overcome with fear of the dark. I pulled the covers over my head, repeated my prayers, and cried again until at last I fell asleep.

The sun was high in the sky when I woke the next morning. I felt stronger than I had the night before. I told myself that I must face my uncertainties as calmly as possible, one day at a time.

Soon after I woke up Mrs. Patrick came into my room. Her nose was very red and her eyelids were swollen. I thought that she must have been crying in the night, likely on my account. She kissed me again and again and asked me to put on the new clothes that she had brought for me. These were very good clothes and they fitted very well, too. I kissed Mrs. Patrick for the new clothes. She said that the clothes suited me and now I looked just fine.

We went down for breakfast. This time my appetite was better than the day before, but still Mrs Patrick did not think that I had enough to eat. She kept me at the table for a long time.

Shortly before noon a team of light dun-coloured horses arrived at the door. Behind them was a fine carriage. A middle-aged man sat on the driver's seat, and held onto the horses' reins. He kept talking to the horses just as if he were talking to another person.

The odd thing about the driver was that he had a broken nose, and whenever he spoke the sound of each word came out of his nose. At the end of every sentence he finished with a sneeze.

"Slow down, Athena! Slow down, Apollo," said the driver and he sneezed twice just as we came out of the house. "Now behave yourself, Apollo. Calm down. Did you hear what I said, Athena? Don't act like a pig or a donkey." This was followed by another sneeze.

Mrs. Patrick and I said goodbye to Mrs. Meynard, and Mrs. Meynard hoped that we would have pleasant weather for our trip. She said that of course she would come to visit Mrs. Patrick at Christmastime.

"Quiet now, Athena. Show some patience, Apollo, while the lady is getting into the carriage," said the driver, and he sneezed once more. "Slow down. That will do."

"Don't use your whip, John Miller, but let the horses run as fast as they can, to please my little parrot here," said Mrs. Patrick. "Did you hear that, John Miller?"

"Do you hear what the lady is saying, Athena? And do you hear,

Apollo?" said John Miller, for that was the driver's name. "You will have to show that you can lift up your feet, since the lady is in a hurry."

"Move those horses," shouted Mrs. Patrick.

"Did you hear that, Athena? A little more, Apollo, a little more." The words came through John Miller's nose, followed by a sneeze. The horses were now running at full speed.

"Still faster, John Miller," shouted Mrs. Patrick, "My little ostrich here wants them to go faster." I certainly did not want the horses to go any faster, far from it.

"A little more, Athena, a little faster, Apollo. The lady wants to go faster." The horses rushed ahead, as fast as they could go. The dust whirled behind our wheels. Trees, houses, gardens seemed to fly past us, out of sight before we knew it.

"Faster, John Miller," shouted Mrs. Patrick.

"This is it," said Jon Miller through his nose

"Do you hear what I am saying?" shouted Mrs. Patrick.

"Do you hear what the lady is saying?" said John Miller to his horses.

"I give the orders, John Miller," yelled Mrs. Patrick.

"Do you hear that the lady is giving the orders?" said John Miller. We fairly flew over straight roads, past more houses and gardens, through parks and woodlands, up hill and down dale. All the time the horses kept up a fast pace and Mrs. Patrick kept up her demands for more speed. Just before sunset we stopped in front of a grand house built from stone.

"Now this is my house, my little pilgrim," said Mrs. Patrick as we entered a stately hall. "This house will be your one and only home from now on! Sit down on the sofa here, my little gem. I am going to ring the bell." I sat down on the sofa and Mrs. Patrick rang the bell impatiently. Immediately a slim woman came forward. She was probably about thirty-five years old. She was wearing a white cap and a big white apron. Her face was unusual, because it was so very thin, shaped almost like the blade of an axe.

"What is the meaning of this, Marianna?" said Mrs. Patrick crossly. "You don't come to the door when you hear the carriage come up to the house? Shame, shame, disgraceful, Marianna!"

"I was in the kitchen, my lady, and I did not hear the carriage arrive," said Marianna, and her head shook a little as she spoke.

"Shame and disgrace!" shouted Mrs. Patrick, "You are a great shame and disgrace, Marianna! Do you hear what I'm saying?"

"I hear, my lady," said Marianna. Her head shook a little as if she could not control it.

"It is good that you hear it, Marianna, that you hear me say that you are shameful!" said Mrs. Patrick, almost out of breath. "Now get yourself into the kitchen and bring some cookies and applesauce for my dear little chick. Do you hear me, Marianna? A full bowl of applesauce!"

"I hear, my lady," said Marianna, her head moving up and down.

"Hurry then, Marianna!" yelled Mrs. Patrick.

"I am going," said Marianna as she was leaving.

CHAPTER 5

Mrs. Patrick's stone house was the most elaborate single family home that I have ever seen. It had been built by skilled craftsmen who paid attention to every detail. It was quite a spacious home with many rooms, both on the main floor and on the second floor. All the rooms were beautifully furnished. Everywhere there were sofas and easy chairs and tables. On the floors were luxurious carpets and on the walls there were fine paintings. The house left no doubt that the owner must be wealthy.

Mrs. Patrick was a widow whose husband had been a judge. As far as I could gather she herself came from a good family in Londonderry, Ireland. She was not Catholic like many Irish people are. Instead, she belonged to the Baptist church, which she claimed was the only true church. I do not know how long she had been a widow at this time, but I know that her husband died when they lived in England. She had never been a mother, or an aunt, or a stepmother, or a foster mother or a godmother. Her neighbours said that she was not known for handing out gifts. Still, they wanted to be on friendly terms with her, and the poorer people were always ready to take on any jobs that she wanted done around the house or garden. She always paid them well for their work and she paid promptly. But it seemed that few cared to live with her. Of all the people in her employ Marianna was the only one who actually stayed at the house. John Miller looked after her horses but he never stepped inside the door unless Mrs. Patrick directly ordered him to do so. The washerwoman came only into the kitchen. The men who worked in the garden, cut the firewood, hauled the water and took care of the cows came only into the woodshed at the back of the house.

My bedroom was beside Mrs. Patrick's room up on the second floor. It was a pleasant room. Two windows offered a view of the fjord. My bed was under one of the windows and under the other there was a small table, made from mahogany, and two chairs. On the table there were books and magazines full of pictures. The bed-clothes were all of the best quality. I was worried about going to bed the first night for fear of wrinkling all this finery. However, I soon fell asleep and rested till morning.

The following day Mrs. Patrick showed me around the house and the garden. Finally she took me into a small room beside the parlour. This, she said, was her favourite room and only people who were special to her ever came into that room. This room was a sanctuary. She had me sit in a chair beside the window and she sat down in a chair across from me.

"So, what exactly is your name, my dear little saint?" she asked, after she looked me over for a little while.

"My name is Eiríkur," I said.

"What, what!" shouted Mrs. Patrick, and she laughed until I thought she would collapse. "What, what! I-rokkur!" (She pronounced the I as in "Irish.") "That is not a name, my dear little jester. Irokkur! That is just a stumbling-stone!"

"My name is Eiríkur Hansson," I said.

"What, what!" said Mrs. Patrick, almost helpless with laughter. "Your name is not just 'Irokkur' but also 'Annsinn.' Bless us, my dear little Hottentot. A name like 'Irokkur Annsinn' is just a tiresome stumbling-stone! Remember that from now on your name is Pat — Patrick Patrick. And when you are a little older you will be baptised Patrick Patrick. Did you hear that, Pat?"

"Yes," I said.

"So what is your name then, sunshine?" asked Mrs. Patrick.

"Eiríkur," I said.

"Watch yourself now, sunshine," said Mrs. Patrick, looking at me with a serious expression. "Your name is Pat. What is your name?"

"Pa-at," I said.

"Correct, my little student," said Mrs. Patrick with a sigh. "God bless us. We will come to understand each other, my sweet. Now remember that you are no longer Icelandic — you are flesh of my flesh and bone of my bone. You are my son! You are Irish, Pat, Irish through and through! Did you hear that, Pat?"

"Yes," I said. I did not dare to say anything more.

"Are you Irish or Icelandic?" demanded Mrs. Patrick and she looked straight into my eyes.

"Ir-ish," I said hesitantly.

"Good, my little charmer," said Mrs. Patrick, looking very dignified. "You must forget that that you have been with Icelandic people. Icelandic people can be good but still they can never be anything but Icelanders!"

"My grandmother is very good," I said, and my heart was beating fast.

"Yes, Pat, my dear," said Mrs. Patrick with a smile. "Your grandmother is very kind, and you will be able to see her when you are big. Of course your grandmother is very kind, Pat, dear."

I asked her whether I would be able to start going to school. She would not think of such a thing, she said, because the boys at school would fight me during recess and I would learn bad things from those boys. No, she said, her treasure would never attend public school. Mrs. Patrick's son would not be going to school. She would rather have some innocent soul teach him at her home, no matter what the cost. Then she asked me about the two books that I had brought with me. I told her that one of the books was the New Testament and the other was a book of poems written by a poet called Jónas Hallgrímsson. She said that the New Testament was a good book but she doubted that an Icelandic version would be an authentic translation and she insisted that I must first read it through in English. The book of poems she said she would like to burn because poems by an Icelander named Ju-nos Hal-grinis-on would likely not be appropriate reading for me. I asked her not to destroy that book because it was very precious to me, and I assured her that Jónas had written beautiful poems. She agreed then to save the book but I was to study the poetry of Thomas Moore who was the best of all poets, and also a lifelong friend of Lord Byron.

A few days later a tall, dignified man came to call. Mrs. Patrick immediately met with him in "the holiest room in the house." That led me to the conclusion that this impressive man must be one of Mrs. Patrick's special friends. They talked privately for quite a long time. Although I was in the next room I did not hear any of their conversation but once I thought I heard the clink of glasses.

When they finally came out of the room Mrs. Patrick pointed at me and said, "This is my son, Mr. Sandford. This is Pat."

"A fine boy," said Mr. Sandford and he patted my head, "a very nice boy. I should say so!"

"He is the apple of my eye," said Mrs. Patrick. "And my dear Pat, this is Mr. Sandford, officer in charge of the police here. He makes sure that bad people don't cause us any harm."

"Ahem," said Mr. Sandford and he patted me on the head again. He probably thought that I would be afraid of him since I had been told that he was the head officer of the police force. But I was not afraid of this handsome and kindly man.

"Now listen to what I have to say, dear Pat," said Mrs. Patrick, "Our friend, Mr. Sandford, head of the police force, has a daughter, a very good and wonderful daughter, Pat, and she has agreed to be your teacher this winter. You are to be a good and obedient pupil."

"Ahem!" said Mr. Sandford. "She is a very good girl, and her name is Lalla."

"Lalla Sandford, my sweet," said Mrs. Patrick.

"Ahem!" said Mr. Sandford. "I'm sure that they will get along well, Mrs. Patrick. I should say so!"

"God bless us, Mr. Sandford," said Mrs. Patrick, "I am sure she will fall in love with my dear little archer (Sagittarius) as soon as she sees him. God blesses us, Mr. Sandford. I know that."

"Ahem," said Mr. Sandford, smiling at me. "This makes me very happy. I should say so!"

After about one week Lalla Sandford came to teach me. She was sixteen years old, tall and slim, with long black hair. Her eyes were kindly and intelligent. She had a high forehead, a straight nose and a particularly pleasant mouth. She was one of the most beautiful, polite and good girls that I had ever known. As soon as I met her I was sure that I could trust her. I would even be able to trust her with my secret wish, my wish to go home. I was to have classes with her for six hours per day with the exception of Saturdays and Sundays. Classes would be given in "the holiest room in the house."

Classes began. I have never had a better or more pleasant teacher than Lalla Sandford and I have never applied myself as diligently to my studies as I did while she was my teacher. I was always so glad when I saw her coming in the morning. I was always overcome by sadness and boredom when she left at the end of her day. I was always homesick and I had a hard time getting to sleep at night.

The very first day that Lalla was my teacher I asked her to call me "Eiríkur" rather than Pat when we were in class and Mrs.

Patrick was out of earshot. She was happy to do that. She was surprised that Mrs. Patrick wanted to change my name. She often asked me about the Icelandic people. She wanted to know how much I remembered about my birthplace and what I knew about Iceland. I told her about my favourite book and that I had memorized some of Jónas Hallgrímsson's poems. She wanted to know about the ideas that he expressed in his work. She thought that Jónas must have been a wonderful man. I was so pleased to hear her say that. Little by little I explained my circumstances, and I told her about my Amma. I let her know how anxious I was about Amma and how much I yearned to go home to see her. Lalla tried to instill in me the idea that it would be best for me to stay as long as possible with Mrs. Patrick, but all along I knew that she understood how I felt and that she sympathized with me. She said that she would be my sister if I would like that. She would ask Mrs. Patrick whether she would allow me to visit at the Sandford home.

Soon we had winter weather. Then it was Christmastime. I received many fine gifts. Mrs. Patrick bought a silver watch for me to give to Lalla. Lalla gave me a copy of Longfellow's poetry in a special binding. Mrs. Meynard came for Christmas and she stayed until after the New Year's celebrations. She said that Amma had sent word to ask me to be a good boy for Mrs. Patrick and not to be thinking of coming to see her until I was grown. She said that I should not be expecting any letters from her. She wanted me to forget the Icelandic language. I pretended to accept this news as it was delivered but even though I was still a child I knew that Amma would never have sent me such a message. I did think that it was more than a little strange that I never had even a note from her. I was not surprised that no Icelandic person had come to see me because none of my people would have any errands in the area where I was living.

Later that winter, thanks to Lalla's kind invitations, I was sometimes allowed to visit at the Sandford house on a Saturday or a

Sunday. I was always received well there, just as if I truly were Lalla's brother rather than just her pupil. Mr. Sandford often said that he wished that he had found me before Mrs. Patrick because he had no son. "A pleasant boy," he said to his wife, "way too good for some people. I should say so."

Soon Mrs. Patrick began to think that I went over to visit the Sandford family too often, and she also thought that when I went there I stayed too long. She started scolding me when I came home, sometimes harshly. She sometimes called me a wretched little wild-cat or a thankless little street sweeper or an insolent little savage. But afterwards there would be kisses, cookies, applesauce or some other treats. Then all of a sudden, I would be her treasure, or her bird of paradise. Always she reminded me that I must not love any-one else as much as I loved her because she was my mother, and she tried to get me into the habit of calling her "Mother." But no mat-ter how good she was to me, I could never bring myself to love her. I was actually afraid of her, and could never believe that she was quite sane. She expressed such exaggerated fondness for me.

The more I saw Lalla Sandford, the better I saw how good and kind she was. She always spoke gently. She tried to make my classes interesting and she tried to make things as understandable as possible for me. She tried to encourage me in every way that she could. I knew that I would never be bored as long as she was my teacher. I dreaded the day when that would end — as I knew it would, sooner or later.

One day, just before Easter, Lalla asked, "Do you never get a let-ter from your grandmother, Eiríkur?"

"No, never," I answered.

"Why would that be?" she continued.

"I do not know," I said.

"Does your grandmother not know how to write?"

"Yes, she knows how to write and she promised that she would write often, but her letters were to go to Mrs. Meynard."

"Do you write to your grandmother?" she asked.

"I am not allowed to write to her," I said.

"Who says you are not allowed to write to your grandmother?"

"Mrs. Patrick," I said in a low voice.

"Just like that," said Lalla thoughtfully.

"I will be very sad when you are no longer my teacher," I said.

"Please don't say that you will be sad, dear child," she said.

"I cannot help it," I said, "I think I will try to run away to be with Amma."

"What are you saying, boy?" said Lalla, looking at me in surprise.

"I am going to try to run away to Amma when you stop teaching. I will be too sad."

"Eiríkur!" she cried, looking pale, "You must not think like that. You will get lost." At that moment the door opened and Mrs. Patrick walked into the room.

"Well, well, well!" wheezed Mrs. Patrick. "What do you call the boy, Miss Sandford?"

"I call him by his Christian name, Mrs. Patrick," said Lalla, bowing to the lady as she spoke.

"And what is his correct Christian name, Miss Sandford?'

"Eiríkur."

"Who informed you of that, Miss Sandford?"

"I found that out on the very first day that I taught him," said Lalla, and now her cheeks were flushed. "I asked him what his name was and . . . "

"And what did he say his name was?" interrupted Mrs. Patrick.

"He said his name was Pat but I knew that was not an Icelandic name, so I asked him to give me his real name. I believe that people should be called by their given Christian names so I have always called this boy Eiríkur."

"You have no business calling this boy by some uncivilized name, Miss Sandford," said Mrs. Patrick, looking at Lalla with a haughty air. "This boy is my son and his name is Patrick and not Irokkur or any other tiresome type of name."

"But since he is Icelandic, Mrs. Patrick," said Lalla, getting up from her chair, "it seems to me only right that his name should be Icelandic, too."

"He is not Icelandic, Miss Sandford," said Mrs. Patrick, stamping her foot on the floor, "He is Irish and his name is Patrick."

"You know just as well as I do that this boy is Icelandic and that is that," said Lalla.

"Miss Sandford!" said Mrs. Patrick solemnly. "Miss Sandford, you are trying to spoil my relationship with this boy. I must ask you to leave the position you have had here this winter. On account of your parents I am sorry that I have to ask you to leave."

"Oh, please, dear mother," I said with tears in my eyes, "do not let Miss Sandford leave. I am so fond of her."

"You be quiet, you little coal digger," said Mrs. Patrick harshly. "One can hear, Miss Sandford, that you have been turning this boy away from me."

"It is not right to talk like this, Mrs. Patrick," said Lalla, "You are speaking against your own better judgement."

"Listen, you little street sweeper," said Mrs. Patrick, turning to me, "which one do you love best, me or Miss Sandford? Answer the question."

"Of course you love Mrs. Patrick best," said Lalla, looking towards me.

"Answer," said Mrs. Patrick, staring at me.

"I love you both very much," I said, although goodness knows I wanted to say that I loved Lalla best.

"Listen, you little wildcat," said Mrs. Patrick, "do you want to stay with me or do you want to go with Miss Sandford and be with her all the time? Answer me."

"Naturally you would rather stay with Mrs. Patrick," said Lalla.

"You be quiet, Miss Sandford. You answer me, Pat. Which would you rather do?"

"You must not put such questions to the boy," said Lalla.

"You be quiet, Miss Sandford. Answer me, Pat. Answer, Patrick."

"Say that you would rather stay with Mrs. Patrick." Lalla was looking very serious.

"I told you to be quiet, Miss Sandford," yelled Mrs. Patrick. "I am talking to the boy and not to you. Answer me, Patrick."

"May I go with Miss Sandford, if I choose that?" I asked in a shaky voice.

"Yes. Answer, Patrick," said Mrs. Patrick.

"I love you, mother," I said, "but I would . . . like to . . ."

" . . . go with Miss Sandford," interrupted Mrs. Patrick, now beside herself with rage. "You have spoiled everything between the boy and me, say I. Shame and disgrace, say I, Miss Sandford. Go home and never set foot inside my door again. Shame! Shame!"

"Farewell, Eiríkur! Farewell, Mrs. Patrick!" said Lalla from the doorway.

"Farewell!" I said to Lalla, with tears in my eyes.

"Leave, Miss Sandford," yelled Mrs. Patrick, and she closed the door.

Mrs. Patrick went into a long tirade, chastising me and laying down the rules that I was meant to follow. She called me the most absurd names and she told me that never again would she allow me to visit at the Sandford home because Lalla was a troublemaker.

I was depressed that evening. I could not sleep that night because I was trying to devise a plan for running away. I made up my mind that I would go home, sooner or later. I felt sure that I would find my way because I had tried to pay attention to the route when we travelled with John Miller several months before. The main difficulty, I told myself, would be to get away from Mrs. Patrick without her discovering it for a few hours. I would have to evade whomever she might send to search for me. It would not be easy because she always took me with her when she left the house, and I was never allowed to go anywhere by myself except when she let me go to visit the Sandford family. I saw no solution to the problem, but I was going to find a way, somehow, to go home to Amma.

The next day I was beside myself from sleeplessness and home-sickness and because I would no longer see Lalla. Mrs. Patrick was also in a bad humour that day. Her nose was very red and her eyes seemed dull as if she had been crying. I had breakfast in the kitchen with Marianna.

"You didn't sleep last night, Pat," said Marianna, and her head was shaking more than usual.

"Oh, yes, Marianna, I slept, but I have a headache," I said.

"I know better, poor you," said Marianna. "You did not sleep last night because of what happened yesterday."

I said nothing.

"You want to go back to the Icelandic people, and that is not surprising," said Marianna. "There you will be most comfortable. There you will have other children to play with. You want to go home. I know that, little wretch." Marianna's head would not relax.

Still I said nothing.

"If I were you, little wretch, I would not be waiting long to run away from here."

"You would not be able to do that," I said.

"Wouldn't I?" said Marianna with a strange little laugh. "I couldn't do it? I would do as the boy did who ran away from my father."

"What did he do to get away?"

"He let himself out the window of his room and he slid down on a rope after everyone in the house had gone to bed and no one knew that he was missing until nine o'clock the next morning. By that time he had travelled twenty miles towards his home. He tied the rope around the bedpost. That is how I would do it if I wanted to run away."

"Did they catch the boy?" I asked.

"No, little wretch, no," said Marianna, and she seemed to shake all over.

I went up to my room when I had finished eating. I started

wondering whether I would be able to escape in the same way as the boy that Marianna talked about. The distance from my window down to the sidewalk was no more than twelve feet. I saw that I could easily get out if I tied the end of a rope to my bedpost and slid down. I was sure that I would be able to get to Ship Harbour by sunrise if I could start off about the time that Mrs. Patrick went to sleep. I worried about my old fear of the dark, but I decided that I would follow this plan nevertheless.

Later that day I was lucky enough to find a roll of sturdy clothes-line in the woodshed and I was lucky enough to take it up to my room unnoticed.

I went up to my room early that evening but I did not get undressed. I put the light out for a short while. I had a dollar bill that Mrs. Patrick had given me one day. I put that in my pocket. I bundled together my books — the New Testament, Jónas Hall-grímsson's poems and my copy of the three works of Longfellow — and I tied a big handkerchief around them. When I thought that Mrs. Patrick would be asleep I opened the window very carefully. Then I tied one end of the clothesline around the bedpost, fastened my book bag to the other end and let the line fall slowly to the ground. Then I climbed up into the windowsill. Imagine my feelings, both excitement and trepidation! I held onto the rope and slid down very slowly, landed safely on the sidewalk below, picked up my books, crept out of the garden and onto the road that led down to the fjord. There was a little frost, with just a hint of snow on the ground. Road conditions were excellent. I started running right away, as fast as I could. I ran past houses and barns, uphill and down. Sometimes I slowed my pace when I ran past houses. Often dogs barked as I passed and sometimes they followed me for fairly long distances. But I was not afraid of any dogs. I was not afraid of anything that night. All that I thought about was getting away as far as possible before Mrs. Patrick realized that I was missing. I ran as fast as I could all night long with hardly a pause.

Just as the sun was rising I arrived at Ship Harbour. I followed the shoreline, around the end of the bay, and up the other side. It was midmorning when I turned east. As I followed the shoreline towards the east, I started to slow down. My feet were getting heavier and heavier. I was covered with sweat and I had a pain in my left side. I kept on until I reached Tangier, the town where Ingvar and I had had lunch the previous autumn. I stepped into the guest house there and ordered some food. I had to answer many questions about my travels. I stopped there longer than I had intended.

When I finally started off into the Mooseland heights I found I was already getting so stiff I could hardly move, but now there were only twelve miles left until I would reach the settlement. I moved along as fast as I could manage. By now the sun was sinking lower but the remaining distance was less and less. The road followed the Tangier River and I crossed on the bridge beside the sawmill. There were only six miles left. I went past the mining town known as Mooseland Mines, only four miles from home! I moved a little faster. I went past the post office, past John Prest's shingle mill. There were only two miles to go to the first cabin in our neighbourhood. On and on I struggled and the anticipation of seeing Amma again gave me the strength to continue. Finally I came to the bend in the road that was one mile from the first house. Just at that point I heard the jingle of bells from horses' harnesses close behind me. I was shocked. I felt sure that Mrs. Patrick's horses were catching up to me. I knew that my own speed was the only thing that could save me. Running off the road and trying to hide would be of no help because the forest there was almost impenetrable. The cabin was less than a mile ahead. Getting there meant safety. Although I was on the point of exhaustion I ran as if my life depended on it. I glanced back and I saw horses with a sleigh come into the bend in the road. They were about one hundred fathoms behind me. The horses were Mrs. Patrick's light-coloured horses! I heard the horsewhip and I recognized the voice of John Miller.

I ran and ran. A place of refuge was just ahead. Through the mist that was coming over my eyes I saw the house on one side of the road and the barn on the other side. I knew the people there and I knew that they would come to my aid as soon as they saw me. I could hardly move my feet, my knees were buckling. There was a ringing in my ears and a blur in front of my eyes.

"Oh, God, help me," I prayed just as I felt John Miller's hand on my shoulder. I had lost the race and I collapsed on the road.

I had run sixty-eight miles in less than seventeen hours. I had lost my chance for freedom.

John Miller stood over me until I was able to breathe again. I wept and I pleaded with him to let me see my grandmother, if only for a few minutes. He didn't say a word. He shook his head a few times. He never said one word.

In retrospect, as I retell this story, I wonder about John Miller.

In later years, when old age and sickness and sorrows overtake him, will he remember how I knelt before him and begged him to let me see my grandmother?

CHAPTER 6

John Miller lifted me up and placed me on the seat beside him. Then he drove back as fast as the horses could go.

My mind was a blank. I did not have any sense of weariness, or hunger, or sleepiness, only a sense of defeat and helplessness. I saw everything through a fog: the houses we passed, the road ahead of us, the forests to the side. I think I may have passed out. I heard John Miller talk to the horses. He told them that the lady wanted them to hurry, the lady demanded that. He told them that he could wager that they would have the best oats in Nova Scotia for the next six months if they were home before twelve o'clock the next day. After each sentence there came a sneeze through John's broken nose.

All at once I felt that the sled was moving backwards, the drone in John Miller's nose faded further and further away. And then suddenly I was in a soft and cozy bed and the bed was at home in Amma's log cabin. Oh, it was so comfortable there. The best part was that Amma stood beside the bed and leaned over me and

Amma looked tall and beautiful and young.

Then, just as suddenly, Amma disappeared, and in her place was John Miller ordering me to get down from the sleigh. We had stopped at a guest house at the head of the fjord. I had fallen asleep soon after I sat down in the sleigh and now it was almost midnight and John Miller wanted to let the horses rest until dawn. I fell asleep again in a good bed at the guest house. Before the sun was up we were on our way again, and around noon we were back at Mrs. Patrick's house.

Mrs. Patrick stood at the front door when we drove into the garden. Her face was white: now even her nose was white. As soon as we stopped she came to the sleigh, grabbed my shoulder and pulled me down. Then she pushed me into the house ahead of her without saying one word to me. In the doorway she turned and called to John Miller.

"Where did you catch him, John Miller?"

"About half a mile on this side of the Icelandic settlement, wasn't that right, Apollo?" said John Miller with a sneeze.

"Disgraceful," shouted Mrs. Patrick. "Tend to the horses well, John Miller, and see that they have the best feed that is available in this town. You come back here yourself tomorrow. Did you hear what I said?"

"Did you hear what the lady says?" said John Miller to the horses. "I told you this last night, Athena. You heard me say that, Apollo. I can't come tomorrow."

"I order it," said Mrs. Patrick.

"Did you hear the lady order?" said John Miller to the horses. "Well, I'll come then, lady." Then John Miller took the horses into town and Mrs. Patrick closed the front door and pushed me ahead of her into "the holiest room in the house." She locked the door carefully and put the key into her pocket.

After Mrs. Patrick had locked the door she walked over to a cupboard that stood in one corner of the room and she took out a thick leather strap. Then she sat down in a chair which stood in the middle of the room and she laid the strap in her lap. I stood in front of her like a delinquent in front of a stern judge. I held my hands together and looked at the floor. I knew very well that I should expect some corporal punishment so I decided that I would try to minimize that to some extent by asking for forgiveness and promising to behave better in the future.

"Who told you to run away from me, you filthy ungrateful scoundrel?" said Mrs. Patrick, pointing at me with the index finger of her left hand.

"Nobody told me to," I said, "and I am going to ask you to . . ."

"Why did you run away from me, you wretched little wildcat?"

"Oh, I did not know what I was doing. I just wanted to see my grandmother." My eyes were wet with tears.

"Aha! So it was your grandmother, and not Miss Lalla Sandford, who made you run away from me. Well, your grandmother can sweep markets and streetcorners and your grandfather too."

"My grandfather died," I said, quavering a little, because Amma might also be dead. Who could say?

"Oh, so he died," said Mrs. Patrick, and it seemed that this knowledge had a calming effect. "Since he is dead I guess we'll leave him out of this. But your grandmother can sweep marketplaces and crossroads! I would like to face up to her."

"Amma is good, and it is not her fault that I ran away. I did not know what I was doing. I was beside myself. Oh, my good mother, please forgive me."

"Oh, you little sinner!" shouted Mrs. Patrick. "You didn't know what you were doing? Perhaps you didn't know that I took you from wretched, dirty Icelanders, that I made you my son and planned to let you inherit all that I own. I was going to make you, you filthy little tiger, into a respectable Irishman, into a respectable and wealthy man. No, you did not know what you were doing; you did not know that you were hurting my feelings. You did not know that you were turning my hair white by running away from my home in the middle of the night. You did not know that I would be afraid for you, that I would be awake, that I would be crying, until I was sure that you had been found and you had not come to any serious harm. No, you could not imagine that I had a heart, a mother's heart, with feelings, a heart that could break. No, you couldn't know these things, you ungrateful little leopard. Your uncivilized nature blinded you so that you could not see your duty towards me, and you could not see the good future that I planned for you. Oh, you little serpent! I have decided to punish you physically, so that you will know what it means to run away from me, but I am not going to beat you as much as you deserve, only five blows!"

"Oh, dear mother," I said, and I fell on my knee beside her, "my dear mother, spare me! Forgive me! I shall never run away from you. I shall always love you and be obedient and good. Don't beat me, dear mother."

"Take off your jacket and your vest, you unfortunate little rogue!" said Mrs. Patrick as she stood up from her chair, with the leather strap in one hand.

I took off my jacket and my vest. "Oh, dear, kind mother, spare me. Forgive your son. You must not beat me. I could not bear it. I am so sick and so tired. Forgive me this time and I will never hurt you like this again!"

My words had no effect on Mrs. Patrick. She was going to beat me. She was in an alarming state of frenzy as she raised her strap and brought down three or four blows one after the other on my shoulders.

"One!" she yelled.

I screamed with pain, got up and ran into a corner, but although she stood in the same place her strap reached me wherever I went because the room was small and the strap was long.

"Two," said Mrs. Patrick after the next three or four blows. I ran from one corner to the other.

"Three!" said Mrs. Patrick as the blows rained down on my head and shoulders. I tried to crawl under the table and still the blows continued.

"Four!" said Mrs. Patrick. I was wild from the pain. I fell in a heap on the floor.

"Five!" said Mrs. Patrick and finally the beating was over.

For a while I lay on the floor, almost unconscious. I was aware that the lady was standing over me, breathless from the exertion. She ordered me to stand up but I did not move. I knew that she bent down and poked at me. Then all of a sudden she screamed and called for Marianna. I was picked up and carried upstairs and into my room. I was undressed and put into bed. Then I drifted off. Now and again I was aware that Mrs. Patrick was sitting beside my bed. She was crying. Sometimes I thought that I could hear her calling me, as from a distance. She was calling to me, so gently and motherly, in terms of endearment.

I woke up late the next day. I felt stiff and sore and worn out. I noticed that things in my room had been rearranged. My bed was now in a different place. The windows were completely changed and these new windows could be opened only a little bit to allow for fresh air. I knew immediately what these alterations signified but I did not care because I had been defeated. My hopes of escaping were now replaced by feelings of anxiety and despair.

I got dressed and made my way down to the parlour. Mrs. Patrick was waiting for me there. She took me in her arms and kissed me. She told me that she loved me very much, and that she very much regretted that she had to punish me, but she added that she had not punished me as severely as I deserved for the wrong that I had done. She said that I could never go over to the Sandford home again — never, never, never. All this trouble was solely Lalla Sandford's fault.

Later that morning I was in the kitchen with Marianna. She

smiled rather coldly when she saw me and her head shook more poignantly than ever.

"You're back, you wretch!" she said.

"Yes," I said, and I looked down at the floor, because I was ashamed.

"Now you know how the lady punishes naughty boys," said Marianna.

I was silent.

"But you certainly deserved this," she said.

"Yes, I know that," I said.

"You deserved this, not because you tried to run away from here, but because you let them catch you."

I stared at her.

"Yes, you can stare at me, little wretch," she said, and then she came up to me, grabbed my shoulder and spoke to me in a low voice. "Next time you try to run away make sure that you manage things better than you did this time because if the lady catches you on the run a second time, she will tear you limb from limb. I know the lady better than you do."

"I will never try to run away again," I said, with a shudder.

"Yes, you are going to try again very soon," said Marianna, "and you would be a fool if you did not make another attempt after all that has taken place here. The lady has begun but she has not finished with letting you feel the sweetness of her strap. I know the lady, believe me." Marianna stood very close to me, her head shaking uncontrollably. I did not know what to say.

Marianna's words certainly did nothing to encourage me to make a second attempt to run home. On the other hand, they filled me with trepidation. I worried about Mrs. Patrick, especially her extreme fits of rage. I distrusted her and I tried to avoid her as much as possible.

Early one afternoon, shortly after this unfortunate escapade, a boy came to Mrs. Patrick's house with word from Mr. Sandford. He needed to discuss some business with her and he wanted her to come to his house, because he was not feeling well that day. Mrs. Patrick went out with the boy. I stood at the front door and I watched as the lady disappeared around the corner of the house. Just as I was about to close the door, I saw Lalla Sandford cross the garden and hurry towards me. I was about to call out to her when she held up her hand to indicate that I had to be quiet. She walked over to me and she kissed me on the forehead. I kissed her in return and gave her a hug.

"Where is Marianna?" she asked.

"She is in the kitchen," I told her.

"That is good," said Lalla. "We have only a short time together, dear Eiríkur, but we have much to talk about," she said and she patted my cheek, just like a sister would.

"Did you see Mrs. Patrick leave?" I asked.

"Yes," she said. "My Dad sent for her and he will keep her busy for half an hour or so, just so that I can talk to you."

"Oh, my dear sister! You are so kind!"

"Dear Eiríkur, you should have come to us, to tell me that you were going to run back to your home," said Lalla.

"I wanted to do that, but I was afraid that you would stop me," I said.

"Yes," said Lalla, "I would have stopped you from running away in the way that you did. I had asked you not to think of doing it that way. You should just have run away to me."

"How did you know that I ran away?" I asked.

"We won't go into all that now," said Lalla. "We were very sorry that we didn't know about it sooner. I am sure that Mrs. Patrick was very harsh with you when she got you back."

"True," I said softly.

"I know, dear child," said Lalla. "She beat you until she was exhausted."

I looked at her but I said nothing more.

"I know that you long to see your grandmother, which is only natural," continued Lalla. "Daddy does not want to take you away from Mrs. Patrick by force, not openly, but he will help you to get away from here, so that she cannot get you back. Once you get back to your grandmother you will have nothing to fear, because Mrs. Patrick has absolutely no claim on you."

"How can I get back to my Amma?" I asked, taking her hand. "I am so afraid that they will catch up to me."

"Don't be afraid, child," said Lalla, "You will be helped this time. Now pay attention to what I have to say to you."

"Yes," I said, full of excitement.

"You see that little hedge back there behind the garden," said Lalla, pointing to a hedge about five fathoms behind the garden.

"Yes," I said, wondering how the little hedge would help me.

"Well," said Lalla, "as soon as the sun sets tonight, you will slip quietly over that hedge when the lady doesn't see you. Don't worry about Marianna. Don't take anything with you, not even your favourite book. I will see to it that you get that later."

"What do I do then?" I asked.

"You don't have to do anything," said Lalla with a smile, "because when you come over the hedge a man will be waiting for you, a man you do not have to be afraid of, because he is an Icelander, and he will take you along a route that John Miller and the lady will never consider. Once you get over the hedge without being seen there will be nothing more to worry about."

"What is the name of this Icelander?" I asked.

"I don't know that but he knows you, whatever his name is. He is a young man and quite handsome. He has beautiful eyes, which tell me that he is a good man. Daddy knew about him and he asked him to come to take you away from here."

"You are so wonderful and so good to me. May I kiss you again?"

We kissed each other and Lalla asked me to write to her as soon as I got home. She asked me to be a good boy always and she wished me well, just as if I were her brother.

When I came back into the parlour, I thought I heard someone walk through into the kitchen. I was a little startled and the idea occurred that Marianna had overheard our conversation, because she was the only other person in the house. I was afraid that Mrs. Patrick would somehow find out about our plan. That was a horrifying thought. Then I remembered that Lalla had said that I need not worry if Marianna saw me leave. Probably she already knew all about this. Perhaps she was a friend of Lalla's, perhaps a partner in this scheme? Perhaps Marianna sympathized with me after all!

I had to follow Lalla's plan and wait quietly until sunset. It was hard to control my excitement. Mrs. Patrick came home and she seemed to be in a good frame of mind. I wondered what Mr. Sandford could have said to make her so pleased. Now she called me her "honeypot" and said that she would let me visit the Sandfords, not right now, but sometime.

"But may I never see my grandmother?" I asked.

"Listen, Pat," she said, now very serious, "I will not allow you to mention that woman by name from now on. I do not like that woman! She can sweep marketplaces and streets. Your grandfather was good enough, Pat, but he has died, you said. Well, he is better off that way. He was good enough, while he was alive."

"Amma may have died, too," I thought to myself. "Who can say about that?"

I sat in the sitting room, beside the window facing west. I had a book in front of me but I was not reading. I was watching the sun slowly going lower and lower in the sky. The strip of blue between the sun and the top of the hill on the west side of the fjord was getting narrower and narrower. It would be sunset soon. Then it was dinnertime. I had no appetite. Mrs Patrick noticed that and asked if I was sick. I said that I didn't feel altogether well. Marianna looked at me. She had a tiny smile on one side of her mouth. Her head jerked up and down a little more than usual. Mrs. Patrick

went into "the holiest room in the house" and locked her door. I
went up into my bedroom and looked for my book of Jónas Hallgrímsson's poems, which I thought I could carry inside my jacket.
My three books were all in their place that morning, but now they
were all gone. I looked around the room but they were not there.
When I came downstairs I saw that the sun was setting. I met Marianna in the dining room. She said that she was going to talk to
Mrs. Patrick in "the holiest room" for a little while. What did I
think of that? She looked at me for a few seconds and smiled. Then
she surprised me with a quick kiss on the cheek and she ran off to
see the lady.

The sun had disappeared behind the hill at the west end of the
fjord. This was the time that Lalla had arranged for my meeting. I
took my hat and I walked out through the kitchen door, to the
woodshed and out into the garden. I stood still for a moment and
looked around me. There was no one to be seen. All was quiet. I
jumped over the fence, stopped and looked around. There was no
one near. I ran over to the hedge and went through it. That only
took a few minutes. A man was standing behind the hedge. I recognized him immediately. He was Eiríkur Gísli Helgi. I rushed over
to him and took his hand. Now I knew that I was out of danger.

"Is this my namesake?" said Eiríkur Gísli Helgi in Icelandic, and
he clapped me on the shoulder.

"Yes," I said.

"Come with me, but don't talk," said Eiríkur Gísli Helgi, and he
led me away.

We walked away from the hedge and through a little grove of
trees. We followed along the edge of the grove and soon we came to
a smooth roadway. There stood a horse with carriage, and the horse
was tied to an oak tree. Eiríkur untied the horse, taking his time.
Then we climbed into the carriage and set off. When we had driven
for a short while a tall well-built man with a wide-brimmed hat
stepped out into the road in front of us. Eiríkur stopped the horse.

The man walked over to the carriage and gave me a small case. "This is your case, my boy," he said, "you will know who it is from when you open it. God bless you! You are a good boy. I should say so." This was Mr. Sandford.

We travelled on and on but we never went fast. Eiríkur said that there was no need for us to rush.

"We are not on the way to Ship Harbour," I said.

"We are on our way through to the Musquodoboit Valley," said Eiríkur.

"When do we get to the place where you live?" I asked.

Eiríkur said that we would be there in the morning.

"What will I do then?" I asked, although I knew that he would help me.

"You can rest now," said Eiríkur. "I will take you back to the settlement. You don't need to be afraid. If anyone is looking for you he will go through Ship Harbour and Tangier." After a while he continued, "Mr. Sandford will make sure that no one will chase you. This Mr. Sandford is a good man, a very good man."

"Yes," I said, "and his daughter has been very good to me, too."

We did not talk much more during our drive that night. I was very tired. I think we may have stopped for a while. I am sure I fell asleep. We arrived at Eiríkur's home early in the morning. No one was up yet but he gave me a snack of milk and bread and then he put me into his own bed for a rest. I went to sleep at once and did not wake up until noon. I thought that we would leave to go to the settlement after we had lunch but Eiríkur said that I would have to be patient until the following morning. I accepted that decision.

I opened the case that Mr. Sandford had given me the previous evening. There I found my three special books, some pens and pencils, some writing paper, a few cookies and some apples and, best of all, a letter from Lalla. She told me that I did not have to fear that Mrs. Patrick would hunt me down again. Her father, she said, would have a word with that lady and explain things to her in such a way that she would actually be glad that I was gone. Along with the letter Lalla enclosed a five-dollar bill for emergencies.

For the rest of the day I entertained myself by exploring the home where my namesake was living. Eiríkur seemed to be very comfortable with the family and he took an interest in everything as if he were at least part owner. It was a pleasant timber house, which stood on the brow of a hill. About a hundred apple trees had been planted around the house. A large barn stood at the bottom of the hill. I saw five or six fine horses, a herd of cattle and some chickens. The husband and wife were very friendly to me. They said that they had a good opinion of all Icelanders, just because of Eiríkur Gísli Helgi. It was good to hear that.

My friend woke me early the next morning. I washed up and dressed quickly. We enjoyed a good breakfast. I thanked my hosts for their hospitality and then it was time to say goodbye. I took my case and climbed into the same carriage that I had been in before. This time we had two lively horses at our command.

We took off at a good pace from the start. We continued on in good form, past farms, over bridges, through villages and market-places. We travelled on beside the Musquodoboit River, past John Higgins' store, past the town of Corback, past Daniel Reid's farm, past Archibald's mill, up into the heights by Bob Miller's farm and from there into the Mooseland forest. We reached the first house in the settlement just before noon. We had driven about thirty-two miles in less than six hours. Here Eiríkur Gísli Helgi turned back to go home. He asked me to be sure to call on him if I needed assistance at any time. I promised that I would do that and I thanked him sincerely for all his help.

I did not stop at any of the houses in the western part of my community. I hurried straight to Amma's house. I walked quickly up the hill toward my home. A woman stood in front of the door. I saw that she was the woman who had moved in with Amma the previous spring. My heart was bursting with happiness. I had arrived. I greeted the woman. "Is Amma inside?" I asked and I didn't wait for an answer. I rushed into the house to hug my grandmother. I looked around but did not find her. I saw that her bed was gone. "Where is Amma?" I cried out. "Where has she gone?"

I turned around to the woman who had followed me in. She did not reply but I saw that her eyes were full of tears. I understood. Amma had died. Good God! My Amma had died! The woman took me in her arms and held me while I cried and she cried with me.

I found out that Amma had died the same day that John Miller caught me on my way home to see her. Twice a man had gone to Mrs. Meynard's house to make inquiries about me, and to try to bring me home. Mrs. Meynard said that Mrs. Patrick had moved with me to Halifax and she did not have her new address. She had promptly returned all the letters that had been sent to me.

The next day friends showed me Amma's grave. I knelt beside her grave and wept. I was overcome with feelings — feelings of love, regret and loss.

I had lost all my family. I had lost my dearest ones. I was left alone in the world, alone in a cold, ruthless world. I had little courage and no means of support. I was twelve years old.

CHAPTER 7

I stayed in Markland for a few weeks at the home of Jón, my friend and former schoolmate. I wrote to Eiríkur and Lalla and explained my circumstances. Eiríkur answered my letter at once and told me to come to see him right away because he knew of a good place where I could stay and work for my room and board. I did not want to miss out on such a good opportunity. I said a sad goodbye to all the neighbours. It was especially hard to leave Jón and his parents. I set off on foot, carrying a bag which contained all that I owned. Most of what Amma owned had gone into paying for medical help during her final illness. As for the farm, no one wanted to buy it, or if they did they had no money to offer. So the farm was deserted.

I walked westward through the Mooseland heights, bag in hand. I walked past Bob Miller's farm, and down the hill into the beautiful Musquodoboit district. I passed Archibald's mill and Daniel Reid's farm and Corback village. From then on I had to stop every once in a while to ask directions to Cooks Brook where Eiríkur lived. The way from Corback to Cooks Brook is hard to follow because this area is quite wide, with hills and many roads running both along the valley and across it. When I had come across with Eiríkur before, we had travelled fast and I had so much on my mind that I did not pay close attention. At sunset I still had about seven miles to go. I walked over to a house that was near the way, thinking I would ask if I could rest there for the night. As I approached the house a middle-aged woman came towards me. I took off my hat and bowed politely.

"What a polite boy! Good evening," she said kindly.

"Could you please give me a drink?" I asked, I wasn't so very thirsty, but I couldn't bring up the question of the night's lodging to begin with.

"Could I give you a drink? Yes, I think I could give a polite boy something to drink," the woman said, smiling. "Come in, lad. You may have as much milk as you like. I see that you have been travelling." She opened the door for us. "You can set your bag down where you are. Just come in." We entered a room that was simply furnished but clean and tidy. The woman offered me a seat and then she sat down herself. She studied me for a moment and then she called to someone in the next room. "Bring in a jug of milk, Maria." Someone answered, "Yes."

"Where have you come from, lad?" the woman asked kindly.

"I came from the Icelandic settlement," I answered, "I am Icelandic."

"Well, this is a surprise," she said. "Bring some bread and butter, Maria." "Yes," came the reply. "And where are you going?" the woman wondered.

"I am going to Cooks Brook," I said.

"Oh, you are going to see the Icelander who lives there," she said. "He is a gentleman. Bring a piece of cake, Maria." Maria said yes, but no food seemed to be coming.

"How is your mother?" asked the woman kindly.

"My mother died when I was a baby," I said.

"Oh, I'm sorry," said the woman. "So you have a stepmother, then, lad?"

"No. I was with my grandfather and my grandmother until they died."

"Did they die too? Maria, put the kettle on and make some tea," said the woman, and I heard the answer, "Yes." The next question was "Where is your father?" and to that I replied simply, "I do not know."

"Lord have mercy on us!" cried the woman. "You'll stay here for the night. Maria, you'll make up the bed in the attic this evening." Then the lady continued, "Tell me more about yourself. Where have you been since your grandparents died? What are you going to do in Cooks Brook?" I told her briefly about my circumstances.

After I had finished my supper, which was ample and very refreshing, the lady, who had introduced herself as Mrs. McLean, said she would like me to meet her mother. Her mother was very hard of hearing but when she finally heard that I was an Icelander she said that she had never seen anyone of that nationality, but she said that her husband, God rest his soul, had seen many Eskimo or Icelanders when he took part in seal hunts near Labrador.

Soon after that I was invited to have a rest in a comfortable bed in the attic. I slept soundly till morning.

In the morning Mrs. McLean suggested that I could come back and spend some time with her if I was not happy with the new job that Eiríkur had found for me. I thanked her for her offer and for all her hospitality. Just before noon I arrived at Cooks Brook.

I spent a week with my friends at Cooks Brook before I went to my workplace. While I was there I received a letter from Lalla Sandford. It was a letter of sympathy over the loss of my Amma and Lalla also assured me of her continued friendship. She stressed that Mrs. Patrick would never try to lay any claim to me again. Then it was time to go to my new home.

The head of the household was a farmer named Ruben Red. He

was not called Red because of his coloring for indeed he had dark hair and dark complexion. "Red" was just a family name which had been given to some forefather, perhaps as a nickname, as in the case of Eric the Red or William the Red, King of England. Names like that are often carried, or passed on, as family names.

Ruben was a tall, lanky man, kindly and well-mannered. He attended church faithfully. Strangely enough, he could neither read nor write, and he was unskilled when it came to looking after his farm or his equipment. His wife, called Mary-Ann, was short and stout and she talked incessantly. She seemed to squander her resources, but she was kind-hearted and generous almost to a fault. Ruben and Mary-Ann had two daughters, Jenny and Rachel. Jenny was sixteen or seventeen years old. She was good-looking, quiet and pleasant in manner, and she had completed public school education. Rachel was a widow in her twenties. She resembled her mother both in appearance and in personality. Like her mother she was a great talker, but she was kind and generous. The family farm was large but the land had not been well looked after. It was located about ten miles from Cooks Brook. The house was old and dilapidated but there were indications that it had once been quite a grand home. The big barn was now quite crooked. The apple trees around the house were scraggly and many of them were no longer bearing fruit. Farm implements seemed to be neglected. I was hired for one year with the stipulation that I could attend the nearby school for at least six months. I would work for my room and board and clothing. I was free to leave if I was not happy with conditions there and, on the other hand, I could stay longer if things were going well.

I was quite satisfied there because everyone treated me kindly, I had good meals and I did not have to work hard. The people there were never cross with each other and never seemed to be out of sorts. On the other hand, I did not learn any new skills through my work experience at that farm.

When I arrived I was surprised to find another Icelander there, a man who had very recently come from the old country. He had been hired for half a year. He was to receive food and clothing and ten dollars per month for his work.

Geir was approaching fifty years of age. He was a very big man, broad-shouldered and such a hard worker that he amazed all around him. It was almost dangerous to be near him, especially if he was felling trees or picking rocks. Old Ruben looked at him, almost in awe, shook his head and said, very quietly, "This man will be the death of me if I don't watch out."

Geir was not attractive in appearance. His face was covered, almost up to his eyes, with a short, untidy, reddish beard. His eyes were kindly, his forehead low. He had worked at sea before he came to America and, according to what he told me, he had often "gone through hard pulling against wind and tide." He had never married, but he had lived for a while with a woman in Reykjavík, and he had good memories of that time. He said that he liked Canada quite well but he admitted that he missed staple Icelandic food. He found it very difficult to learn English. As long as I knew him he could never manage a proper sentence in English, but he was able to make himself understood by using gestures. He was well-liked by the womenfolk because he was obliging and always willing to help with odd jobs. He could mend clothes, fix shoes, knit mittens, and so forth. This sort of help was well-appreciated.

"Icelandic men are very handy, and quick, too, and I think all Icelanders are like that," remarked Mary-Ann one day, when Geir was fixing Rachel's shoes. Rachel agreed with her mother, but added that not only was Geir multi-talented and quick, but he was also ingenious and showed a lot of foresight. Jenny never made any comments about Geir, and Ruben only said, "That man will be the death of me if I don't watch out."

One evening Geir and I sat under the trees in front of the house. Geir was smoking and I was looking at a newspaper. Suddenly Geir took out his pipe and he said, in Icelandic of course, "Listen, mate."

I looked up. "Yes?" I said.

"Listen, mate, you understand every single word in English, don't you?"

"No, far from it," I said.

"But you talk to people, just as if you were an Englishman."

"I can carry on an ordinary conversation," I said, "but that does not mean that I know every word."

"I think so, though," said Geir.

"Not so, Geir," said I.

"Listen, mate," said Geir, "what does *my love* mean in Icelandic?"

"*Ástin mín,*" I responded, "or *elskan mín.*" I was quite surprised. Geir filled his pipe again and began to smoke. After a while he said, "Listen, mate, how do you say *gæska* in English?"

"I think I would say *darling,*" was my answer.

"*Darling,*" Geir repeated and he nodded to himself, as if to say "this might come in handy sometime." He wrote this word in a little notebook that he always carried with him. He said that he was only asking me about these words for fun and he asked me not to mention this to the family.

A few days later Rachel called me into her room and she asked me whether I had been teaching Mr. Reykjavík some English. Geir had taken the name Reykjavík when he first arrived in Canada. He said this was appropriate because he had spent so much time in that city.

"No, I am not teaching Mr. Reykjavík English," I said.

"Yes, you have taught him to say *darling,*" said Rachel, pretending to be a little angry, "and you have taught him to write it, too. Oh, you are a bad boy, teaching Mr. Reykjavík to say *darling.* I am sure that he does not understand what that means."

"I am sure he does understand that," I said.

"Are you quite sure about that?" asked Rachel, smiling. "And Mr. Reykjavík writes so well! He must be an educated man. But tell me how does one say *darling* in Icelandic?"

"*Gæska,*" I said.

"Oh, is that really so? Mr. Reykjavík is a true gentleman. But you must not tell him that I said that. But you say that *darling* is *gæska* in Icelandic. Am I saying it correctly?"

"Yes," I said. Then she gave me a big apple and asked me not to tell anyone about this nonsense.

And so it went on. Another night as we sat in the garden under the trees, Geir asked me what the word "sweetheart" meant in Icelandic. Geir had the habit of scratching his head behind his ear when he was thinking. After a little while he spoke again. "What does *your wife* mean in Icelandic?" I told him what that meant.

Then he filled his pipe again and he looked very thoughtful as he sat there and smoked.

The next day Rachel called me into her room and asked me if I knew whether Geir had ever been married. I told her that he had always been single.

"Is it not surprising that such a good-looking, clever man was never married? Please don't tell him that I said that he was good-looking." I promised that I would not tell him about that, and then she gave me another good apple.

This continued day after day for a long time. Geir wanted to learn a few English words and Rachel wanted to learn a few words or a few phrases in Icelandic.

I lived at the farm for half a year, then Eiríkur Gísli Helgi came to get me. He wanted me to stay with him and attend school in Cooks Brook. The family protested and tried to persuade him to let me stay longer, but he was firm. He thought that it would be in my best interest to make this change and in the end I left with him.

Just around this time I received a long letter from Lalla. She wrote to inform me that she and her parents were planning to move to Halifax because her father had been offered a good position with the police force in that city. They had not found a home yet so I did not have a new address and I had to wait to answer her letter.

About a month after I left Ruben Red's farm, Geir came to see us. He took a seat and filled his pipe. "Mates," he said, "I have something to tell you."

"Well?" said Eiríkur Gísli Helgi.

"Yes, it's a strange story I have to tell you," he said, "very strange."

"Well?" prompted Eiríkur.

"I'll be damned if I'm not, all of a sudden, duly married. It's a strange thing."

"Well?" said Eiríkur.

"Yes, mates," said Geir, "for some time now Rachel and I have been on very good terms. Ever since I first met her Rachel has always been thoughtful and good to me, but I believed it was just kindness until yesterday I began to think that we were married, and I still think so."

"And why do you think so?"

"I'll tell you why," said Geir, as he took out his pipe. "It was this way. Yesterday morning Rachel brought me a brand new set of clothes to put on. I thought this must be some sort of holiday and started to put on my new clothes. Then Rachel came all dressed up and took my hand and led me outside. There was a horse and carriage, with a driver sitting up front. Then Jenny came out and she was all dressed up. We all got into the carriage and started up at a good clip. The sisters were always talking to me. But, darn it all, I could not understand what they were saying. Then after a while we arrived at a big house, which looked to me pretty much like a church. Two men were standing there and one of them held a book. Rachel and I stood in front of him while he read something from the book. While he spoke to us Jenny stood beside Rachel and the other man stood beside me. He was a very handsome man, I must say. Then all of a sudden Rachel said "yes" and I was told to say "yes," too. Then we went home and we sat down to an excellent lunch. I was called Mr. Reykjavík and Rachel was called Mrs. Reykjavík, which I thought was odd. Then I was really surprised when Rachel kissed me right in front of her sister. Today they moved furniture into the little house on the hillside where I think Rachel and I are going to live. I think that we are married, mates."

"There's no doubt about that," said Eiríkur.

"But was that a reverend who married us? There was no sign of cassock or chasuble."

"Pastors in this country do not always wear gowns," said Eiríkur. Geir scratched behind his ear as he pondered the situation.

Geir spent the night with us. The next day Eiríkur went with him to find out the truth about this matter. He understood right away that Geir and Rachel were united in marriage and that they were going to make their home on the farm that her former husband had owned. Eiríkur said that Jacob worked and waited for years to win Rachel but Geir won his Rachel in just a few months.

BOOK II

THE STRUGGLE

CHAPTER I

When I was thirteen years old I was not as big or as tall as the average boy of my age. I was probably more mature, however, than many a thirteen-year-old. I had travelled from one country to another, and I was growing up with two different cultures. I had enjoyed good times and I had been happy and healthy; and I had also been lonely, grief-stricken and afraid. I was learning to become more self-reliant, but I was also learning that it is not easy to go through life without a friend. I needed a friend I could trust, a friend who could understand my hopes and fears.

I had been fortunate. I had been nurtured by people who had done everything within their means to make my life as good as possible. However, these good angels had been called away while I still depended on their support and love. More than once I had been left alone; but always, within a short time, someone had come along to offer a helping hand.

My mother's grave was overgrown with grass in a churchyard in

Fljótsdal district, far away in Iceland; yes, overgrown and forgotten. Afi and Amma's graves were in the little cemetery in the Mooseland heights. Flowers planted there had bloomed and faded more than once. My father's grave could be in Brazil, or in Australia, who could say? My closest relatives had died and most other relatives were scattered here and there in North America, but far away from me.

Eiríkur Gísli Helgi had taken my father's place, although he was no kin of mine. He had looked after me ever since Amma died. He had tried to make sure that I received the education that public schools in Nova Scotia could provide. He truly cared for me and he was always kind to me. He did not possess that which youngsters need as much as growing plants need sunshine and warmth in order to thrive, namely, a cheerful outlook, but he was sensitive, and he was a good man. I was fond of him and I had a great deal of respect for him but I craved fun and action and he could not understand that. He was a man of few words, and once he had made a decision he could not be swayed.

Eiríkur seemed to be getting more and more despondent. He often hinted that he would like to return to Iceland. What I really wanted was to go to Halifax, especially because Lalla Sandford was there. She often wrote to me and mentioned all her activities in the city. I felt certain that she would be able to help me to find some interesting work to do there. Eiríkur Gísli Helgi would not consider that. "Don't go to Halifax!" he said.

"Where should I go then?" I asked.

"It would be better to go to Tangier," he said.

"To the gold mine in Tangier?" I asked. "Would that be better?"

"Much better," he said. "Not so much stuff going on."

"As you wish," I said.

"It will be easier for me to know how you are doing if you are in Tangier rather than if you were in Halifax," he said.

"All right then," I said. I was not too pleased but I tried to hide my disappointment.

So it was decided that I would go to Tangier to work as an errand boy for about six months. Eiríkur's employer had a friend who was a foreman at the mine and I was to be entrusted to his care. But before I went to Tangier my guardian wanted me to spend a month or so with the Icelanders in Markland.

Families in the settlement would be preparing children in their fourteenth year for Confirmation in the spring. Eiríkur Gísli Helgi wanted me to be part of that class. He had me read and re-read the *kver,* the old Icelandic catechism that I had studied with Amma before I left her.

For several years a pastor had visited the settlement, once in the spring and then again once in the fall. The pastor was German but he conducted services for us in English. He travelled about two hundred miles to serve this congregation but he always refused remuneration of any kind.

I stayed with my old friend Jón and his family. His father prepared us both for Confirmation, based on Icelandic texts. Our Confirmation was solemnized in English by the German pastor. I was pleased to be officially a member of the Lutheran Church.

Altogether I spent five full weeks in Markland and greatly enjoyed being with Jón for the whole time. We were best friends and we vowed that we would keep that friendship for the rest of our lives. That promise has not been broken. If Jón should read these lines someday I know that he will remember the days of his childhood in the Mooseland hills and he will remember his friend Eiríkur Hansson.

I returned to Cooks Brook and Eiríkur was ready to drive me to Tangier. I was looking forward to having a job that would actually earn me some money. Six months' employment at twenty-five cents per day seemed pretty good compared to other jobs that I'd had in the past. The future looked bright.

We set out one morning in early June. We travelled through a beautiful area. The apple trees were in full bloom, wildflowers were everywhere. The buckwheat, oats and barley were already growing in the fields. Birds were singing, bees were busily collecting nectar. The sea breeze was refreshing. Nature was at its best. On such a day it was good to be alive!

But my companion did not pay attention to anything but the road and the horses' reins. He did not talk to me at all. He was thinking, just thinking. But what was he thinking about? Were his thoughts all in the past? Was he remembering childhood days? Was he recalling a time when he was full of hope, and looked forward to a good life? Was it loss of a loved one? Or loss of his home? Did something even more painful happen to him? Could it have been a breach of troth? I only know that something left him so broken that he could never recover. My poor friend, poor Eiríkur Gísli Helgi!

We arrived at Tangier late in the evening. We slept at the boarding house where I was going to stay during my term there. The next morning Eiríkur found the foreman, a man by the name of Harris. He was rather short, but sturdily built, very lively and cheerful. His grey eyes fairly sparkled with glee. He had a wooden leg, a "peg leg." He had lost part of his right leg, below the knee, in 1863 in the American Civil War.

After I was introduced to Harris he grabbed me by the shoulders as if to test me to see if I was of solid build. Then he looked me directly in the face, and laughed out loud. He told Eiríkur that he would dump me into one of the pits in the mine and he would pay me sixty cents a day if I worked like a skunk and did not eat any of the gold. Eiríkur seemed satisfied with that. He said goodbye to Harris and me and left to go back to Cooks Brook.

I was pleased too. I looked forward to working in the mine with lively men and a foreman as cheerful as Harris seemed to be. Best of all, I would be earning some cash at last.

Tangier was a small mining town on the south shore of Nova Scotia about twelve miles from the Icelandic settlement. It was the main marketplace for the settlers. The land around Tangier is rather rough and there was little farming there. The townspeople were mostly miners and gold was the chief product, but the yield was small and the profits low after all the labour costs were taken care of. On the north side of the town a range of hills ran from west to east. From the top of the nearest hill there was a striking view of the wide fjord, both sides of the fjord thickly settled with cottages. At the base of this hill, north of the town and even in the town itself, mine shafts were scattered, most of them from one hundred to three hundred feet deep.

I spent my first day in Tangier exploring the area. I visited several sites and I saw the miners going up and down the stairs into the shafts. Each man had a lamp on his hat. As the men went down the stairs the lamps on their hats looked smaller and smaller in the distance. I was awestruck as I watched. Then I went to the mill that ground the rock and sorted out the gold. The noise from this machine was unbelievably loud. I saw rocks come up in big buckets. I thought at first that the rocks were mostly gold because I saw pieces that looked like shards of gold but this turned out to be a different metal altogether. I learned that, as the saying goes, "All that glitters is not gold!"

In the evening I walked down to the seashore. I looked at all the ships out in the bay. I saw the lobster, mackerel and herring that the fishermen were bringing in, for in the Tangier area there were good fishing grounds. I had not had a chance to sit down in the sand and relax since I was a little boy picking shells at Seyðisfjörð.

Six years had gone by since I left Iceland. Still, I did not yearn to go back "home" that day. That yearning came later. That evening I just thought about growing up and getting rich, and travelling far and wide, having adventures and fun. I built my own "Alhambra Castle" and gave myself Aladdin's lamp. In my daydreams I held sway as the ruler of a magical island. I allowed myself to relax there for a while, and then I came back to reality and I found my way back to the boarding house where I was going to stay for the next few months.

The boarding house was a large frame house painted white and it was usually called the White Castle. The manager was called Mrs. Ross. She provided my food and lodging for six or seven months. The food cost me thirty cents per day (ten cents for each meal), and it was five cents per day for my bed. When I subtracted thirty-five cents per day from my salary of sixty cents per day I saw that my earnings were not quite as good as I had thought at first. On Sundays of course we did not work but we still had to pay for our room and board.

Mrs. Ross was always nice to me while I was there. No one ever complained about the meals: Mrs. Ross always put out plenty of food for her house guests. There were forty to sixty miners there, men of all ages. Her husband, Mr. Ross, had moved to California and he worked in a mine there. He always wanted his wife to come to California, but she insisted that he come back to Tangier. Neither of them moved, with the result that they had not seen each other for some years.

It is not easy to describe Mrs. Ross. It was said that no one in Tangier could look at two pictures of her and see that they were of the same person. That was because she was never in the same mood for more than a few minutes at a time. She could be furiously angry at sunrise, everyone's darling at nine o'clock, weeping at noon, full of jokes at dinnertime or singing at bedtime. She was not tall and slim, but you could not say that she was short and stout either. She was not beautiful, but it would be wrong to say that she was homely. Her eyes had no particular colour; rather they seemed to combine all colours of the rainbow in equal proportion. And so it was with her hair; it was not black, not blonde, it was not red, or brown, neither was it golden or chestnut-coloured. It was as if all these colours were together in her hair, which was neither long nor very short. In other words it is impossible to describe her. However, it does not really matter because she only supplied me with a bed and meals for a short time and she was never unkind to me — and neither was she ever particularly good to me.

The second morning that I was there I woke up when I heard someone calling loudly outside the house.

"Mrs. Ross! Mrs. Ross," someone shouted.

"Shame on you, Harris!" shouted Mrs. Ross.

"Oh, don't be so shy, my dear," called someone from outside.

"Shame on you, Harris," shouted Mrs. Ross.

"Oh, don't be like that, Mrs. Ross, my dear. I was just going ask you to call the Icelandic laddie, because the cocks are crowing already!" said the voice outside.

What is he talking about? I asked myself. I was sure that it was Mr. Harris, my foreman, who was shouting. I got dressed in a hurry.

"Look after your Icelandic laddie yourself," said Mrs. Ross.

"Good morning, Mrs. Ross, my dear," said Harris as he came into the room. "What a sight to see your nose! It's as blue as the nose of the parish priest, if I say so myself!" Harris laughed heartily at his own joke.

"Shame on you, Harris! You talk to me like a street kid," said Mrs. Ross. "I'll tell Mrs. Harris about this!"

"Yes, do that," said Harris, "and I will tell her about the other, that is about the kiss!" and Harris was almost convulsed with laughter.

"The kiss? What kiss? Do you think you could make anyone believe that I kissed you, you old wooden leg?" said Mrs. Ross in a rather high-pitched voice.

"Well, my dear, get the laddie up and give the poor guy a good bite to eat because he is going to be in the pot today for the first time in his life. I hope he is fit for the job."

Just then I arrived in the dining room. There were men sitting all around the table, hurriedly eating their morning meal.

"There he comes," said Mrs. Ross as she saw me come in.

"Good," said Harris. "I am going to sit here on the steps until he has finished eating so I can take him to the pot but he has to hurry because the Black One is heating up."

I sat down at the table and tried to eat but I had no appetite. First of all, I was up earlier than usual and, secondly, I was anxious about the pot and the Black One.

"Oh, I say, Mrs. Ross, my dear," cried Harris, "have you heard any squawks from that crow of yours out west?"

"What a way to speak, Harris!" said Mrs. Ross. "People might think that Mr. Ross was some sort of weakling. But since you have asked about him I can tell you that he wrote to me just recently and asked me particularly to say hello to you."

"Oh, bless him," said Harris, laughing. "We had fun, your crow and I, when we were in Richmond that year. We kissed the black girls and took a 'sex-tour' at the Hotel Rio de la Plata."

"Shame on you, Harris," said Mrs. Ross, pretending to be very angry. Harris didn't answer; he just laughed and banged the steps with his wooden leg.

I got up from the breakfast table, picked up my straw hat, and walked over to Harris. "Oh, there you are, laddie," he said and he shook me again, his eyes sparkling with good humour as before.

"I am ready to work," I said as bravely as I could, although I worried about the "pot" and the "Black One."

"Come with me then, laddie," said Harris and he hurried down the main street. He walked so fast on his wooden leg that I had to run to keep up with him. "I am late because I came to get you but I thought that I should take you to the pot myself," he said.

"To the pot?" I asked.

"Yes," he said, "the pot will be bubbling soon. Now this is Miller's store," he said. "Don't ever buy anything from Miller." He indicated a large store on the north side of the street.

"Does the pot boil?" I asked.

"Yes, the pot boils when the Black One comes," said Harris and added, "Here is Forest's store. Buy what you need here, because old

Forest has been whitewashed."

"What is the Black One?" I asked.

"Oh, the Black One boils over in the pot," he said. "And where is the rooster who was with you the day before yesterday?"

"The rooster?" I asked, surprised.

"Yes, the rooster," said Harris, laughing. "That was definitely a rooster, that bird. I saw his crest even though he didn't crow too much."

"If you are talking about the man who brought me here, he went home," I said.

"We have to hurry," Harris said, and he rushed along so fast that I could hardly keep up with him.

Finally we arrived at the site that Harris supervised. Several miners greeted us and they all seemed to be on good terms with their foreman.

Harris called to a man named Samuel. "Take the lad to the pot. Let him help the Chinaman stuff the coffin."

"Yes, sir," said Samuel.

"Don't let the falcons pull him to pieces. I promised my friend that I would look after the laddie," said Harris, smiling.

"Yes, sir," said Samuel.

"This is an Icelandic boy of good family," said Harris.

"Just so," said Samuel.

"It is best to send him down in the coffin. Don't let him climb down the skeleton," said Harris, looking me in the face and smiling.

"Yes, sir," said Samuel.

I did not like all this reference to coffins but I tried to look brave. Samuel patted me on the head and whispered that the gold mine was really not a scary place.

I was told to step into a large bucket. The bucket was supported by a very heavy rope, which was wound around a wheel that was turned by a steam engine. One bucket came up full of rock or water while another went down. I went down very quickly in the bucket but it stopped safely. I stepped out of the bucket and realized that I was now in a large cave that the miners had created. There were many men at work. Some were picking holes in the rock with chisels and others were banging with sledgehammers. The sound of their blows echoed through the cave. Where was the Chinaman that I was supposed to work with? Where was the pot? Where was the Black One? All of a sudden a very big man approached me.

"Are you the boy? Are you the one who is supposed to assist me with this difficult work? Oh, oh!" said the giant.

"I was told that I was to work with a Chinaman," I said.

"That is so, my boy," said the big man and he picked up a shovel. "That is right. I am the Chinaman that you are to help in this awful pot. Oh, oh!"

"You do not look Chinese," I said.

"I am not born Chinese, my boy, not born in that mighty empire, but I was there for many years. Oh, oh!" And this "awful" man grimaced as he said that but he did not look at me.

"What am I to do?" I asked, and I was not at all pleased with this new boss that I was to work with.

"You have to shovel, boy, shovel, shovel as if your life depended on it, so we won't be buried alive in this awful pit," he said, and he began to shovel from a heap of broken rock into the empty bucket.

I picked up a shovel too, and I shovelled rock into the bucket. I thought it would never fill, but finally we had it loaded to the brim. Then the giant pulled on a rope and the bucket went up to the ground level and another bucket came hurtling down. We picked up our shovels and began filling anew.

After we had filled several buckets in this way I was brave enough to address this awful Chinaman. "Is there a pot here?" I asked.

"We are in the pot, my boy, we are in that awful pot, and many a man has been cooked to death in this pot, cooked until he was cooked into mush. Oh, oh!" I shuddered when I heard this.

"What is it that the men call a coffin?" I asked.

"This is the coffin, my boy," said the big man and banged the bucket with his shovel. "This is that awful coffin which has carried many a good man lifeless from this awful pot. And who knows, maybe it will carry us, too, in the same condition. Oh, oh!"

I felt a chill sweep over me.

"And what is this skeleton that they talk about?" I asked, because I had to get to know this "awful" place.

"The skeleton is over there, my boy," he said and he pointed to the stairs that led up through the shaft.

"Tell me," I said, "Where is the Black One, who boils over?"

"Oh, don't mention him," said the big man, and I thought that I heard something like suppressed laughter. "Oh, please don't mention that one, because that is the most awful thing in the mine."

"I have to know about the Black One," I said.

"Oh, that monster simmers and boils, my boy, boils just like a hot spring. Oh, oh."

"Is it dangerous?" I asked.

"Dangerous? He is danger itself."

"Are the men afraid of him?" I asked.

"Afraid of him?" asked the giant, "Yes, I should say so. The miners are not afraid of anything in the mine except him!"

"And who is he?" I asked.

"I must not say that out loud, my boy" he said. "I must not let that secret echo through the shafts. That is a terrible secret."

"I have to know about this," I said.

"Don't mention this to anyone if I tell you this awful secret, my boy. Promise that you will not tell anyone about this. Oh, oh."

"You can trust me," I said innocently.

"I am going to trust you then, my boy, and tell you who he is, this terrible one who simmers and boils. But if you fail me — well, it doesn't matter. I will trust you."

"You don't need to worry," I said.

"Pay attention now, my boy." The Chinaman looked around as

if he was making sure that there was no one nearby. He whispered so low that I had to strain to hear what he said, "The Black One who always simmers and boils, the one that all of us in the mine fear more than anything else, do you hear, is none other, are you sure you are hearing me? is none other than our foreman, Harris, with the wooden leg. Oh, oh."

For a long moment I was stunned by this unexpected revelation. I had almost begun to think that the Black One was some supernatural creature who haunted the mine from time to time and was occasionally sighted by the workers. But to connect the Black One with Harris seemed impossible, especially since he, that very morning, had referred to the Black One that hissed and boiled. Then suddenly I realized that all these stories had been crafted in fun. They were all a joke, and the miners, including Harris himself, were jokers.

Soon I began to feel quite comfortable in the pot since I no longer had to dread meeting the Black One. I never climbed the skeleton although the miners went up and down those stairs like cats. I always enjoyed going up and down in the bucket. I was often tired after I shovelled the bucket full, but my Chinaman never made me work harder than seemed necessary. The falcons never tore me to pieces. They were the miners who worked on the team that Harris supervised. They were always good to me.

While I was in Tangier I worked day after day with this Chinaman who was actually a Scottish Highlander. In his youth he had travelled to Hong Kong and after that his friends called him Sing Song although his name was Roderick McIsaac. The longer I knew him, the better I liked him. He never tired of telling me stories. Some of them may have been true, some half-truths, and some pure fiction. I decided to treat them all as entertaining stories. What a storyteller! Mark Twain was not his equal. Don Quixote from La Mancha was lacking in comparison.

One day I asked Sing Song, I didn't feel like calling him Mr. McIsaac, whether there were any other Icelanders working in the mine.

"What are you saying, boy?" he said. "Are you Icelandic?" He pretended to be shocked. Finally he admitted that there was one Icelander up on deck. He was a terrible man. "Oh, oh." He pressed his lips together and he shook his head at the thought of this frightful man.

"Up on deck?" I asked.

"Yes, up on ground level, my boy, up on the good green earth where the sun shines equally on the sinners and the righteous. Up there is a frightful Icelander, with broad shoulders like a gorilla, and calves like Goliath. He is frightening. Oh, oh."

"Is he a young man?" I asked.

"Young, my boy?" said Sing Song, "He is neither young nor old. He is of that awful age when men are neither young nor old. He is frightening, but still altogether different from the Icelanders that I saw in China, altogether different."

"Did you see Icelanders over there?" I asked.

"Yes, my boy," said Sing Song, "over there I saw two frightful Icelanders, two frightful-looking Icelanders! One of them was called Sandy, and the other was called Andy. They were kept like souvenirs in a tower, a tower made of pure porcelain. They were kept in dangerous material. Oh, oh!"

"They were kept in what?" I asked.

"In alcohol."

"In alcohol?" I repeated.

"Yes, my boy, in a large glass chest, full of purest alcohol."

"Why?" I asked.

"So they would not rot, my boy" said Sing Song looking rather amused. "So they could be preserved indefinitely. How terrible. Oh, oh!"

"Now you are testing me," I said.

"Oh, far from it, boy," said Sing Song, innocently. "Far be it from me to try to fool you. I saw two Icelanders in the Pagoda Tower in Nanking. They were in a large glass chest full of alcohol."

"Then they were dead," I said.

"Dead, my boy, long dead, killed by blows long, long ago, quite dead. Oh, oh."

"Killed by blows?" I said, not knowing what to make of this story.

"They were killed by blows, my boy, killed up north, in the Arctic Ocean, in that terrible, freezing ocean."

I stared at Sing Song.

"Listen, my boy," he said in a low voice, and he bent down and whispered. "Listen, I am going to tell you a secret, a terrible secret."

"I can keep a secret," I said, quite innocently.

"Listen, my boy," he whispered. "These two poor Icelanders, pay attention now, were actually — are you sure that you hear every single word? They were actually two very fat and clean seals. Oh, oh!"

Once again I was very surprised, but I was relieved to know that two seals had been killed by blows but not two of my countrymen.

"You have travelled far afield," I said after a little pause.

"Yes, very far," said Sing Song as he watched the next bucket come down the shaft. "I visited all the greatest empires in the world but I spent most of the time in Peking and Nanking because the emperor's sister did not want to let me leave the country. She was terrible, my boy. She wanted to turn me into a Mandarin, a terrible Mandarin. She fed me soup made from birds' nests, what a soup that was! And they had me walk on snow-white shoes and I had a long braid on the back of my head. I had to drink tea day and night; always I was drinking hot tea, because I was supposed to turn into a terrible Mandarin. Oh, oh!"

"The emperor's sister would not let you go?" I said.

"Don't mention her, my boy," said Sing Song sadly. "Oh, that terrible witch! I still bear the marks from her claws. She wanted to keep me so that I could become a terrible Mandarin."

"And she scratched you when she wanted to keep you?" I said.

"She patted me with ice-cold claws," he said, and he shivered all over. "She patted me because she loved me, she loved me terribly. She clawed at me with her claws because she loved my life. She felt for my heart and wanted to hold it and squeeze it, to squeeze it terribly, so that I could feel how much she loved me, so that in the end I could become a Mandarin, a terrible Mandarin. Oh, oh!"

"She must have been insane," I said.

"Terribly insane, my boy," he said sadly. "Finally she tied me to a bed with ice-cold iron bands. Then she licked the muscles off my bones. Oh, oh!"

"How could she boss you?"

"She was strong in those days, my boy," he said, "and she had plenty of help."

"And who helped you in the end?"

"A cunning doctor from London, my boy. That doctor was full of tricks and he knew the emperor's sister from years before and he knew what would stop her craziness. That was terrible craziness. Oh, oh!"

"If the emperor's sister had not been insane would you have loved her?"

"Listen, my boy! The secret is, listen carefully, the emperor's sister was none other than that terrible cholera! Oh, oh!"

Again I was astonished. I would never have thought that anyone would describe cholera as "the emperor's sister." I was going to ask Sing Song more about his travels but just then a horn sounded from the deck above to announce the time had come for our mid-day meal. I thought that morning had passed very quickly.

"How did you like the pot and your Chinaman, laddie?" asked foreman Harris when I came up on deck.

"I liked him very well," I said. Harris nearly choked with laughter.

"And how did you like the laddie, Sing Song?" asked Harris and he kicked Sing Song's rump with his wooden leg.

"Well, sir," said Sing Song, trying to keep from falling, "I like him awfully well, oh, oh."

 I worked in the mine for a little more than half a year. At that point Harris was laying off some of his workers. He indicated to me that I could have a job there again the following spring if I so desired. It never came to that, but before I go on to the next chapter of my life I cannot resist relating the story of one incident that happened at the mine while I was there.

It happened one afternoon just after lunch that some unusually large blasts were taking place in "the pot" and no one could go down through the shafts until the explosions were concluded. This took longer than had been expected. Meanwhile forty or fifty men were sitting "up on deck," as they called it, with nothing to do. They were all strong, energetic men. Soon someone suggested that they should have some entertainment while they were waiting. Nothing would be better than a good wrestling match. This idea was generally well received.

At this suggestion a tall, heavily built man got to his feet. This man was Christopher O'Brian. He was known as the strongest man in the town, and indeed he was closely related to the giant MacAskill who was by far the strongest man ever known in Nova Scotia. MacAskill, the giant with the heart of a child, had died a few years earlier, before the Icelandic settlers came to the province. I had heard many stories about his almost unbelievable feats of strength, and also about his remarkable sensitivity and his kindness. I had also heard many stories about his kinsman, Christopher O'Brian. He was certainly known far and wide for his strength, especially for weight-lifting. He was frequently involved in various contests, and he was so good at boxing that his equal was not to be found between Halifax and Tangier.

So now it was none other than Christopher O'Brian who stood up and took his stand in front of the crowd of miners. I stared at him because there was something about him that I had never seen before. First of all, I had rarely seen such a tall and thick-set man so handsome and so graceful in all his movements. The other thing that I noticed about him was his attitude. With every movement he seemed to invite someone to call him out, to invite someone to a struggle. He carried his head high and his bearing showed unlimited self-confidence. I imagined that Achilles himself must have looked very much like Christopher.

Christopher had curly black hair and a bushy black beard. His eyes were black and sharp. They seemed to say, "Come on if you dare." He had strong jaws and a wide chin, his nose was high and thin and slightly hooked like an eagle's beak. His forehead was well proportioned to the rest of his face. On his head he wore a grey, wide-brimmed hat that was tipped slightly to one side. He stood very straight and he looked over the crowd like a general looking over his legions.

"Good fellows!" he said in a very deep voice. "You would like to see some wrestling. Well and good, if someone would like to take me on I will be ready for a match." As he said this, he crossed his arms across his chest, stamped his right foot and looked over the gathering. No one spoke and some looked away.

"Good fellows," said Christopher again, "I see that you would rather watch others wrestle with me than let others watch you wrestle with me."

"You hit the nail on the head, Christopher," said someone who was sitting quite near him.

"Good fellows!" said Christopher, raising his voice. "I have heard that Icelanders are famous wrestlers and that they are usually willing to test their skill in that sport. Now, as it happens, we have been lucky to receive a few men from that nationality into this community. We should not hesitate to learn how they conduct themselves in a good wrestling match. If there are any Icelanders in this group I would invite one of them to tangle with me."

"This is awful, my boy," said Sing Song, who was sitting beside me. "This is awful for the poor Icelanders! Oh,oh!"

"Good fellows!" shouted Christopher when he saw that no one was coming forward, "I thought there were a few Icelanders in our mine.

At least there are some in Ferguson's mine, a few lively fellows."

"There are two of them here with us," said someone who was sitting down.

"Good fellows!" shouted Christopher. "If there is a full-grown Icelander here let him try his skill against a Bluenose!"[16]

"Good fellows," shouted Christopher, louder than before, "if there is any Icelander here who hears and understands my language, but does not dare to come forward and wrestle with me, then I will say that all Icelanders are cowards!"

I was about to stand up to say something in defence of my countrymen when I saw that a man stood up and walked quietly toward Christopher. Although he was a complete stranger to me, I saw right away that he was an Icelander. He was a man of average height, but of sturdy build, and vigorous in his movements.

"Very good!" shouted foreman Harris when he saw the man come forward.

"I don't understand you very well," said the Icelander calmly to Christopher and it was clear that he had difficulty with English.

"Come here, laddie," said Harris and pointed to me. "Come here and tell your countryman what Christopher has to say."

I hurried forward and explained the situation to the man, stressing that much depended on this performance. The man's name was Bergvin and he looked to be about twenty-five years old.

"I don't mind having a round with this man," he said in broken English, after he studied Christopher from top to toe. "I don't worry about falling."

"Well said," shouted Harris and he gave Bergvin a pat on the back, "and I will say that you Icelanders are good men if you can keep up this fight for one round."

According to local custom, assistants measured the distance between the combatants and put them in their places. They were to run at each other and then they could take holds on each other as they chose. Christopher took off his jacket and his vest and Bergvin took off his shoes and his hat. Then Harris called out, "One, two, and three!" As soon as the opponents met it was clear that Christopher meant to bring Bergvin down by sheer strength, whereas Bergvin depended on skill and Icelandic strategy.

"Very good!" shouted Harris. "I'll tell you that Icelander is made of good stuff!"

The wrestlers tried every trick they had to bring each other down, but they seemed to be at a stalemate. Bergvin was much shorter than Christopher and therefore Christopher had a hard time keeping his opponent from getting under and lifting him up. Christopher knew that if he did not stand solid he would be in danger of taking a fall, so he used all his strength to try to push Bergvin over. Bergvin quickly realized that if he could lift Christopher up even a little bit, then he could easily topple him.

For quite a long time neither one seemed to be gaining. But then the onlookers noticed that Christopher was getting short of breath and his face seemed to darken, whereas Bergvin didn't seem to be out of breath and his color remained good. Although Christopher was very strong and was used to competing in wrestling matches, he did not have very good endurance, likely because he had been drinking alcohol for some years and had damaged his lungs by smoking. Bergvin on the other hand had good lungs and had good endurance because he was used to hard work.

"Christopher O'Brian," shouted some of the miners, "are you going to let the Icelander beat you?"

"Keep it up, Icelander," called Harris. "You are going to win! Don't worry about letting him fall. He is my cousin and I know his bones won't break!"

Bergvin heard and understood what Harris said and he pressed on even harder. Christopher seemed to be on the defensive rather than trying to attack, although he tried every now and then to push Bergvin over.

"Christopher O'Brian," shouted some of the miners again. "Give it all you've got, drive the Icelander to the ground!"

"Hold on, Icelander!" shouted Harris and he stamped with his wooden leg. "Think of your great-grandfather, friend. Hold up the honour of your family. You have courage. You should have been the son of Richard the Lionheart or my forefather the Black Douglas. You are going to beat him, friend, I will bet my boots on that. He is beginning to weaken, he is giving up, take him down!"

"Christopher O'Brian, watch out!" shouted the others.

Christopher was stronger than Bergvin, but Bergvin was quick. Christopher lifted himself up a little, hoping to throw his full weight on Bergvin to drive him down, and this gave Bergvin his chance. He quickly caught Christopher's heel and he followed through so strongly that Christopher leaned back a little — and then he fell, with Bergvin going down on top of him.

Harris shouted, "Bravo! Very good! Well done, friend!"

All others were quiet except for me. I shouted, "Hurrah, hurrah!" and I jumped for joy.

When they both got up, Christopher rolled up his sleeves and was ready to get into a boxing match, and that would have meant disaster for Bergvin because he was altogether unskilled in that sport.

As soon as he saw how things stood Harris stepped between them. "If you want a boxing match, Christopher O'Brian, you will have to take me on. You invited the Icelander to wrestle, not to box. He won in an honourable way."

Christopher put on his vest and his jacket and left. He was obviously far from pleased with this outcome.

"You did very well," I said to Bergvin as he was putting on his shoes.

"Oh, well," he said, "it was just the old Icelandic backheel[17] that took him down."

That evening Christopher walked over to Bergvin and shook his hand and said that he would like to be his friend. Bergvin was the only man who had ever brought him down. After that the two were good friends but they never wrestled again. Bergvin was afterwards held in high regard in the mine.

CHAPTER 2

Near the end of July, that summer while I was working in Tangier, my special friend Jón and two other Icelandic boys from Markland came to the mine to see me. They and their parents and all my old neighbours were leaving to go to Manitoba. They could not leave, Jón said, without coming to say goodbye to me. The boys spent two hours with me, then they had to leave to get home that evening. I did not have a chance to talk to them as much as I would have liked because I was working in the pot when they arrived. They had to get special permission to come down there to see me. I asked them all to write to me as often as they could. I wished that I could have gone west with them but I did not talk about that. I said that I would come later, when I had earned enough money to pay my way.

I knew that I would miss my Icelandic friends after they were gone. I had not spent much time with them during the past two years, but I had known them for a long time and they had always treated me with affection and helpfulness. I had always felt safer somehow, when I was on my own working out in the wider community, just from knowing that these good people were living in their old homes. I knew that if I ever came to them in need they would help me in any way that they could.

My guardian, Eiríkur, was still my main support; but he could die, and then who would be there to help me? I must not forget, I did have one other friend and that friend was Lalla Sandford. But she could die also. There was no denying it, I was sorry that all my friends from the Mooseland heights were moving away and I was sorry that I could not go with them. I had no money so I could not leave right then. My guardian had no money either. He never had a cent in his pocket because he never asked for any pay. In fact I think that he sometimes felt that he did not need to ask for any money because he was the rightful owner of the farm.

My Icelandic friends were leaving Nova Scotia to go to the old home of the buffalo and the Indians. They were going to the huge grasslands of western Canada, where the soil was fertile and free from rocks and stubborn roots. All that was needed was to put the plough to the ground, drop in the seed, cover it lightly with the harrow and wait for the wheat to ripen, the best wheat under the sun, the yield as much as forty bushels to the acre. There one could sit in comfort on the binder or the mower and still accomplish as much as twenty men using ordinary scythes and sickles. Out there in the west the weather was not unpredictable. It was warm while the crop was growing and then it was cool when harvest was over.

My friends were going west where towns and cities were springing up and where every small job brought in a good wage. They were all going to Manitoba or to Dakota, where one could become a wealthy farmer in just a few years. They were going to the fertile Red River Valley, or to Winnipeg!

Much work had been put into those Icelandic farms. Around every house thirty to fifty acres had been cleared and several acres had been smoothed and turned into fields. Each farmer had built a barn and had carefully fenced his land. Every house had been neatly improved. The farmers, in co-operation, had made plans for setting up a sawmill and a gristmill. It was hard to give up after all that effort. Still, the farmers felt that they would never prosper financially there, and that their children would have to leave sooner or later.

Furthermore, they had come with the understanding that more immigrants would be welcome and that friends or relatives could join their group. Now they were told that government land was no longer being offered. Indeed, one group of Icelandic immigrants bound for Nova Scotia had been stopped in Quebec and sent on to Manitoba. Meanwhile boom conditions in Winnipeg had been reported in the newspapers of 1880 to 1882 and letters from Icelanders in that city corroborated these claims. This combination of circumstances led to the decision to abandon the colony.

One day in August, 1882, these good people left Markland. They had spent time and energy on all their endeavours. They had come empty-handed and now they left empty-handed. Some sold their land for a few dollars, others could not raise any money from their farms. Sale of their animals barely paid for the journey to Winnipeg. Some only managed to cross the Great Lakes, then had to stop to earn money to continue on their way. It took courage and determination to leave Iceland to go to Nova Scotia; it took courage to leave the Mooseland hills to move to Manitoba.

Some thirty to forty families had settled in Markland. One-tenth of the original settlers had died, many children had been born there. Icelanders did not seek public office or take part in public debates in Nova Scotia; neither did they get involved in any disputes or litigations.

Their neighbours from other communities were sorry to see them leave, and said they had never known more hardworking and law-abiding people. And I am sure that all the Icelanders themselves would say that they remembered friends they had met in Nova Scotia with gratitude and respect.

I worked at Tangier until the first part of December. After paying Mrs. Ross for my board and room I had $25 left. I bought myself a set of clothes and a few odds and ends that I needed, and I had only a few dollars left in my pocket when I started off for Cooks Brook. My guardian, Eiríkur, had no money but it had been decided that I would stay with him at Cooks Brook for the winter.

Instead of going directly from Tangier to Cooks Brook I thought I would walk to the old settlement first and then go on from there. Although it was December there had been no snow. This time I did not hurry as much as I did when I was running away from Mrs. Patrick. That time I had been looking forward to reaching the community. Now I dreaded it, knowing that my friends were gone. Still, I felt that I must stop there one last time. I had enjoyed many happy times there, and there were Afi and Amma's graves. At the very least I needed to stop beside their graves.

I crossed the river on the bridge by the sawmill, went past the mining town called Mooseland, past Jakob Hillsey's farm, past John Prest's shingle mill, past Isaac Young's house, past the swamp on the north-west side, down the hill on the other side, into the forest, and onto the path that led to the first house in the settlement. Just one half mile east of that house John Miller of the broken nose had caught up to me when I ran away from Mrs. Patrick's house the first time. I stopped at that spot for a moment and unpleasant memories came back.

I walked up to that first house. The door was ajar, some windows were broken. A few small stones lay on the floor, likely the ones that had broken the windows. The trap-door into the basement had been removed, leaving an ominous dark hole in the floor. A few kitchen utensils remained, and a table and three good chairs. I sat down briefly and thought about the woman who used to live there. She had told me many a good story, and shared with me many a pleasant verse. Her grave is now near the Pembina Hills in North Dakota.

No one lived in the next house or the next one after that. I stopped at one house after another. All were vacant. When I got confirmed in June of that year, all these houses had been occupied. Now it seemed as if a scourge or a pestilence had removed all life.

I walked up the hill where the house stood, the house where Afi and Amma had lived their last days. The doorway and the windows had been boarded up so I did not go in. The path around the house, with its inlaid stones, had already been damaged, likely by animals wandering around. Weeds had grown up in the garden over the summer. Grass had invaded the path that led up the hill from the main road. Signs of neglect were everywhere. But the tall white birch tree was unchanged. It spread its sheltering branches over all. From high up on the hill it stood like a monarch presiding over the yard and all the other trees.

I stood awhile under the birch tree and thought about days gone by. All around was quiet. Then suddenly I heard a screech. There was a squirrel sitting on a branch just above my head. He was nibbling away as squirrels do and he stopped now and again to look at me. Soon he forgot about his lunch and he hopped around from branch to branch as if in celebration. "They're gone!" he seemed to say, "All gone! All gone!" As he ran up and down he seemed to scoff. "I can live here, I live here, I live here." From the topmost branch he shook his head at me and he was full of fun and frolic.

I stopped awhile at the cemetery. Flowers had been planted on Afi and Amma's graves in the spring and they had been tended during the summer. The fence had been improved.

I went from house to house. All were empty, all except one. Professor Cracknell and his family were still there. I spent the night with them. He was very kind and he never said, "Blunder" or "Fiddlesticks." He said that he missed the Icelanders very much. As soon as he could manage it, he thought that he would return to old Scotland. "There is no place like home!" he said. His work was finished now that the Icelanders had gone. Only because of them had he been willing to live in a rough area like the Mooseland heights.

The next morning he walked with me a little way. He wore his hat, not the big Scottish cap. He was in a good mood. He said that he was sure that I would become a City Councillor in Winnipeg if I decided to go west. He shook my hand on leaving and sincerely wished me well in the future. Then he turned to go home and I made my way down from the hills and into the Musquodoboit valley. I reached Cooks Brook that evening. I was likely the last Icelander to walk through the Markland settlement.

When I arrived in Cooks Brook I found that the household there was in a state of confusion. All the family, Eiríkur included, were about to move away from the Mosquodoboit area to a place about a hundred miles away from Cooks Brook. It was Bridgewater in Lunenburg County. The wife's parents lived in Bridgewater and had long hoped that their daughter and her family could find a farm in their neighbourhood. As it happened a man from Bridgewater wanted to move to the Musquodoboit district, so it was decided that the two families would switch farms.

Of course Eiríkur was to go to Bridgewater too. The family had long depended on his help. It had been planned that I would join them at the new farm the following spring after they had settled in. Meanwhile, Eiríkur had found a place for me for the winter months. I was to be errand-boy for Dr. Braddon at Gays River, only a few miles away from Cooks Brook. I was to receive room and board and clothing but no other wage. At New Year's Eiríkur and the family went to Bridgewater and I went to Dr. Braddon's house.

CHAPTER 3

Dr. Braddon's house stood on a high hill and from a distance it looked like a castle. There was a palisade fence around it, and two large gates. The house was very well finished, both outside and in.

There were many rooms in that house, some of them never used. All the rooms were fully furnished, although I must say that the furniture had neither the style nor the quality of the furniture in Mrs. Patrick's house. The doctor had a large room to himself. This was his office where he received patients and other people who came to call on him. In this room he had two daybeds, a couple of easy chairs, and a very large table. There was a cupboard with many shelves, stocked with bottles of medicines and various tools of his trade. When the doctor was at home he spent most of his time in this room and he often slept there. In truth, he was often away from home. He made frequent trips, which sometimes involved considerable distances. People in the neighbourhood rarely sought his help, either because they were unusually healthy or because they had little faith in him. On the other hand, he seemed to get many calls from people who lived in other communities, even though they had their own doctors nearby. For these reasons he was often travelling.

I soon found out that my job would be to travel with Dr. Braddon and to look after his horse. The horse was a lively grey called Daniel. Daniel was known to kick and bite on occasion, but he also had the reputation of being steady and not easily frightened.

Dr. Braddon was tall and well-built, and quite imposing in appearance. He had a black beard which was always very well-kept. His skin was white as milk and as smooth as silk. His hands were unusually small, for a man, and always very clean. He spoke quietly and always wore a smile on his face. When he spoke one saw his white teeth glisten behind his black beard. Those perfect teeth looked like pearls. Every hair on his beautiful beard seemed to have a life of its own whenever he spoke, but his eyes revealed nothing. He never seemed to look at people when he talked to them. Instead he always seemed to be looking at something far away. When he was travelling he wore a tall black top hat on his head, and on his hands he wore expensive gloves that buttoned at his wrists. He wore a long tailored cloak that reached down to his ankles. On cold days he had a large Scottish shawl over his shoulders.

He seemed to typify the medical profession itself. He seemed to have at the tips of his fingers the names of all medications and all diseases that chemists and doctors had discovered from the days of Hippocrates to the present time.

When I arrived at his house, Dr. Braddon was at home. He was in his office and he was preparing for a journey. I was shown into his room by a maidservant. He was standing at the table beside his medicine cupboard and he was packing a travelling case with medicine bottles, small packages, and various tools of the trade. He looked up from his work when the maidservant brought me into his office.

"Good day," I said, bowing, with cap in hand.

"Good day," said the doctor, smiling but looking over my head into the hallway as if he were expecting someone else to come in and wish him a good day.

"Take a seat," he said in a gentle voice.

I sat down and he kept on arranging bottles in his case. I noticed that each time after he added a glass or a package or an instrument he stood quietly for a while as if he were in deep thought and with the thumb of his right hand he touched the tips of the fingers of the left hand like a child who counts on his fingers. Each time that he touched a fingertip I heard him repeat a word from a language I did not understand, but which I assumed must be Latin. During the coming winter I heard these same words so often that I knew which finger of the left hand designated a certain medicine or a plant. For example the tip of the thumb could be *Papaver somniferum* or *Atropa belladonna* or *Humulus lupulus.* The tip of the index finger was *Viburnum opulus,* the middle finger indicated among other things *Asclepias tuberosa,* the ring finger called for *Aconitum napellus* and others and the little finger carried a number of names, such as *Rhem palmatum* or *Oleum ricini* and others. I thought that the fingers of the right hand represented various diseases or conditions, for example the tip of the thumb indicated insomnia, the index finger represented cramps, and the middle finger meant chest trouble or consumption. The ring finger meant fever, the little finger represented digestive problems. Dr. Braddon was both a doctor and a druggist.

After I had been sitting there for a while he said, "Where do you come from, my dear?"

"I came from Cooks Brook," I said.

"Oh, this is our little boy," said the doctor, smiling nicely and looking out the window as if he were expecting to see someone coming up the hill. "This is our workplace," he continued and his white teeth sparkled under his black beard.

I said something to the effect that I found the workplace very pleasant. He kept on counting on his fingers and arranging bottles into his bag.

"Insomnia," he said to himself, and he touched the left index finger to the tip of his right thumb. He thought for a few moments and then he said "*Humulus lupulus*" and he touched the right thumb to the tip of his left thumb.

"What is your name, my dear?" asked the doctor as he was packing a bottle which he called "*Nux vomica*."

"My name is Eiríkur," I said.

"Oh, like Eric the Red," he said, but he pronounced it "Erik Roddi." "I read about him when I was a small child," said Dr. Braddon, smiling. "That is a wonderful name."

"My name is Eiríkur Hansson," I said.

"Oh," said the doctor, "the man who arranged for you to come here gave us your name. It is a beautiful name." He continued with his packing. "We will travel to Upper Musquodoboit early tomorrow morning," he went on. "We have a very small patient who is anxious to see us. You and Daniel will have to get to know each other today. Daniel is our horse. He is a willing horse but sometimes he kicks or bites those who are not good to him. Be good to him and then he will be good to you, my dear." The doctor smiled as he said this but he was looking at a picture that was hanging on the wall above my head.

"I am afraid that I will not know how to handle him if he kicks and bites. I am not very brave around horses," I said.

"O-o-oh," said the doctor smiling, "we'll see about that, we'll see about that." As he said that he added a few bandages into his case.

At that point the doctor's wife came into the workroom. She was a small, delicate, sad-looking woman.

"Hypochondria," said the doctor, and he touched his index fingers together as his wife came into the room. Then he put his right thumb on his left index finger and he said, "*Asafoetida ferula!*"

Then he took a tiny pillbox and added that to his kit, which seemed to hold an endless supply of materials.

"Is this the boy who is going to stay with us?" asked Mrs. Braddon. I greeted the lady.

"Yes, dear," said the doctor, bowing slightly to his wife. "This is our errand boy, a very sensible young lad, it seems, and his name is Erikk Roddi."

"My name is Eiríkur Hansson," I interrupted.

"O-oh," said the doctor, smiling, and he looked over his wife as if he saw someone behind her. "Excuse me. 'Eiríkur Hansson' is his name, a wonderful name. That reminds me of a Danish friend I knew years ago in Halifax. That was Captain Hansen!"

"He will not be happy here, I can tell from the expression on his face already," said Mrs. Braddon sadly.

"Let's hope that he will not be unhappy here, dear," said the doctor and smiled kindly. "I've been told that Icelanders are never bored, and they can feel at home anywhere."

"They are lucky," said Mrs. Braddon, and sighed deeply, "but does the boy understand English?"

"Very well, dear, and he uses proper grammar, too, which proves that he has been with good people in this country and perhaps he has even attended school a little bit," said the doctor. As he spoke he looked at a lamp that was hanging from the ceiling and his face lit up with a big smile.

"Is he healthy?"

"He seems to be very healthy. I am told that Icelanders are very healthy people," said Dr. Braddon.

"They are blessed," said his wife and she sighed deeply once again.

"Show him his room, dear, and talk to him while I go out to check with Jacob and explain what he should be doing while I am away." As soon as he said that he locked his case, put on his hat and walked out.

Mrs. Braddon watched her husband leave in silence, put her left hand over her heart, sat down in a chair. She put her head to one side and studied me for a moment.

"Oh, I know that you will be bored," she said and she sighed again.

"I am sure I'll be fine," I said.

"Oh, I know it," she said drearily, "everyone gets depressed in this house. Even my husband gets depressed. He can never stay at home. Maybe it is because of me, because I am always sick, always sick." I saw tears run down her cheeks. I was silent.

"Life is difficult when one is always sick," she said, "because then one has no friends, one is always lonely, always, always lonely."

I did not say a word, but I was shocked to see how sad and broken the poor woman appeared to be.

"I will take you to your room," she said after a short pause, "I know that you will be depressed here. Everything is so depressing here." Then I followed her up a curved staircase with my bags in hand. Mrs. Braddon took me into a large bedroom near the staircase. In the room there was a bed, all made up, a table and a chair, and a small cupboard. There was also a washstand, with a wash basin, a large jug of water, a towel, and a soap dish, along with a brush and comb.

"This is your bedroom. I know you will find it tiresome, like all the others who have been here before you," said Mrs. Braddon. I tried to reassure her that all would be well but it seemed to be of no avail. She left the room after she told me that I would be called when dinner was served.

I opened my bags and began to hang up some clothes on hooks on the back of the door. Then I took up my books and laid them on the table, so they would be handy if I had some free time to read. Then I walked to the window and looked out. The view was very pleasant. There was a little snow on the ground and I saw horses and sleighs on the main road below the hill. I could see many farmhouses near the Gays River. I saw a mill, a church and a schoolhouse.

All of a sudden I was aware that someone had crept quietly into my room. I looked around and saw a small, sickly-looking boy about seven years old.

"My name is Benjamin," said the little boy.

"Hello, Benjamin," I said.

"Jacob told me that there was an Icelandic boy here."

"He told you the truth," said I.

"Where is he then?" said Benjamin.

"You are talking to him," I said.

"You are not Icelandic!" said Benjamin.

"Yes, I am Icelandic," I said.

"But Jacob told me that the Icelandic boy wore seal-skin clothes, and his hair stood straight up, and he had one eye in the middle of his forehead," said Benjamin as he looked me over from top to toe.

"Then Jacob has been telling you a lie," I said.

"Jacob never lies," said Benjamin. "There must be an Icelandic boy with one eye in the middle of his forehead, and I have to find him. I'll be furious if I don't see him. He has one single eye in the middle of his forehead, and he wears seal-skin clothes."

"You will never see an Icelander who looks like that," I said.

"Yes, I will," said Benjamin and he stamped his feet on the floor. "I will find him. He is hiding somewhere. Jacob always tells the truth, he wouldn't dare to lie to me, Benjamin, the son of Dr. Braddon. I have to see the Icelandic boy who has an eye in the middle of his forehead!" I couldn't help smiling at that although I saw some look in Benjamin's eyes that made me a little uneasy. "I will search for the Icelandic boy," he shouted. "I will!"

Benjamin searched the room. He searched the cupboard in the corner, he looked under the table, he crawled under the bed, he lifted the bedspread and the pillow, and he raised the mattress on one side. He looked through my suitcase.

"You have hidden him somewhere!" he screamed. "Let me see

him right away, let me see the Icelandic boy with the eye in the middle of his forehead, or I will get you!" He threw himself at me and I found that he was surprisingly strong for such a small boy. I had to watch that he did not push me over and seriously scratch my face. Mrs. Braddon heard his screams and she came into the bedroom. With great difficulty she pulled him away.

"I want to see the Icelandic boy with one eye in the middle of his forehead!" said Benjamin as he struggled with his mother. "I will not stop until I find him!"

"You see the Icelandic boy over there," she said.

"But he has two eyes and neither one in his forehead," yelled Benjamin. "More than anything else in the world I want to see the Icelandic boy with one eye in the middle of his forehead!"

"Stop this nonsense, child!" said his mother. "All little boys have two eyes in their right place."

"But Jacob said it," shouted Benjamin. "He saw an Icelandic boy with one big eye in the middle of his forehead. Jacob does not lie."

"You must never be bad to the Icelandic boy," said Mrs. Braddon, "because then he will feel worse."

"I only want to see the Icelandic boy who has one eye in the middle of his forehead," said Benjamin.

Then the two of them went downstairs, but not without a tussle on the steps.

Soon after that I walked out towards the barn. A young man with a fork stood beside the barn door. I guessed that this must be Jacob.

"Is it you?" asked Jacob, and his eyes were full of mischief.

"Yes," I said.

"I expect that you will want to get acquainted with Daniel," he said.

"Yes, I would like to see him," I said. We went into the barn together. There I saw a big strong-looking horse in a stall, and his harness was hanging on a beam beside him.

"There you see him," said Jacob, "but you haven't tried him yet."

I approached this beautiful grey horse, slowly and carefully, and

I saw that Jacob enjoyed seeing how tentative I was. The horse seemed to accept my advances quite well. He turned his head to look at me briefly as if to say, "I am not as crafty as Jacob over there."

"I guess you know Tom Nelson," said Jacob with a smirk.

"No, I don't know him," I said.

"He was errand boy here and he left before Christmas," said Jacob. "He had enough of Daniel before he left. Still, Tom was always good to Daniel — just like you are now."

"What happened?" I asked.

"Daniel bit off his nose," said Jacob with a grin.

"That was a bad accident," I said, trying to pretend that I was not surprised to hear such news. Jacob could be telling the truth but I had already decided that he should not always be taken seriously.

"Yes, that was an accident," said Jacob, "but that was nothing compared to what happened to Johnny Smart who was here before Tom."

"What happened to Johnny Smart?" I asked, although I felt sure that Jacob was going to tell me another tall tale.

"So you know Johnny?" asked Jacob.

"No," I said.

"Daniel hurt him badly, although Johnny was good to the horse, just like you. Daniel bit Johnny through the back and he is crippled for the rest of his life."

"Oh, that's awful," I said, still cautiously stroking the horse's neck.

"And what happened to Willie Monk was even worse. Willie was here before Johnny," said Jacob. I could see that he had been looking forward to seeing my response to his stories.

"What happened to Willie?" I asked, but before Jacob could tell me about that Dr. Braddon came into the barn. All of a sudden Jacob became very proper and quiet.

Dr. Braddon asked me what I thought of the grey one, and I said that I liked what I had seen of him so far. Then the doctor gave me many suggestions regarding the care of this favourite horse and I found all this information stood me in good stead as time went on.

Next we all went into the house for dinner. We all sat at the table together, the doctor and his wife, little Benjamin, Jacob, and I. The maidservant ate in the kitchen after she had served the rest of us.

Dr. Braddon fastened his napkin into the second-last button on his vest, Mrs. Braddon laid her napkin across her lap and Benjamin had his napkin covering the front of his shirt. I had mine across my lap and Jacob had his across his left knee. Benjamin glowered at me from across the table. It was my fault somehow that he did not see the Icelandic boy with one eye in the middle of his forehead. I could see that Jacob was waiting to see me make some mistake in table manners but I managed quite well, thanks to Mrs. Patrick, for she had trained me well in that regard.

I went up to my room early that evening. I had bought a copy of Walter Scott's *Ivanhoe* for fifty cents and I looked forward to reading for a little while. There was no lamp in my room so I read by candlelight but soon I blew out the candle and went to bed. It was still early but I wanted to be ready to travel the next morning and I needed a good rest.

I fell asleep quickly and I slept soundly for a while. Then I woke up with a start. I sat up in the bed, almost breathless with fright. The room was in total darkness and at first I could not remember where I was. But someone or something had touched my door. I leaned back on my pillow and tried to go back to sleep. I had long suffered from a fear of the dark, especially if I woke up in the middle of the night and was alone in a room. I was going to try to overcome that weakness this time and go back to sleep. Just as I was about to fall asleep again I heard something brush against my door. I held my breath and listened. I heard someone walking back and forth on bare feet in the hallway just in front of my room. I was sure I heard breathing. Then I heard someone whispering right at the keyhole, but I could not make out any words. I was frightened but I didn't dare to call out for help. I pulled the covers over my head. I repeated all the prayers that I knew, not once but over and over like a monk on the alert. Finally I heard someone walk away from the door and I heard something being dragged along the floor.

Even though this person had moved away I was still frightened. I was sure that something strange was going on in this house. Superstitions that I had learned as a small child came back to haunt me. In my imagination I recreated a host of horrible ghosts, with deathly pale faces, faces without noses, faces with toothless gums or empty eye sockets, ghosts with bare bones rattling in wasted limbs, ghosts that groped their way through the darkness, with long fingers and sharp nails. Some ghosts seemed to carry with them an eerie light that was felt rather than seen. Some ghosts could glide wherever, or slip through keyholes. Some grew very tall, awesome because of their height.

It took some time before I could relax enough to fall asleep again. I was tired when Dr. Braddon came into my room. He asked me to get dressed quickly and feed the grey and then come in for breakfast. After that I should harness the horse and hitch up the sleigh. I hurried to do as he asked and the doctor and I sat down to breakfast by ourselves. Edith, the servant girl, had been roused to get the meal on the table and I found her looking tired and pale. She looked at me sympathetically because, like her, I had to get up so early.

Dr. Braddon and I set off on our trip to Upper Musquodoboit, where he had to visit three patients. I soon began to feel sleepy and I started to yawn.

"You must have gone to sleep too late last night," said Dr. Braddon as he studied the road ahead.

"I went to bed early," I said.

"Oh, you did not sleep well. You must have been homesick." Why would I be homesick? Where was home?

"No," I said. "I woke up and I thought I heard someone at my door. I couldn't get back to sleep right away."

"Oh, you must have eaten something that did not agree with you last night. When your stomach cannot digest your food you will often find that you have bad dreams. The stomach is an amazing part of the body." He smiled as he said that, and he looked up the path to a house that we happened to pass by just then. I didn't want to disagree with him because he was a learned man, so I said nothing.

When we reached Upper Musquodoboit, the doctor stopped in at some of the houses. I stood outside and held the horse's reins. The weather was cold and damp that day and I often shivered because I was not warmly dressed.

At one point the woman of the house stepped out the door with Dr. Braddon. "Your boy is cold," she said.

"This is my Icelander, my dear," said Dr. Braddon as he buttoned up his gloves. "Icelanders are never cold. They have grown up with fire and ice."

"He is just a child," said the woman.

"He is also an Icelander," said the doctor. His white teeth sparkled behind his black beard.

We spent a few days in Upper Musquodoboit. On our way home we stopped briefly at the post office in Cooks Brook. There were three letters waiting for me there. One was from my guardian, Eiríkur, one was from Lalla Sandford, and one was from my special friend, Jón. They were all well. Jón was working in a store in Winnipeg. Lalla was attending a Women's College in Halifax. Eiríkur was getting everything organized at the farm in Bridgewater, but he said that he would never feel at home there. I replied to all these letters as soon as I returned to Gays River and I asked them all to send their next letters to the post office there.

That evening I went to bed early and I fell asleep quickly. Then I woke up with a start just like the first night that I slept in that house. Once again I could hear someone moving back and forth in front of my door. This time these strange activities did not last as long as before, but I was nevertheless seized with uncertainty and fear. It was a long time before I was able to fall asleep again. I mentioned this to the doctor next morning. He smiled kindly as before and said that my stomach was a little upset but that would correct itself in time. "*Mens sana in corpore sano* — a sound mind in a healthy body. There is a remarkable connection between our digestive system and our brains."

I found it very difficult to talk about this but I tried to explain it to him. "I clearly heard someone at my door and then I heard someone walk away."

"Oh," said the doctor, and he seemed to be looking at something far away. "There must be a good explanation for this. Maybe you heard the cat prowling around."

"No, this was a person." I did not want to mention ghosts or anything like that.

"Oh," said Dr. Braddon, "the house is locked every night, so no thief can come in. There is nothing to be afraid of. This is all the result of a little indigestion, which we can soon fix. And if you think there are ghosts around here that is just nonsense. There are no ghosts! Those who die lie quietly in their graves. We doctors know that. We do the deceased an injustice if we think that they are moving around after death. *De mortuis nil nisi bonum!* — avoid saying anything but good about those who are gone."

I never mentioned this again to Dr. Braddon because he would just think that I was not in my right mind. Often during that winter I heard someone outside my door in the middle of the night. Sometimes the person was there for a long time and sometimes for only a few minutes at a time. Strangely, I noticed that this seemed to happen either the night before the doctor and I left to go on one of our trips, or on the night after we came home from our travels. I wondered whether it did have something to do with my digestion or with excitement with regard to comings and goings. I wondered whether the sounds were indeed coming from somewhere else in the house even though it seemed to be just in front of my room. Finally I stopped waking up in the night and slept until morning even if there was some movement in the hallway.

I was often sent to the store or the post office at Gays River, for that was not far from Dr. Braddon's house. I soon found out that people in the neighbourhood did not have much respect for the doctor and there seemed to be something about him that people disliked. People did not speak ill of him, but they shrugged their shoulders or raised their eyebrows whenever he was mentioned. People seemed to shy away from me when they heard that I worked for Dr. Braddon.

Around the middle of February I caught a cold and I developed a persistent cough. I never had warm clothes and I had to stand outside with the grey one in all kinds of weather while the doctor was visiting his patients. I thought that Dr. Braddon would notice my cough and perhaps give me some remedy, but he did not give it any attention. Finally I told him about it and asked him what I could do to feel better.

"This is nothing serious, my dear," he said, "you just have a little cold and it has affected your trachea. The trachea is very sensitive. Drink a little ginger tea tonight before you go to bed." This was the only advice he offered. Of course, no such drink was mentioned after that and I did not ask for it. The cough lasted throughout the winter.

CHAPTER 4

One day in late February Dr. Braddon and I drove down towards Musquodoboit harbour, which extends ten or twelve miles inland. There had been thaws for a few days and the snow had disappeared from most of the roads. We drove in a two-wheeled cart called a sulky or a gig. The cart was partially canopied with a black waterproof material. We drove for some distance along the west side of the bay and we stopped at a farm home that was actually located on a peninsula, which protruded from the west bank about five miles from the mouth of the harbour. We spent the rest of that day and the following night at the farm. There had been freezing temperatures during the first day and during the night, so when we left Dr. Braddon judged that we could drive on the ice across from the peninsula to the east side of the bay.

Daniel's horseshoes, admittedly, were worn. It was getting close to noon when we started across the bay and a northwest wind was coming up. The bay is wide and quite open, and since we were far out in the bay the wind was coming directly at us. As we moved further out into the bay the wind grew stronger and the cart was being pushed sideways. Our grey horse was having a hard time keeping his direction and he skidded time and again. We continued for a while but gained only little by little. When we got about halfway across the storm had become relentless. There was no snow but it was bitter cold. Daniel could not make headway. He faced the weather and struggled against the odds but the wind and the cart pulled him back, slowly at first, then faster and faster, towards the open sea at the mouth of the harbour.

The storm grew in intensity, rushed unimpeded down the frozen surface of the bay, and filled the canopy over the cart. The poor horse struggled with all his might but he could not get his footing and finally he fell on his side and that broke one of the shafts off the cart. We were now in serious danger. Dr. Braddon got out of the cart, still holding onto it. I shook and shivered from cold and fear. The doctor looked a little pale but he kept on smiling. He tried to stop the cart and he tried to get the horse up but to no avail. Daniel tried again to get up but he could not do it.

"We will be helped, my dear," said Dr. Braddon looking towards land on the west side. I looked in that direction and saw that four men on skates were coming towards us but I thought they would likely not reach us in time. Then I saw that men were coming from both sides. We were close to a large break in the ice. We passed another break in the ice and narrowly escaped. All of a sudden seven or eight men surrounded us. After a struggle they managed to stop the cart and they were able to get the horse back on his feet. More rescuers arrived and they were able to pull horse and cart to land. They got us into a house that stood near the bank. Dr. Braddon thanked the men individually and showed them all his white teeth with his smiles.

I overheard one of the men say that the doctor "kept his cool" and did not show any white feather, even though death looked him

in the face. I did say to Dr. Braddon that we'd had a narrow escape
and help had arrived just in time.

"Oh, my dear," he said, "it is always certain that *labor improbus
omnia vincit! Ergo!* Determination overcomes all! Therefore one
must never lose courage, but keep on working till the end." I had
to look up to him at that moment, and admire the courage of this
learned man. I felt that he was so far above me, a weakling, full of
fear, and ignorant.

I had not spent many weeks in Dr. Braddon's house when I first
realized that Mrs. Braddon had the idea that whenever I went to the
store or the post office in Gays River "people" would approach me
and ask me questions about the family, about herself, her husband
and all that went on at their house. As time went on, she became
more and more convinced that this was so. I tried to assure her that
no one had talked to me about the family, and that was the truth.

She would call me into her private sitting room and ask me to
move the carpet or move the furniture from one corner to another.
Then she would mention how insincere people were, how they
talked about her and used all their cunning to gather stories about
her. Of course, these stories were all lies.

"You must have heard people in the store and in the post office
talking about us," she would say.

"No. People have never talked about you or your husband in my
hearing," I said, truthfully.

"But you have heard people talk about Jacob and Edith?" she said.

"No," I asserted again.

"Boy, I know that they often talk about us and say many things
that are not true," she said, and she sighed deeply. "People in this
neighbourhood are prejudiced against me. If any of our neighbours
are ill they never call on Dr. Braddon. It is all because of me,
because I am always sick, so sick."

I said nothing and she continued, "I know that they have asked
you to tell them all about us, just like they asked the other boys who

were here before you. They are so clever at fishing for information. It would be only right if you would tell me what it is they want to know about us. That way we could avoid those who are not friendly toward us."

She often talked to me like this, and the more I tried to convince her that I had not heard people speak ill of them, the more convinced she was that the neighbours talked behind her back. In the end, she always started crying and cried until she could hardly breathe. Later in the winter she began to suggest that I was untruthful and indeed that I was among those who stood against her.

One spring day Dr. Braddon called me into his workroom. "There is something I have to tell you, my dear," he said, smiling in his usual manner.

"What is that?" I asked.

"I have decided to ask you leave my service," he said, smiling more kindly than before.

I must confess that I was rather taken aback, although in truth I was not very disappointed at this news.

"Now, my dear, I am not going to explain the reason why I want you to leave, and I hope you will not be asking me what it is."

I stared at him.

"Yes, my dear," he said. "There is a reason for everything. I will admit that I have always appreciated you because you have been a willing helper but still I am forced to have you leave." I saw every single white tooth as he said this.

I had nothing to say. I gathered my things together.

Where would I go? My guardian was one hundred and fifty miles away from Gays River. Lalla Sandford was fifty miles away in Halifax. I decided that I would go to Halifax and find Lalla, and then I would write to Eiríkur and let him know what I was doing. I was sure that in the capital city I would find some good employment.

The next morning I was ready to leave. I went into Mrs. Braddon's sitting room to say goodbye to her. She said that she was sorry that

I was leaving, but she added that I could have stayed longer if I had been more faithful to them and had not talked to the neighbours. From that I gathered that Mrs. Braddon had no small part in my dismissal. I did not say goodbye to little Benjamin because he was still sleeping. I said goodbye to Edith in the kitchen. She was going to say something more but hesitated. I did not forget to say good-bye to the grey one. I gave him a pat. I was sorry to leave him because he had always behaved well for me and had never tried to harm me in any way. Jacob was in the barn and I said goodbye to him. He was surprisingly friendly. He took my hand and said that I was not a bad kid. I asked him to be good to my horse and we left it at that. Finally I said goodbye to Dr. Braddon himself. He smiled at me and said that I must not expect any money from him because the agreement had been simply that I would get food and clothing. I had indeed received good food during the winter but I did not get much in the way of clothes. He said that I could contact him if I ever needed a letter of reference. Then he offered me his soft white hand and wished me good luck.

When I had gone a short distance from the house, I heard some-one calling me. I looked back and saw that Edith was running towards me. I stopped and waited for her, thinking that I must have forgotten something. "This is for you to keep," said Edith, as she pressed a dollar bill into my hand. "It is not much but it might come in handy. Please don't spend this dollar on anything that you don't really need."

At first I pretended that I did not want to take the dollar but at that time even five cents would have been helpful to me. I looked around to see if anyone was watching and then I put my arm around her neck and gave her a kiss. I blushed. I don't know why, because I had often kissed girls before, girls who were more respectable and prettier than Edith.

"May God bless you and protect you, and be with you always," she said. "Always remember to say your prayers, especially when you come back from a journey or when you are going to start out on a journey." I promised to do as she said and thanked her for her concern.

"You did not know," she said seriously, "that all winter I said prayers for you whenever you and Dr. Braddon were planning a long trip, and every time when you came home again."

"Thank you very much, Edith," I said.

"But do you know where I said these prayers?" Edith asked. "I always said them in front of the door to your bedroom when I thought you were asleep."

"You were very good to me," I said. I realized then that it was Edith that I had heard whispering in front of my bedroom door so often in the winter. She was praying for me like a mother prays for her sleeping child. I had at first thought that there were ghosts in the house and at my door, but Dr. Braddon had insisted that I had indigestion and therefore could not sleep well at night. But we were both wrong, because it was Edith praying for a poor boy, who she thought would not know any prayers or would not remember to say them, because he had no one to encourage him to do so. Now the mystery was solved. Poor Edith! She was childish and simple but she was kind and sensitive. Poor Edith! May God bless her! I kissed her again and then she turned back to the house and I continued down the hill towards the main road.

I started off down the road and all of a sudden it occurred to me that it would be nice to have a visit with my old friend Geir before I left the neighbourhood. He lived about ten miles from Cooks Brook but about twenty miles from Gays River. I had not seen him since he got married, and I decided that I would like to see him again. He was now the only Icelander that I knew of in Nova Scotia, aside from myself and my guardian.

Much later, I found out that there were about twenty other Icelanders scattered here and there around the province at that time.

I left my suitcase and my bag at the post office in Gays River because

I would have to come back that way when I set out for Halifax.

I arrived at the farm where Geir lived just before sunset. I saw him working away picking rocks from the field.

"Hello," I said. He looked up and stared at me. "Hello! Don't you recognize me? Don't you know your little Eiríkur?"

"Oh, is it you, mate?" said Geir. "You have changed so much." And then he slapped me on the shoulders. After that he asked one question after another. He wanted to know where I was going and what I had been doing since we last saw each other. He was very surprised when I told him that all the Icelanders had left from the Mooseland settlement and that my guardian had gone to Bridgewater. He hadn't heard anything about this.

I found that it was difficult for Geir to speak Icelandic and he could barely manage a sentence in broken English. He had almost created a new language for himself. He soon asked me to come home with him because Mrs. Reykjavík would be happy to see me. Rachel welcomed me and said I should spend a few days with them. As it turned out I visited with them for a week and I enjoyed that time very much.

The last evening I was there, Geir came up to my room and seated himself on a chair across from me. I thought he must have something important to say. "Listen here, mate," said Geir, taking out his pipe.

"Yes?" I answered.

"You're going to be rich, "said Geir.

"Well, we will see about that," I said.

"Don't you think," said Geir, "that you will be going back to Iceland sometime when you are rich?"

"I won't ever be rich," I said. "But of course it would be nice to go back to Iceland."

"Well, I believe you will be rich some day," said Geir, "and I'm going to ask you one last favour."

"I'll be glad to do you a favour if that is possible," I said, wondering what the favour might involve.

"If it happens that you become rich and travel to Iceland then I want to ask you to publish my life story, which I have been writing."

"Your life story?" I asked, surprised.

"Yes, mate," said Geir, chewing on his lip. "I have noted the main events in my diary, but I hope that you could maybe rewrite it a bit for me so it would sound better. That book should pay for itself. Would you do me that favour?"

"I'll think about that if I travel to Iceland sometime, but why don't you want to publish the story in English?" I asked.

"Because I want my friends in Reykjavík to read my life story so that they know how I have managed in America. I have never written to them since I came to this country."

"So, do you want me to take your diary with me and look after it for you?" I asked.

"No, no," said Geir. "I may still want to add a few things to the story. When I die you should write to Rachel and ask for the book, and if Rachel has died then Jenny will send it to you." Geir seemed sure that Jenny would outlive the others.

"But how will I know when you die?" I asked. Geir had not thought about that.

"Now that is the question," he said, and he scratched behind his ear.

"Maybe it would be best that I write to Jenny when the time comes that I am going to go to Iceland," I said.

"There we have the answer," said Geir, very pleased. "Now that is decided, and, listen, when you mention my marriage be sure to explain that my wife wanted the marriage just as much as I did. I would like my friends at home to know that."

"I'll remember that." I said.

"And listen, friend," said Geir. "Could you make it understood that the people around here think that I'm hard-working and that I accomplish a lot. Perhaps you would note that I called myself Mr. Reykjavík as soon as I came here. This is an honour for the city of Reykavík because I could have chosen another name if I wanted to."

"I shall mention that when the time comes," I said.

"Then I won't worry anymore," said Geir. All of a sudden we heard Rachel call out. "George, George!" she shouted. "There is something going on in the barn."

"I'm coming," said Geir, as he stood up and started down the stairs. When he was halfway down the stairs he stopped for a moment.

"Listen there," he said looking back at me. "I want you to mention that Rachel is always called Mrs. Reykjavík."

"Yes," I said.

"George, dear George, hurry!" shouted Rachel.

"I'm coming," said Geir and he went down the stairs and ran out to the barn. As soon as Geir left, Rachel came upstairs to talk to me.

"Would Mr. Reykjavík like to go west to Winnipeg with the other Icelanders?" she asked.

"No, no," I said.

"Wasn't he talking to you about that?" she asked.

"No," I said. "He was asking me to get his life story printed if I went back to Iceland some day." I decided it was best to tell her that right away because I realized that she was anxious to know about my conversation with Geir.

"Oh, was it just that?" said Rachel. "That was nice of Mr. Reykjavík to see about having his life story published, because his life has been quite remarkable. Now you must get to sleep so you will be ready for your travels tomorrow." Then she went back downstairs. Soon after that Geir came back and told his wife that all had been well in the barn.

The next day I said goodbye to Geir and his wife and I arrived in Gays River that evening. I spent the night at the home of the postmaster, who had taken care of my suitcase and bag while I was away.

CHAPTER 5

I could choose between two routes to go to Halifax from Gays River.

I could go to the railroad station at Shubenacadie, which was only a few miles from Gays River, and travel forty miles by train to Halifax, or I could walk to Dartmouth along the main road and then take the ferry across to Halifax a distance of only about one mile.

If I walked to Dartmouth, I would save the price of the train ticket. I had six one-dollar bills and fifty cents in silver coin. I thought that it would be sensible to save my money as much as possible, so I decided to walk to Dartmouth.

I left Gays River early in the morning. I carried my suitcase on my back and my bag in front. These bags were not heavy but still I began to feel their weight after a few hours. I stopped frequently and sat down by the roadside to rest. Every once in a while I would walk over to a house near the road and ask for a drink, and to inquire about the way to Dartmouth.

I felt isolated and alone. I did not expect to see anyone that I recognized until I arrived at Number 70 Grafton Street, in Halifax. I was indeed a lonely traveller. Many people passed me by along the way. Most did not seem to notice me. I was only fourteen years old and rather small for that age. One old man gave me a ride in his carriage but soon we came to a crossroads and he went one way and I went another.

At noon I stopped at a store and ordered a meal. The merchant, Mr. Clark, asked whether I had money to pay. I pulled twenty-five cents from my pocket and paid beforehand. He served me a hearty meal, which gave me the strength to continue. Mr. Clark wanted to know where I was going but did not ask where I had come from. Then I continued on my way when I had finished my meal.

That night I spent at the home of a farmer who lived in a little valley about eighteen miles from Gays River. The people there asked many questions and it was difficult to find answers for some of them. The farmer would not accept pay for my overnight stay, just because I was Icelandic, he said. I thought that was remarkable. I thanked those good people and set out once more on my way to Dartmouth.

Early in the afternoon I came to the north end of a long narrow lake. There was a high hill on the east side of the lake and the road wound along between the lake and the hill. I saw a large herd of goats up on the hillside. Houses were far apart in this area. There was no eating place along the way so I had no lunch at noon. I went to one house and asked for a drink of water. The lady also gave me a slice of bread with syrup.

Just before sunset, I came to a large house close to the road. A sign over the door indicated that this was an inn. I decided that I would spend the night there regardless of cost, because I was tired and hungry. I knocked on the door but there was no answer. I knocked a second time, because I could hear voices within. I knocked a third time, louder than before. Finally a voice called out, "Come in." I walked into a large salon and I soon realized that this was a bar. There was a long table on one side of the salon. Behind the table there were shelves with many wine bottles and glasses and a large mirror. Behind the table stood a man who I thought must be the manager, and in front of the table there were five men who were drinking from large glasses. I thought they were rather wild-looking. They all turned around and stared at me for a moment and they seemed surprised to see me.

"Can I spend the night here?" I asked timidly because I did not feel comfortable with this gathering.

"Wait a few minutes," said the man behind the table, hesitantly. His speech was slurred.

I sat down on a chair near the door and waited, expecting that I would be taken into another room.

"Here, chum, come over here," said one of the men, "and show us your teeth."

"I am happy to sit here," I said, trying to smile.

"Who are you, son?" said a small man who stood by the table next to the door.

"My name is Eiríkur Hansson," I said.

"That's a smart-looking fellow," said the small man to his drinking companions. "Are you Danish?" asked another man.

"I am an Icelander," I said.

"An Icelander!" shouted all the men and laughed as if this was a huge joke.

"Listen to that! I am going to marry an Icelandic girl next month," said the small man.

"I wish you good luck," I said.

"Listen to that! He's not so wet behind the ears, this one. Come here and have a drink!" said one of the men, beckoning to me.

"I don't drink liquor," I said.

"That's a likely story!" said the little man. "We'll get him to sing an Icelandic song for us."

"Yes, yes!" said the others in chorus.

"I can't sing," I said.

"Yes, you have to sing for us, and start right now," said the little man.

"I don't know any tunes," I said.

All the men laughed uproariously.

"Then you'll dance for us," said the little man.

"Yes, by all means, dance an Icelandic dance for us," said the others.

"I can't do that," I said.

"Then I'll teach you to dance," said the little man, pretending to be very serious.

I stood up, picked up my bags and moved toward the door.

"No, you're not leaving until you dance for us," said the little man and he blocked the doorway. I was still going to leave and I put my hand on the doorknob, but the little man pushed me away.

"Leave him alone," slurred the manager behind the table but the little man would not stop.

"He will dance," said the little man. "I am going to teach him how to dance a jig!" Then he grabbed my shoulder and tried to pull me forward.

"It's best to leave him alone," said the manager.

"No, he will dance," said the little man and he pulled my shoulder. "If you don't dance, I'll let you dance on your head for a whole hour."

"Let me go!" I said, and I tried to pull away from him. "Let me go!" but he held me still. He was a small man, but I was just a child.

"Let him dance," said one of the men. "It won't hurt him one bit." The little man tried to get me to dance, but I tried to pull away from him. I asked him over and over again to let me go because I was tired and did not know how to dance. I called over and over to the men at the table and asked them to make him let me go so that I could leave. But they just laughed at me and said that no one was hurting me and I was a strange kid who neither wanted to dance nor sing.

The bartender was the only one in the group who tried to help me, but he was far too drunk to have any effect on these men. They ordered him to be quiet if he tried to say anything. Gradually the little man got impatient, because I would not cooperate .He started shaking me roughly. I grabbed his arm with both hands and tried to protect myself. But just the same, tears ran down my cheeks.

All of a sudden, I noticed that a side door opened and a tall dignified woman stepped into the room. The little man relaxed his hold on me immediately, walked over to the table and took off his hat. The other drinkers did so as well, but the woman paid no attention to them. She walked directly to me and told me to come with her. I bowed to this dignified woman, picked up my belongings, and followed her into another room next to the salon. Two young girls, likely maids, were sitting in that room and I saw from their expressions that they had heard the goings-on that had taken place next door. They brought me a hearty supper, and I soon fell asleep in a good bed.

The next morning I started off again. I was told that Dartmouth was only nine miles away and that I would have no trouble finding my way there. I had not gone very far when I caught up to a two-wheeled cart which was pulled by a cow without horns. The cow moved slowly and chewed her cud as she moved along. Two old women sat in the cart and they were both smoking short clay pipes in a leisurely manner. These women had red complexions, high cheekbones and foreheads which narrowed and sloped back to the scalp. Their eyebrows were well-defined and their eyes were small, black and quick. Their noses were rather flat and their mouths unattractive. The lips were dry and pale. Their cheeks were sunken and wrinkled. The veins in their necks and the backs of their hands stood out and seemed to lie almost on top of bare bones. I realized right away, from their colouring and general appearance, that these women belonged to a tribe of native Indians. I had never met any of those people before and indeed there were not many natives left in Nova Scotia at that time. A few of them lived in huts north of Dartmouth. Generally speaking, they are good-looking people. Most of the men are about six feet tall with broad shoulders, very muscular and agile. They are usually calm and quiet but they are said to be rather lazy. Some of them lived in poor huts made of a few stakes rammed into the ground and thatched with birch bark. They are mainly of Catholic faith because the Jesuits were the first white men that they met. In the last few years they have increased in numbers, which is unusual in countries where white men have taken over and dominated for some time.

When I caught up to the cart and was about to pass it these two old women called out to me. They were both talking at once and they were so similar in looks and in voice that I decided that they must be sisters.

"*Kva* (hello)," they both said, removing their pipes from their mouths. I wished them a good day and took off my hat.

"*Hva venin kel?* (Who are you?)" they shouted in very high voices. I told them in English that I did not understand them.

"*O, hvo, hvo!*" they said as if they were surprised at something. They gestured to me that I should put my suitcase and my bag into the cart. I accepted the offer although I felt that the cow moved too slowly and perhaps it was not right to add my burdens to the load. Also I was not sure that I wanted to be a travelling companion to these two old women.

We moved along our way, with the cow chewing her cud and the ladies smoking leisurely. I walked after the cart and tried to push it to lighten the load for the cow. I saw that the old women noticed that, and I thought they were saying that I was a good boy.

"*O, hvo,*" they said over and over again. "*O, hvo, Eirkjú hasú.*" I have never been able to get a translation of those last two words, which they repeated often in their high voices. I thought these words were surprisingly similar to my name and I wondered if it was possible that they knew my name, but I could not get an answer to that question.

When we had travelled along for a while, we met a carriage pulled by two horses. A few young men sat in the carriage and they were talking loudly and laughing in a silly way. I saw right away that they were drunk. When they passed us, they shouted at us and said a few rude words to the old women. One of the fellows stood up and waved a bottle over his head.

"*O, hvo*," said the old women, shaking their heads. "*O, hvo, viktuk!* (They like the taste!)" and their black, sunken eyes seemed sharper than before. The young men shouted "Hurray" over and over again and laughed like they were crazy.

"*O, hvo*," said the old women. "*Ga-gogg! Ga-gogg!*" And I thought those were suitable words although I did not understand what they meant.

We had travelled about two or three miles further when the cart stopped beside a hut by the roadside close to a lake. A tall, broad-shouldered young native man came out of the hut and spoke to the old women in words which I did not understand. He unhitched the cow and took it down to the water. The women climbed down from the cart and one of them passed my belongings to me as she went. I took a twenty-five cent piece from my pocket and gave that to one of them. They studied the money carefully, and said something which I understood as a "thank you."

"*Tabúinskak-nan cents* (twenty-five cents!)," they said in surprise. They exchanged a few words and one of them ran into the hut and returned to give me a small basket made from blue and white twigs. She let me understand that I was to keep it in return for the money. I thanked them for the gift, bowed to these kind old women, put the basket into my bag and continued on my way.

Now I was coming closer to Dartmouth and there were more and more houses beside the road. These houses seemed to be in better condition than most of the houses that I had seen along the way. The gardens seemed to be more carefully tended. The carriages, the horses, and the people themselves seemed to have a different look than I had been accustomed to in Cooks Brook and Gays River, and I soon began to feel that this didn't suit me well. Somehow the people were not as friendly as the country folk I was used to meeting. I began to feel a little anxious, perhaps a little fearful.

Now the road seemed smoother and wider, and soon houses lined the way on both sides. I had arrived in Dartmouth.

When I was passing one of the first houses in the town I saw a big, ugly dog coming towards me. He barked fiercely and looked as if he were going to bite me. I had long been afraid of strange dogs, even those who looked harmless compared to this one. I turned off the main road, thinking that I could go around a fenced-in yard and possibly avoid the beast that way. The dog realized that I was afraid of him and he hurried after me. I threw my suitcase and my bag over the fence and climbed over myself. As I did so, the dog bit my leg. I came down in the garden just where there was a mound of loose earth. My feet left deep marks in the soil. I was just picking up my baggage when a big man came rushing out of the house. He was very excited and he waved his arms and yelled at me.

He was an elderly man with a droopy, grey moustache and bushy eyebrows. He was tall and thick-set and obviously very angry. "What the devil are you doing?" he asked.

"Nothing," I said timidly.

"Nothing?" yelled the man, shaking his fist. "Don't you see what you've done, you rascal?" and he pointed at the mound.

"That was not intentional," I said.

"A likely story! I buried my dog there, poor old Rover, poor Rover, and I don't want any rascal messing around on his grave. He should lie there in peace, I say!"

"I could not escape anywhere else," I protested.

"Escape? Don't bother telling me any lies, you scoundrel. Escape? Escape from what?"

"A big dog was following me," I said.

"Were you followed by a big dog?" asked the angry man in a quieter tone.

"Yes," I said.

"Was he ugly and very shaggy?" asked the man, his tone much quieter now.

"Yes," I said.

"And yellow?" Now the man was very interested.

"Yes," I said.

"Aha!" he said, "That was Sam, that damn Sam, the dog that killed my Rover, poor harmless Rover. Rover was old, but Sam is young and strong. I hate that dog! And you say he followed you?"

"Yes," I said.

"Well, no doubt it was that damn Sam! And I wouldn't be surprised if old O'Hara and his boys sicced the dog on you. They are scoundrels, O'Hara and his kids! They sicced Sam on Rover, when they knew I was not at home, and they helped Sam to snuff the life out of my poor old Rover. I still have to get them for that dirty business, and I'm going to kill that Sam." He said the last few words very low, as if he wanted to say, "I'm telling you that just between you and me." I said nothing, just stared at this old man who had changed his tune so quickly. "So, he was going to bite you, was he?"

"Yes," I said.

"He would have torn you to pieces if you hadn't escaped over the fence. Isn't it amazing that you should just land in the garden where Rover is buried? Isn't that amazing? And who are you, kid?" asked the man.

"I am an Icelander," I said.

"Stop it now," said the old man.

"That is the truth," I said.

"An Icelander?" he said after he studied me awhile. "Can that be? Is that true?"

"It is true," I said.

"Well, darn! This is interesting! You had better come to the house with me," said the old man. I followed him with my suitcase and bag. As we walked towards the house, a young girl came out.

"Listen here, Kate," said the man, "bring a bowl of milk and a good slice of bread with syrup, and be quick for once!"

"Yes, Grandpa," said the girl.

"Interesting, interesting!" said the old man to himself. "If the boy is Icelandic, that is interesting!"

The girl returned quickly with a big bowl of milk and a thick piece of bread with syrup. I accepted this food gratefully because I was both hungry and thirsty by this time.

"Listen, Kate," said the old man. "This boy says he is from Iceland."

"Really?" said the girl shyly, looking at me.

"You have been to school, Kate. You can tell me whether the people who live in Iceland are like us. In other words, are they white?"

"I think they are white, Grandpa," said the girl, "but to be sure about that I'll run and get my geography book."

"Do that, Kate," said the old man. The girl ran into the house again and soon returned with a big book in her hands. I saw that this was the geography text that was used in elementary schools in Nova Scotia at that time.

"The people of Iceland are white," said the girl.

"Altogether white? Interesting," said her grandfather.

"It is cold in Iceland, isn't that so?" asked the girl.

"Yes, isn't it really, really cold?" asked the old man and he pretended to shiver at the thought.

"Sometimes it is fairly cold there," I said.

"Interesting," said the old man.

"The capital city of Iceland is Reykjavík, is it not?" said the girl.

"What is the name of the largest city in Iceland, where most of the people live?" asked the old man.

"The capital city is called Reykjavík," I said.

"That is a name I could never say, even if my life depended on it," said the old man.

"The main exports are fish, eiderdown and wool," said the girl.

"Yes," I agreed, "those are the most important products."

"Interesting, that's interesting," said the old man. It wasn't until Kate and her grandfather had finished asking all their questions about Iceland, that I could start off again.

When I had gone a short way, the old man called out to me, "Listen, lad, tell me one more thing? Did you walk all the way from Iceland?"

"No," I said, "I came to America on a ship." I thought this question was very strange.

"That's very interesting. Thank you for your answers," said the old man. "Watch out for that damned Sam, that Sam that killed my poor Rover."

Then he turned back to the house and I continued on the road to Dartmouth.

Dartmouth is a neat little town directly across from the city of Halifax, on the east side of the harbour. The town is built on a high slope. A short, swift river flows through a large section of the town. This river comes from the lake that I followed earlier.

The population of Dartmouth is about five thousand. There are some large factories in the town. They produce steam engines and all sorts of tools made from iron. I noticed a number of interesting buildings. One of them is the Mental Health Hospital, which is operated by the provincial government. This is a large, attractive building, and the view from there is beautiful. The road on which I had travelled all the way from Gays River had now become a wide street with expensive houses and stores.

It was well past noon when I reached the middle of the town. I had travelled only a little more than nine miles. I inquired about the way to the ferry. Unfortunately, when I arrived at the pier the steamship had just left. I was told that I would have to wait for at least half an hour. I bought a ticket for the ferry for five cents. Then I sat down to wait.

The city of Halifax lay before my eyes. The city stands on a hill-side, its population about forty-five thousand. There are impressive fortifications here, and Halifax has been long known as a fortress city. There are also excellent docks. Ships are moored at many long piers, all sorts of ships — battleships, merchant ships, passenger ships, yachts, sailing ships, steamships, large and small, and ships from many lands.

As I watched, steamships were travelling back and forth, and boats of various shapes and sizes were busy. The smoke from the steamships and the factories settled over the town. While I sat there I noticed that a dark fog slid over the harbour. The ships gradually disappeared from view. The fog crept over the city and over the pier where I sat. Finally it wrapped itself around me like a wet, cold blanket.

I waited on the pier for an hour and a half. Finally our ferry arrived. The fog had caused the delay. A few passengers and two carriages with horses came off the ship. I hurried on board as soon as possible, along with a few men who had been waiting rather impatiently. When we were all settled, the crew indicated that we were ready to leave. The ferry crawled away from the pier, into the fog, heading across the bay.

Nothing remarkable happened on the ferry, which was a fairly large steamship. The fog hid everything from view. On the ferry, I became interested in two passengers. One was a rather short man with a big paunch. He was rather broad-faced, without a beard. The other one was very tall and very slim with a long, thin face. He looked rather dour. They were both well-dressed. They carried on a discussion all the way across the fjord. The tall man seemed to be telling the other one some sad story, because his face and his voice seemed very subdued. The strangest thing was that the short fat man laughed at everything that the other one said. He laughed so hard that he looked as if he might burst. He laid both hands on his paunch, as if he was worried that it would break open. I couldn't hear what the tall man said, but the other one said over and over between fits of laughter, "They're all going to be bankrupt, all going to be bankrupt!" and the tears flowed down his cheeks — tears of happiness, it seemed to me, because they were going to be bankrupt.

All of a sudden, the ship stopped at a pier in Halifax. I took my suitcase and my bag and walked up the dock. There were many men and boys eager to drive people and baggage around the city.

There was so much commotion and noise that I could not concentrate. The men, the horses and wagons, the tall buildings, and everything around me seemed threatening as I ventured into the city in the fog.

As I walked up the pier, a driver ran up to me, grabbed my suitcase and was about to throw it into a wagon. I ran after him and asked him to give me my case. He said it was far too heavy for me to carry. "I will haul it for you for only twenty-five cents," he said. "No," I told him, "I prefer to carry it myself."

"I will take it for you for only fifteen cents," said the man and he refused to give me my case even though I tried to take it from him.

"I would rather carry it myself," I repeated.

"I will haul it for only ten cents," said the man. I thanked him for his offer, but insisted that I would rather carry the suitcase because I was short of money; but he was still insisting. He would likely have started off with my suitcase, but a man stopped beside us and ordered the driver to drop the suitcase.

I walked up the pier and soon found myself on a fairly wide street, which I later learned was called Lower Water Street. The traffic on the street was almost overwhelming. There were people running and horses with wagons hurrying by. Newsboys were shouting and vendors were selling fruit and snacks.

I inquired about Grafton Street, and was told to walk up a certain street that led up a hill. After I had walked awhile and asked directions now and then, I found myself on Grafton Street. It was a wide street, and cobbled. I checked the numbers on the doors and decided that the house that I wanted must be close by. I started to feel easier because I had almost reached my destination. I had arrived in the capital of Nova Scotia. I was on Grafton Street. I was sure that Lalla Sandford and her parents would receive me with open arms and make me welcome. I was sure that now my problems were at an end and my struggle would be over. The future looked as bright as a sunny day, and the past was like a sad dream.

CHAPTER 6

Number 70 Grafton Street was a seven-storey apartment block on the corner of Grafton and another street that went all the way from the ocean up the hill.

I knocked on the door and waited. I was half expecting that Lalla herself would come to the door. No one came so I knocked again, louder than before, because there was no doorbell. Still no one came. I knocked a third time and then I heard footsteps.

An older man came to the door but he was dressed in coat and hat and was on his way out. I asked him whether Mr. Sandford lived there. He did not stop but he said, "Go in and inquire." I went in but I saw no one around. At the end of a long hallway I saw some stairs. I went upstairs but there was no one to be seen up there either, only another long hallway. There were many numbered doors on either side but there was no one I could talk to. I went up three or four stairs. Finally I met a woman who was carrying a basket. She was obviously on her way out.

"Could you kindly tell me where Mr. Sandford lives, which number and which floor?" I asked.

"You want to know where Mr. Sandford lives?" said the woman.

"Yes, Police Officer Sandford," I said.

"Do you need to find Mr. Sandford rather than other police officers?" asked the woman.

"Yes, I need to find Mr. Sandford and his family," I said.

"Oh, that's it!" said the woman, "They are your friends and you have come to visit them?"

"Yes," I said.

She explained that many families lived in this building and she did not know half of them. "I will take you to see Mrs. Flanagan, who is the manager here. She will be able to give you the information you need." She took me down to the first floor and she stopped at a door that was next to the main entrance where I had come in off the street. She hesitated briefly. Then she set down her basket and knocked.

The door was opened immediately by a slim woman probably between thirty and forty years old. She wore glasses and she held her head high. She looked at us from under her glasses. She had thick black hair that was wound up on top of her head. At first glance one might have thought that it was some sort of hat. She was round-faced and freckled. Her forehead was low, her nose was flat and her eyes were far apart. Her mouth was not attractive, and her jawbone exceptionally strong. This was Mrs. Flanagan. She did not invite us into her apartment but I saw her front room quite well from where I stood. The room was large and full of furniture but it was not very well arranged. A man was sitting in a big chair by the window which faced the street. His face was hidden behind the large newspaper that he was reading.

"I have brought this boy to see you, Mrs. Flanagan," said the woman who was with me. "He wants to know the apartment number where Police Officer Sandford lives."

"You have brought a boy who wants to find a police officer?" asked Mrs. Flanagan.

"Mr. Sandford and his family are friends of this boy and he has come to visit them and stay with them for a while," explained the woman who was helping me.

"Mr. Sandford and his family are friends of this boy. Is he perhaps a nephew?" asked Mrs. Flanagan.

"No," I said.

"Well, then," said Mrs. Flanagan, "I can tell you that his family lived in Apartments 23 and 24 and he and his family were the most pleasant and reliable people. They lived in numbers 23 and 24 and those are the nicest rooms on the first floor."

"Does Mr. Sandford live on another floor now?" I asked.

"Mr. Sandford and his family were the most agreeable people," said Mrs. Flanagan.

"Does Mr. Sandford no longer live here?" asked the woman who stood beside me.

"Mr. and Mrs. Sandford have moved from my building," said Mrs. Flanagan, "and I am sorry because their rent always came in on time."

"Where did they go?" I asked in a low voice because my throat was strangely tight.

"Mr. Sandford and his family moved out a little more than a month ago but where these good people went I have no idea. Between you and me, when people leave my apartments it does not occur to me to ask where they are going. Perhaps Mr. Flanagan can give you some information."

"Mr. Flanagan gives no information about this or anything else," said a gruff voice from behind the newspaper.

"What should the boy do?" asked the woman who was with me.

"I guess the boy does not know the city very well," said Mrs. Flanagan.

"I do not know the city at all," I said. My throat was hurting.

"Since I really liked the Sandford family and since this boy is probably related to them I would like to give some suggestions to this boy, and I am sure Mr. Flanagan would be willing to do that."

"Mr. Flanagan is not willing to do anything," said the voice from behind the newspaper.

"I do not know what street Mr. Sandford works on or what his hours might be," continued Mrs. Flanagan, "but I would suggest that the boy should go straight to the police station and inquire about Mr. Sandford's home address."

I thought that this was a good idea. "Where is the police station?" I asked.

"I must admit that I do not know that," said Mrs. Flanagan, "I have never had occasion to enquire about that. I am sure Mr. Flanagan knows where the police station is."

"Mr. Flanagan does not know anything about that," said a very impatient voice from behind the newspaper.

Finally it was decided that the best thing for me to do would be to talk to one of the policemen on the street. I thanked both the women for their help, picked up my suitcase and bag and made my way out onto Grafton Street. I looked around and soon I saw a policeman and he was walking towards me. I could see his helmet from far off because he was taller than most of the other people on the street. He walked rather slowly and looked from side to side as if he were checking the windows in the stores. I stood on the sidewalk waiting for him but he was going to continue on without giving me so much as a passing glance.

"Would you be so kind as to tell me where Mr. Sandford lives?" I asked.

The policeman stopped, looked around him for a moment and then he turned to me.

"What Mr. Sandford?" he asked.

"Police Officer Sandford," I said.

"What do you want with him?" he asked.

"I came to see him," I said.

"Where did you come from?"

"I came from Gays River," I said.

"Where is that place?"

"It is about fifty miles away," I said.

"Where did you think Mr. Sandford lived?" asked the policeman.

"At number 70 on this street," I said.

"He has moved away," said the officer.

"And where did he go?" I asked.

"I don't know that," he said.

"Where can I find out?" I asked.

"Go to the Police Station," he said.

"I don't know the way there," I said.

"You know where Upper Water Street is, don't you?"

"No, I don't. I do not know the city at all," I said.

"Go down this cross street," said the officer, pointing, "and when you come to a building with a high tower you turn north along that street and from there someone will be able to show you where the police station is." I thanked the officer and said goodbye to him.

I walked down the street as I had been directed. I saw another policeman. He was even taller than the first one and much heavier. I spoke to him and asked him whether he knew where Mr. Sandford lived. He did not answer immediately but drew himself up to his full height and looked me over. He asked me what Mr. Sandford I was looking for, where I had come from, and where I had expected to find Mr. Sandford. Finally he advised me to go to the police station and he gave me some directions, a little more precise than those that the first officer had given. Soon I found myself in front of a large grey stone building and this was the police station. A man who walked with crutches actually showed me the place and then he asked for five cents for his trouble.

By this time it was starting to get dark and lamplighters were making their way along the streets. Lamps were beginning to appear in store windows. There was still some fog and my clothes were damp. I felt chilly and I was both hungry and tired. Now I wondered whether I would be able to get to Mr. Sandford's home that evening. Would I be able to find lodging for the night? After my last experience I did not want to go to an inn ever again.

After some hesitation I walked up the wide stone steps and opened the big door, with my suitcase in one hand and my bag in the other. I found myself in a large room. There were chairs and benches along the walls, and two large tables stood in the middle of the room. The far end of the room was separated off by a lattice framework and a door. Several officers were seated in that end of the room. One of them sat at a desk and was busy with some papers. Two of them were playing a game of chess, and others seemed to be standing by. I felt very small when I came into this room because there everything seemed to be on such large scale — the chairs, the tables and even the men themselves. When I opened the door all the men looked at me. A man who was dressed a little differently than the others came up to the divider and waited to talk to me. He was a middle-aged man, tall and impressive. His hair was black and curly, and he wore a big, well-kept moustache. His eyes were small and dark but sharp and quick. He gave me a questioning look as if he wanted to say, "What have you been up to, young fellow?"

I greeted the official politely and he responded with a nod. "What would you like, boy?" he asked.

"I came here to find out where Mr. Sandford lives," I said, trying to meet the man's gaze.

"What Mr. Sandford?" he asked.

"Police Officer Sandford," I said.

"Which Officer Sandford?" asked the man.

I said, "Is there no police officer in the city by the name of Sandford?"

"What is the given name of this Mr. Sandford that you are looking for?" asked the man.

I had never heard Mr. Sandford's given name so I said, "Is there more than one officer by that name?"

The man did not answer my question. Instead he said, "What is your name, boy?"

"Eiríkur Hansson," I said.

"Are you Danish?" he asked.

"No, I am Icelandic," I said and at that I noticed that the other men got up and all of a sudden they seemed to be paying attention to this conversation.

"But you speak Danish," said the man I had been dealing with.

"No," I said, "I speak Icelandic."

"How do you say '*bad boy*' in Icelandic?" he asked.

"*Vondur drengur,*" I answered quickly.

"Where are your parents?" asked the sharp-eyed man after glancing at the other men who now seemed to be listening to my answers.

"My mother died and I have never seen my father," I said.

"Who raised you?"

"My grandparents," I said.

"Where are they?" was the next question.

"They died." The officers looked at one another.

"Where is your home?"

"I have no home at the moment," I said.

"On what street was your last home?"

"I have never lived in this city," I said. "I do not know the city at all, but I am looking for Police Officer Sandford."

"What do you want with him?"

"I am going to stay with him for a while," I said. The gentlemen looked at one another. The next question was, "Where did you come from?"

"From Gays River," I said.

"Who were you with in Gays River?" they wanted to know.

"Dr. Braddon," I said.

"Why did you leave him?" they asked.

"He didn't need my help anymore," I said.

"Did you know Rev. Samuel Reid in Gays River?"

"No," I said, "and I do not think he lived in Gays River. Rev. William Banning was there."

"Where were you before you went to Gays River?"

"I was in Cooks Brook," I said.

"Did you ever shop at Donald's store there?"

"There is no Donald's store in Cooks Brook," I said.

"Who runs the store there now?"

"Hinrik Taylor runs the store in Cooks Brook," I said. "Now, would you please tell me where Mr. Sandford lives? I have to find his home this evening."

"I guess you know his boys?" asked the official instead of answering my question.

"When I last knew him he had no sons," I said.

"Where did you get to know him?" was the next query, and then "How long have you known him?" I told them that I had known Mr. Sandford for more than two years.

"How many daughters did he have then?" I told them that there was one daughter.

"What was the daughter's name?" I told them that the daughter's name was Lalla.

"Where did you expect to find Mr. Sandford?"

"At number 70 Grafton Street," I said.

"Did you go there?"

"Yes," I said, "but he has moved away from there."

"Who told you that?"

"The manager," I said.

"Could the manager not tell you where Mr. Sandford had gone?"

"No, but I was advised to come here to get that information."

"Who gave you that advice?"

"The manager at number 70 Grafton Street gave me that advice and also two police officers that I talked to on the street."

"How did you know that Mr. Sandford had lived at number 70 Grafton Street?"

"I had his postal address", I said.

"Where did you get his postal address?" asked the sharp-eyed officer.

"From letters that I have received," I said.

"Who has written letters to you?"

"Miss Sandford." The men in the office looked at each other once more.

"When did you get your last letter from her?"

"A little more than a month ago," I said.

"Do you have the letter with you?"

"Yes, but it is in the suitcase over there," I said.

"Whose suitcase is that and whose bag is that?"

"They are both mine," I said.

"Where did you get that suitcase?"

"I bought it in Tangier last fall," I said.

"Where is Tangier?"

"It is the next harbour on this side of Spry Bay," I said.

"You speak good English if you are Icelandic as you say," said the man who had all the questions.

"Oh, thank you for that," I said, "but my reason for coming here was to find out where Mr. Sandford lives. If you know that, will you please tell me because I am anxious to see him tonight."

"I have to ask you one more question. Can you show me an Icelandic book?"

"Yes," I said. I opened my suitcase and pulled out Jónas Hallgrímsson's book of poems. He took the book, looked at it quickly and passed it over to one of the men who stood beside him. He was himself looking at my suitcase, which was open. "I see a letter there. Is that the one you received from Miss Sandford?"

"Did you want to see the last letter that I received from her?" I asked.

"Yes, if you don't mind," he said, his voice much softer now.

I pulled out the letter and handed it to him. He looked quickly at the address and the signature on the letter, and then he gave it back to me. While this was going on the other officers were studying Jónas Hallgrímsson's book. Now the man with the questions grabbed the book and gave it to me.

"Read four or five lines for us," he said. I was pleased to do that so I read ten or twelve lines.

"That will do," he said. "Now, again, how do you say 'bad boy' in Icelandic?"

"*Vondur drengur,*" I said. He looked at the man who had been writing at the table, and that man nodded briefly.

"Then, how do you say 'good boy' in Icelandic?"

"*Góður drengur,*" I said.

"All right, lad," he said. "You will find out where Mr. Sandford's home is. I know where it is but there is no point in telling you that now. I am sorry that I can't have someone take you there right away."

"Why can't I find out where they live tonight?" I asked.

"That is because Mr. Sandford and his family are not at home at this time."

"Not at home?" I said and suddenly I felt numb.

"The family left the city a few days ago on vacation and they will be away for some time, possibly three or four weeks, likely not much longer than that."

"Where did they go?" I asked.

"I can't say about that," said the man kindly.

I felt as if the room began to turn. I had a hard time standing on my feet. I grabbed hold of something so I wouldn't fall. Somebody brought a chair for me and somebody else brought me a drink of water. I heard someone say that I must be tired and likely hungry. The drink of water helped a lot.

"What will I do?" I asked. "I don't know anyone. Where will I stay tonight?"

"Do you have money to stay at a reasonable boarding house until Mr. Sandford comes home?"

"I have a little money," I said but I did not say how much.

"That is very good. We will get you into a safe but inexpensive boarding house. You can stay there until Mr. Sandford comes home. You can call in and see us once in a while if you like. In any case we will be in touch as soon as Mr. Sandford comes home."

Then he asked one of the officers to take me over to Sailors' Home.

I said goodbye to the officers and thanked them for their help. The man who accompanied me carried my suitcase and my bag. After we had walked some distance we stopped in front of a fairly large house. The officer rang the doorbell. A man came to the door quite quickly. The officer took the man aside and talked to him briefly in low tones. Then he said goodbye to us and went his way. I went into the house with the man who had met us at the door.

CHAPTER 7

Sailors' Home was on Upper Water Street not far from the police station. It was a three-storey house and was built from grey stone like many other houses on that street. Over the door there was a white board with large blue Gothic letters that spelled *Sailors' Home*.

The man who came to the door was the manager himself and his name was Clifford. He was a middle-aged man of medium height, and kindly manner. He was teary-eyed and he had a rather weak voice. I found out later that he had taken courses in theology, but for some reason he had never been ordained. For a few years he had worked as a missionary in Siam in the service of the Baptist Church. He had to give up that work because he could not tolerate the climate over there. After that he moved to Halifax and established a boarding house for sailors and foreigners. Sailors' Home was usually full to capacity with men, especially seamen, from various countries.

Mr. Clifford brought me into a very large dining room. There were many tables covered with white cloths and laid with dishes and cutlery. There were no men there because the dinner hour was over by this time. From the look of the tables one could guess that the management would be prepared to look after guests at odd times as needed.

"Take a seat at the table there, my boy," said Mr. Clifford, pointing at one of the tables. "You are hungry and need some refreshment." He wiped his eyes with a silk handkerchief, which he kept inside his vest.

I put my suitcase and my bag out of the way in a corner of the dining room, and then I sat down at the table that Mr. Clifford had indicated to me. Clifford rang a little bell that stood on my table. Immediately a woman came in to us, and I felt sure that this was his wife. She was nicely dressed, good-looking and dignified. I stood up right away and greeted her, and she received me kindly. "Officer Inkster asked us to look after this boy, my love," said Clifford, a little apologetically.

"Right," said Mrs. Clifford, "but who is this boy?"

"Well, that is a story in itself," said Clifford, "He is an Icelander, according to the officer who brought him here."

"An Icelander?" said Mrs. Clifford as she looked at me. "This is strange."

"This is strange, my love," said Clifford, "and also somewhat mystic. I think that he is . . . (he took out his handkerchief just to have it ready) I think that he is one of the lost lambs of the house of Israel, one of those lost little lambs, which, God be praised, has been found." Then the handkerchief went up to Clifford's eyes.

"But who pays for his stay here?" asked Mrs. Clifford.

"He will be here only two or three weeks and he has money to pay for himself for that length of time. If he cannot manage that we are to notify Officer Inkster. Therefore there is no worry about taking this young foreigner into our house, my love."

"He seems to be a nice boy. He has a kindly look about him," said Mrs. Clifford.

"He looks very kindly," agreed Clifford, "and he could be fairly intelligent, praise the Lord!"

"Perhaps he is motherless," said Mrs. Clifford, and she looked at me sympathetically.

"Perhaps motherless," said Clifford, wiping his eyes, "and also perhaps fatherless, which is just as sad."

"But does he understand English?" asked Mrs. Clifford, as if she had suddenly woken up.

"Unfortunately that is something that I have not investigated," said Clifford, looking rather serious. "Likely he understands a little bit. I'll inquire about that right away." Then he turned to me.

"Do you understand some English, my boy?" he asked.

"I understand a little," I said.

"He understands a little, my love," said Clifford to his wife, "and, what's more, he speaks, too, much better than the boy we had with us in Siam."

"Have you had dinner, my dear?" asked Mrs. Clifford kindly.

"Have you had anything to eat or drink, my boy?" asked Clifford and he pointed at his mouth and gestured as if he was eating and drinking so that I would understand him better.

I said that I had not had dinner. Mrs. Clifford indicated that she was sorry that she had not asked me about that right away because I must be very hungry. She brought food to the table herself. Her husband arranged the dishes in such a way that I could reach everything conveniently. I enjoyed this good meal, but meanwhile I had to answer one question after another to satisfy Mr. Clifford.

"Do you know the Lord's Prayer, my boy?" he asked after I started to eat my supper.

"Yes," I said.

"Please say it for me," he said.

I recited the Lord's Prayer in English. Mr. and Mrs. Clifford both seemed quite surprised. Mrs. Clifford gave me a little pat and said that I was a good boy, and she told her husband that I spoke good English.

"This is glorious!" said Clifford, wiping his eyes. "This shows that our missionaries have travelled even to cold Iceland and that seeds of the faith have taken root among the glaciers there. Yes, the blessed book is known even in that frigid wasteland. Glorious! Glorious and wonderful!"

"Can you read and write, my dear?" asked Mrs. Clifford, very kindly.

"A little bit," I said.

"This is a matter that is worth consideration," said Clifford, rather haughtily. "Doesn't this clearly show the accomplishments of the missionaries? What wonders the missionaries have brought about! My love, I am going to send a letter about this to the Missionary Board in London!"

"Have you ever seen an Icelander before?" said Mrs. Clifford to her husband after she thought about all this for a while.

"No, I have never seen an Icelander before, my love. I have seen Norwegians, and Swedes and also Danes, Dutch, Belgians, Germans, and also Frenchmen, Hungarians, Austrians, Swiss, Russians and Portuguese, also Spaniards, Greeks, Finns, Poles, Turks and Basques and men from Romania, Bulgaria and Serbia, men from all nations in the northern hemisphere, but Icelanders, never!"

Clifford explained later that my board and room would cost forty cents per day and that would be payable at the end of each week. He asked me to let him know ahead of time when my funds were getting low because he would seek help from my friends. I thought that he was referring to the Sandford family and I asked him whether he knew their address. He said that he did not know that but he did know where Police Officer Inkster lived. From that I understood that Mr. Inkster was going to pay my bills if need be, and that he would forward the account to Mr. Sandford when he returned. I would certainly not want to bring debts with me when I went to stay with the Sandfords. If the family did not return within two weeks, I would either have to take a loan, or I would have to find some kind of work to pay my expenses. I had five dollars and a few cents which would barely last for two weeks but, I thought, Lalla and her parents could be home by that time.

Clifford and his good wife asked about my name, and age, and circumstances. They said that they were surprised that a foreigner of my age could understand and speak such good English. Mrs. Clifford wished me a good night and prayed that God would be with me. Her husband took me to a small room on the second floor.

In the room there was a neatly made bed, a table and one chair. I brought my suitcase and bag upstairs with me and I was thankful to have this room to myself. Clifford knelt down by the bed and recited a long prayer and then he said goodnight.

I was tired and glad to get into a comfortable bed in a safe place. I could not remember any other day so full of adventure. I had not travelled very far but I had seen a lot and I had talked to people of different ranks and different personalities. I had come from the quiet country life into the hustle and bustle of the city. I had found my way through a maze of streets. My joyful expectations had ended in confusion and disappointment but somehow I had kept my courage up. I had met people who viewed me with distrust but in the end they had lent a helping hand. On this day I had been faced with many questions but I had managed to concentrate and to answer as carefully and as courteously as I could.

I fell asleep quickly and had a good rest.

When I came down the next morning most of the guests had finished their breakfast. Only three or four young men were sitting at one of the tables. I thought that they must be sailors. They were chatting in English but their accent was different from the English that I had learned. A tired-looking young woman brought my meal.

Then Mrs. Clifford came to say good morning to me. She told me that there was a reading room up on the third floor, and she said that I could make myself comfortable there whenever I wanted. She warned me against having any dealings with gangs of boys that I might see on the streets.

I did not hesitate to go up to see the reading room. In the stairway I met a few men who wore unusual clothes and they spoke a language that I had never heard before. When I walked into the library I found that there was only one man there. He was not reading. Instead he was sitting beside a window and looking out. He was a young man, no more than twenty-five years old. He was short and rather stout. He was broad-faced and beardless and he had a big mouth. His nose was big and flat, his neck was thick and his jawbones were strong. His forehead was low and wide and his hair was black and curly. His eyes were dark and shifty and there was something peculiar about the wrinkles around his eyes. This man spoke to me right away in broken English. His tongue was quick but his talk was gibberish. He kept this up so I had no chance to look at the variety of magazines and newspapers that were on display. Although he spoke in broken English I was able to get some sense of what he was saying.

He said his name was Jacob Goldenstein. He said that his people were Jewish of the highest order, because he was a German Jew. Russian and French Jews, he said, were notorious schemers but the German Jews used no tricks. He said that he had travelled all over Germany and much of Austria. And he said that he knew Berlin, Bremen, Breslau and Hamburg just as well as the room that we were sitting in. He said that his brother, Solomon, was an important merchant in Dresden, and his half-brother, Abraham, was a bank manager in Frankfurt. He had an uncle on his father's side in Nürnberg and his mother's sister lived in Stuttgart. His grandfather was once a weaver in Aix-la-Chapelle and his father bought wheat in Danzig. He said that he himself wanted to travel all over the world to see how it looked.

All of a sudden he asked me whether I didn't own a knife. I said I did own a knife. He wanted to see it, so I showed it to him. It was an attractive knife and I was fond of it. He studied it carefully, then shook his head and said, "Oh, this knife doesn't have a good bite. It is actually a fake." Then he pulled out an ugly old knife and said that this was a tool that was worth talking about. He said that he would trade knives with me if I would give him ten cents as well. I thanked him for his offer, but said that I would rather have my own knife even if it was poor. Then he offered to trade knives if I would give him five cents. No, I didn't want to do that. Then he offered to trade for three cents. Again I said no. What about one cent, would I trade for just one cent difference? Then he offered to exchange with no money difference. I still did not want to trade. Then he offered to exchange with me and he would give me one cent! Then he offered to give me two cents and then three! Finally, I stood up to leave the room. He sat still, put his knife in his pocket and was looking out the window again. As I left the room I thought I heard him say, *"Ach, ich bin so gar ein armer Mann!"* which I thought meant "Oh, I wasn't such a poor man yesterday!" but which actually means "Oh, how poor I am!" By that evening Jacob Goldenstein had traded his knife three times and had made a profit of twenty-five cents.

"Ein Sperling in der Hand ist besser als zhen auf dem Dache, mein Freund! (A bird in the hand is better than ten in the bush, my friend!)" he said to me when he showed me the money and the knife that evening. I didn't know what this meant at the time.

A few days went by and nothing remarkable happened. I dropped in at the police station frequently to find out whether they had any news from Mr. Sandford. The officers became very friendly to me and I noticed that they seemed to pay special attention to me whenever I was out on the street, especially if there were gangs of boys around or large crowds. From the first days it seemed that every policeman I met recognized me.

I did not just sit around. I travelled around the city from one end to the other. I walked along every single pier because I loved to see the ships and watch the men unloading the cargo. I walked around the citadel on the hill, and I often looked at the cannons and watched the soldiers moving back and forth. Sometimes I walked around the famous Halifax city park, stopping wherever there were breaks in the fences; but I never spent any of my money to pay admission. I studied all the various wares on display in store windows. One of my favourite places was the 7 Cent Store. Every item in that store was available for seven cents. The goods on offer included toys, games and so forth. I was often tempted to go inside but lack of funds prevented that. Twice I did go into a store close to Sailors' Home and each time I bought some candies for one cent. The candies came in many colors and shapes, and they were so tempting.

On my travels across the city I also saw many sad and unpleasant sights. I felt sorry for horses pulling heavy wagons. I felt sorry for the tired men who unloaded freight at the piers. Sometimes they had to keep working for a long time with hardly a pause. Worst of all was the plight of those who searched in vain for any kind of employment so that they could earn a few cents.

I felt sorry for the children who walked the streets, barefoot and dirty and dressed in rags. My heart went out to children who were hungry and sick, children who might well be homeless orphans. There were children who had to rely on handouts to keep body and soul together.

I felt sorry for boys who made their living by polishing shoes. I felt sorry for boys who wore pants that fit badly, with twine for suspenders, who had neither shirts nor socks and wore worn-out and ill-fitting boots. Probably their only home was a dump, or a little hole under some building or a barrel with a bit of straw for a bed. Some boys probably had parents who beat them if they didn't come home with money for a pint of whiskey or a couple of pints of beer. Some boys had known nothing but ugliness and coarseness. They had never enjoyed the warmth of a mother's love or had a chance to call someone "Pabbi" or Papa. There were boys who didn't know their own names or how old they were. Such boys distrusted everyone they met and looked at everyone who passed by with a mixture of hatred and fear in their eyes. There were boys who sneered like savages, spit tobacco juice and swore. Yet, in spite of everything, these boys had seeds of goodness and generosity in their souls, seeds that lay covered with frost and rubbish, but that could still spring to life and thrive if they were tended.

I pitied the poor old women who sold fruit at marketplaces or street corners even though they were worn out and crippled. Perhaps they had once been beautiful, they had loved and been loved, but now they were old and they had no one who could look after them. It was painful to see the beggars who sat on benches along the busy streets. They were men who had once been young and strong and full of courage. Now they were ill or crippled or nearly blind and in need of help. They had to sit and wait, hoping that some passers-by would have a few coins to spare for them.

Amid all this poverty I saw wealth, luxuries, frivolous spending and all sorts of entertainment.

After I had spent a few days at Sailors' Home it occurred to me that perhaps I could earn a few cents by selling newspapers. So I left very early one morning and hurried to the print shop of the morning paper "The Halifax Herald" and I bought ten papers for ten cents, at one cent each. Because I knew that one paper sold for two cents on the street I thought that I would gain ten cents.

About fifty boys had gathered around the print shop when I arrived. Several of them bought from twenty-five to a hundred papers each. I didn't get my papers until all the others had taken theirs and rushed outside. I was told that happened because I bought so few papers and especially because I was the "new boy." I hurried as fast as I could and shouted with all my might that I had the morning paper to sell, but most people had already bought from the boys ahead of me. I did sell five papers that day. I had not lost money but I had not gained anything for all my efforts. The next day things went much the same, except this time I only sold four of my ten papers, so I lost two cents that time. On the third day I bought only five papers and I sold three so I earned one cent that day. In total, over the three days, I had lost one cent. Of course I couldn't return the papers that I did not sell, so I decided that this business venture was not going to be of any help to me. I thought of buying a shoe-shine kit but I gave up that idea. I went to several stores and offices and factories to try to get work as an errand boy, but none of these places needed that kind of help.

Day after day went by and still there was no news from the Sandfords. My money was disappearing and I knew that soon I would have to accept help from strangers. All of a sudden something happened that changed my situation.

CHAPTER 8

One afternoon after I had spent nearly two weeks in Halifax I was standing beside the window of the 7 Cent Store, looking at the items on display on their windowsill. I had not been there long when someone grabbed my shoulder. I turned to see who would dare to approach me like that on a busy street. I can't describe how shocked I was when I saw that the man was none other than John Miller, Mrs. Patrick's driver. I jerked quickly to loosen his grip, but John Miller was not going to let me go and he held me on the spot no matter how I struggled.

"This is Pat," said John Miller as if he was talking to a third person. He sneezed and I noticed a strong smell of liquor on his breath. "As I live and breathe," he said, "this is Pat, the little scoundrel himself."

"Let me go," I said.

"Mrs. Patrick is here in the city, just nearby. The old woman would be glad to see little Pat face to face, because she is still fond of the boy," said John Miller.

"Let me go at once!" I said and I raised my voice as much as I could.

"I must take Pat to see the lady," said John Miller. "She would never forgive me if I let this bird fly away, since I was lucky enough to catch him."

"Let me go, or I'll call for help," I said.

"I must take Pat to his mother," said John Miller, and he sneezed again. "No one on earth is going to stop me. For once Johnny Miller will perform his duty." Then he dragged me along with him for a short distance, and I thrust my feet down and resisted with all my might.

All of a sudden I saw a police officer coming in our direction. He noticed our struggle and he hurried toward us.

"Leave the boy alone!" said the policeman, who recognized me immediately.

John Miller was startled and he let me go. As soon as I was free I ran off, but I heard John Miller tell the policeman that I was the son of his employer, whose name was Mrs. Patrick. I was sure that he would go on to say that I had run away from her under very mysterious circumstances, but I did not hear him say that because I did not wait around. I looked back as I turned the corner and I saw that John Miller and the officer were still talking to each other.

I ran directly to Sailors' Home and up to my room. I closed the door and sat down on my bed. I thought about this unpleasant event that had taken place in front of the 7 Cent Store. I got the idea that if Mrs. Patrick found out that I was in the city she would do all in her power to find me and take me home with her. I thought that she and John Miller would tell their story to the police and they would be believed whereas I was just a child and had no one to vouch for me. To let her take me home with her once again was unthinkable. I didn't dare to go down to the police station and tell Mr. Inkster about my problems because that would likely lead me right into the grip of Mrs. Patrick. It would be useless to enlist the help of Mr. and Mrs. Clifford because they would not want to be involved in such controversy. I had to do something. The only solution that I could find was to leave the city immediately. But where should I go? I could not go to my guardian, Eiríkur. He was far away and I did not know the way to Bridgewater. It was too late to write to him and ask for help under the circumstances. My funds were almost gone. Geir was the only person I could ask for help. If only I could get to his place I would be safe. I did not want to take the route that I had taken when I came to Halifax, so I decided that I would try to make my way to Shubenacadie. From there I could go to Gays River and then on to Cooks Brook. To go to Shubenacadie by train would only cost forty cents, provided that I could go by half-fare. I thought that would likely work since I was small for my age.

I checked to see how much money I had left after I paid for my board and room. I found that I would have only twenty cents left.

I decided that I would travel as far as I could by train for twenty cents. I picked up my suitcase and bag and went down to the sitting room where I found Mrs. Clifford. I gave her the money that I owed them and told her that I was leaving.

"And where are you going, my dear?" asked Mrs. Clifford kindly.

"I am going to my friends," I said.

"I am happy to hear that," she said, thinking that I meant the Sandford family. "It is so good to be with friends. That is so good!"

I asked her to say goodbye to her husband for me and I thanked them both for being so kind to me. She asked me to call in often to see them. She asked whether I did not want help with my luggage but I said that my bags were not heavy and I could carry them easily. I had my suitcase on my back and my bag in front.

When I left Sailors' Home I looked around carefully to see whether there were any policemen around. I wanted to get to the railway station unnoticed. If any officers saw me carrying my suitcase on my back and my bag in front they would ask where I was going. I went along Upper Water Street at first and then I turned to go down Lower Water Street. There I noticed a policeman so I crossed that street and went down to the ocean. For a while I walked past the warehouses and then I went back to Lower Water Street again for a little while. Soon I caught sight of another policeman coming towards me and I went down to the sea again. I did not make quick progress there because of all the barrels and boxes beside the warehouses. Once again I went up to the street. My path took many twists and turns, up this street and down the next, sometimes on the east side and sometimes on the west side and finally I arrived at the railway station.

The railway station in Halifax was quite impressive. There were many train tracks and there were four trains lined up side by side waiting for their next journey. I left my suitcase and bag behind a large pile of trunks and I walked over to the office where tickets were sold. I knew that I would not be able to buy a ticket for twenty cents but I asked about the trains and the schedules. I found out that one train left for Truro at four in the afternoon but did not stop at Shubenacadie. Another train left for Truro at 6:30 in the evening with a scheduled stop at Shubenacadie at 8 o'clock. The time now was ten minutes before four, but there was no choice. I would have to wait for the second train. I returned to my luggage and sat down to wait for the time to pass.

The first train left for Truro. At 4:30 another train left for Annapolis. At six o'clock a train came in from Antigonish. People came and went. I always sat in the same place. At 6:10 a train left for Pictou. At 6:15 another train arrived from Point Levis. Twice policemen walked by but neither of them noticed me huddled behind the trunks.

Finally it was 6:30. The steam engine was hissing away, people hurried into the passenger seats. All of a sudden a bell rang and the train began to move. I just managed to get into the second-last car before the train pulled out of the station. I would have moved sooner had I not seen an officer walk by just as the first passengers were getting on board. He must have seen me jump on board but he likely thought I was I was just one of those youngsters who are always doing things at the last moment.

I sat down on the only empty seat that I saw. I put my suitcase and my bag under the bench. The train was soon moving along at full speed and I sighed with relief.

After we passed the town of Richmond, just north of Halifax, the conductor came through to collect tickets. He was a big man with a red beard.

"The ticket," he said as he approached my seat.

"I don't have a ticket," I said.

"Money, then," said the conductor.

"Can I go for half fare?" I asked.

"How old are you?"

"I am fourteen years old," I said, "but I am so small, many twelve-year-old boys are bigger than I am."

"Where are you going?"

"To Shubenacadie," I said.

"Half fare there is forty cents."

"I have only twenty cents," I said as I gave him my last coins.

"You will only get half way there for this money," said the big man with the red beard.

"I will be happy to stand on the steps outside if you will let me stay on the train for the rest of the way for nothing," I said.

"Nothing?" said the conductor. "I don't understand that word."

"There is such a word in Webster's dictionary," said a one-eyed man who sat across the aisle from me. He had a strong smell of liquor on his breath.

"That word does not exist in the dictionary of the Intercolonial Railway Company," said the conductor haughtily.

There were a few other brief exchanges between the one-eyed

man and the conductor before he went on to collect the rest of the tickets. He had not answered me when I asked whether I could stay on the steps for the last part of the trip so I was hoping that would still be the case. The train stopped briefly at Bedford, and again for a few minutes at Windsor Junction where the Annapolis railway connects with the Intercolonial railway. At three or four miles past the Windsor Junction the train stopped again and at that moment the red-bearded man stopped at my seat and told me to go out. I was about to say something to the effect that I would pay the rest of the fare later if he would be kind enough to let me stay on but he grabbed my collar, pushed me ahead of him and practically threw me down the steps so I had a hard time to keep from falling on the ground beside the tracks. At the next moment the train was gaining speed again. I realized that my suitcase and my bag were still under the seat. It was too late to do anything about that. I stood there by myself for a few moments, not knowing what to do, while everything that I owned was carried away at high speed.

The railway stop where I got off was very small. There were only four houses to be seen nearby. The country seemed rough and desolate. On the east side of the tracks there was a hill and I saw a few goats grazing there. It was getting close to sunset. It would have been good to find a place to rest for the night but since I had no coins left that was hardly an option. I asked a man who was at the station which way I should take to go to Gays River or Cooks Brook. He pointed to a road that lay to the northeast by the hillside.

After I had walked for a while I came to a house that stood beside the road. A small vegetable garden had been fenced off and I saw a man working there. He had a spade in his hands. Nearby was a young fellow who was leaning on his fork as I came along. I greeted the two of them and the older man nodded but the younger one just stared at me as if I was some strange creature. The man asked me where I came from and where I was going. I told him that I had come from the railway station and I said that I was going to Cooks

Brook. I asked if he could tell me the shortest way to get there.

"You will walk along this road for quite a long way," he said, pointing to the way I had come, "until you come to the crossroads. Take the road that leads north. After a while you come to crossroads again. This time you take the road that leads southeast. After a short time you will come to a house...."

"And that is the schoolteacher's house," interrupted the young fellow, "and if he gets hold of you then he will drag out of you all that you know and then some."

"Then you come to a house, which is the schoolteacher's house," continued the man. "There it is best to go north along the wire fence until you reach a road which goes east beside the hill."

"And I'll bet my shirt that your trousers will be ruined on the fence," said the youth. "It is a barbed-wire fence."

"On the other side of the hill you come to a big house," said the man. "There is a barn with the letters O and K, large white letters."

"They are so big that even a blind man could see them," interrupted the youth.

"From there you go straight east over the meadow until you come to the main road again," said the man.

"But if old Donald sees you when you walk over his meadow, he will squeeze the life out of you before you can count to ten," said the youngster.

"Oh, he's not quite that dangerous," said the man.

I could not handle any more directions so I said goodnight and continued on my way. I had at first thought that I might ask the man for lodging for the night, but I had changed my mind by this time.

The sun was going down and twilight was creeping around me. The weather was clear and perhaps the night would not be very dark, although there was as yet no moon. I tried to walk as fast as I could while the light lasted. Maybe I would still come to a house where I could have a rest.

I passed two horses eating grass by the side of the road. They stopped to look at me for a few moments and then kept on eating as if they were thinking, "We do not have to be afraid. This is not the one. He is only some poor harmless boy."

Soon after that I saw a few sheep nibbling away in a little clearing. The sheep were startled and ran off at first but soon they stopped, watched me leave and then began to eat again. It was as if they might be thinking, "We don't have to be afraid. He won't be sending a dog after us, not this boy!"

Two owls sat in a clump of trees, one on each side of the road. They were calling to each other. It seemed as if they were telling each other that there was no need for them to move at all because I would not be throwing stones at them. I was in too much of a hurry to bother about that. "Who-oo! Who-oo!" they said.

As I ran along it was starting to get dark. The brush along the roadside was a little frightening. I could hear some animals moving through it from time to time. I did not like the idea of sleeping out under the open sky, away from houses, but I was getting tired and I felt that I would soon fall asleep. I left the road and lay down behind a thicket. I folded my hat together and used it for a pillow.

I lay awake for awhile. The sky was clear and the stars had come out. The evening breeze was warm. I felt comfortable and for once I was free of night fears. I did not even worry about snakes although they are not uncommon in Nova Scotia. I thought about all the things that had happened to me during the day. The worst thing was losing the books that I had in my suitcase. I felt very much alone. I began to think about my friends, Lalla, my good old friend, Jón, and my guardian, Eiríkur. What would they think if they knew about my circumstances?

Strangely, the stars seemed to drift away and I was drifting too. I thought all of a sudden that I had died, but there was nothing painful or sad about it. I felt very comfortable. It seemed very pleasant to be dead. I did not need to struggle any more in the world. I thought it strange that my spirit did not roam from star to star until I came to the spirit world. I tried to break away from my body but that was not to be. I and my body were inseparable.

Then all of a sudden people were gathering around me. The people leaned over me and shook their heads. "No there is no sign of life in him," they said.

John Miller of the broken nose was there with his horses, but they were worn out and thin. I could count their ribs. John Miller sneezed till I thought he could not recover. "I told you, Athena and Apollo, that Pat would not live long," he said to the horses but the horses shook their heads as if they were surprised that life could be so short.

The one-eyed man that I met on the train was there. He had thought of a new line to say to the conductor, "Man comes into this world with nothing, and he leaves with nothing — except his reputation." The conductor only shook his head.

Mrs. Patrick was there, leaning on Dr. Braddon's arm. "It was his digestive system," he said to her, "there was always a problem with his digestion." Mrs. Patrick had never thought of that. "Well, well," she said.

"Then there was a problem with his trachea, always a problem with his trachea," said Dr. Braddon, "but he was always a willing helper. *De mortuis nil nisi bonum!*"

My old friend Geir was there. He was scratching his head behind his ear. He could not believe that such a robust kid would just lie down and die.

I woke up. Grass was blowing over my face, birds were singing in the trees around me. It was good to be alive on such a beautiful morning.

I looked around and got my bearings. I walked along briskly and soon I saw a big house. I saw smoke coming out of the chimney so I knew that someone was up although it was still early. I could not bring myself to knock at the front door so early in the morning to ask for a drink of water. Instead I went to a door that I thought might lead to the kitchen.

I knocked on the door and I heard someone say, "Oh, I know who you are!" It was a woman's voice. I knocked a second time. "Oh, I know who you are. You are not going to fool me into opening the door for you like I did yesterday." I knocked a third time. "Oh, you can open the door for yourself. You are not going to get me to come. I have too much to do." I opened the door and I saw a small woman who was churning. The churn was very big and so tall that the woman had to stand on a stool to apply her strength to the work.

"Good morning!" I said as I stood on the threshold, hat in hand.

"And good morning to you, too," said the little woman and she continued to work the churn as fast as she could. "Do you think I don't know you, you rascal?"

"No, I think that you take me for someone else, because we have never met before." I hesitated and then I said, "Would you be so kind as to give a drink of water?"

"There is water in the bucket by the stove if you are thirsty and you can have some buttermilk when I finish churning."

I helped myself to some water from the bucket, and just then an older woman came into the kitchen and said good morning to me. "Who is this boy?" she asked.

"This is Joseph Willford," said the little woman at the churn, "He is always trying to play his tricks on me."

"I think you are mistaken, Nena, my dear," said the older woman. "This is definitely not Joseph Willford. I have never seen this boy before." Then, turning to me, she introduced herself as Mrs. Dallas. "And what is your name, my lad, and where are you going?"

"My name is Eiríkur Hansson," I said, "and I am on my way to Cooks Brook."

"And where have you come from?" asked Mrs. Dallas.

"I came from Halifax," I said. "I am an Icelander."

Nena said that she was surprised that she had made such a mistake. Mrs. Dallas offered me breakfast. She said that her husband, Dr. Dallas, would be happy to meet me. She went into the next room and I waited in the kitchen. I was busy answering Nena's questions. I soon realized that she was almost blind.

Mrs. Dallas soon returned and invited me to sit down to breakfast with her husband. We walked through to a little sitting room, which was near the front door. There a small table with a white cloth was set for two people and there were several bowls of food already prepared for us.

At one end of the table sat an older man. His chin and upper lip were shaved but he had thick grey sideburns. His eyes were bright and lively. His movements suggested that he had been a man of action in his younger days. He got up from the table when I entered, shook my hand warmly and invited me to sit down and join him for the morning meal. After Mrs. Dallas poured our tea we began a long conversation. He was not a medical doctor, but a "Doctor of Philosophy." He asked me about my journey and about my circumstances in general. I told him a little bit about myself, as much as I thought was appropriate in this situation.

"You are a bright boy," he said, "a very bright Icelander. Please help yourself to another slice of ham and another egg."

"I was reading a book just yesterday about a great man who was an Icelander," Dr. Dallas continued. "Can you guess who he was?"

I thought for a few moments. "Was it Egill Skallagrímsson?"[18] I asked.

"No, no, no," said Dr. Dallas, "I've never heard of him. He does not appear in this story."

"Was it Njáll?"[19] I asked.

"Tsk, tsk! That name does not appear in the story."

"Then it must have been Snorri Sturluson."[20]

"That name is mentioned in the story, to be sure, but he is not the one, this man is greater. . ."

"Was it Grettir, Gunnar or Skarphéðin?"[21]

"No," Dr. Dallas shook his head. "No, those men must have been Vikings and raiders. No, the man I was reading about yesterday was the artist Albert Thorvaldsen. Have a piece of spice cake."

"Thank you," I said. "I remember now that I have read about Albert Thorvaldsen." I had read about him in the magazine *Fjölnir* and I had seen a picture of him.

"So you have read about him," said the doctor, looking pleased. "Good. But where was he born?"

"He was born on the ocean, between Iceland and Denmark," I said.

"That was unfortunate for you Icelanders," said Dr. Dallas, "because if he had been born in Iceland instead of being born at sea then the whole world would have called him Icelandic. People of many nationalities, including Englishmen, think that he was Danish because his mother was Danish. For my part, I think that everyone is of the same nationality as his mother. Please have another cup of tea." Then he continued, "I saw an Icelander once before. I saw him in Oxford, England. He was a teacher at the University there. That was Dr. Vigfússon[22]. I don't suppose you have heard of him. You Icelanders don't often hear about your few great men, because they usually work abroad. What could you offer them? Nothing but stones!"

"I have heard of Guðbrandur Vigfússon," I said.

"So you have heard of him," said Dr. Dallas. "You are a well-informed young man."

All of a sudden the doctor got up and started walking back and forth, with his hands behind his back. "You Icelanders are proud of your country and your origins. I agree that your forefathers were highly esteemed and great men in their way. But what are you now? Nothing but shepherds and fishermen, quiet and slow. Your forefathers did form a small republic, but it lacked executive power. And what good did it do, since you were taken over by a monarchy?

Still I think you are fortunate to be under Danish rule. The Danes are a skilled people and everything that is modern you have learned from them. From your forefathers you inherited a good deal of literature, the Sagas and the Eddas, but you did not know how to take advantage of that treasure. You have had many poets but they have all been minor poets, not one in the first class, none even that compare with Savage or Otway."

I thought that Dr. Dallas belittled our nation, which was bad enough, but what hurt me most was that he should take all Icelandic poets (including Jónas Hallgrímsson, Bjarni Thórarensen and Hallgrímur Pétursson) and rank them below Savage and Otway. To be sure, I did not know anything about Savage or Otway but I thought that they were not famous in English literature since he compared them to Icelandic poets.

"I thought that Jónas Hallgrímsson would compare with many excellent English poets," I said rather hesitantly.

"Tut, tut!" said Dr. Dallas. "In the history of literature that man is not even mentioned. Not only do you not have any poets, you have not produced any novels, not any!" He paused and looked me in the face. "I see that I have been too critical, lad. You are an Icelander through and through! I am glad to see that. Maybe we should talk about something else."

I agreed. That discussion had gone far enough.

"So you are going to Cooks Brook," said Dr. Dallas. "Now if you want to relax here today, then you can travel with me to Gays River tomorrow. I am going to drive there. I plan to set out early tomorrow morning."

I thanked him for his offer. I had really appreciated his wonderful hospitality. I had not been happy with his opinion of Iceland in general, but I knew that he had not had a chance to become acquainted with recent Icelandic literature, so I was ready to forgive him.

"So you are willing to wait here until morning," said the doctor.

"Come out with me to see my horses. I hope they will compare well with the best horses in Iceland." He smiled as he said that.

In the barn we found two chestnut brown horses in their separate stalls. I saw that they had been fed some cornmeal that morning. "I have my horses in the barn every night even in the best weather. I feed them each morning. I like to take care of my horses myself. This horse is named Mohammed V and this one is Mercury XII." Then he traced the horses' pedigrees for several generations. "I have always loved horses," he said. "No other animal compares with a good horse."

The next morning Dr. Dallas hitched his chestnut brown horses to a fine carriage and the two of us started off for Gays River. I saw that Dr. Dallas was an experienced driver. Indeed only a good driver could have handled that team for they were a lively pair. On the way the doctor told me stories of many different horses that he had known.

We arrived at Gays River just before noon. Dr. Dallas suggested that I have lunch with him and the postmaster. He planned to stop there for about three hours and then he would return to his home. I accepted his offer with thanks.

There were three letters waiting for me at the post office in Gays River. All of them had arrived just a few days after I left to go to Halifax. One letter was from my special friend, Jón. He had moved with his parents to Winnipeg and from there they had moved to North Dakota. Now he had found an office job in the town of Pembina. Another letter was from my guardian, Eiríkur. He was not happy in Bridgewater. He said that he hoped that I would stay as long as possible with Dr. Braddon. Indeed, he might come back to Cooks Brook before long. The third letter was from Lalla Sandford and had been written in Cape Breton. She mentioned that she had travelled to visit friends and that they had planned to be away for six weeks but they expected to return to Halifax on June 15. She explained also that the family had moved from 70 Grafton Street just before they left on their holiday and they would now make their home at 126 Harriet Street. My next letter should be sent to that address.

On checking the calendar I realized that this was June 11 so the Sandford family would be back in four days. Now I had to reconsider my decision. Should I continue on to Cooks Brook or should I return to Halifax? Should I even think of going back there when I had no money? I turned that question over in my mind for a while and then I had an idea. I asked Dr. Dallas to let me speak to him privately and he came out to the postmaster's horse barn. He sat down on a beam, prepared to listen to my concerns. I explained the situation fully and asked him whether he would dare to lend me money to pay for a train ticket to Halifax, so that I could get to the Sandfords' new home on the day after their return. He smiled and said that he would help me to get to Halifax. However, instead of lending me money he would hire me for four days. He said that he would pay me fifty cents per day and that way I could start off with two dollars. That would be much nicer than coming to the city with a debt on my hands. I thanked him very much for that good offer. Suddenly I felt much better. Dr. Dallas had given me new courage.

That evening I went back with Dr. Dallas. I worked in his garden for four days. It was not very hard work and I enjoyed listening to the stories that he told me because he worked along with me all the time. His wife and Nena were very kind to me and wished that I would stay even longer.

On the morning of June 16 the doctor gave me two dollars and drove me to Oakfield, which was the nearest railway station. There he bought me a ticket and accompanied me into the railway coach. "Farewell, my little Icelander," he said. "May you be blessed in the years ahead."

CHAPTER 9

The train carried me quickly towards Halifax. Houses and barns, hills and valleys, shelter belts and little lakes came into view and disappeared as we hurried on. I counted the posts that carried the telegraph wires. The telegraph wires followed the Intercolonial Railway lines and telegram messages were interpreted at the railway stations. I knew that there were approximately thirty posts to every mile, and I knew that the distance from Oakfield to Halifax was approximately thirty miles. I was very anxious to return to Halifax. I tried to imagine what the house at 126 Harriet Street would be like. I was sure that it would be a fine house simply because it was Lalla's home. I wondered just how I would be received. I felt sure that I would be welcomed and that never again would I be reduced to a beggar's lot. Never again would I have to be afraid of John Miller and Mrs. Patrick. I thought about many things but I kept on counting the posts and the miles. This was not the same train that I had travelled in before and the conductor was not the same, either in his appearance or in his manner. There was no one-eyed passenger who questioned the rules of the Intercolonial Railway Company. All the passengers were quiet and courteous, like parishioners at a church service.

Finally, we came to a stop within the large railway station at Halifax. I didn't want any of the police officers to see me until I had talked to Mr. Sandford, and because I now had a little bit of money I decided to ask a driver to take me to 126 Harriet Street. I did not want Lalla to see me arriving in a carriage either like a helpless invalid or a man of means, so I told the driver that I did not want him to stop directly in front of the house but rather I wanted to stop a couple of houses on one side or other of number 126. The driver asked me to pay him before we started off. No doubt he thought that it was strange that I did not want to stop right at the house. I paid him fifty cents and we were soon on our way. After a short ride I got down and walked a little further on. As it turned out number 126 was a neat little frame house, painted white. From the gate to the front door there was a curved path of inlaid stones and around the house there was an attractive garden. I saw a big man working in a flower bed near the gate. I recognized him immediately. It was Mr. Sandford. He was not dressed in uniform. I was delighted to see him and now I was sure that Lalla must be home as well.

I lost no time opening the gate and stepping into the garden. "Good day, Mr. Sandford!" I said, offering my hand.

"Ahem!" said Mr. Sandford, looking up from his work and taking my hand in his. "Good day, my boy. Ahem! Is this Eiríkur? You have grown so big now, so very big!"

"I am Eiríkur, Eiríkur Hansson," I said.

"Ahem!" said Mr. Sandford, smiling at me. "You are always welcome. I am very happy to see you. I am very happy."

"And I am very happy to see you, Mr. Sandford," I said.

"Ahem!" said Mr. Sandford, still holding my hand. "I wasn't really expecting to see you at this moment. I did hear this morning that you had been in the city a while ago. Now you appear in my garden as if by magic. You have caught me by surprise! I should say so!"

"Is Miss Sandford at home?" I asked because that was so important to me.

"Ahem! Lalla has just walked into the house. I can tell you that she will be very glad to see you because she has been thinking about you ever since we heard that you suddenly disappeared from Sailors' Home. I can also tell you that our policemen have been searching for you all over the city for several days. I guessed that you had left Halifax after you were bothered by John Miller. I sent a letter to the postmaster at Gays River, because I felt sure that you had gone there. He will receive that letter tomorrow. And now suddenly you are here. I am very surprised! Come into the house with me. You are welcome!"

We walked into the house together and he offered me a chair in a small sitting room.

"Ahem!" said Mr. Sandford, "I am going to call Lalla." Then he called into the next room and said that they had a visitor, someone the ladies would be happy to see.

"This is Eiríkur!" said Lalla, as soon as she entered the room.

"Ahem!" said Mr. Sandford. "And now he is a big boy. See how he has grown!"

"Dear child!" said Lalla. "I am so glad you have come to be with us!" I put my arms around her neck and kissed her. Then I was a little embarrassed because her father was looking on.

"Ahem!" said Mr. Sandford. "You don't have to be shy. You are a fine boy!"

Just then Mrs. Sandford came into the room. She welcomed me back, she said, after the horrors I had been through!

We all sat down together and they asked me to tell them the whole story. They wanted to know why I set out for Halifax in the first place. Then they wanted to know all that had happened from the time that I first left Gays River until I arrived at their doorstep. Lalla held my hand as I told my story and once in a while she gave me a little pat in sympathy. Her mother smiled at me in encouragement and Mr. Sandford nodded his head again and again. "Ahem," he said, "I should say so. I should say so!"

"You did the right thing when you decided to come to us, dear Eiríkur," said Lalla, "but you should have written to me first to tell me about your plans. You could have waited with your Icelandic friend at Cooks Brook until you heard from me. Then things would have gone better."

"Ahem!" said Mr. Sandford. "Then everything would have gone better but not one in a thousand would have considered all that in his circumstances. But all's well that ends well. The boy has come to us safe and sound, and he will stay with us. He will be one of us and this will be his home for as long as he wishes. He will be a fine son. I should say so!"

Lalla and her mother both welcomed me sincerely into their family. I thanked them all. I said that I would be happy to be there as long as it suited them. Soon we had lunch and then Mr. Sandford went down to the police station. He mentioned that he would try to get information about my suitcase and bag. I gave him a good description of the two pieces. He also asked for a description of the red-bearded conductor.

After lunch Lalla showed me to my own room. The room was upstairs and it faced the street. It was a neat room, pleasant in every way. Then she invited me to come out to see the sights of the city with her. Of course I was happy to do that. We spent the rest of the afternoon in the beautiful city park. We saw many rare birds and animals. There were two or three large fountains, one of which was supposed to be a miniature reproduction of the famous Geysir in Iceland. Two black swans were swimming in a small lake. We took a boat out to an island in the middle of the lake. The ride cost one cent for each of us. Here and there in the gardens there were hedges and flower beds. There were many benches and chairs made from willow branches and these seats looked as if they had just grown up from the ground. In some cases the legs were laced with moss, which made them look even more like a part of nature. I was thrilled with the beauty of the park and Lalla said that we should plan to spend some time there every Saturday afternoon until the end of summer.

We got home just in time for dinner. I don't think I ever spent a more enjoyable afternoon. That was because Lalla was with me and she was so kind. I felt as if I had left all my cares behind. Probably I appreciated everything so much because I had experienced hard times before. I felt my whole life was changing and now a new chapter was about to begin. Now I had hope for the future.

Mr. Sandford came home for dinner. He brought my suitcase but the bag seemed to be lost. Indeed, it was never found. I did not worry about that because it contained only my work clothes and the basket that the old women had given me when I was on my way to Dartmouth. I was very happy to have my suitcase because it held all my books and all my letters.

"Ahem!" said Mr. Sandford that evening as we relaxed in the little sitting room. "Now, Eiríkur, my dear," he said, "it is time for you to begin to study Latin and Greek, and other subjects which are taught in schools of higher learning in this country. You will be a well-educated man in the future. I should say so!"

"Oh, Daddy! You are so good!" said Lalla. She knew how eager I was to learn and to get an education.

"Ahem!" said Mr. Sandford. "Tomorrow we will buy some new clothes for Eiríkur. The day after tomorrow he will start lessons with Professor Harrington. I have arranged with the professor that he will tutor Eiríkur this summer so that he can start his studies at the Dalhousie Latin School in the fall. I should say so!"

And so it happened that two days after I came to Mr. Sandford's house I started my lessons with Professor Harrington, who was a wonderful man in every way. I studied with him for four hours each day, five days per week for most of the summer. I passed the entrance examination for the Dalhousie University in September. I was almost fifteen years old.

I wrote to my guardian, Eiríkur, and to my friend Jón shortly after I came to Mr. Sandford's house and told them about the changes that had taken place in my life. They wrote back to say how pleased they were to hear of my good fortune and they hoped that I could stay on with these good people for a long time.

One day, a few weeks after I came to stay with the Sandford family, I came home from my work with Professor Harrington and found Lalla in the sitting room. She was talking to a young man. She introduced us by giving him my name, saying that I was like a brother to her. She told me that the young man's name was Alphonso Picquart and his home was in Cape Breton. She explained that Alphonso was her friend and a friend of her parents. She said that she hoped that he and I would become good friends too. Alphonso and I shook hands and greeted each other very politely. He was a man of average height and very well proportioned. He was very gentlemanly in manner. His hair was black and just a little bit curly. His moustache was well-kept and attractive. His face was very handsome. Somehow I could not decide anything about his character from first impression. His eyes were quick and clear but his gaze seemed cool. I felt sorry about that because he was a friend of my good friends.

This young man, who was of French descent, had dinner with us and after that he spent a few hours with us. He talked to Lalla most of the time. I sensed that he would prefer to have the sitting room free while he was talking to Lalla but somehow it happened that either Mr. Sandford or his wife, or sometimes both of them, sat in the room that evening.

A few days later the same young man had dinner with us again and again he stayed on for a while in the sitting room and talked to Lalla. From what I heard of the conversation he did not seem to have anything special to talk about.

He came a third time and a fourth time and a fifth time and each time he seemed to stay longer and longer and he always had more and more to say to Lalla. One time she went with him to church and another time she went with him to the theatre. For a long time he did not come again and I was told that he had gone to his parents' home in Cape Breton but that he would return to Halifax later in the fall.

From the beginning I was not quite sure how I felt towards Monsieur Alphonso Piquart, even though he was handsome and polite. For some reason he seemed to draw Lalla's attention from me to himself, which I found hard to understand because Lalla treated me just the same as always even though he came to our home. He seemed to create a wall between Lalla and me. I had a feeling or state of mind that some might call jealousy.

One Saturday evening late in the summer Lalla and I were sitting on one of the benches in the city park. It was a clear evening and the moon had come out. Under the moon there was a bank of clouds. At the top there was a long narrow cloud and below it was another slightly shorter cloud. The third and fourth cloud layers were shorter and darker. Finally at bottom there was a short dark cloud. This was such an unusual formation that Lalla and I studied it for awhile and we talked about it. We were sitting side by side and she held my hand as she often did when we were together.

"This is a beautiful sight," I said. "The cloud at the top is brighter than the one below, and the next two are darker, and then the last one is the darkest."

"The layers are just like our family," said Lalla with a smile. "Daddy is at the top, then Mama, then you are the third one and I am at the bottom."

"No," I said, "I am at the bottom because I am the youngest. But who is the last one?"

"Maybe that is Alphonso," said Lalla, and she smiled at me.

"Maybe," I said, but I was not too pleased to hear him counted as one of us.

We said no more for a little while. We just sat there and watched all the people passing by. All of a sudden I thought of something and even now I don't know why I spoke up.

"May I ask you something?" I said to her.

"Oh, what is that, dear Eiríkur?" she asked.

"Do you think you could have an Icelander for a husband?" I asked rather shyly.

"Do you mean could I have an Icelander for a husband as far as his nationality is concerned?" said Lalla.

"Yes," I said, "Supposing a young and good-looking Icelander asked you to be his wife, would that be a possibility? He would of course have to be a good man, tall and well-built."

"Of course I could marry an Icelander, just as well as an English-man or a Scot, because I know that Icelanders are just as good and just as handsome as the others, but why do you ask such a question, dear child?"

I felt very small all of a sudden, when I heard those last words. She thought I was just a child, even though I was almost fifteen years old and preparing for university and almost as tall as she was. If I was still a child, as she said, then wasn't it ridiculous that I should mention marriage to her? Of course I had not asked her to be my wife.

Still I did have myself in mind when I asked her that question. Oh, it was ridiculous and childish of me to mention anything like this to her. I felt smaller and smaller until I was almost reduced to nothing.

"Oh, I asked that without thinking," I said. "I didn't really mean anything by it."

Lalla squeezed my hand a little tighter and smiled as she looked me in the eye. I am sure that she knew more or less what I was thinking.

"It really doesn't matter, dear Eiríkur, that you asked me about this, and I can assure you that I consider Icelanders just as handsome and lovable men as my own people. And I am going to tell you something else. I am going to start learning Icelandic. I am going to start tomorrow and you are going to be my teacher. Maybe I will someday be able to read for myself the words of your favourite poet, the one who wrote the beautiful poem about the little bird that lay frozen beside the moss, and the poem about the hero who turned back after he had been exiled from his fatherland. You told me so many things about this man when we were together in the room at Mrs. Patrick's house."

I was very happy to hear about Lalla's plan. I assured her that I would be very pleased to teach her Icelandic. I was so happy about this that I wanted to kiss her, and I probably would have done that if we had been at home. Suddenly I felt big again.

"But now I am going to tell you something," said Lalla, and she looked around to see whether there were any people nearby. Then she spoke in a low voice.

"And what is that?" I asked attentively, because I had an inkling that she had something important to tell me.

"You remember Alphonso, the young man who came to see us a few times last spring?" said Lalla.

"Yes, I remember him well," I said, and suddenly I had a foreboding about what she was going to tell me.

"Alphonso and I," said Lalla, and she leaned towards me, "are engaged. We will be married soon."

I quickly looked at her face and I knew that she was telling me the truth. She and Alphonso were engaged. I was not happy to hear that. For some reason it actually distressed me. But was it really any of my business whether they were engaged or not? I asked myself that question. And the answer was that it concerned me a great deal because I was not happy that she was engaged to anyone other than — well, that she was engaged to anyone other than . . . whom? What was I *thinking*? Wasn't I just a boy less than fifteen years old and she was well past nineteen? What nonsense! I wished her happiness and gave her my blessing. Then we said no more about it.

For a long time after that I felt that the days were not as bright as before. The city park was not as pleasant. My studies seemed more difficult. Everything seemed to have taken on a different hue, everything except Lalla. She was still the same as before, still my beautiful, kind sister.

BOOK III

ASPIRATIONS

CHAPTER 1

Time passes quickly. I was now in my sixteenth year. This is the time of life when people start assessing their own circumstances. It is the time when we start wondering about the meaning of life, and of existence itself. This is the time when we encounter crossroads. Which path should one take? Whose lead should one follow? What part should one play in the real-life drama? One wants to play an important part but, in practical terms, just what can one do to live a worthwhile life?

This is the time of life when every little excitement stirs the blood and every nerve and muscle responds. This is the time when our thinking and our sensitivity and our ability are at their best. This is the time when we tend to be happy and light-hearted, affectionate and optimistic. This is the time when we look for respect and crave independence. This is also the time when we yearn for freedom, fun and action. It is the time when we think we don't need to be told what to do or to be reminded of this or that. It is also the time when we are most subject to influences, whether good or bad.

This is the time of life when we begin to read romantic novels and enjoy romantic scenes enacted on stage. Young men notice red lips, rosy cheeks and full bosoms. Entertainments such as dances and theatre are suddenly important. Feelings almost beyond control can lift our spirits to new heights, or draw us down into shyness and self-deprecation.

I was almost sixteen years old. I was happy and healthy and full of energy. I enjoyed all kinds of fun. Memories of my struggles during my younger years had been pushed aside, but perhaps they had taught me a certain caution that helped me now.

I loved the green fields and hills, the wildflowers, and the forests filled with sunny glades and singing birds. I loved the brooks with their clear water and I loved rivers with waterfalls. I loved sea breezes. I loved the sea with all its changing faces. I loved the ebb and rush of the ocean. I loved the night when the heavens were clear and I marvelled at the stars and the galaxies and the moon. I loved the sunshine, the sunrise and the sunsets. I loved animals, and birds, and ants and honey-bees. I loved people too, like Lord Byron, who said, "I love not man the less, but Nature more."

Yes, I loved good men and good women, people who were sensitive. I loved good music and song. I dearly loved poetry. I loved being with people who were happy, but I could also cry with those who grieved.

By now I had spent nearly two years with the Sandford family. I had been very comfortable there. Mr. and Mrs. Sandford had been caring parents and their daughter, Lalla, had been a loving sister. She was not married yet but wedding plans were under way. By this time I had spent a winter at Dalhousie University. I was eager to learn and I had proved to be of average intelligence. I would have liked to have some choice with regard to the reading material. I was not happy with the curriculum. When I was supposed to read Caesar's *De bello Gallico* I would have preferred to read from the *Aeneid*

about the loves of Dido. When I was supposed to read about Aeneas
I read instead Vergil's *Ecloga Quinta* in the *Bucolicon*.

I well remember my first day at Dalhousie University. Mr. Sandford came down to the school with me that morning. As he put it,
he came "to make peace with the school board and to make the necessary arrangements" on my behalf.

We walked into a small office near the main entrance. An older
man was sitting at the desk and looking through some papers. He
was the secretary-treasurer for the school. His name was Robert
West. He was a very mild-looking man, tall but lean, and he had a
long face. His upper lip and his chin were shaved but he had thin
dark sideburns. His lower lip was full and partially covered his
upper lip. The corners of his mouth turned down, giving him a sad
expression.

"A-hem!" said Mr. Sandford. "Good morning, Mr. West."

"Good morning, Mr. Sandford," said Mr. West, setting his
papers aside. "What a beautiful day."

"Ahem," said Mr. Sandford, "I should say so."

"Right, Mr. Sandford," said Mr. West.

"Ahem!" said Mr. Sandford. "I have with me the lad we talked
about this summer, Mr. West. He is a good boy and intelligent."

"Quite right, Mr. Sandford," said Mr. West, holding his chin in
one hand while he looked me over. "An intelligent-looking young
man and he resembles you very much."

"Ahem!" said Mr. Sandford, smiling. "I am very glad to hear
that."

"What is his Christian name, Mr. Sandford?" asked Mr. West as
he opened a big book.

"Ahem!" said Mr. Sandford. "His name is Eiríkur."

"Quite right," said Mr. West, taking up his pen, "and how do
you spell that?"

"Ahem!" said Mr. Sandford, looking towards me. "Spell your
name for Mr. West, Eiríkur."

I spelled my name.

"Quite right," said Mr. West, writing very carefully in his big book. "So his name is Eiríkur Sandford."

"Ahem!" said Mr. Sandford, "His name is Eiríkur Hansson."

"Quite right!" said Mr. West, and he looked at us, turning from one to the other. "In fact, I thought that the young man was your son, Mr. Sandford. I thought that."

"Ahem! Strictly speaking, he is not my son."

"Quite right!" said Mr. West and his face looked longer than before. "We don't have to discuss that any further, Mr. Sandford."

"Ahem!" said Mr. Sandford. "As it stands, the boy is now under my care, and he is just as dear to me as if he were actually my own son. He is an Icelander."

"Quite right! And he is truly an Icelander?"

"Ahem! He is an Icelander from the top of his head, down to his toes."

"And was he born in Iceland?"

"Ahem! He was born in Iceland," said Mr. Sandford.

"Right! And how old is he, Mr. Sandford?"

"Ahem! He is fifteen years old," said Mr. Sandford.

"Right," said Mr. West, as he was writing something in his big book. "Will he stay at the school while he is studying with us?"

"Ahem!" said Mr. Sandford. "Yes, I would prefer that, but still I would like him to come home on weekends."

"Right!" said Mr. West, and he wrote that down. "He would be quite happy to share a room with one of his classmates?"

"I trust he will be happy with that arrangement," said Mr. Sandford, "but his roommate will have to be a good boy, a very good boy."

"Absolutely right!" said Mr. West.

"Ahem!" said Mr. Sandford and he gave Mr. West a few ten-dollar bills. "This, I hope, will cover his costs until Christmas." School fees at Dalhousie University were looked after by the government of Nova Scotia, but students had to pay for room and board.

"Absolutely right, Mr. Sandford," said Mr. West after he carefully counted the bills and entered this information into his big book. Then Mr. West quickly wrote a receipt and gave it to Mr. Sandford. As soon as this business was completed Mr. Sandford said goodbye to the two of us and he left the school.

Soon after that the school bell rang and I was shown into a large classroom. There were between eighty and one hundred new students gathered there. This was probably about one fifth of the entire student body. That day classes were just being organized and no teaching was actually taking place. One of the teachers gave a short speech. We were told to spend the rest of the day getting settled and getting acquainted with each other.

I left the classroom and entered the assembly room, and noticed an elderly man standing beside the door to the next classroom. He seemed to be paying particular attention to me, and soon he walked over to me and offered his hand. It was Dr. Dallas, who had helped me so much when I was in trouble about six months before. He looked so different that I did not recognize him until he spoke. Now he was dressed altogether differently. He had a beard on his chin and his sideburns were gone.

"I am happy to see you here, my young Icelander," he said. "You Icelanders belong in schoolrooms, because you are fond of learning. But I did not recognize you at first," he said.

"And I did not recognize you, Dr. Dallas, until you spoke to me." I said.

"That is not surprising," said the doctor, "the beard on my chin changes my appearance so that even some of my old friends did not know me at first. I stopped shaving my chin when my dear Mohammed died. I will never have a horse like him again."

I said that I was sorry to hear that he had lost his fine horse.

Doctor Dallas told me that he was going to teach Latin and Greek at Dalhousie that winter. He told me to be sure to look him up if I needed any help as far as my studies were concerned. He did indeed give me helpful advice and he was always kind.

I was very comfortable while I was studying at Dalhousie University because Mr. Sandford made sure that I was looked after as well as possible. I went back to the Sandford home every Saturday afternoon and stayed there until Sunday evening and sometimes until Monday morning.

My roommate was Hendrik Tromp. He was about my age and also a newcomer at Dalhousie. He was not a very big boy but he was healthy and lively. He was round-faced with fair hair and fair complexion. His grey-blue eyes were full of good humour and at the same time they revealed a sensitive nature.

I introduced myself. "My name is Eiríkur Hansson," I said.

"Where are you from?" he asked.

"I am an Icelander," I said.

"We are from Holland," he said.

"Were you born in Holland?" I asked.

"No, I am sorry to say that I was not born in Holland but my parents were born and raised there. I was born in America and my parents live in Lunenburg. Where are your parents?"

"My mother died years ago and I don't know where my father is. I have no relatives in this country," I said.

Hendrik looked at me for a few moments as if he was assessing me and then he spoke. "Listen, Eiríkur Hansson, here is my hand. Let's be friends." We looked into each other's eyes as we shook hands.

Likely we were drawn to each other partly because we were both "foreigners." This was in itself a bond between us. In general, though, our classmates were friendly and accepted us well. I was, as always, proud of my Icelandic heritage and Hendrik was every bit as proud of his Dutch ancestry. He thought that their literature surpassed that of any other nation. He was proud of the naval victories of his people' and he traced his lineage to the grandfather of the famous Admiral Tromp.

Two boys from the Annapolis region shared the room next to ours. Sometimes in the evenings, after homework was done, they would come to our room and we would take turns telling stories. Hendrik's stories were always the best. Hendrik spoke excellent English and neither his accent nor his grammar would suggest that English might not be his first language. Yet there was one expression that he used when he wanted to suggest that he didn't quite understand something that was said to him and that was, *"Kannitverstan."*

Hendrik's birthday was in late October. He celebrated the occasion by inviting me and the boys from Annapolis to dinner at a restaurant not far from the school. Hendrik entertained us by telling us Dutch folk stories. Just to offer an example of the kind of story that Hendrik told us, I will try to relate the story that he told us on the night of the birthday party.

The Story of Lúðvík

It was around the middle of the seventeenth century that a man came to a certain small town not far from Rotterdam. He was called Lúðvík. He was an older man and he had a large scar on the right side of his neck. He had with him a large horse, stone-coloured, with many scars all over its body. Lúðvík did not have anything else with him so far as anyone could see. No one in that neighbourhood had ever seen this man before, and no one knew where he came from. When he had spent a few days in the town he bought a large piece of land not far from the village. Then he hired carpenters and stonemasons and architects and had them build for him a very spacious and beautiful palace with several hundred rooms. When the building was completed all the workmen disappeared and no one knew what had become of them; no one except Lúðvík himself and he never said anything about that because he was a man of few words. Now Lúðvík hired many attendants and maidservants and he paid them twice the wages that were customary in the country at the time. More people would have liked to work there. Every New Year's Eve he announced to his staff that in the coming year their working hours would be shortened by half an hour and their wages would be substantially raised.

This arrangement meant that the servants at Lúðvík's palace had to work for only a few hours each day, as time went by, and within a few years they were all quite well off. Lúðvík had many large rooms set aside for his own use and few people ever entered there, and those few who entered never said anything about what they had seen there. Lúðvík never went out or in through any door that could be seen or that others knew about. Instead he went in and out through a hidden doorway that no one knew about except himself.

Sometimes he disappeared from the palace and was gone for weeks at a time. No one saw him leave and no one saw him return. But each time he was gone from home some stranger would come by and ask for the master. It was never the same man twice. Yet when Lúðvík was at home no strangers came to ask for him.

When it was storming outside and snowing some melancholy music was often heard from Lúðvík's rooms. He usually sat at table with his servants and his seat was always at the end of a long table that was placed lengthwise in the grand dining room. He left orders that the first visitor who came after he left would be given the seat at the head of the table. That command was always followed.

People tried in every possible way to find out who this Lúðvík really was, because he seemed to be as rich as the Count of Monte Cristo, and as mysterious and as widely known as the magician Cagliostro, but no one reached any real conclusion in that regard. Some thought that he was a wealthy nobleman from a foreign country who had been exiled on account of some political blunder, and a few even imagined that he was Charles I, King of England, who had tricked old Cromwell and escaped to Holland while some traitor had been executed in his place. Others, who thought he was the devil himself, were reluctant to come near the palace.

Twenty years after the palace was built, Lúðvík disappeared once and for all. Soon afterwards the mayor of Rotterdam announced to all within hearing that he had Lúðvík's will in his hands and that he would open the same and declare its contents in public on a certain day that Lúðvík himself had named long before. The appointed day arrived and the document was opened. It was found that Lúðvík had willed to his servants all his money, and this was worth so much that each person received the price of a small county in Germany. The palace he gave to the citizens of Rotterdam for a hospital. No one found out where he came from or where he went or what his intention was when he built this great palace near Rotterdam.

But some thought that they did have information about one chapter of Lúðvík's life story. There had been one guest who came to Lúðvík's palace and asked for a bed for the night when Lúðvík was not at home. The guest said he needed to see the master but he said that he could not wait for him beyond the darkest part of the night. The guest sat at table with the servants for the evening meal. He was seated in the place where Lúðvík usually sat.

"Your master is a hard man to deal with," said the guest.

"No, he is not a demanding employer," said the household manager.

"He is kindness itself," said the housekeeper.

"He must have had a change of heart," said the guest, "because he was a real tyrant when I knew him."

"Did you know him a long time ago?" asked the household manager.

"Yes, that was many years ago," said the guest. "It was during the great war that I saw him first."

"During what war?" asked the manager.

"During the great war," repeated the guest. "He came to the encampment one morning about dawn and he rode on a stone-grey horse. No one knew who he was or where he came from.

"He sat for a long time in discussion with the commander in charge, and the commander gave him permission to choose fifty men from the cavalry division to fight under his direction. He spent two days choosing these fifty men. They all rode on stone-grey horses and they were all excellent swordsmen. Ten men were giants, ten were of average height and very thickset as well, ten were tall and slender, ten were men of average height and rotund build, and ten were short and stout, and I was one of that last group. Those were hard days. We dashed at full speed around the enemy's outposts and engaged them in skirmishes. Before the main battle began eighteen of those fifty men had been killed. Lúðvík delivered a eulogy to each man who had fallen and called the others cowards."

"Then came the main battle. It took place down by the ocean. That day we fought from morning to evening. The enemy suffered defeat. By the time the battle was over that night only four of our fifty famous cavaliers remained. Lúðvík lay among the slain, with terrible wounds on his chest and on his neck. His horse was covered with wounds. Lúðvík ordered us to keep watch over him until midnight and we were not allowed to go to the encampment until he gave his permission. We were very tired and hungry and terribly thirsty. We saw the fires at the encampment about a mile away and we knew that our soldiers were having refreshments but we could not move from Lúðvík and his horse. Just before midnight, Luðvík took a little lantern from the saddlebag that we had put under his head. He ordered me and another man to go down to the ocean, light the lantern and wave the light seven times over our heads, then cover the light while we counted up to fifty, then take note to see if anything happened. Next we were to wave the lantern three times, cover the light again and wait to see whether anything happened while we were counting up to thirty. Then we were to wave the lantern four times, and after that return to Lúðvík. We did as we had been directed. We went down to the ocean, we lit the lantern, and we waved the light seven times. Then we saw that a light appeared four times in a row out on the fjord. Then we waved the lantern three times and three times we saw a light appear out on the fjord. Finally we waved the lantern four times and we saw a light appear seven times in a row out on the fjord. We returned to Lúðvík and told him what we had seen. He told us then to light the lantern and to hold it high. Shortly afterwards two horsemen arrived and they said a few words in a language which I did not understand. Lúðvík spoke to them in the same language in a commanding voice. They took his horse and disappeared into the dark. Lúðvík raised himself up on his elbow and ordered us to take him down to the sea and we did that right away. When we got there he had us light the lantern again and wave the light four times. A light appeared briefly out on the fjord. Then Lúðvík told us to wave the light three times. Across the water a light appeared twice in a row. Then we waved the lantern twice and the light out in the fjord appeared three times in a row. Then Lúðvík told us to hold the lantern still for a little while. Almost at the same instant we heard the sound of oars and soon a large boat landed close to us. Luðvík asked us to carry him out to the boat and to come along with him. The boat started out into the fjord. Before we knew it we were at the side of a big ship. We all went on board and we carried Lúðvík below the deck. Then we came into a large salon, which was hung with silk and other rich fabrics. This big room was well-lit with many candles. We laid Lúðvík down on a soft daybed and now he seemed close to death. As soon as we laid him down a young, beautiful and dignified woman came from an adjoining room and knelt down beside the bed. She hugged Lúðvík and kissed him over and over and wept. Lúðvík said that we were free to go now and we were taken up on deck again. There we were given food and drink and each of us was given a large purse full of gold coins. After that we were taken back to land again by rowboat. Since then I have not seen Lúðvík but I heard recently that he lived here. I thought I would like to see him but since he is away that will not happen. I am pressed for time."

This was the story that the guest told the servants at Lúðvík's

Palace. In the morning when the servants got up the guest had left and he was never seen again. It was the same with all the other guests who came to see Lúðvík; they all arrived late at night and were gone when morning came.

Hendrik's stories were all like this. They were reminiscent of *A Thousand and One Nights*. Many were about men or women who appeared from nowhere and departed mysteriously. He said that all his stories were folk stories from Holland but I think myself that many of them were his own creation.

"The end of this tale is similar to *The Death of King Arthur*," said one of the boys from Annapolis, when Hendrix finished the story.

"In fact," said Hendrik, "*The Death of King Arthur* was no doubt an imitation of the story of Lúðvík because Dutch authors would never copy an English folk tale."

CHAPTER 2

One evening Hendrik and I had just returned to our room after dinner and we were about to start doing our homework when Mr. West came to see us. He said that there was a man downstairs who wanted to talk to me. I asked Mr. West to have the man come up to our room because I thought that this must be someone that I knew quite well. A few minutes later there was a knock at our bedroom door.

"Come in," I said. The door opened immediately and in walked a man I had never seen before. He was about twenty-five years old, of medium height, and very well dressed. Indeed his clothes fitted so well they might have been custom-made. He had an expensive cloak thrown over his shoulders but under it he wore a tailored jacket fully buttoned. He wore a felt hat, which he did not remove when he came into our room, and on his hands he wore thin leather gloves. His skin was white and his complexion was very clear. He had an attractive black moustache and black hair. His hair was curly; indeed, the curls were so perfect that a curling iron must have been used. His curls showed under his hat, behind his ears and at the back of his head. His eyes were dark and clear and he had a well-shaped mouth. He had obviously not grown up in poverty. Good manners seemed almost inborn in him.

As he entered our room he paused and proceeded to slowly take off one of his gloves while he studied Hendrik and me.

"Which one of you is called Hansson?" he asked.

"I am called Hansson," I said, wondering what this young man could possibly want with me.

"May I talk with you privately, Master Hansson?" he asked, looking at Hendrik as he said that.

"I will step outside," said Hendrik.

"Thank you very much," said the stranger, bowing slightly before Hendrik.

As he was leaving I heard Hendrik say, *"Kannitverstan."*

"You are an Icelander, Master Hansson?" asked the stranger.

"Yes, I am an Icelander," I repeated.

"Can you read and write your mother tongue fairly well?"

"I can read and write my mother tongue reasonably well," I said.

"In other words, would you be able to write a personal letter in Icelandic?" he asked and he looked directly into my eyes.

"I think so," I said.

"Good," he said. "You would do a big favour for me and my friends if you'd write a letter for an Icelandic girl who is too ill to write herself. I can assure you that you will be well-paid for your time and trouble. Not only will you be doing a favour for me and my friends, but you will also be doing a good deed."

"When do you want me to write the letter?" I asked.

"This evening," he said. "A driver with a carriage and two horses is waiting for us in front of the building. If you will come with me right away I will guarantee that you can be back here before midnight." He pulled a gold watch from his pocket and looked at it. "It is now exactly seven o'clock."

"Can we leave it until tomorrow night?" I asked.

"No, that could be too late," he said. "The letter must be written tonight because the girl in question is very sick."

"What is the girl's name?" I asked.

"I don't know that, but she has been staying with my aunt, who lives at 48 Rosemary Street."

"Where is that street?" I asked.

"The street is south of the hill, on the edge of town."

"What is your aunt's name?" I asked.

"Mrs. Hamilton."

"And what is your name?"

"Edward Ferguson," he said, "but will you please tell me whether or not you are willing to do us this favour?"

I said nothing for a moment. I was not comfortable about going, but I did not like to refuse.

"I want to say again," said Mr. Ferguson, "that you will be doing a good deed if you come with me, and I stress that the person involved is a sick girl of your own nationality."

I still did not answer.

"If you come with me I will leave my name and address with the supervisor of the school. In other words I will get his permission for you to leave with me."

I was still hesitant.

"But if you cannot or absolutely will not come with me, then I must ask you to suggest someone else who could write in Icelandic." Mr. Ferguson had risen to his feet.

"I don't know of any other Icelanders in the city," I said.

"That is too bad," he said, now very serious.

"I will go with you," I said.

"I am very grateful," he said, and a look of relief spread over his face, "but can you come right away?" He started pulling on his gloves.

"I'll come right away," I said, putting on my jacket and my hat.

"Don't you want to let your friend who was here with you know that you will be away for a few hours?" asked Mr. Ferguson.

"Yes, I'll do that," I said. I looked for Hendrik but he was not in the hallway and he was not in the next two rooms either, so I wrote a note and left it where he would be sure to see it. I explained that I was going into the city. I asked him to please let the night watchman know that I would not be back before the usual curfew, which was eleven p.m., but I would be back before midnight.

"Should I talk to the supervisor and let him know that you are going into the city with me?" asked Mr. Ferguson.

"No, that is not necessary," I said, because I felt that would show that I did not altogether trust him.

"As you wish," he said.

We walked out of the school and out to the road. In front of the building we found a coach and two horses waiting for us. In the driver's seat sat a man holding onto the horses' reins. It was starting to get dark outside. I could not see the driver's face. He was wearing a wide-brimmed hat and the collar on his coat was turned up. I could not see any number on the coach, though all drivers for hire in Halifax at this time had numbers on their carriages on both sides. Actually I had very little opportunity to check the coach or the driver because Mr. Ferguson lost no time. He opened the side door of the coach and told me to sit in the front seat. Without so much as a word to the driver he climbed in himself and sat down on the back seat. Soon we were off at a good pace. I had never before travelled in a coach that had glazed windows. I noted right away that the windows on both sides were covered with a thick material so that not even a glimmer of light came in from the street lamps. I found this rather uncomfortable. To be sure, though, these heavy drapes may have been intended to make the coach a little warmer. It was quite cold outside and rather windy.

Up to this time I had not considered that this journey might be in any way dangerous because Mr. Ferguson had not given me time to think about it. But now that I was in the coach I started thinking about the possibilities. Might this Mr. Ferguson had something different in mind, something other than getting me to write a letter for an Icelandic girl? Why was Hendrik Tromp not allowed to hear what I was being asked to do? This trip was seeming quite mysterious.

I began to think about different stories that I had read about men who had been asked to travel in the middle of the night and had been taken in covered coaches to places which were altogether unfamiliar, taken there to do something that was totally against their principles. I remembered the story of a certain doctor who was woken up at night and asked to come to see a dying man. He was taken in a covered coach to a house in some undisclosed location but the task which he was asked to do was to remove a hand from a healthy man. I also recalled the story of a priest who was approached late one evening and asked to administer the sacrament to a dying man. He also was taken to an unknown house in a covered coach and he had to witness the murder of a man who, he felt sure, was innocent. I also thought of the story of a locksmith who was visited one evening by some strangers who asked him to come with them to the house of a particular friend of his. This friend, they said, was in need of his help. In fact he was moved in a covered coach to an out-of-the-way place and he was forced to make a key. He felt sure that these men were robbers who planned to use the key to open a safe that belonged to a certain wealthy man. Was it possible that I would be forced to do something like these men had to do? Of course I was neither a doctor, nor a priest, nor a locksmith.

"How did you know that I was an Icelander and that I lived at Dalhousie University?" I asked.

"Mrs. Hamilton had that information."

"How did she get that information?" I asked.

"I do not know that with certainty, but I think she probably sought information from the police department. Those people are usually called on for help under these circumstances."

"How did you know that I was called Hansson?"

"I did not know that until Mr. West told me," said Ferguson.

These answers seemed reasonable and for the moment distrust faded away. Then I noticed that the coach had turned corners several times. Sometimes we seemed to be going up the hill and then we seemed to be going straight down but always we rushed along over the cobbled streets. I could not see anything because of the covered windows. We turned a corner and suddenly I asked, "Are we on Church Street?" although I don't know why I said that.

"You are correct," said Ferguson, "Now we are going south on Church Street."

"And now we are driving south beside the city park," I said after a while.

"No, this time you are mistaken. We are now on Kingsway."

I felt that this trip was taking a long time. If someone had told me that we had travelled several times around the city I could have believed it. Again I began to think how queer this journey really was. Suddenly a thought came into my mind, an awful thought, a mental picture of Mrs. Patrick. Once again I was gripped with dread. Could she be behind this mysterious journey? In her cunning way might she be seeking to capture me again? I shuddered at the thought and wished that I could somehow escape. Then I tried to regain my courage and I told myself that I must meet whatever lay ahead sensibly and calmly.

"Where do you live?" I asked.

"I live at 9 Rosemary Street," answered Mr. Ferguson. "I am an accountant at the Bank of Nova Scotia."

Very soon after that the coach stopped. Ferguson got out ahead of me and spoke to the driver in low tones. Immediately the driver pulled two blankets off his seat and covered the horses. We were on a wide street, but the houses seemed to be quite far apart. All the houses were big and showed signs of wealth and privilege. The house in front of us seemed to outshine all the others. There were tall trees in the garden and three or four stone steps led up to the front door of the house. Strangely, there were no lights to be seen in the windows of this house, although all the surrounding houses had lights.

"Does Mrs. Patrick live here?" I asked, to see how Ferguson would react.

"Mrs. Hamilton lives here," he said quietly. He rang the doorbell and then he opened the door himself, which showed he was familiar with this house. He had me walk in ahead of him. We entered a large foyer, which was well-lit by two gas lamps. Likely the windows had looked dark because the drapes were exceptionally heavy. To the right of the hallway there was a wide staircase, and the steps were covered with a rich carpet. On the left there was a sitting room.

As soon as we entered a middle-aged woman in a light blue silk dress stepped out of the sitting room. "Is this the young man?" she asked.

"Yes, Mrs. Hamilton," said Mr. Ferguson, "this is Master Hansson." Then he turned to me. "Master Hansson, this is Mrs. Hamilton." I bowed to the lady. She asked me to step into the sitting room and find a seat, and she followed. I looked back into the hall and found that Mr. Ferguson had disappeared. I had not heard him open the door again and neither had I seen him go up the stairs.

Mrs. Hamilton sat across from me and she seemed to look me over very carefully for a few moments. I studied her as well. She was a rather small woman. She had fair hair and blue eyes. She had fine features, with delicate skin, seemingly free of blemish or wrinkle. Her face reminded me of a marble statue of the goddess Diana that I had seen in a museum in Halifax.

"You are an Icelander," she said.

"Yes," I said.

"You can read and write Icelandic," she said.

"I can read and write Icelandic fairly well," I said.

"You came here to write a letter in Icelandic," she said.

"Yes," I said.

"Wait here for a few minutes," she said, and she left the room. After she left I looked around the sitting room. There were expensive chairs and two elegant couches. Several costly ornaments were displayed on tables here and there around the room. There were thick carpets on the floor. On a long, narrow table beside the window were many different varieties of geraniums.

On the walls there were pictures in gilt frames. I particularly noticed three of the pictures. One was a picture of Nelson, standing on his ship *Victory* just before the battle at Trafalgar. This suggested that the homeowner was English and proud of English victories. The next picture, not surprisingly, was of Queen Victoria. The homeowner must be a loyal subject and a law-abiding citizen. The third picture that I paid particular attention to was a picture of Jesus blessing the children. From looking at this last picture I judged that the homeowner was a Christian who loved all things right and beautiful.

Mrs. Hamilton returned and asked me to come with her. We crossed the hall and she indicated that I should go up the stairs and she followed me to the second floor. Upstairs there was a long hallway with many doors on either hand. Mrs. Hamilton opened one of the doors, invited me to enter ahead of her, and then closed the door quietly. This room was rather small and two areas, one on either side, were curtained off. In the middle of the room there was a small table and two chairs. On the table were paper, pen and ink.

Mrs. Hamilton asked me to sit down on the chair next to the door, and she sat down on the other chair. Then she passed me a letter that lay on the table, and asked me to read it for myself. The letter was not in an envelope but I saw immediately that it was written in Icelandic. It was written in blue ink. The lines were close together and the letters were very small, but overall the script was attractive and neat. More than three months had passed since the letter had been written. It had been written in Skagafjörð, in Iceland.

The letter began, "My beloved daughter!" The writer thanked

her daughter for a long and interesting letter from the previous year, mentioned that her own health was fairly good, and that she would be with the same family for the next year. Then there was a lengthy description of the weather conditions, followed by news of shipwrecks, deaths and marriages, etc. The letter ended with sincere good wishes for her daughter's health and happiness, and was signed by her loving mother, Kristín Björg Jóhannsdóttir.

The lady asked me to read the letter in a fairly loud voice. Before I started to read I looked around to see whether there would be anyone besides the lady herself to hear what I said. I saw no one else. I asked whether I should read in English.

Mrs. Hamilton said, "Read the letter in Icelandic." I read it in Icelandic. I could not tell from the lady's expression whether she understood any part of what I had read.

"Read the letter again," she said, when I was going to give it back to her.

So I read the letter a second time, and returned it to her. She stood up and walked into one of the adjoining rooms and stayed there for a short time. I did not hear any conversation take place in the other room. When the lady came back she sat down across from me and asked me to take pen and paper and write in Icelandic what she was going to dictate for me in English. The letter was very short. It began, "Dear mother!" The mother was thanked for the letter she had sent. The author mentioned that she was well and that she was still with the same woman. She mentioned that her father had died during the previous summer and had been buried according to Christian tradition. She discouraged her mother from planning to move "out west." She sent regards to all her friends and promised to write again soon. The letter ended with the words "Your loving daughter...."

When I had written the letter I expected that the lady would tell me what name I should write at the end, but instead she asked me to read out loud what I had written. I did that. "But what name do

I put at the end?" I asked.

"Write on this envelope," said Mrs. Hamilton as she passed a square envelope to me, and pretended that she had not heard my question.

I wrote on the envelope the name of the woman who had written the letter from Iceland, and also the name of the farm which was written at the top of her letter, and finally I wrote Skagafjörð, Iceland, Europe. The name of the parish where the farm was located I could not add on the envelope because I could not find it in the letter.

"You are sure that this is the full address?" asked Mrs. Hamilton.

"I think so," I said, "but should I not sign a name to the letter?"

"You have written all that you have to write here," said Mrs. Hamilton, and she folded the letter that I had written and placed it in the envelope, but did not seal it. "Tell me how much I should pay you for your trouble,"

"I do not want any pay for this," I said as I stood up.

"I will feel insulted if you do not accept any pay from me," said Mrs. Hamilton as she stood up, but I did not see any sign of displeasure on her face.

"Far be it from me to insult you, Mrs. Hamilton, but I have to tell you that I would never accept pay for writing a letter for a patient, especially when that patient is someone from my own nationality."

Mrs. Hamilton stood there very quietly for a moment and looked at me. "So you will not accept any pay," she said.

"No, nothing," I said, "and if this patient needs to send another letter then I would be glad to write it for her."

"The patient is very grateful to you," said Mrs. Hamilton, with the hint of a smile on her lips.

And just then I thought I heard, it may have been my imagination, but I thought I heard a little sigh in the other room.

I would gladly have written a hundred letters if only I had been allowed to see the patient for a moment, and I felt that she would have liked to see me, but the way things stood I knew that it would not be appropriate to say any more about that.

Mrs. Hamilton and I walked downstairs and I picked up my jacket and my hat. When she opened the front door for me she said, "Just step into the carriage that is waiting in front of the house and you will be taken home directly. Good night!"

At 11:30 that evening I came back to my room at Dalhousie. Hendrik was sitting at the table and said he was glad to see me alive and well. He had gone outside, seen the coach and waited nearby until he saw us start off. He tried to follow us a little while but he soon lost sight of the coach and turned back to the school. He found my note and talked to the night watchman. I told him the whole story and he thought there was something mysterious about this exchange of letters. *"Kannitverstan!"* he said.

Whether or not there was anything mysterious about the situation, I vowed that I would try to see and talk to this Icelandic girl in Mrs. Hamilton's house on Rosemary Street. My friend Hendrik said that he would help me in any way he could.

During the next few days I could think of little else. At night I dreamt about her. I imagined that she was beautiful with golden hair and blue eyes. I thought that she was staying at Mrs. Hamilton's house against her will and that she needed my help to get away.

The following weekend I went back to the Sandford house as usual. I told Mr. Sandford about the Icelandic girl who lived at Mrs. Hamilton's house on Rosemary Street.

"Ahem!" said Mr. Sandford, with a questioning expression. "Do you know this girl?"

"No," I said, "I have never seen her."

"Ahem!" said Mr. Sandford. "A sick Icelandic girl is very lucky to be in Mrs. Hamilton's house. She will be better off there than in a hospital. Florence Nightingale herself would not nurse her better than Mrs. Hamilton."

I told Mr. Sandford that I had been approached for help and had been taken to the home to write a letter but I had not been allowed to see the girl and I had not been given her name. I thought that was very strange.

"Ahem!" said Mr. Sandford. "This is understandable. You were called upon to write a letter, not to meet a girl."

Then I told Lalla the same story, and mentioned that I really wanted to speak to the sick Icelandic girl and find out about her circumstances.

"The girl could not be better off anywhere than with Mrs. Hamilton," said Lalla.

"But why could I not talk to her, or even learn her name?" I asked.

"Possibly friends thought that it would not do you any good to get acquainted," said Lalla. "You should stop worrying about her, dear Eiríkur. I can assure you that the people she is with are good to her."

I felt clearly that the Sandford family, for some reason, did not want me to meet the Icelandic girl. That attitude only made me wish more than ever to get to know her. Many times that winter I walked by Mrs. Hamilton's house in the vain hope that I might see her. I never saw Mrs. Hamilton or Mr. Ferguson either. Finally spring arrived and I moved back to the Sandford home to be with the family until it was time for school again in the fall.

CHAPTER 3

As I mentioned earlier, Lalla Sandford was engaged to Alphonso Picquart, a young man of French descent. I had expected that they would be getting married in the fall when I began my studies at Dalhousie. As it turned out, Alphonso spent one month with the Sandfords that fall and then he returned to Cape Breton to live with his parents. He did not come to Halifax during the winter. In the spring, just after the school holidays began, he came back to the Sandford house, and then I was told that Lalla and Alphonso would be married after just two weeks.

Mr. Sandford and Alphonso's father had grown up together and were good friends. Lalla and Alphonso had known each other since they were young children and had seen each other every year because the Sandford family spent a few weeks each summer in Cape Breton with friends and relatives who lived there. I had often heard Mr. Sandford say that he did not know a better man than Mr. Picquart, Alphonso's father. No doubt he thought that Alphonso was like his father. Otherwise he would not have been happy about the marriage.

In spite of Mr. Sandford's high regard for Alphonso, he never appealed to me. In fact I felt an aversion to him the first time we met. Although Alphonso was always polite and well-mannered I always felt that his attitude towards me was cool. Even though he always spoke to me courteously he was never inclined to carry on any conversation with me. Most likely he, in turn, felt that my responses to him were cool. For some reason it seemed impossible that Alphonso and I would ever understand each other or become really friendly. Indeed, I could not see how Lalla and Alphonso could live together comfortably and happily, so different were they in their approach and, seemingly, in their attitudes.

I knew that Lalla loved me, too. She had done more for me than any other person, except my Afi and Amma. She had been my best teacher, and she had studied Icelandic with me because she knew that would make me happy. For years she had protected me in every way that she could and I was treated as the brother she never had. She was dearer to me than anyone else in the world. Then along came Alphonso Picquart, this man whom I disliked, and took her away from me. Obviously she loved him with all her heart or she would not have become engaged to him. I could not say anything against him.

Soon the wedding day arrived. The weather was cool and fog carried with it an air of melancholy. For me the mood was one of grieving rather than of celebration. Mr. and Mrs. Sandford were very happy and so was Alphonso Picquart. Lalla looked confident and happy. She looked at me and smiled as she stepped into the carriage that was waiting to take her to the English Church. I saw her walk into the church in her wonderful bridal dress. I have never seen a more beautiful and dignified bride than Lalla. I had always thought that she was outstanding among other young women but never had I seen her look as lovely as she did that day. Never had her voice sounded so beautiful as it did when she repeated the customary vows in the English church. The rose is most fragrant when it is picked, and Lalla was most beautiful when she gave her heart and hand to Alphonso.

I was sitting near the front of the church while the long ceremony went on. I sat there with a heavy heart because I felt that my lovely Lalla was leaving me forever. The priest's remarks seemed to carry an air of finality, rather than of rejoicing.

Then the holy ceremony ended. Alphonso and Lalla had promised to love one another in sickness and in health and the priest had said that only death could separate them. The priest had introduced them to those who were gathered there as Mr. and Mrs. Picquart. Miss Lalla Sandford had disappeared from the scene, and there was no longer a beautiful girl by that name. In her place there was now Mrs. Picquart.

After the ceremony a group of guests gathered at the Sandford house to congratulate the newlyweds. When the visitors had offered their good wishes to the couple, I walked over to Lalla, took her hand and wished her happiness and blessings in the future. She smiled at me very sincerely as if she wanted to say, "Even though I am married, dear Eiríkur, I will always be your sister, just the same."

I shook hands with the bridegroom and wished him all the best. He thanked me and smiled rather coldly, as if he wanted to say, "You cannot call my wife your sister because she is no longer Lalla Sandford but rather she is Mrs. Picquart." But I would not think of calling her Mrs. Picquart. She was my sister, Lalla; and Lalla, my sister, she would remain.

The day after the wedding Lalla and Alphonso went to Annapolis Royal for a short holiday. Annapolis Royal is the oldest city in Nova Scotia. They were gone for about one week. After their return to Halifax they planned to travel by steamship to Cape Breton. They were going to live with Alphonso's parents for at least a year because the parents had a large and beautiful home in Sydney. Mr.

Picquart had a business there and had had two ships engaged in trade with the West Indies. For some reason Alphonso's parents had not been able to attend the wedding in Halifax. Instead, they had arranged for a big reception in Sydney when the wedding party arrived there. Mr. and Mrs. Sandford wanted to accompany their daughter to Sydney and they had planned to spend three or four weeks in Cape Breton as they had done every summer for years.

I had been thinking that I would take that time to visit my old friend Eiríkur Gísli Helgi, who lived near Bridgewater. I had not seen him since he left Cooks Brook but I had received letters from him now and again. He had indicated to me that he was most anxious to return to Iceland. I was fond of him and wanted to see him.

However, Mr. and Mrs. Sandford had taken for granted that I would go with them to Cape Breton. Of course I was eager to spend as much time as possible with Lalla so I decided in the end to put off my trip to Bridgewater and go instead with the Sandfords.

Our journey on the steamship went very well. We landed at Louisburg, a town famous in Canadian history. It had been a French fortress city at one time and its construction cost $6,000,000. We took a train from Louisburg to Sydney. We arrived there early in the morning and were immediately taken by carriage to Mr. Picquart's house. The house was at the edge of the town but likely it is now in the middle of the city because Sydney has grown so much since I was there. Near the city there are important coal mines.

Mr. and Mrs. Picquart received us with a warm welcome. I saw immediately that Mr. Sandford and Mr. Picquart were close friends. Mr. Picquart was in his late fifties, kindly and courteous in manner. His wife was an exceptionally beautiful woman in spite of advancing years and she carried herself proudly. Alphonso resembled his mother and her side of the family. Mrs. Picquart, I soon discovered, thought that her son was the most wonderful man under the sun, and Lalla, she thought, was the luckiest woman born in the nineteenth century.

Two days after our arrival a wedding reception was held at the Picquart residence. Everything had been well-rehearsed and guests were graciously received. Over a hundred people sat down to a sumptuous meal. Many wonderful treats were offered. Alcoholic drinks, I noted, were not on the menu.

Many of the guests were prominent citizens of Sydney or enterprising young businessmen. I noticed one man who seemed to stand out from the rest. He seemed to be on his own, yet everyone addressed him as "Uncle." He always replied with "mon cher" or "ma chère" and often referred to the battle of Sedan (1870).[23] He was a Frenchman through and through. He was a small man but nimble. His hair was quite long and silver-grey and his moustache was the same color. His face was thin, his nose hooked. His chin was firm and his jaws were strong. His brow was furrowed. His eyes were black and quick. On one cheek he had a large scar, which gave him an odd appearance. He wore blue denim trousers, very wide at the bottom, and a blue jacket with a dark woollen shirt underneath. He stood very straight and held his head high. He kept moving through the crowd, holding his pipe in his hand as he visited. As soon as he stepped into the garden in front of the house he would light up his pipe. He never stopped talking, always about the battle of Sedan. His listeners would always smile kindly and politely and say "Yes, Uncle, yes Uncle." No one was at all interested in talking to this man, likely because they had heard his story so often.

I was intrigued by this unusual man so I asked Alphonso about him.

"Oh, that is Uncle Jean," said Alphonso, shrugging his shoulders. "He is an old soldier and he is half-crazy. Pay no attention to him."

I had been thinking of approaching him but he always seemed to pass me by. Then all of a sudden I ran into him in the garden and he fastened his gaze on me. "Do you dare to look me in the eye?" he asked.

"Yes, I dare to look you in the eye," I said, smiling.

"You would not have dared to do that if you had been in the

Prussian army at the battle of Sedan," said Uncle Jean.

"Yes, just the same," I said.

"Mon cher!" said Uncle Jean. "Mon cher, you are the only one who has dared to say that, and the only one who has dared to look me in the eye since I came to Sydney. You could become a good soldier. I will tell you how things happened at the battle at Sedan."

Then he told me a long story about the battle, about the events that led up to it, and about the after-effects. He told the story well, paying attention to detail. He hated Bismarck and the Prussians. He criticized Jules Favre and he blamed Napoleon III for the defeat.

"The French are born soldiers," said Uncle Jean. "No soldiers anywhere can compare with them."

"And still they were defeated both at Waterloo and at Sedan," I said.

"Mon Dieu!" said Uncle Jean. "We lost at Waterloo because Napoleon was foolhardy and believed too much in Marshall Ney. In Sedan we lost because we had a useless commander who was sick at heart and physically ill as well. No, mon cher, the problem was not with the French soldiers but rather with the officers."

"I have always thought that the French soldiers did not compare with the English or the Germans," I said.

"Mon Dieu!" said Uncle Jean, pulling on his pipe. "You are the first who has dared to say such a thing in my hearing. Do you think we are children since you rank us below the English and the Germans?"

"No," I said, "I have always thought of you as athletes, artists and poets."

"Yes, mon cher," said Uncle Jean. "Athletes we are and the best soldiers in the world. But artists and poets we are not."

"Victor Hugo and Alexandre Dumas are two famous French writers," I said.

"Alexandre Dumas was a lanky fellow who wrote a bunch of lies," said Uncle Jean with a grimace, "and Victor Hugo combined truth and fiction and ruined both with ridiculous philosophies. Mon cher, French soldiers have maintained the honour of their country, much more than the French writers."

"Good!" I said. "So you think that French soldiers surpass all other men?"

"Yes, mon cher," said Uncle Jean. "Let's discuss this later, when we have more time. Come to see me tomorrow in my cabin up there in the hillside. I will show you my sword."

I promised to see him the next day. We went into the dining room and we did not talk to each other any more that day.

The next day I visited Uncle Jean. He was sitting on a three-legged stool in front of his door and he was quietly smoking his pipe.

"Good day," I said.

"Good day, mon cher!" he said. "You have a good memory."

"Why do you think that?" I asked.

"I think that because you remembered to visit me."

"It was only yesterday that you invited me to visit you."

"You are the only one that I have met here in Sydney in eight years who has remembered a similar invitation," said Uncle Jean.

"Has no one visited you?" I asked.

"No, no one that I have invited has come. They all have memory loss, mon cher. Please come in," said Uncle Jean.

We walked into his little house. It was probably about twelve feet long and about eight feet wide. There was no loft and there were no dividers. All was very tidy. Along one wall there was a small well-made bed. Along the other wall there was a table and two three-legged stools. Near the door there was a small stove and close by there was a counter with a few cooking utensils. Everything in the house was clean and polished. There were three large items hanging on one wall. One was a picture of the battle of Waterloo and another was a picture of the battle of Sedan. The third item was a sword.

"This is my sword, mon cher," said Uncle Jean when he saw that I was studying it. "This is the sword that kissed my cheek during the battle at Sedan. That was a rough kiss, mon cher!" Uncle Jean stroked the scar on his cheek.

"Was it your own sword that wounded you like that?" I asked in amazement.

"Yes, mon cher," he said. "My face was cut by this sword, but I did not own it then. It belonged to one of the soldiers from the Prussian cavalry. He was one of several Prussian riders who tried to break through our infantry line. He sat on a spirited horse, spurred him on, waved this sword, bellowed a battle cry and headed straight towards me. I waited for him calmly as becomes a French soldier. I put the butt of my gun into the ground. I checked to make sure that the bayonet was well fastened to the barrel of the gun. The rider steered the horse in such a way that he could just squeeze past me through the gap between me and the next soldier, but I knew that trick. I turned the gun slightly to the side just as the horse, with his rider, was about leap past me. The bayonet was buried in the horse's chest and the poor beast fell on his side. At the same time the rider brandished his sword and managed to inflict a considerable injury to the left side of my face. In a fury, I rushed at the rider and grabbed away his sword. I was about to cut through his head as he lay, half under the horse, but I swooned and collapsed. When I came to the battle was over but the sword was still in my grasp. The rider was gone and I have never seen him since. That is how this excellent sword became mine. Mon cher, only a French soldier can display the weapon that the enemy used to maim him."

"You speak good English even though you were born and raised in France," I said.

"I speak reasonably good English but I was born and raised here in Sydney, and lived here until I was twenty-one years old. I spent only twenty-five years in France."

"You have relatives here," I said, "and they all call you 'Uncle'."

"I had many relatives here, mon cher," said Uncle Jean, looking into the distance, "but now most of them are gone. Picquart Senior is now the only one who can rightly be called a relative. Our fathers were brothers."

"Then you can also say that Alphonso is your relative," I said.

"We won't count Alphonso," said Jean as he shook the ashes out of his pipe.

"Why do you say that?" I asked.

"His ways are not my ways," said Uncle Jean. "He will be like his great-grandfather, his mother's grandfather. The sins of the fathers reappear in the descendants in the third and fourth generations."

"What about this great-grandfather of his?" I wondered.

"Mon cher, he was the worst drunkard and carouser who ever walked on God's green earth," said Jean, "and the sins of the fathers reappear in the third and fourth generations. The Bible says so, and doctors agree, and experience shows that too. All indications are the same."

"But isn't it possible that Alphonso will follow his father's side rather than his mother's?" I asked.

"No, mon cher," said Uncle Jean, shaking his head. "He is the living image of his mother and the sins of her grandfather will emerge in him sooner or later. He will be a drunkard and a carouser. Too bad! Too bad!"

I was sorry to hear this prophesy for Lalla's sake. Sadly, Jean knew Alphonso better than I did. I wanted to turn this discussion in another direction.

"What is your full name?" I asked.

"My name is Jean Picquart," he said.

"Why does everybody call you 'Uncle'?" I asked.

"They think that is an honour, I suppose," he said with a strange little smile.

"Did you not have children?" I asked.

"I had a son, mon cher," he said, "but he is dead. The Prussians killed him in the battle at Sedan."

"Where is your wife?"

"She died, mon cher, she died long ago." A look of tremendous sadness passed over his face. He sat quietly for a long time, or so it seemed to me, and stared into the distance. I guessed that his thoughts were all about a lonely grave in a cemetery on the other side of the ocean.

I said goodbye to Jean and he wished me well and asked me to visit him again sometime in the future. He stood in the doorway and watched as I walked down the hill.

I did not stay in Sydney as long as I had expected because Mr. and Mrs. Sandford had to return to Halifax earlier than they had planned. I cannot say how hard it was to leave Lalla. I asked her to come to me if she ever had any problems. She smiled and asked me to come to her if I ever needed help. She would always be my sister. She asked me to work hard at my studies, and always be their good boy.

"We will see each other after a little time, dear Eiríkur," she said and she grasped my right hand in both her own hands, "we'll see each other, happy and contented. May God bless you."

"We will hope so," I thought to myself. We will hope that I will see her happy and content and in good health, not saddened, tired and pale. We will hope.

CHAPTER 4

Halifax is famous for its fortifications and even more famous for its beautiful city park. Here nature and man's ingenuity have together created an earthly paradise. Here you may find all the most beautiful and fragrant flowers and the loveliest trees that grow in the temperate zones. Here are songbirds and many other interesting birds. There are little hills and dales, little streams with waterfalls, little lakes with islands, little meadows and fields with hedges and fountains. There are paths inlaid with stones throughout the park and around the beautiful flowerbeds. Everywhere there are benches so that people can sit down to relax in sunshine or in shade. Here visitors are often charmed by birdsong, and sometimes by instrumental music. Here nature offers an opportunity for refreshing rest and peace!

All who live in Halifax have at some time visited this park. During the summer season some people may visit every month, some every week, some every day, and some may spend time there more than once each day.

Rich people come to the park when they are tired of the theatres and the dance salons and the parties. City councillors come to the park when difficult decisions await them. Newspaper editors, journalists, judges, lawyers and priests all come to the park to reconsider opinions, to dispel unpleasant information and sometimes to ease the voice of conscience. Merchants and accountants come here to forget, briefly at least, all about dollars and cents. Clerks come here to forget the smells of soap and syrup, smoked hams and salted herring. Policemen come here when they are off duty and dressed in regular clothes. Here they can walk around without being noticed and without feeling that people shrink away from their discipline. Here come the sailors, tired from tossing about on the ocean, happy to walk on solid ground. Here they can enjoy the fragrance of flowers instead of the salty smell of the ship, and here birdsong replaces the sounds of the sea. Here come the soldiers, seeking relaxation after long hours of training. At the end of the day come the workers from factories and warehouses, the carpenters and the men who maintain and build the piers. For the time being, at least, all are able to enjoy their freedom. Here come the students and here come the teachers, here come the poets and the painters. Here come the mothers and the little children. Here young lovers meet. Often orchestral music will be heard as part of the attraction. People come from every walk of life, men and women, children and old people, the poor and the rich, in times of rejoicing and in times of grief.

I was one of those who visited the gardens frequently during the weeks after Mr. and Mrs. Sandford and I came back from Sydney. I had spent many happy hours in the park with Lalla. Now we were all missing her. Mr. Sandford did not want me to take a job during the school holidays. He felt that I should enjoy this time, rest and prepare for classes in the fall. The best place to spend leisure time was in the park. I followed the paths that I had often taken with Lalla and I lingered beside her favourite flowers.

I wrote letters to Lalla every week, and I wrote letters to Eiríkur Gísli Helgi, to my good friend Jón, and to Hendrik Tromp. He was in Lunenburg for the holidays.

One day in late summer I saw a woman who seemed vaguely familiar. I could not think just then where or when I might have seen her before. She was sitting on a bench in the park and she had two young women sitting on either side of her. The girls looked to be about my age, sixteen or seventeen. I could not see the woman's face because she was wearing a large hat decorated with feathers.

I walked past the bench and suddenly it occurred to me that this woman was none other than Mrs. Hamilton. For some time now I had not thought at all about the sick Icelandic girl for whom I had written the letter. I had been very anxious to become acquainted with her at the time, but if I had not seen Mrs. Hamilton in the garden all thoughts of her, of Mr. Ferguson and of the Icelandic girl would likely have been abandoned.

Suddenly I became very anxious to see the lady again and to study the two girls who were with her. I felt sure that I would be able to tell which girl was Icelandic from some indefinable expression or look which I could not define.

I had only gone a short distance from the bench when I decided to turn back. I walked slowly and pretended to be deep in thought. When I came back to the bench there was no one there. I walked all over the gardens for the rest of the afternoon, but there was no sign of the ladies. But now I was determined to meet the Icelandic girl.

A few days later I was lucky enough to see Mrs. Hamilton and the two girls walking around in the park. I noticed that one of the girls had black hair and the other girl had golden blonde hair and blue eyes. She was not really pretty but she had a pleasant, intelligent face. She had a good figure and there was something about her bearing that appealed to me. I thought that Mrs. Hamilton would recognize me if she actually looked at me, and I was going to be ready to lift my hat should she indicate in any way that she remembered me.

I chose my paths in such a way that they would be sure to meet me again. I met them a second time, a third time, and a fourth time and there was never the slightest hint of recognition on the part of the lady and my hat stayed on my head all afternoon.

Hendrik Tromp returned to Halifax one week before classes started at Dalhousie University. He visited me right away and told me that he was going to spend this week having some fun, and he invited me to join him. The first day we went across to Dartmouth and we rented a boat and rowed until we were both exhausted. Rowing and bird hunting were Hendrik's favourite sports, but while we were having fun together hunting was not on the list of activities. We visited Dartmouth several times that week. We toured the town, visited factories, walked along the shore and did some more rowing. On Saturday morning, two days before classes were to begin, Hendrik suggested that we spend the day in the city park. I enthusiastically agreed with this idea. Noon hour on Saturdays, when the weather was good, was a busy time at the gardens. A crowd of people had gathered near the gate. Hendrik pushed his way through to buy our tickets for admission. I waited for him outside the gate. Soon he returned and handed me a ticket.

"See, Eiríkur, there he is," said Hendrik, pointing to the area where the tickets were sold.

"Who?" I asked, scanning the crowd.

"The man who made you come with him to write the letter for the Icelandic girl last winter," said Hendrik.

"Oh, Mr. Ferguson," I said. Then I saw Mr. Ferguson approaching the gate with another young man

"Yes, indeed. Had you forgotten him?" asked Hendrik.

I did not answer his question because just then I saw Mrs. Hamilton about to enter the gate and with her were the two girls.

"Do you see the lady in the light blue silk dress, Hendrik?" I asked.

"Is that the woman with the big hat?" he asked.

"Yes, and do you see the two girls who are walking with her? Do you see them?" I asked.

"Yes, and who are these women?" asked Hendrik.

"The woman in the light blue dress is Mrs. Hamilton and one of the girls with her is the Icelandic girl," I said.

"So you managed to get acquainted with her this summer," said Hendrik, teasing me.

"No, unfortunately. I have only seen her three or four times, walking with Mrs. Hamilton."

"You have never had a chance to talk to her?" asked Hendrik.

"No," I said.

"Then how do you know that she is Icelandic?" asked Hendrik.

"I imagine that she is Icelandic because I know that Mrs. Hamilton has an Icelandic girl in her home."

"So you imagine that," said Hendrik, "and which girl, in your imagination, is Icelandic?"

"The fair-haired girl," I said. "They are coming into the garden now."

"I do not think that the fair-haired girl is Icelandic. I have seen many English girls who look like her. I think the black-haired girl is Icelandic. She looks more like a foreigner."

"Icelandic girls are usually very good-looking," I said.

"That may be," said Hendrik, smiling, "but how are we going to solve this question?"

"I have no idea," I said.

"Are you sure that the Icelandic girl who was with Mrs. Hamilton last winter is still with her?" asked Hendrik.

"I imagine that she is," I said.

"Supposing that your imagination is correct, and it turns out that the girl is still with Mrs. Hamilton," said Hendrik rather smartly, "can you still imagine, dear Eiríkur, that she is there as a maid?"

"Yes, I can easily imagine that," I said.

"And if she is there as a maid, is it possible that she goes out walking day after day with her employer? It is not customary in this country for prominent ladies to go out walking with their maids."

"That is true," I admitted, "but still I am convinced that the fair-haired girl is Icelandic."

"Very good," said Hendrik, "you will have the truth before the sun sets this evening."

"How am I going to manage that?" I asked.

"That is very simple," said Hendrik.

"Maybe you think that I will walk up to the girl, bow politely and say 'Are you Icelandic?'"

"No, I am not suggesting that, Eiríkur," said Hendrik. "Let me explain my plan. We'll go into the park and find the ladies. We will walk one or two fathoms behind them and try to make sure that others do not come in between us and them. Then you will start talking in Icelandic about something or other. You have to talk loud enough to make sure that they will hear what you are saying. So it doesn't seem like you are talking to yourself I will answer you from time to time by saying 'yes' or 'no' in Icelandic."

"And how will you know whether to say 'yes' or 'no'?" I asked.

"When you want me to say 'yes' you will jab my side with your elbow, and when you want me to say 'no' you will pinch my arm," said Hendrik.

"And what next?"

"Nothing," said Hendrik. "I can assure you that if one of the girls is Icelandic, then she will turn her head to see who is speaking in her mother tongue."

"But one or other of the girls might look back just to see who is speaking in a foreign language," I said.

"That is possible, but not likely," said Hendrik. "We'll try it out."

I taught Hendrik to say "yes" and "no" in Icelandic. He had no trouble saying "*nei*" for "no," but to say "*já*" for "yes" was more difficult. It always sounded like "*yow–ow*," just like a cat's "meow."

Soon we saw Mrs. Hamilton and the girls. They had taken a path around the little lake in the middle of the park. In no time we had caught up to them and we slowed down at least a fathom behind them. Now we kept pace with them. I had decided that I would address Hendrik as "Nonni."

"I wish that I could find the Icelandic girl I was telling you about, Nonni," I said, in Icelandic, while I gave Hendrik's side a good poke with my elbow.

"*Já-á á*," meowed Hendrik.

The fair-haired girl showed no reaction at all.

"If she only knew how important it is that I find her, then she would try to contact me," I said in Icelandic and I gave Hendrik a sharp poke with my elbow.

"*Já-á-á*," meowed Hendrik. Neither the fair-haired girl nor the others seemed to pay any attention to us.

"Have you seen her, Nonni?" I asked in Icelandic and I was going to pinch Hendrik's arm but just then two boys passed us roughly and my elbow hit Hendrik's side.

"*Já-á-á*," meowed Hendrik. I pinched his arm in my excitement.

"*Nei*," said Hendrik.

Still the fair-haired girl did not respond in the least.

"Do you know where she lives, Nonni?" I asked in Icelandic, and I pinched Hendrik's arm.

"*Nei*," he said in Icelandic. "My arm hurts," he said in English.

Just then Mrs. Hamilton and the two girls walked over to a near-by bench and sat down. Hendrik and I walked on.

"This is not going very well," I said to Hendrik.

"But now you know that your fair-haired girl is not Icelandic," he said.

"No, I still maintain that she is Icelandic," I said.

"Then we will try another approach and see what happens," said Hendrik. "We'll follow them again after they have a rest and you'll say that the fair-haired girl is about to lose her hairpin. If she is an Icelandic girl and she hears your words she will automatically put her hand to her hair."

"Now, that is a good idea," I said. We walked quickly around the little lake and when we approached the bench the ladies were standing up. They set off once again with Hendrik and me following them.

"Listen, Nonni, do you see that the fair-haired lady ahead of us is about to lose her hairpin?"

"*Já-á-á,*" meowed Hendrik.

The girl didn't check her hair, but, to our great surprise, Mrs. Hamilton raised her left hand and touched the comb that kept her hair in place. Hendrik and I looked at each other. Was this sheer coincidence, or did Mrs. Hamilton understand what we had been saying?

"*Kannitverstan!*" said Hendrik.

"Now you'll say that there is a bit of moss on the shoulder of one of the girls who are walking ahead of us," whispered Hendrik.

After a little while I said, in Icelandic, "Nonni, do you see that bit of moss on the shoulder of one of the girls who are walking ahead of us?"

"*Já-á-á,*" said Hendrik. There was no reaction at first. Then all of a sudden one of the girls stroked her left shoulder as if to remove something that should not be there. It was the black-haired girl.

I looked at Hendrik and bit my lip in dismay. "She is Icelandic," whispered Hendrik.

"That is not true," I said. Just then a large group of people came to meet us and we lost sight of the ladies. We did not see them again that day.

"Do you still think that the fair-haired girl is Icelandic?" asked Hendrik on the way home.

"I have never been as sure about that as I am now," I said, but I didn't give him my reasons.

"*Kannitverstan!*" said Hendrik, and he shook his head. "*Kannitverstan!*"

CHAPTER 5

Studies at Dalhousie University resumed at the scheduled time, and I was now in second year. This year I did not have room and board at the school, as Mr. Sandford wished that I would come home every evening. For one thing, this would be less costly for the Sandfords. Hendrik was sorry to lose his roommate. Now he had another student with him and the two were not very compatible.

Time went by. The days were getting shorter and the nights were getting longer. The weather got colder and colder. Ducks and geese came from the north and continued on their way. Leaves changed color, fluttered through the air, and fell to the ground. Roses and lilies and violets were long gone. Some drooped and died after the first frost. Other flowers recovered, lived out their allotted lifespan, then, in turn, faded and died. The sunflowers survived longest because they were of sturdy build from the beginning. Then came the snow. The city park was closed for the season. The gates would not be opened until spring returned. I was upset when the park closed because that was the only place where I had hopes of seeing the fair-haired girl, who I was sure was Icelandic. Now I would not see her until the winter was over.

There were three things that bothered me at this time. First of all were my classes. Secondly there was my wish to meet the Icelandic girl. And, third, I missed having Lalla in Halifax.

One evening, after we finished our dinner, Mr. Sandford turned to me.

"Ahem! Do you know of many Icelanders here in the city, Eiríkur?"

"I do not know of any, except myself, and the girl who stays with Mrs. Hamilton," I said.

"Ahem! So you do not know of an older Icelandic man here in the city?"

"No," I said.

"Ahem! A man came to the police station today and asked us whether we could tell him where he could get in touch with an Icelandic boy named Eiríkur Hansson. He said that he was Icelandic and he was very anxious to see that boy."

"What did you tell him?" I asked.

"Ahem! We told him to come back tomorrow."

"How did he look?" I asked.

"Ahem!" said Mr. Sandford, "I would guess that he is nearly sixty years old. He is a big man, slightly bent, with huge hands and feet and his beard covers most of his face. He looks harmless. I should say so."

"Does he have a tuft of hair on his nose?" I asked.

"Ahem! That is quite possible," said Mr. Sandford, smiling. "He is a very homely man with a very low forehead. I should say so!"

"Did he give his name?" I asked.

Mr. Sandford took a small book from his pocket. "He said that his name was George Reykjavík."

"I know him well," I said. "He lives a few miles from Cooks Brook."

"Ahem! He doesn't live there now. He lives in room 14 or 15 on the fourth floor of number 70 Grafton Street."

I was very surprised. Was it possible that Geir had moved to Halifax? But whether he had moved to Halifax or not I was sure that he needed my help since he was looking for me.

"I would like to talk to him," I said.

"Ahem! I will tell him to come here at 7 o'clock tomorrow evening," said Mr. Sandford.

The next evening, at precisely 7 o'clock, there was a loud knock at the door.

"Ahem! Here is Mr. Reykjavík," said Mr. Sandford. "I will invite him into the sitting room. You wait for him there."

I went into the sitting room and moments later Mr. Sandford brought in the visitor and left the room himself. The visitor was none other than my old friend, Geir.

Geir stood for a moment in the doorway, holding his hat in one hand and making a face as if he wanted to say, "I don't know this fellow."

I said, "Good evening, Geir. Come in and sit down."

"Good evening, mate!" said Geir, relieved. "I could hardly recognize you, you are so changed." Then he took my hand in his and squeezed it long and hard. He clapped me on the back till I shook from his pounding. Then he shoved his hat into his coat pocket and sat down on the nearest chair.

"You have also changed, Geir, my dear," I said. "It seems to me that your hair is turning grey."

"Right you are," said Geir, shaking his head.

"When did you move to the city, Geir?" I asked.

"This fall, in October," said Geir.

"Will you be here for a long time?" I asked.

"I don't know, mate," said Geir. "But listen, mate, I have much to tell you and some of it is mighty strange." At that he took his pipe out of his pocket.

"Please don't smoke here. Mrs. Sandford cannot stand tobacco smoke."

"Alright, mate," said Geir, putting his pipe back into his pocket, "but I have a story to tell you!"

"Yes, of course," I said, full of curiosity.

"Well, mate," said Geir, "it was this way. Last summer, not this past summer but the summer before, Jenny, my Rachel's sister, moved to Halifax to learn how to sew dresses and how to make all kinds of fancy things. Jenny is awfully good with her hands, you know. She was right away at the top of her class in her sewing school. She could do embroidery and frills just as well as her teachers. You can just imagine what the young men thought when they saw how capable she was. Well, mate, when Jenny had been here in the city for a few months she wrote to Rachel and said that she was engaged to a young and clever officer in the army. After the letter came Rachel spent the whole day laughing and crying by turns. She says that Jenny is the luckiest girl in the entire Red family, and her mother says the same, but old Ruben said that he would like to see a picture of the officer before Jenny made plans to marry him. After a few months Jenny wrote again and said that she was already married and she sent a picture of her husband. He was a handsome fellow, it seemed, in a regular soldier's uniform. There was no fancy stuff on his shoulders like there should be on an officer's jacket. But my Rachel said that the man was very good-looking and therefore it didn't matter what position he had. Then after a few weeks Jenny wrote again. But darn if I heard anything about what that letter said. Then a few days later my Rachel wants us to move to Halifax. We rented the farm out for one year and we moved here last fall and we live now at number 70 Grafton Street, on the fourth floor, and Jenny is in the next apartment. Her husband is only home for two nights in each week, which I think is a strange arrangement. There is something crazy about that marriage, mate. Rachel and I have to provide almost everything that Jenny needs to get by. We have to pay the rent for her apartment, which I think is very odd. I work every regular work day at the sugar refinery and get $1.50 per day and still I never have a cent left over at the end of the week. All this is just a lot of fuss. But listen, mate, now Rachel wants to talk to you, and she wants you to come to see us tomorrow."

"What does she want to talk to me about?" I asked.

"Darn if I know what she wants, mate," he said and he scratched behind his ear as if he would like to say, "That is just mighty strange."

"I'll come after lunch on Saturday," I said.

"All right then, mate," said Geir and he took out his pipe.

"Please do not smoke in here," I said, "because Mrs. Sandford...."

"All right, mate," said Geir, putting his pipe back in his pocket. He scratched behind his ear again, as if he would like to say, "That's a queer woman who can't stand the smell of a pipe." Shortly after that Geir said goodbye and left.

Next Saturday I went to visit Geir and Rachel. As it happened, that day Geir was not at work at the sugar refinery. Instead he sat beside the stove at home and was smoking his pipe when I arrived. Rachel was washing up the dishes and her sister, Jenny, was sitting on a stool beside the window and she seemed quite depressed.

"What! Is it possible that this is Eiríkur?" said Rachel after I greeted them all. "How the dear child has grown! My mother said that he would grow to be a big boy. That has come true. Aren't you altogether surprised, Jenny, my love?"

"Yes," said Jenny sadly.

"And aren't you very surprised, my good George?" asked Rachel, turning to her husband.

"Yes," said Geir, scratching behind his ear, as if he would like to say, "He will never be as broad-shouldered as I am."

"I think that all Icelanders are as big as giants," said Rachel, surveying her husband with satisfaction. "They are not only tall, but they are also exceptionally broad. See, Eiríkur, what I have gained since you visited us last." She pointed to a one-year old boy who was on the floor.

"A beautiful child," I said, flushing a little for no apparent reason.

"This is our little Ruben," said Rachel, and she picked up the little boy and kissed him. "Whom does he look like, Eiríkur? The blessed little sweetheart!"

"He looks like you," I said.

"'No, I am like my Daddy,' he says," said Rachel, lisping a little, like a small child. "'I have my Daddy's eyes and forehead and nose,' he says, and 'I will be big and strong like him, and when I get older I will wrestle with you, Eiríkur, my dear,' says he, 'and then you will have to watch out,' says he. Yes, he says all that. Doesn't he say that, George, my love?"

Geir said nothing. He scratched behind his ear as if he would like to say, "He doesn't really say that, he just thinks that."

"What do you work at, Eiríkur?" asked Rachel. She put the little boy down on the floor and gave him two balls to play with.

"I am studying at Dalhousie University," I said.

"Aren't you just surprised, Jenny, my love?" said Rachel. "Aren't you just amazed, George, my darling? All this has happened to the blessed child! Now he is studying at the University and he will be a doctor or a reverend before we know it. This is wonderful. And my mother always believed that this would come to pass. 'Eiríkur will become a learned man,' she said. Now, George, dear heart, please go and fetch a bucket of water at the street corner. That water is so much better than the water from the pump in the hallway downstairs. I am going to make some tea for Eiríkur."

"No, no," I said, "that is far too much trouble."

"Don't say a word about it," she said shaking her head. "Just go right away, George, my love, and stop at the bakery and buy some cream tortes."

Geir scratched behind his ear, as if he would like to say, "My Rachel is brewing something now." He picked up the bucket and prepared to walk out.

"Oh, what a dear man!" said Rachel, and she blew him a kiss as he was leaving.

"You remember my sister Jenny, Eiríkur," continued Rachel after Geir left. "Now she is no longer Jenny Red, she is Jenny Smart, as Mr. Reykjavík has no doubt told you already."

"I have not forgotten her," I said and I smiled at Jenny who was now sitting at the table.

"It is with regard to her that I have to talk to you," said Rachel. "Her husband, Mr. Smart, is in the army, which is in itself an honourable position, but because he is just a regular soldier, not an officer, he was not supposed to get married so soon. Indeed, he was married without the knowledge of his superiors. He did tell them about it right afterwards. Then they gave him permission, very kindly, to come home to his wife twice each week. Such kindness! That would have been all right if things had remained as they were for the three years he still has to serve in the army. That was not to be. Recently he was told that his regiment is to go early this spring to India[24] and he will be there for the next three years. Now what do you think of that?"

"Can his wife go there, too, and live close to the place where the soldiers are located?" I asked.

"Yes, she could do that, but in the first place she doesn't have the money to get there, and then she would have to have an income to live on once she arrived. Mr. Smart gets only fifty cents per day in pay and fifty cents per day does not pay for food, clothing and household expenses for a child, never mind for a mother and child."

"What are you thinking that you can do about the situation?" I asked.

"Jenny and I and Mr. Smart have come up with a good plan, but we cannot manage it without the help of good people. You and Mr.

Reykjavík could help us as necessary, and I know that Mr. Reykjavík is ready to do that but he doesn't understand us very well because it is so hard for him to learn English. I don't say that to criticize him because I love Mr. Reykjavík as much as any woman could love her husband. He can't help that he finds it difficult to learn English. That is only natural. Now Jenny and I want to ask you to help us to execute this plan that we have thought of, and we ask you to explain everything to Mr. Reykjavík. I know that you will not refuse. You are so good."

"I would be glad to help you," I said.

"Oh, you are such a wonderful young man," said Rachel.

"God bless you," said Jenny, and now a happy expression crossed her face.

"But what is this plan that you have thought of?" I asked.

"I will tell you about it because I know that we can trust you," said Rachel. "This is how it is. Mr. Smart is going to run away from the army and we are going to help him to get to the United States. When he gets there he can get work because he is a good carpenter. Then he will send money to Jenny so that she can join him there and then our problems are over. We have thought of doing this next week. He will shave off his moustache and we plan to dress him in Mr. Reykjavík's Icelandic clothes. They are not worn at all and are stored in his *koffort*. Mr. Smart is going to be an Icelander while he gets to Boston. We are going to ask you and Mr. Reykjavík to take him in a rowboat just past the mouth of the harbour on the day that the ship sails to Boston, get him on board the ship and tell the captain that this man is an Icelander who doesn't understand English, pay his fare for him and ask the ship's crew to look after him until he arrives in Boston. You could add that his friends will meet him there. And you could make it understood that you are coming from Cole Harbour, rather than Halifax. This should all work out if you will be so kind as to help us in this way. We do not know anyone that we can trust, except you and Mr. Reykjavík."

"There is harsh punishment for soldiers who desert," I said, "and it is against the law to help soldiers to run away."

"It can be called unlawful," said Rachel, "but it is not a sin to help a man to run away so that he can support his family. It would be sinful to break up the marriage of two people who love each other. Jenny and Mr. Smart must not be separated, and they shall not be separated until death does them part so long as we have the courage to help them. Help us, Eiríkur, and you will never regret it because you are only doing a good deed. I know that it is a soldier's duty to remain in the army as long as he has promised, but it is a holier responsibility to look after his wife. It is his duty to break laws and army regulations rather than leave his wife to depend on others for her welfare and subject her to a life of sadness and grief."

Then Geir arrived with the water and the cream tortes. Rachel prepared the tea and set the table while I explained the plan that his wife had in mind. He paid close attention, grimaced from time to time, and scratched behind his ear, as if he would like to say, "This is a most unlucky and dirty mess, mate." Still, he agreed to do his utmost to help Mr. Smart to escape.

I had tea and cream torte, and I assured them that I would come to them on the day that the ship sailed to Boston. I listened to a long oration in which Rachel sang my praises. Then I said goodbye to them all and went home.

Then came the day we had talked about. In the morning I told Mr. Sandford that I would not be home that evening because I was going to stay at school with Hendrik the next night and I gave some reasons for that. Mr. Sandford allowed that but he stared at me while I told him about this arrangement at the school. I went directly to number 70 Grafton Street and came into Geir and Rachel's apartment just as Geir was about to shave off Mr. Smart's moustache. They were very glad to see me because I was to play an important part in the drama that Rachel and Jenny had plotted. They were all talking in whispers. Rachel was pale, and Jenny had obviously been crying. Mr. Smart was nervous. Geir seemed very calm. He scratched behind his ear a few times, and grimaced as if he would like to say, "Now, today we'll have to give it all we've got!"

Mr. Smart was almost twenty-eight years old, a man of average height, well-built and of medium weight. He was quite handsome, with fair hair and grey eyes and he didn't look very severe. They were now quickly preparing him for his reckless journey, for reckless it was and much depended on it. It took more than half an hour to remove his moustache. Geir was not a gentle barber. He was too heavy-handed for that type of work. He didn't stop until the moustache was gone with only a few small cuts in its place. That changed Mr. Smart's appearance considerably and when we had dressed him in Geir's woollen suit he was transformed. The trousers were too big, and the pant-legs had to be turned up a little. They looked like a grown man's pants worn by a twelve-year-old boy. The fit of the jacket was even worse. The sleeves were way too long and of course the jacket was far too wide. They folded a large shirt and placed it under his vest between his shoulder blades so that the jacket almost fit. Now Mr. Smart had a decided humpback. On his head he wore a large seaman's hat that belonged to Geir and around his neck he had an Icelandic scarf of a reddish brown color. We wondered what should be done with Mr. Smart's uniform. He couldn't take the clothes with him because customs officials in Boston might examine his bag. There was no safe place in the apartment and it could be expected that a search would be conducted there. Finally it was decided to open the mattress in Geir and Rachael's bed and shove the clothes into the straw filling.

Now Mr. Smart was dressed in his new outfit and he had packed a few things to take with him into a worn old suitcase. He tried to encourage his wife, who was weeping bitterly. He embraced her very tenderly. I saw that his eyes were wet, for soldiers have feelings.

We said goodbye to the sisters and walked out into the street. We had only walked a short distance when we saw that two army officers were coming towards us.

"There come two of my superiors," said Mr. Smart, and he gripped Geir's arm. "They are on their way to check on me. They've thought it strange that I did not report to the barracks this morning as I usually do. I want to cross the street."

I saw that the men were walking at a brisk pace and they would meet us very soon. It occurred to me that it would attract their attention if we all of a sudden hurried out of their way and I decided that it would be better to step into the next store on the street and let the soldiers pass. There was a store just ahead where tobacco was sold. As we approached it I pulled at Mr. Smart and I walked into the store. Geir followed me. Just as we closed the door behind us, the soldiers walked by. Mr. Smart's forehead broke out in a sweat and he was so shaken that he had to steady himself at the counter. Old Geir scratched behind his ear and grimaced a little, as if he would like to say, "That was a close call, mate." We bought a little tobacco for Geir, so that it would look like we had an errand there. Then we hurried along because we knew that within minutes the soldiers would know that Mr. Smart was running away and a search would be on to find him.

We managed to get safely down to the dock where Geir had left the boat he had rented the day before. It was a small boat, intended for four men. We rowed out to Devil's Island, near the mouth of the bay, and waited for the ship that was scheduled to leave for Boston that day. The sun was already low in the sky when we saw the ship coming out of the harbour. We had been waiting for it since shortly after noon. As the ship approached I waved a flag and shouted, "Steamer ahoy!"

"Boat ahoy!" came the response from the ship. Then a bell rang and the ship slowed down. We rowed quickly over to the ship and scrambled on board. One of the crew asked us to explain our errand as quickly as possible. I told him that we had come from Cole Harbour with an Icelander who did not speak English but wanted to travel to Boston. A friend of his would meet him at the pier. I paid his fare, and asked the crew-member to look after him on the way. He smiled and said that no one would hurt him while he was on the ship. He indicated that Mr. Smart should follow him and he asked Geir and me to hurry into our boat.

When we were back in our boat and the ship started off again, the sun was about to set. Now we noticed that we had come a considerable distance south of the mouth of the bay. Devil's Island lay far to the northeast. We hadn't stopped long to get Mr. Smart settled but the ship had moved quite a bit in the meantime. There was a strong wind coming up from the northeast right in our faces and the waves were already crested with foam.

"Listen, mate," said Geir after he took his seat by the oars and studied the weather, "we'll have to make it past the mouth of the bay before it gets dark."

"The sea doesn't look so good," I said as I sat down on the back bench.

"No," said Geir, "there's a stiff breeze and it's going to be damn hard to fight against it." Now Geir was in his element. He rowed deftly. He let the oars stay down quite long each time, and then at the end of each stroke he jerked so hard that the bulwarks creaked. Geir managed to keep the boat in line with Devil's Island. The wind grew stronger until it became an intractable storm. The waves got higher and higher. I realized quickly that we would not reach the mouth of the bay before dark. Things did not look good, to say the least. I shivered from cold and fear. Soon we had water in the boat.

"Listen, mate," said Geir, all of a sudden. "Bail, mate!"

"Are we in danger, Geir?" I asked.

"No, mate," said Geir. "Bail, bail!" I took the scoop and started bailing the water that kept coming into the boat. The effort warmed me up and helped to quell my fear. It was getting dark and the waves rose higher and higher. The island was still far away.

"We are in serious danger, Geir," I said.

"No, mate," said Geir. "Bail, mate." I kept on bailing.

Darkness fell. The storm continued. The boat moved up with the waves and fell down again. I thought that death lay ahead.

Old Geir seemed to put more and more weight on the oars. He used all his strength with each stroke. Our lives were literally in his hands.

"Aren't you tired, Geir?" I asked.

"No, mate," he said. "Bail, mate."

A little later I said, "Would you let me take a turn, Geir?" Geir didn't answer.

All night I sat on the back bench and bailed. All night long Geir rowed with an even pace and without stopping. Once in a while the smell of sweat came back to me and I heard a rattle in his throat or lungs. I could hear that he cleared some froth out of his mouth. I knew that he was very thirsty. Several times I asked him whether he was tired but he never answered. Maybe he said to himself, "I am no weakling." He used all his strength just to keep the boat from drifting and to keep it from going over.

Finally dawn came and the storm began to ease a little. I saw that we were about half a mile from the mouth of the bay. Geir applied more power than ever to the oars and I was actually shocked by his efforts and his endurance. He seemed to gain new energy with the morning light. We found shelter beside the island just as the sun was rising. There Geir rested a while. He was very tired and short of breath. I saw that his fingernails were bleeding. He wiped off the sweat and scratched behind his ear as if he would like to say, "Many a battle I've had with wind and tide in my time, mate, but never quite like this one."

Now I took one oar and we rowed together under his watchful eye. We reached Halifax about noon. We had gone to land before that to have a drink of water. Rachel and Jenny were more than a little relieved when they saw us. They had long since concluded that we must have met with disaster. They were thankful to hear that

Mr. Smart had boarded the ship safely. They praised Geir's courage and hardihood when I told them about our overnight ordeal. Geir and I slept till six o'clock that afternoon, then Rachel did not want me to leave until I had dinner and I accepted her offer.

When we sat down at the table Rachel said, "There was a knock at the door just after you left yesterday morning. I opened the door and there stood two soldiers. 'What would you like?' I asked. 'We have come here to inquire about Mr. Smart,' said one of the men. 'This is not Mr. Smart's apartment,' I said. 'What do you want with Mr. Smart? Isn't he in the barracks?' I said. 'No, Mr. Smart went home to his wife last night,' he said, 'but he did not return to the barracks this morning as he usually does,' he said. 'Where is his wife's apartment?' he asked. 'What?' I said. 'Did he not return to the barracks this morning? Maybe he is sick,' I said. 'I will go and ask Jenny, my sister, about it.' So I went to see Jenny. I told her what to say if the men came in to talk to her. Then I came back here. 'Mr. Smart didn't come home last night,' I said. 'Something must have happened to him. You'll have to look for him' and I pretended to be very worried. 'Poor Jenny thought that he was at the barracks, and if anything has happened to him, please be careful how you give her the news because she has a serious heart condition.'

"Just as the clock there on the cupboard struck four two great big fellows from the army burst into the apartment without warning. Jenny and I were sitting at the table and we were startled. 'What do you want?' I asked, and I was cross. 'I am Major Hopp,' said the older one. 'We are here to look for Mr. Smart. We know that he was here last night, and either he is hiding here or he has run away with your help, and you know where he is,' says he, 'and which one of you is his wife?' says he. 'My sister over there is his wife,' says I, 'and I will never believe that he has run away from his wife, and to suggest that he is hiding here is an insult to his wife and to me,' I says. 'I will take responsibility for searching for Mr. Smart, because I have a warrant to do so,' says he. 'You can search all you like, Major

Hopp,' I says, 'but I can tell you right off that you will not find Mr. Smart here and you should be ashamed of yourself for scaring his wife by telling her that he is missing.' Jenny started crying and I picked up the broom.

"'You should know enough to be ashamed of yourself, Major Hopp, and if you don't get out of here I will make you hop on your head down all the stairs.' The two of them took to their heels and rushed out as if the Devil himself was chasing them. They only touched every third or fourth step. We have not seen them since."

Geir didn't take a bite while his wife was talking. Then he scratched behind his ear as if he would like to say, "My Rachel is quite a diplomat, and that's a fact!"

After dinner Geir, Rachel and Jenny wished me all the best in the future and said that they hoped that they could do something to repay me for my help. Then I went home.

Mr. Sandford asked me right away whether I had a good sleep the night before. I said yes. He said that judging from my appearance he didn't think so. A few days later he told me that Mrs. Reykjavík's brother-in-law had deserted from the army. He said that he hoped that I had not had anything to do with helping him to get away. I was silent, and he understood my silence.

I must add that Mr. Smart arrived safely in Boston. He soon found a good job and he sent his wife money to pay for her fare. In the spring Geir and Rachel moved back to their farm near Cooks Brook. They did not fail to say goodbye before they left. They were all well when I last heard from them. Geir said that I must not forget to see that his life story was published if I ever returned to Iceland. "There are some high points in that story," he remarked. Indeed I think that his story, like the account in his notebook, would be full of dots and dashes, a story of purposeless struggles, for he was like a strong boat without a rudder.

CHAPTER 6

Spring returned after the long winter. Sunshine and warm weather were welcomed by all. Ducks and geese stopped briefly on their way to their nesting grounds further north. Leaves came out on the trees and early flowers burst into bloom. The south wind stirred new energy everywhere. The gates to the Halifax city park were opened. School holidays began. Hendrik Tromp went back to his parents in Lunenburg.

Lalla and her husband came to Halifax and spent a week with us. Lalla seemed happy and yet once in a while I thought I detected a hint of sadness in her beautiful dark eyes. Alphonso was just as he had been when I last saw him. One evening when he sat down to dinner with us I thought that I smelled wine but maybe I imagined that. The words of Uncle Jean were uppermost in my mind whenever I was near Alphonso: "The sins of the fathers reappear in the children in the third and fourth generations." Mr. and Mrs. Sandford did not go to Cape Breton that summer so I did not go either, although I would have liked to go.

Once again my greatest pleasure was strolling through the city park. Several times in early summer I saw Mrs. Hamilton out walking. Sometimes she was alone, and sometimes she had the fair-haired girl with her. The dark-haired girl was not with them anymore. Just as before, Mrs. Hamilton gave no indication that she recognized me.

One day I saw Mrs. Hamilton and the fair-haired girl sit down on the bench where they had often rested the previous summer. I walked past them two or three times but made no sign that I knew them. Then I noticed when they stood up and started off that the fair-haired girl had left her parasol under the bench. Then I saw the girl turn around. I was quick to take advantage of this opportunity. "Isn't this your parasol?" I asked in Icelandic as I lifted up my hat. "Thank you," she said in English but I saw a smile on her lips as she took the parasol, bowed politely and left.

Even though the girl had answered me in English I felt quite sure that she was Icelandic. I felt that I had made great progress in becoming acquainted with her. Later in the day I saw the ladies again. Mrs. Hamilton was talking to another woman and the fair-haired girl stood aside from the two as if she didn't wish to be involved in their conversation. She noticed me right away, smiled quickly and bowed. I smiled also, lifted my hat and continued on my way. "Another step in the right direction," I thought to myself.

About one week later I was walking by their favourite bench and I saw that the girl was sitting there by herself. As I approached she bowed slightly and smiled.

"Good afternoon," I said in Icelandic.

"Why do you speak to me in a foreign language?" she said in English.

"Because that is your mother tongue," I said, in Icelandic, but perhaps a little hesitantly.

The girl smiled. "How do you know that?" she asked in English.

"I have thought that up to this time," I said, "but now I do know it."

She laughed. "I guess you've won the chess game this time," she said, in Icelandic. "I am happy to say that I am Icelandic. I think that you must be the young man who wrote the letter for me when I was sick in bed."

"Yes," I said. "I wrote that letter. May I sit on the bench and talk to you for a few minutes?" It took a lot of courage to ask the question.

"You are welcome to talk to me for a few minutes. As far as the bench is concerned, I have to say that I don't own it any more than you. So if you sit down, then that is your own responsibility, not mine." I saw that she was teasing me.

"I thank you for allowing me to talk to you for a little while. I am so happy to speak to someone who can understand Icelandic. I think that we are the only people in this city who speak our language." I sat down at the end of the bench.

"Well then, Hansson," she said. "Let's speak Icelandic while we have the chance. I am happy to hear my mother tongue. I have not spoken Icelandic for two full years."

"So you know my name?" I said.

"No," she said, "I do not know your name, but I know whose son you are." She was laughing again. "Mrs. Hamilton always calls you 'Master Hansson' so I know that you are the son of someone called Hans."

"My name is Eiríkur," I said.

"My name is Aðalheiður Einarsdóttir.[25] You can call me Heiða if you wish."

I thought that she was being a little forward because in Iceland we never call anyone by their first name unless we know them very well. "I thank you for allowing me to call you Heiða," I said. "Do people here call you Heiða?"

"No, no", said Aðalheiður. "They could never pronounce my

name. Mrs. Hamilton calls me 'Ethel,' and others call me 'Miss Einars.' You can call me that if you would rather."

"I would rather call you Aðalheiður. That is such a beautiful name. I don't know you well enough to call you simply Heiða."

"You don't expect me to believe for a minute that you think my name is beautiful," she said, laughing.

"Anyway, you said that Mrs. Hamilton calls me Master Hansson. Does she remember me?"

"Yes, she remembers you."

"But she doesn't recognize me even though she sees me."

"Oh, yes, she recognizes you but she doesn't care to let you know that."

"What is the reason for that?"

"She has never told me the reason," said Aðalheiður, and she was teasing me again.

"Where were you when I wrote the letter for you?" I asked.

"I was in the next room. I heard all that was said, and I was half wanting to see your face. But I was very sick and everyone thought that I was going to die, except myself."

"And why did I not write your name at the close of the letter?"

"Mrs. Hamilton did not want that for some reason."

"Are you working for Mrs. Hamilton?" I asked.

"Mrs. Hamilton took me in when my Dad died. I did not have anyone here and my mother is in Iceland." For a moment Aðalheiður looked very sad.

"Who is this Mrs. Hamilton?"

"She is a wealthy widow from a noble family, but I do not know any details."

"Is she good to you?"

"I would not stay with her if she wasn't good to me."

"I understand you," I said.

"No," she said, "you do not understand me." She was teasing me again.

"Have you seen me before?"

"Yes, many times. You were following us last summer every time we came to the park."

"Did you ever hear me speak in Icelandic?"

"Yes, once," said Aðalheiður, smiling. "You were with another fellow who was practising meowing. It was hard to keep from laughing that time. You were trying to make me turn around. And when you said that the fair-haired girl was about to lose her hairpin I told Mrs. Hamilton to fix her comb. I enjoyed that. When you said that one of the girls ahead of you had a bit of moss on her shoulder I told Miss Wilford that she needed to brush something off her shoulder. It was fun to trick you that way."

"I can tell you that was when I thought you must be Icelandic. I saw that you were playing games with me."

"You have a sharp eye, I suppose. But why have you been following me? This could look very bad."

"I wanted so much to meet you because you are the only Icelander that I know of around here."

"Well now you have met me. Are you satisfied?" She kept on teasing me.

"I am happy for the moment, but I would like to talk to you again," I said.

"Now there's a problem. Mrs. Hamilton doesn't want me to talk to young men that she doesn't know. She will be coming here within the next half hour. You will have to leave. I am to wait for her here."

"Will I never have a chance to talk to you again?" I asked.

"I don't know," she said, looking into the distance. "It is possible that I will be here next Saturday afternoon, but I am not sure about that. I have enjoyed talking to you. You are so funny."

"I am glad to hear that," I said. She laughed.

"Do you have any Icelandic books?" I asked.

"I have a book of poems called *Snót,*"[26] she said.

"I'll have to see that book," I said. "I love to read poetry."

"I thought that you'd have enough reading to do since you are going to school," she said.

"But I have only two Icelandic books, the New Testament and Jónas Hallgrímsson's poems," I said.

"Well, then, if you lend me Jónas Hallgrímsson's poems, I will lend you *Snót.*"

"That is agreed, then," I said.

"Good," said Aðalheiður. "Mrs. Hamilton will be here soon. Goodbye. Don't forget, Saturday afternoon. Bring the poems."

"Goodbye," I said, bowed and left.

I waited impatiently to see her again. On the following Saturday I was at the park in the early afternoon. I had brought Jónas Hallgrímsson's book of poems. I sat down on the bench where we had talked before. Soon Aðalheiður arrived with her copy of the book called *Snót,* and immediately drew my attention to Bjarni Thorarensen's *Sigrúnarljóð* (Ode to Sigrún). This type of poetry, she said, was much to her liking. I was impressed with her choice.

We exchanged books. We talked a little bit about Iceland and memories from our childhood. She remembered more than I did. Although we were the same age she was older when she left the country than I had been when I left with Afi and Amma. She had often kept watch over the "*tún*" (the homefield) and during her last summer in Iceland she had gone up into the mountains to look after the sheep. She had come to Canada with her father, who was a carpenter by profession. She had spent very little time with her mother but she spoke of her with respect and warmth. I understood that her parents had been together for only a short time. It was difficult for Aðalheiður to talk about her parents. Strangely, her sadness seemed to lend dignity to her face. We planned to meet again the following Saturday, depending on her circumstances. She told me not to come to see her at her house because Mrs. Hamilton would not approve. She laughed a bit as she said that.

"Do you attend the Latin school?" she asked before I left.

"Yes," I said.

"Are you going to be a pastor?" she asked.

"No."

"A doctor?"

"No."

"Oh, I understand," she said, laughing again. "You are going to be *nothing*."

The next Saturday Aðalheiður came to the park but Mrs. Hamilton was with her and neither of them paid any attention to me. I went home in a bad mood.

I saw her three times after that. Once I recited a poem I had written one evening when I was disappointed because I did not find her at the park. This was the third poem I had put together. I was very hesitant and I told her I was sure she had not heard that poem before.

"Let's hear it," she said. "I will listen carefully." I started the poem.

> *Have you not come on a mid-summer's day*
> *to the elm woods?*
> *There the southerly breezes gently play*
> *through the lofty leaves and flowers gay*
> *by the red rose.*

"The elm trees over there are beautiful," said Aðalheiður, looking at the elm trees that stood nearby, "but continue on with the poem."

> *So peaceful to stroll in the morn of day*
> *through the elm woods,*
> *as the breezes waft and the branches sway,*
> *fall asleep and dream your cares away*
> *by the red rose.*

"A gentle breeze through the branches would not put me to sleep," said Aðalheiður, smiling. "I am too fond of the morning sun for that. But go on with the poem."

> *There wandered a lad with a heavy heart*
> *to the elm woods,*
> *no friend or relation to take his part,*
> *alone in the twilight, a soul apart,*
> *to the red rose.*

"I would have chosen to stroll through the wood in daylight," said Aðalheiður, "but I expect that all sad young men would choose to wander around in the dark. Poor fellows! How sad! Continue."

> *How often in carefree mood he'd strayed*
> *in the elm woods*
> *and there embraced that lovely maid*
> *whose promise of heart and hand would fade*
> *like the red rose.*

"What a stupid girl, to promise heart and hand so casually!" said Aðalheiður, looking away into the distance. "Please continue."

> *Often he'd sauntered, his heart on fire,*
> *to the elm woods*
> *through flow'rs soft-blown, in summer attire.*
> *but hope would die and his heart's desire*
> *like the red rose.*

"Yes, even the red roses die," said Aðalheiður. "The poor young man! It was very sad that his hopes died. But let's hear more of the poem."

> *Heartbroken he'd plod on a summer's day*
> *into the elm woods*

"That has been mentioned before," said Aðalheiður.

Tho' kissed by the breeze in the gentlest way

"The breeze was so kind to him," said Aðalheiður. "Surely things will improve."

He ended his life in the brambles' bouquet.

"It was good that he died since life was a burden," said Aðalheiður, "but he should not have gone to the trouble of going into the woods to die."

Red grow the roses.

"The poor roses must have suffered because the young man died among them," said Aðalheiður. "Continue."

"That was the end of the poem," I said.

"That was an abrupt ending," said Aðalheiður.

"And you don't like the poem," I said.

"The poem is not bad," said Aðalheiður, "but the style is not to my liking. Still, the undertone is pleasant. Who wrote this poem?"

"I don't remember," I said.

"You have written it yourself," said Aðalheiður, with a teasing expression on her face. "My advice to you is that you should never again write about young men who kill themselves because that could bring on a real depression. That happened in the case of Thomas Chatterton, who wrote that sort of stuff and died before he was eighteen!"

Her comments about the poem hurt me, I must admit. She seemed to try to distract me as I recited and she seemed to make fun of me. I vowed that I would never show her another poem. I decided that I would never write another poem. There were plenty of poems around anyway.

In spite of it all I saw that she had an appreciation of poetry and that she had her own opinions. I realized that Aðalheiður had a tendency to tease. The more I noticed that the more I cared for her.

Soon I found that I loved her.

Then the summer was over. School holidays ended. It would be impossible for us to meet during the winter. I would be busy with my studies and she was going to attend a women's college. We decided to exchange letters. I would send mine to her college so that Mrs. Hamilton would not see them. She would send hers to Dalhousie University.

CHAPTER 7

The Moose River gold mine was located only three miles west of the old Icelandic settlement. A few of the Icelandic farms had been bought by miners, and should the area of the mine, or miners' homes, move closer to the old settlement then the farms would rise in value. Mr. Sandford realized this, and he determined that I should try to sell the farm that my grandfather had owned, since I was the only heir. He said that it would be better to sell the farm at a low price than to leave it deserted. But because Afi and Amma hadn't left a will, Mr. Sandford said, I would require the assistance of a lawyer before I would be in a position to sell the farm.

So it was that one day Mr. Sandford asked me to go with him to the office of an attorney named Gordon to look into this matter. The office was on the third floor of a large stone building on Upper Water Street. We found that the building had lawyers' offices on every floor. We found Mr. Gordon's office but unfortunately he was not in that day. In fact he was away for three or four days.

"Ahem!" said Mr. Sandford. "I am not going home without talking to a lawyer since there are so many around here." On one of the doors we saw the name of a lawyer called Mr. Sprat.

"Ahem!" said Mr. Sandford. "We'll have a chat with Mr. Sprat." We walked into the office, which was a large room. Beside a table in one corner sat a small, sick-looking boy. He was addressing envelopes. He had a hat on his head and he was chewing something.

"Ahem!" said Mr. Sandford. "Good afternoon, my boy! Is Mr. Sprat here today?"

"Good afternoon," said the boy in a very high-pitched voice. "He will be back right away. Please take a seat." There were plenty of chairs, perhaps ten or twelve. There were no other customers there but on some of the chairs there were books and papers. After a few minutes Mr. Sprat came back. He was a middle-aged man, agile in his movements. He strode into the room as if he was in a foot race. "Ah! Good afternoon, my friends," he said. "Good afternoon."

"Good heavens!" cried Mr. Sprat as he walked over to the little boy in the corner. "Good heavens! Are you going to let the hair rot on your head, boy? Take your hat off right away!" The boy took his hat off hastily.

Mr. Sprat shook hands with us. "Ah! I have seen you before. You are Mr., er...."

"Ahem! My name is Sandford."

"Ah! Now I remember. You are Mr. Sandford. I am very glad to see you," said Mr. Sprat.

"Ahem!" said Mr. Sandford. "I am happy to see you."

"You work at . . . er . . . you are . . .?" said Mr. Sprat as he hung up his coat.

"Ahem," said Mr. Sandford. "I am with the police force."

"Ah! You are still with the police force, Mr. Sandford," said Mr. Sprat.

"If you are not too busy, Mr. Sprat, I would like to get down to business."

"Ah," said Mr. Sprat, "I am always busy but I will take time to talk to you, my friend, yes for an hour or longer. You wanted to talk to me about...?"

"Ahem! It is with regard to the young man who is with me..." began Mr. Sandford.

"Ah!" said Mr. Sprat. "I understand! I understand! This young man has run into debt with some fellow and he doesn't feel like paying it back with interest. Ah! I shall fix that for you, my young friend."

"No," said Mr. Sandford. "It is quite a different matter."

"Ah!" said Mr. Sprat. "Now I understand. My young friend has gotten into a little wrestle with one of his friends, and has been a little too rough. Ah, somebody got a black eye. I'll fix that, my young friend..."

"No, Mr. Sprat," said Mr. Sandford, smiling. "It is not that bad."

"Ah!" said Mr. Sprat. "Not that bad, not quite, just a little argument or two. That will be easier to look after, young friend."

"Ahem!" said Mr. Sandford. "It is with regard to an inheritance."

"Ah!" said Mr. Sprat. "Now I understand at last! Of course it is with regard to an inheritance. Of course the other heirs don't want to give up their rights, my young friend. I will show them the other side of the story."

"Ahem! No, Mr. Sprat," said Mr. Sandford. "This young man is the only heir. But..."

"Ah!" interrupted Mr. Sprat. "The stubborn old fellow is changing his will because the girl is poor. I understand! I understand! I'll talk to the old codger!"

"Ahem!" said Mr. Sandford. "His grandfather is dead."

"Ah! So he is dead. Of course he is dead. And he has forgotten to leave a will."

"Ahem!" said Mr. Sandford. "That is correct. He did not have a will."

"Ah!" said Mr. Sprat. "My good young friend needs to get

'Letters of Administration.' I shall look after that for him. How big is the estate?"

"Ahem!" said Mr. Sandford. "The property is one hundred acres of land in the Mooseland heights."

"Ah!" said Mr. Sprat. "There is gold in the earth in those parts, and a hundred acres should be worth about . . . er . . . five thousand dollars. A nice sum for my dear young friend. I will look after all of this for him."

"Ahem!" said Mr. Sandford. "How much does it cost to get these 'Letters of Administration'?"

"Ah!" said Mr. Sprat. "It would cost in all, through me, Mr. Sandford, let's say, about . . . er . . . er . . . Is my dear young friend related to you, Mr. Sandford?"

"Ahem!" said Mr. Sandford. "He is under my care."

"Ah!" said Mr. Sprat. "I understand. I understand very well. It makes a big difference that my dear young friend is under your care. I will do the work as reasonably as possible since you are involved."

"Ahem!" said Mr. Sandford. "Thank you for that."

"Er . . . Willie!" shouted Mr. Sprat to the boy in the corner. "Bring Blackstone, the book on the table beside you. You don't have to be afraid. The book won't bite you."

"Oh, thank you," said the sick little boy, and he brought the book very quickly.

"Good heavens!" cried Mr. Sprat as he grabbed the book. "Your fingers will rot if you don't wash your hands, boy. Go into the closet and wash right away."

"Yes, thank you," said the poor little boy. He looked as if he would like to disappear through the floor. He probably earned twenty-five cents each day.

"Get going and wash up," said Mr. Sprat in a loud voice. "Don't use my soap, though."

"Yes, thank you," said the poor sick boy. Swollen glands and tuberculosis and Mr. Sprat drained all his strength. He had no advocate. "Thank you." "Take a seat." "If you please." Those three little statements were all he could say. He had no one but Mr. Sprat to speak for him.

"Ah!" said Mr. Sprat. "Will you please wait a few moments, Mr. Sandford, while I look this up in my Blackstone manual?"

"Ahem!" said Mr. Sandford. "I should say so."

"Ah!" said Mr. Sprat, laying aside his book. "What was your grandfather's name, my dear young friend?"

"His name was Egill Þorsteinsson," I said.

"Ah!" said Mr. Spratt, as he picked up pen and paper. "That sounds very foreign."

"Ahem!" said Mr. Sandford. "He was Icelandic. I should say so!"

"So my dear young friend is part Icelandic," said Mr. Sprat.

"Ahem!" said Mr. Sandford. "He is all Icelandic and he was born in Iceland."

"Ah!" said Mr. Sprat. "So he was not born in the British Empire. Oh, so I will have to get him citizenship papers. Oh, I will arrange all these things for my dear young friend! . . . er . . . How do you spell his grandfather's name?"

"Ahem!" said Mr. Sandford. now rather serious. "We won't bother about writing that down until we agree on what to pay you for your trouble."

"Ah!" said Mr. Sprat, raising his voice. "We'll agree, my good friend. Of course we'll agree. We will not argue about a few dollars. We will first note down on paper all the items that relate to this matter. After that we can always discuss the fee."

"Ahem!" said Mr. Sandford, "No, Mr. Sprat, it is best to decide from the beginning whether we agree on the fee."

"Ah! My dear Mr. Sandford, the fee will be very small, because you are involved in this situation."

"Ahem!" Mr. Sandford was looking a little annoyed. "Give me your total fee for the work."

"Ah!" said Mr. Sprat. "Because you are so involved, my dear

Mr. Sandford, the fee will be no more than, say . . . er . . . er . . . about seventy-five dollars, which is . . . almost nothing, and only a small part of that goes . . . into my own pocket."

"Ahem!" Mr. Sandford cleared his throat a little. "I find the fee rather too high!"

"Ah! My good friend," said Mr. Sprat, "the fee is almost nothing, because the work is . . . ."

"Ahem! That may well be, but I am going to discuss this matter with another lawyer and find out how much he would charge."

"Ah!" said Mr. Sprat. "No lawyer would charge less than that for all this work, Mr. Sandford, my friend, not one cent less. We lawyers are all in agreement as far as that is concerned."

"Ahem!" said Mr. Sandford, standing up. "That may well be. Goodbye, Mr. Sprat."

"Ah," said Mr. Sprat, "My time is worth money, my dear friend. I would be glad to spend time talking to my friends, but still . . . my time is worth dollars and cents."

"Ahem! How much do I owe you, Mr. Sprat?"

"Ah! Because my time is to me like dollars and cents, shall we say . . . er . . . two dollars?"

Mr. Sandford took two dollars from his pocket and gave them to Mr. Sprat.

"I thank you, my friend," said Mr. Sprat. "Goodbye, my good friend, and . . . goodbye, my young friend. I am sure I will see you again."

Mr. Sandford and I went home. A few days later we went to the office of the lawyer Mr. Gordon. He was a good-looking man and very courteous. He listened carefully while Mr. Sandford explained the whole situation. He provided "Letters of Administration" for me, sold the farm for $250 and charged very little for his efforts. Mr. Sandford put the $250 into a bank account for me.

A few days later, in the month of September, two men came to see me. One was Eiríkur Gísli Helgi, and the other was the farmer he had worked for over the years. I was glad to see Eiríkur because I had not seen him since he moved to Bridgewater. But now I saw that he was a changed man. He was thin and sick and bent. Instead of a strong man in his late thirties he now looked old. His hand shook and his knees were weak. His face was pale, his hair was grey, and his eyes which used to be so blue and beautiful were downcast and seemed to have a strange glint. He seemed engrossed in thought and unaware of what was going on around him. The farmer said that my friend was mentally ill. He seemed to be rational but he would not admit that he was sick. He wanted to go home to Iceland, and home he had to go, no matter what the cost. He greeted me in a friendly manner but asked me at once whether I knew of a ship that would be sailing soon. Then he sat down and stared blankly around him.

"Have you decided to go to Iceland?" I asked.

"Yes, I have to see mother before she dies," he said.

"Don't you want to wait till spring? It would be more pleasant to come home in the spring," I said.

"Mother will be dead by then," he said.

"No, no, she'll still be alive."

"It would be too late, too late. I have to go today," he said.

"The mail-boat doesn't leave till next week," I said.

"I'll take another ship then," he said. He sat down with a vacant look on his face.

His long-time employer bought a ticket to England for him, gave him one hundred dollars in gold, and said goodbye to him as if he were parting with a well-loved brother.

"Kiss little Maria for me," were the last words that Eiríkur said to the farmer. "Kiss little Maria."

Eiríkur Gísli Helgi spent four days with me in Mr. and Mrs. Sandford's house before he set off across the ocean. I tried to make his stay as pleasant as I could. I took him walking with me in the city and tried to show him things that might be of interest to him.

He seemed to be in a dream and paid little attention to anything.

"When does the ship leave?" he asked each day when we returned to the house after our walks. "I have to see mother before she dies. Poor mother!"

I took him on board the mail-boat just before it was to set sail. I said goodbye to him and I did not forget to thank him for all that he did for me when I was a lonely and faint-hearted kid. I could not hold back my tears when I left that good and generous man for the last time. I never heard anything of him after that. Either he returned to his childhood home to die or he died on the way. Who can say?

"Dear friend!" I said, as I watched the ship depart. "Farewell, dear friend."

CHAPTER 8

I was soon going to be eighteen years old. I had studied at Dalhousie for three years. But what was that compared to being engaged? Yes, I was engaged and my fiancée was Aðalheiður. I will not mention all the daydreams and the hopes that we shared. I will not go into detail about our courtship. I will not describe the first time that the lovelight came into our eyes, when our hands met and our lips touched.

It took a long time for Aðalheiður to confess that she actually cared for me. She held back and often told me that it was ridiculous and even foolishness for youngsters of our age to talk about love. When I finally decided to ask her whether she would marry me she laughed at first. Then she pretended to be a little frightened and said that maybe the right thing would be to stop seeing each other altogether.

"You are a child and you don't know what you are talking about," she said. Our relationship was off and on for some time. Sometimes she scolded me and told me how silly I was and at other times she praised me. She went through almost as many phases as Thetis when she was courted by Peleus. Finally she became my gentle, charming, dear Aðalheiður.

"Yes or no?" I said.

"You have won," she said.

"Yes or no?" I said.

"Yes," she said.

Aðalheiður and I were betrothed.

We agreed that we would not get married until after I graduated from Dalhousie, and perhaps not until I had found a good occupation, maybe as doctor, pastor or lawyer. However things did not work out like that. I did not graduate from Dalhousie University. I did not become a doctor, pastor or lawyer.

As it happened Aðalheiður and I were married shortly before we were eighteen years old. One day soon after our engagement, Aðalheiður came to meet me at the city park. She told me that her kind guardian, Mrs. Hamilton, was moving back to England permanently. She took it for granted that Aðalheiður would go with her.

"Now what do we do?" asked Aðalheiður.

"You refuse to go with her," I said.

"She says that it is my duty to go with her."

"But I will tell her that you are my fiancée."

"Then things will go from bad to worse."

"I will tell her then that you are my wife."

"And how are you going to prove that?"

"With verification from the minister. We will have to get married right away."

Aðalheiður said nothing, but covered her face with her hands.

"Will you agree, dear Aðalheiður, that we get married right away?"

Aðalheiður looked away.

"Yes or no?" I said.

Adalheidur said nothing.

"Yes or no?" I said.

Aðalheiður offered me her hand.

"Yes or no?" I said.

"Yes," said Aðalheiður, "but we must not live together until we are twenty-one years old."

"That will be just as you wish," I said, squeezing her hand.

The following day I found a Methodist minister and asked him to marry Aðalheiður and me that evening. He agreed cheerfully and asked about our age. I told him that I was older than I actually was. I bought a marriage license and waited for Aðalheiður at the southeast corner of the park. When she arrived I called on a driver who had a carriage nearby. He took us to the home of the Methodist minister, who married us right away. The witnesses were the minister's wife, her servant girl and the driver. I gave the minister ten dollars for his trouble and he gave me a marriage certificate signed by himself, his wife and the driver. Now Aðalheiður and I were one before God and man. My wife and I parted at the park. I went back to Mr. Sandford's house and she went back to Mrs. Hamilton's house. Neither of them had any idea that we were engaged, never mind any notion that we were married. To be sure, I had asked Mr. Sandford the night before to lend me twenty dollars, which he did right away, no questions asked. He likely thought that I needed to repay some debt.

Two weeks later, I received a letter from Mrs. Hamilton asking me to come to see her right away. I put the marriage certificate into my pocket and left at once to pay my respects to her. I must confess that I was not looking forward to this meeting although it meant that I would have a chance to see my wife again.

I rang the doorbell at 48 Rosemary Street and the door was opened by a servant girl. She ushered me into the sitting room. I waited only a few minutes and then both Mrs. Hamilton and Aðalheiður came into the room. Mrs. Hamilton's face showed neither sadness or pleasure, neither arrogance nor complacency. It was like a beautiful marble sculpture.

I stood up and bowed. "Good evening, Mrs. Hamilton," I said, "and good evening Aðalheiður."

"Good evening, Mr. Hansson," said Mrs. Hamilton as she sat down.

"Good evening," said Aðalheiður, smiling as she took her seat.

"You received my letter," said Mrs. Hamilton. I could not tell from her voice whether that was a question or a statement.

"Yes, and I thank you for that," I said.

"You know what I want to talk to you about."

"I have no idea," I said. I found that my face reddened a little bit.

"It concerns Miss Ethel Einars." She pronounced Einars as Eenars.

"Indeed," I said.

"I have recently received the news that you and Miss Einars have come to know each other over a very short time, and that your acquaintance has gone quite far."

"That is right."

"No, that is not right. You and Miss Einars had no permission to get to know each other. I am going to forbid any further acquaintance by taking her with me to England this autumn."

"You have no right to do this, Mrs. Hamilton," I said.

"Why not?" asked Mrs. Hamilton.

"Because she is my wife," I said.

"That is impossible," she said.

"Please read this," I said, and I handed her the marriage certificate.

"I do not want to see that," she said.

"That shows that we are married," I said.

"No man has the right to join two under-age youngsters in marriage. Your marriage is in every way illegal," said Mrs. Hamilton.

"I look on that differently," I said.

"Who gave you her hand?" asked Mrs. Hamilton.

"She gave me her hand herself," I said.

"She had no right to do that," said Mrs. Hamilton.

"Who has that right?" I asked.

"I have that right," said Mrs. Hamilton.

"I thought that her mother alone had that right," I said.

"She is in Iceland," said Mrs. Hamilton.

"I have her address," I said.

"You are going to write to her?"

"I have done so." Now I had lied again. Aðalheiður stared at me.

"You are still a child, and so is Miss Einars," said Mrs. Hamilton, "and this undertaking of yours is childishness, pure and simple. I blame this whole thing on you, Mr. Hansson."

"And I am thankful for that, Mrs. Hamilton," I said.

"That is good. But can you support your wife?"

"Yes," I said. Again I did not speak the truth.

"You must not think that I have anything in particular against you, Mr. Hansson," said Mrs. Hamilton. "I know that you are an intelligent and good young man and you will be a good husband to Ethel, but it was an unspeakable childishness on your part to be getting married so young. That is what has caused all these problems."

"And now it is too late to change things."

"I wish it were not too late. I love Ethel as if she were my own child and I find it very disturbing that she should go and marry an underage youngster without my knowledge. But since it has come to this it is best to accept this calmly and try to avoid further problems in this regard. What I do want is that Ethel will come with me to England and stay with me until you come of age and have taken a good vocation."

"I am not opposed to that," I said, and this time I spoke the truth.

"You have promised Ethel that you two will not live together until you are twenty-one years old."

"I promised that."

"And you will live up to that promise."

"But does she want to go to England?" I asked, and I looked at

Aðalheiður, hoping that she would say no.

"She is ready to go, and she will go," said Mrs. Hamilton. Aðalheiður bowed her head slightly and looked at me.

"How long is she supposed to stay with you in England? What assurance do I have that I will see her again?" I asked.

"What God has joined, let no man put asunder."

We were all silent for a little while.

"I will let my wife decide in this matter," I said. "If she wants to go then I will allow that, but if she does not want to go then only death can take her from me."

"You talk like a knight from the Middle Ages," said Mrs. Hamilton, "and at the same time you talk as becomes a sensible young man. You will never be sorry that you obey me in this, Mr. Hansson. I want her to love you as well after three years as she does now. I will call her Ethel and everyone else will call her Mrs. Hansson. You may write to each other as often as you wish, every week if you want. I shall let you know the day before we leave so that you can say good-bye to your wife, but in the meantime you will not see each other."

"Why not?" I asked, frowning.

"It will only make it harder for you to part if you see each other again."

We were all quiet again for a short time. Aðalheiður and I looked at each other.

"You know, Mr. Hansson, that I wish all the best for Ethel," said Mrs. Hamilton.

"Yes," I said.

"You know that this plan will be good for both of you in the end."

"Yes." I was not sure about that, though.

"And you know that you will see each other again."

"Yes." But how was I to know that?

"God bless you, children," said Mrs. Hamilton. "God bless you."

I said goodbye and went back to my home.

For some time I was very angry because Aðalheiður had to go so far away from me and had to be away for so long. I thought that at least it was better that she was my wife before she went away.

Though I was at first very angry with Mrs. Hamilton I soon realized that her plan was best for us. She did love Aðalheiður as if she were her own daughter. After I got over my anger I began to realize that my marriage was in fact ridiculous childishness on my part because I was still a boy. That is not to say that I regretted having married Aðalheiður. No, quite the opposite. But what would my fellow students think if they knew that I was married? They would howl with laughter. What would Mr. Sandford say? "Ahem!" he would say, "Ahem! This was nonsense on your part, my dear Eiríkur. I should say so." My nerves were on edge. If one of my fellow students said, "Hey, do you know what I heard today?" I would turn red. I was always startled if Mr. Sandford said, "Ahem! I want to ask you about something, Eiríkur."

The day before Mrs. Hamilton and Aðalheiður were to leave to go to England, a boy delivered a letter from Mrs. Hamilton. She asked me to come right away to say goodbye to my wife. Aðalheiður and I had only a short time to talk. We sat in the sitting room and Mrs. Hamilton did not leave for one moment. I embraced my wife and kissed her. Tears ran down my cheeks. Aðalheiður wept. Mrs. Hamilton sat by and watched us like a beautifully chiselled marble sculpture.

"You'll see each other . . . again," she said as I was leaving. I felt that the hesitation was so long that she could have added in the word "never."

I went home and I felt as if my heart was broken. For many days after that I could not relax. I wandered around in a sort of dream. I went to the park but there was nothing to interest me there, nothing except the bench where we used to sit. Now I sat there alone and the wide Atlantic Ocean lay between us. My thoughts were always on the other side of the ocean. I thought I heard her whisper carried on the wind, "Dear Eiríkur, dear, good Eiríkur!" And my own inner voice said, "Aðalheiður! Lovely Aðalheiður!" and I thought the birds in the park said "Aðalheiður! Aðalheiður! Aðalheiður! She comes, she comes, she comes." And when I went to bed at night I thought that the breeze on the window pane whispered "Eiríkur! Dear Eiríkur!" But the big clock in the hallway downstairs always said "Aðalheiður! Aðalheiður! Aðalheiður!"

Aðalheiður wrote to me as soon as she arrived in England. She was staying with Mrs. Hamilton in a small city in Devonshire. She said that she was well and happy but I read between the lines that she was missing me. She wrote to me regularly and I did the same for her. I did not hesitate to say how much I missed her.

CHAPTER 9

Shortly after Aðalheiður left Halifax I received a letter from Hendrik Tromp. He said that he hoped I could come and spend the last week of the summer holidays with him. I thought that would be a nice change, and Mr. Sandford agreed. He said that he had never seen me look as downhearted as I had been during the past few weeks. He thought that this visit would be good for me. So off I went to Lunenburg. Hendrik and his parents gave me a warm welcome. Hendrik's mother was a fairly young woman, his father much older. As far as I could see they lived happily together.

One day Hendrik mentioned that there was going to be a "barn raising" at a farm not far from the town. Afterwards there would be a great feast as was the custom in Nova Scotia on such occasions. Many people were invited and Hendrik was one of them. He wanted me to go with him and I went along. When we arrived at the farm men were already working on the barn and women were preparing meals for the day, especially for the big dinner that would be served in the evening.

The framework had been put together and lay in four sections on the ground. Poles and beams and rafters had been prepared ahead. In an amazingly short time, the framing was up, the roof was shingled, the walls were clad, the floor was laid. Doors were installed and vents were looked after. The barn was finished.

Tables were set up in the new barn for the men, and tables were set up in the farmhouse for the women. After the dinner a dance would be held in the new barn and the fun would go on till morning. The tables were loaded with food. A five-year-old ox, well-fed, had been slaughtered for the meal. There were all types of vegetables so well prepared that the more one tried the more one wanted to sample. There were many types of bread, various kinds of fruit, baking and beverages. Alcoholic drinks would not have been available even if life depended on them.[27]

There were many men there but the hosts had made sure that there were enough tables that all could sit down to their meal at the same time. At the end of the largest table sat a man who seemed different from the rest. He wore a striped shirt and he had a silk kerchief tied around his neck, with the knot at the back. He had a "parrot nose" and a distinctive voice. He seemed to be in charge of his table. He talked incessantly and all the men listened to him with interest. Hendrik told me that this man had been away from Lunenburg for many years and had only recently returned. "He likes to talk about his adventures and put on airs," added Hendrik.

"I am going to eat like an Icelander," said the man with the parrot nose.

"Oh, have you seen some Icelanders?" asked one of the men.

"Have I seen them?" asked the man with the parrot nose. "I have seen many of them, probably hundreds. I saw many of them in the gold mine in Tangier and worked with them there. They used to live up in the Mooseland hills. Now they have all left. I believe they went north to Hudson Bay. It was too warm for them here. They have a strange language. They say 'm-yow-ow' for yes and 'n-a-ay' for no. They call girl '*stelka*' and boy '*drinka*'. If they say '*blessa manskja*' they are very good, but if they say '*anda fjanda*'[28] then you're going to catch it."

Hendrik jabbed me with his elbow.

"Do they like to eat?" asked one of the men.

"Do they like to eat? You can't fill them up! They eat anything, cooked or raw.

"They don't always find the food they were used to in Iceland. For example, 'Iceland moss.' A lot of this moss grows in Iceland. They dry it there, then grind it up and make bread out of it, and sometimes they make porridge. When they came to the Mooseland hills they saw that lots of moss grew on the maple trees. Here you know that this moss is used for dye, never for food. But the Icelanders were happy to see the moss on the trees. They picked bagfuls of it. They tried to cook pots of the moss but the longer they boiled it, the tougher it became, and so they had to throw it out."

All the men laughed except Hendrik and me.

"Are they good-looking men?"

"They are big people. The men are like giants and the women are as stout as barrels but the girls, you could say they are beautiful. Their hair is a golden color and their cheeks are like red roses in the snow. At least that's what Benjamin Ford thought. Benjamin lived out near Spry Bay. He has a mole on his nose and he is also a bit cross-eyed. He is well over six feet tall and a good strong build at that.

" 'You're never going to find a wife, Ben dear!' said his mother.

" 'Is that so? We'll just see about that!' said Ben.

" 'Maybe you could catch one of those Icelandic girls up there in the Mooseland hills,' said his mother. So Ben hitched up his old grey to the buggy and headed straight-away up to the Mooseland heights. He thought he would introduce himself with a little gift, a half barrel of herring. He walked into one of the cottages. He set the barrel down beside the bed. The Icelanders have their bedroom, sitting room, dining room, pantry, and kitchen all in one. The farmer was lying on the bed with his hands behind his head and he was chewing on a plug of tobacco. Two old women were standing beside the stove, and the farmer's daughter was sitting in a corner of the room. Ben thought the daughter would be a bonnie wife. He tried to explain that to the farmer, and he tried to explain that to the two old women and finally he tried to talk to the girl herself. He hoped the half-barrel of herring would help him plead his case but the people did not seem to understand him at all. They sent for an interpreter from the next house. In the meantime Ben had three cups of strong tea and a big bowl of blueberrysauce.

" 'The Icelanders make a good blueberrysauce,' Ben reported later, 'but the tea is strong enough to kill an ox.'

"When the interpreter came he couldn't understand what Ben wanted. They sent for another interpreter but that was of no help either. 'I'll have to think of a way,' said Ben to himself. He pointed to his heart, and he took the girl in his arms and kissed her. No interpreter was needed after that. The old women howled and the girl screamed and the old man got up from his bed. He pulled the plug of tobacco out of his mouth and stuck it into his vest pocket. He walked over to Ben, took hold of his shirt collar with one hand and the bottom of his pants with the other hand and he threw him headfirst out the window and the window sash followed.

"Was Ben hurt? Yes he was hurt. Both shoulders were dislocated and his nose broken too. Then the old man went out, grabbed Ben's right hand, put one foot in Ben's armpit, and jerked the shoulder joint back into line. He did the same with the left side. Then he tossed Ben into his buggy, threw the half-barrel of herring in with him, untied the horse and sent them off. The horse didn't stop till they got back to Spry Bay. Ben went pale every time Icelanders were mentioned after that!"

"Those Icelanders must have the strength of giants," said someone in the crowd. Hendrik jabbed me with his elbow.

"Oh," said the man with the parrot nose, "I will tell you another story about that.

"One day they brought in a new anvil at the Mooseland mine. The anvil weighed three hundred and twenty pounds. Several men got together to try to lift the anvil as a test of strength. Many of the men could not budge the anvil, some lifted it just a few inches from the ground, a few men lifted it as high as their knees, and two men lifted it up to their chests. At that point Archibald came by. He is more than six feet tall and he looks like a three-headed monster, his shoulders are that big. Archibald walked over to the anvil. His mouth twisted to one side in a sneer and he rolled his eyes. He put his palms under the corners of the anvil, lifted it up to his chin, stretched out his arms and let the anvil fall.

" 'That's off the shoulders,' said Archibald. He sneered his one-sided sneer and he rolled his eyes again.

"An Icelander happened along in time to see these goings-on. He was carrying four bushels of potatoes to sell. He threw down the potatoes (he had two bags on his back) and he went over to the anvil. He took hold of the two corners.

" 'Stand down on the anvil, Archibald,' he said. He did not speak very good English. 'Stand down into the anvil,' he said, 'and hold all your hands around all my shoulders.' Archibald jumped up on the anvil and put his hands on the shoulders of the Icelander. 'Up-p!' said the Icelander, and he lifted the anvil and the man up over his head and threw the whole lot behind him. Archibald landed four fathoms behind him and the anvil a little closer.

"That came from the shoulders,' said Archibald. He stood up, shook himself, rolled his eyes and walked away. Was he sneering? No, not Archibald. He just rolled his eyes and walked away."

"The Icelandic men are obviously known for their strength," someone remarked, "but are they honest people?"

"Oh, honesty itself!" said the man with the parrot nose. "One time an Icelander bought a pound of tea from Taylor, the merchant at

Corback. Soon after, the Icelander came back, reached his hand over the counter and he said, 'These are yours, Mr. Storekeeper. They were put into the tea by mistake.'

" 'Wha- wha- wha- what?' said Taylor. He stammered quite badly and he never managed to overcome that problem. 'Wha- wha- wha- what is that?' He asked again.

" 'Those are lead shot, shot for a shotgun,' said the Icelander.

" 'P- p- p- put them into the keg over there,' said Taylor.

" 'First we will put them onto the scales over here,' said the Icelander. Onto the scales went the shot. 'Two ounces,' said the Icelander, 'two ounces of tea.'

"Taylor was flustered and by mistake he put out eight ounces of tea. 'No,' said the Icelander, 'just two ounces and no more.' Then he left with his tea. There was never any lead in Taylor's tea after that."

"Do the Icelanders like tea?" asked one of the men.

"Oh," said the man with the parrot nose, "they drink a lot of tea. I'll give you an example of that. You've all heard of Jacob Prest, that famous hunter who killed forty-two bears in one winter. He killed one of them with an ordinary axe, and he wrestled with another one and broke its back. That one weighed 570 pounds. That was some hunter, that Jacob Prest! He had an Icelandic man working for him. That man worked like a trojan, but could he ever eat! Mrs. Prest did not spare food on the table, and she never begrudged what the Icelander ate, but could that man drink tea! Mrs. Prest had a hard time keeping up with the tea he needed. It was quite a long way to go to the well to get the water."

"Are they intelligent people?"

Hendrik grinned as he glanced at me out of the corner of his eye.

"Oh, they can be clever and shrewd," said parrot-nose. "It is not easy to fool those guys. I can tell you a good story about that.

"There is a man named Joseph Red. He lives in Upper Musquodoboit. He is a prosperous farmer, also known as quite a trickster. 'Listen here,' said Joseph Red to four of his neighbours, 'do you want to hear how I am going to play a trick on one of the Icelanders?' 'Yes,' said the neighbours. 'Well,' said Joseph, 'I know of an Icelander who wants to sell a cow. I am going to offer to buy the cow but then I am going to prove that I don't have to pay for it. Of course I am going to pay for it sometime later on.'

"Joseph and his neighbours went up to the Mooseland settlement and found the Icelander who wanted to sell a cow.

" 'What are you asking for the cow?' asked Joseph.

" 'How much are you willing to pay for the cow?' asked the Icelander.

" 'Fifteen dollars for each of her horns when she arrives at my farm,' said Joseph slyly.

" 'I'll agree to that,' said the Icelander innocently. Then Joseph gave the Icelander a note saying that he would pay fifteen dollars for each whole horn and he would pay the money after one month, at the office of Mr. Reid, the old justice of the peace.

When the cow arrived at Joseph Red's farm, she had no horns on her head because Joseph had hired a veterinarian, en route, to cut off the horns.

The Icelander arrived at Mr. Reid's office at the appointed time. Joseph and his four neighbours were already there and the cow was tied to the gate. The Icelander passed Joseph's handwritten note to the justice of the peace.

" 'Did you write this note, Joseph?' asked Mr. Reid.

" 'Yes,' said Joseph, 'and here are the witnesses.'

" 'I understand then that you are to pay thirty dollars today,' said Mr. Reid.

" 'No, I don't have to pay a cent because the cow had no horns when she came to my farm,' said Joseph Red, 'and here are the witnesses.'

" 'I swear that the cow had horns when she came to his farm,' said the Icelander, 'and furthermore, I swear that those horns are still there.'

" 'They are not whole horns,' said Joseph, 'and in the note it says "fifteen dollars for each whole horn.'

" 'I swear that the cow had whole horns when she came to his farm, and they are still there,' said the Icelander.

" 'We'll look into that,' said the justice of the peace and they all walked out. 'Indeed the cow has no horns,' said Mr. Reid, 'That is obvious.'

" 'She has four feet though,' said the Icelander.

" 'True enough,' said Mr. Reid, 'but feet are not mentioned in the note.'

" 'On each foot she has a cloven hoof and each hoof is whole,' said the Icelander.

" 'That is quite right,' said Mr. Reid, 'but the handwritten note does not mention those.'

" 'So the cow still has eight whole horns,' said the Icelander, 'and the note says fifteen dollars for each whole horn. So I ask for one hundred and twenty dollars in payment.'

" 'The hoofs are not horns,' said Mr. Reid.

" 'Are they bone?' asked the Icelander.

" 'No, they are not bone,' said Mr. Reid.

" 'Are they cartilage?' asked the Icelander.

" 'No,' said Mr. Reid.

" 'Is there meat in them?' asked the Icelander.

" 'No, of course not,' said Mr. Reid.

" 'What are they made of then?' asked the Icelander.

" 'Horn, I guess.' Mr. Reid sat, chin in hand, and thought. Joseph blinked. The neighbours looked at him and at the Icelander by turns. They didn't know whom to support at this point.

" 'One hundred and twenty dollars in payment,' said the Icelander, rubbing his hands together.

" 'You will have to pay that, Joseph,' said the justice of the peace, 'because what is written must be honoured.'

" 'I don't have so much as one cent,' said Joseph Red.

" 'I'll take the cow back then,' said the Icelander, 'and three more cows with her.'

" 'I guess you will have to agree to that,' said the justice of the peace.

" 'Mercy! Mercy!' said Joseph Red. The Icelander did not understand that word. His English was not very good, he said. A few days
later he had three more cows than he had the year before."

"Oh, those fellows are something else," said someone in the audience.

"Here is another good story," said parrot-nose. The after-dinner
entertainment continued.

"There were hard times among the Icelanders in the Mooseland
heights. They were short of good clothing. Their brothers in faith
here in Lunenburg sent them stores of clothing and yard goods.
Old Rev. Paterson from Halifax was asked to allot these gifts
because he is a very fair-minded chap. Among the Icelanders who
received gifts there was one healthy-looking young man. He didn't
say, 'Give me, give me,' like some of the others. Instead he examined the yard goods. 'Take it, take it,' said Rev. Paterson. 'This
could be used for a suit for the oldest boy,' he said. 'Take it, my
friend, take it,' said Paterson. 'This would make a nice dress for my
oldest daughter, and this would make a christening gown for the
youngest child,' 'Take it, take it,' said Rev. Paterson and he gave the
young man one piece after another. 'All for the wife and children,'
he said. 'How many children do you have, my friend?' 'The sixth
and the last one will be one year old when the eldest will be twelve
years old.' 'Bless me! What a large brood to look after and he is still
so young!' said Rev. Paterson. When the parson was told later that
the young man had neither wife nor children, he was very angry.
'You lied to me,' he said. 'You have no children, and not even a
wife!' The young man glowered at the parson. 'I never told you that
I had a wife and children. I said that when my youngest child
would be one year old, my oldest would be twelve years old. And if
I do not have a wife and six children in twelve years' time then you
can take back all the goods that you have given me today.' Old Rev.
Paterson wiped the sweat off his brow and said, 'Bless me! Bless my
soul! If Nova Scotia had one man like that in the legislature then
our financial standing would be safe and sound.' He knew that

there would be no point in arguing with an Icelander."

This was met with laughter around the table.

The man with the parrot nose said, "Their tolerance is absolutely unbelievable. I had an Icelandic friend once. He was something else! He lifted a barrel of kerosene up on the counter. He took a sip from a barrel of Danish Brandy just as if he was holding a two-pint jug. He told me that where he came from he was just a weakling compared to the other guys. Then he broke his leg. The doctor had to amputate but his tools were dull and in poor shape. The procedure was taking a long time. 'I am going to put you to sleep with chloroform,' said the doctor. 'No, no,' said my friend, 'I prefer to stay awake to see how the job is done.'

"And I have one more story," said the man with the parrot nose. When I was working in the Caribou mine there was an Icelander there. We called him Jonky. (He pronounced Jonky as Yonkey.) Of course that was not really his name but we couldn't say his name. There were about fifty letters in that name and it ended with 'son.' They are all somebody's sons. We often had fun with Jonky. You couldn't make him angry. We tried to tease him in any way we could think of. We thought it would be a sight to see an angry Icelander. We put a little bit of powder in with his tobacco, so there were little explosions in his pipe when he was smoking. But no, Jonky didn't get upset over a little thing like that. We put salt in his tea, but he just drank it as if he did not notice. We did all we could to annoy him. He never got angry. 'An eye for an eye, and a tooth for a tooth,' said Jonky but he never gave us tit for tat. But when we were about to go to sleep then Jonky started to sing Icelandic songs. That singing was enough to kill us all. The tune was always the same, a very tiresome tune, and each part always ended with a refrain that was almost as long as the tune itself. Oh he was just killing us with that song. 'He is singing Psalms,' said Harry Lee, the foreman. 'You can't deny anyone the right to sing the Psalter.' No one suffered more from the singing than Harry Lee himself because he liked to sleep in the evening. Finally the singing became so unbearable that he bought a pound of cotton so he could plug his ears. After that he could tolerate the noise. 'An eye for an eye and a tooth for a tooth,' said Jonky but we did not understand what he meant at the time.

"Long afterwards Jonky built a cabin for himself, about a mile and a half from the Caribou mine. At that time he was cutting fire-wood for Harry Lee. One night in the middle of winter the cabin burned down and Jonky narrowly escaped, dressed only in his underwear, and not able to save anything that he owned from the cabin. That night he walked barefoot to the Caribou mine. The temperature was reported to be five degrees below zero Fahrenheit. Jonky was not chilled and his feet were warm. This sort of thing was unheard of. 'Who would have set fire to the cabin?' asked Harry Lee. He thought that someone must have intended to burn Jonky in the blaze. Jonky thought the same. 'It was Andy Scott Fantor,'[29] said Jonky. 'We'll have to find that scoundrel,' said Harry Lee. 'Does anyone know of that man?' No one had heard of that name and he was never found."

"It would be fun to meet an Icelander," said one of the men. "Here is one," said Hendrik, pointing to me. At that the man with the parrot nose looked at me, grabbed his hat and ran out. I never saw him after that. He must have gone home and he did not return to dance that evening.

CHAPTER 10

Hendrik travelled with me to Halifax. We arrived three days before my classes were to begin at the Dalhousie University, but it was not meant to be. The very evening that I came home Mr. Sandford became seriously ill. He had not been feeling well for a few days but he had continued to go to work. The morning after I came home he was worse than the day before. He did go to work but he came home before noon.

"Ahem!" said Mr. Sandford. "There is some strange drowsiness in my head. I feel hot. I should say so!" Mrs. Sandford and I saw that he was very ill. We got him into bed and I went right away to find the doctor, who happened to be a good friend of the Sandford family. He looked very serious when he emerged from Mr. Sandford's room. "Go quickly to the drug store and pick up this prescription," he said to me and this I did. Mr. Sandford seemed to be getting worse as the day went on. When the doctor came back in the evening he stayed for quite a long time. When he left he looked more serious than before. Mrs. Sandford and I now knew that the situation was dangerous.

"Ahem! Where is Lalla?" asked Mr. Sandford. "She will be here soon," I said, and I ran out to send her a telegram. If she was able to leave right away, it would take her twenty-four hours to come home. She would have to cross the Strait of Canso and take the train from Port Mulgrave to Halifax.

Three doctors took turns looking after Mr. Sandford, and Mrs. Sandford and I took turns at his bedside.

"Where is Lalla?" asked Mr. Sandford. "She will be here soon," we said. "Ahem!" he said. "God bless you! God bless you!" Then Lalla came and her husband with her. Lalla was very pale. "Has Daddy died?" she asked. "Dear mother, dear Eiríkur! Has Daddy died?"

"No," said Mrs. Sandford through her tears.

Lalla went into her father's room and knelt at his bedside. She kissed her father on the forehead, patted his hand and wept. "Dear Daddy!" she said. "Don't you know me, Daddy? This is your Lalla, your little Lalla. I have come here to be with you." It seemed at first that he didn't know her but then all of a sudden he smiled. "Ahem! Is it you, dear Lalla? I – am – so glad. God bless you, my child!" Then he seemed to drift off again. "Ahem," he said a little later, "where is Lalla?" "I am here, dear Daddy. I am here to stay with you."

The day passed, and the next night and the next day, and Mr. Sandford was getting weaker all the time. Everyone in the house was very quiet. People spoke in whispers. We walked on tiptoe. We all seemed to hold our breath. Many callers came and went, moving through the house like ghosts. The policemen came, one after another, slipping quietly into the sickroom and out again.

For some time Mr. Sandford had been unconscious. Then all of a sudden, "God bless you, Jenny," he whispered. Jenny was his wife. Then "God bless you, Lalla! God bless you, Eiríkur! God – bless – you – all!" Then he faded into a sleep again. The doctor held his left hand and his wife held his right hand. Their minister stood by the headboard, and Lalla knelt beside the bed. The others stood by. The doctor gave the minister the sign and the minister announced to us all that Mr. Sandford had died. We all wept.

"Blessed are the pure in heart, for they shall see God."

The funeral service was very impressive. The coffin was handsome, there were many wreaths and there was a large gathering. The newspapers in Halifax carried a picture of Mr. Sandford along with a short account of his life. He was praised for his endurance, for his devotion to duty in the police force, for his dedication to his family as a loving husband and father, and for his loyalty to his many friends.

Now he had died. The editors had not noticed all his virtues until he was gone. It hurts me to think that often good people are not properly acknowledged until it is too late.

Mr. Sandford had died. He did not leave behind gold or silver or real estate. He did not even own the house that he had lived in. His salary from the police force had only sufficed to look after the requirements of his family.

Instead he left behind love and respect in the minds of all who had known him. For that reason so many friends were eager to help and to encourage his widow in her time of sorrow.

Alphonso had come to Halifax with his wife a few days before Mr. Sandford died, but he did not spend much time with us at the house. He was often out somewhere in the city, and when he came back I could often smell alcohol on his breath. I had to conclude that he had become a chronic drinker, and I remembered what Uncle Jean had said.

The day after the funeral Alphonso went back to Cape Breton but Lalla stayed to help her mother. The plan was that after a couple of weeks we would all go to Sydney because Lalla wanted her mother to come to live with her, and that was Mrs. Sandford's wish as well. It was decided that I would stay with them in Sydney until Christmastime and then go back to resume my studies at Dalhousie after the New Year, with help from Lalla, or rather from Alphonso, because Lalla did not seem to have much control over their money.

Lalla now had a little daughter, named Juliet in honour of Alphonso's mother. Lalla had left little Juliet with her grandmother in Cape Breton when she came to Halifax to care for her father. Of course, Lalla was looking forward to going home to be with her little girl.

Now it happened that a few days before we were planning to leave I suddenly took sick myself. I was up and about for one or two days, and then I was confined to bed. I had never in my life been seriously ill and in the beginning of this sickness I really thought that my days were numbered. Around this time I received a letter from Aðalheiður. I was not able to write to her myself so I asked Lalla, who was nursing me, to answer the letter for me. I told her how things were, that I was married and that Aðalheiður was my wife. I told her to use her own judgement as to what to say about my illness, because the doctor had probably told her what he thought about it all.

Lalla listened to my story and said nothing for or against my decision to get married. She just patted my cheek like the good sister that she had always been. I knew that she wrote to Aðalheiður. I remember that she read the letter for me, but I do not remember the content of her letter because I was soon "out of it" myself.

I became disoriented and unaware of what was going on around me. I realized vaguely that Lalla sat beside my bed and that she leaned over me from time to time and tried to get me to drink something. I was aware that someone held my wrist and I thought that it was Hendrik Tromp and that the boys from Annapolis Royal were with him but they all disappeared. I also thought that Dr. Dallas and Mr. West were there. Soon they were gone too. I was swimming and swimming, close to drowning. Then a boat came sailing over the sea. I managed somehow to climb into the boat. There was someone sitting at the oars. It was old Geir. "Bail, mate, bail, bail, bail!" he demanded over and over. We were caught in a waterspout. The boat was tossed up, up, up, higher and higher — and finally I was thrown right up into the moon. It was awesome to look down at the earth. I felt dizzy. I could see the western hemisphere, much of the Atlantic Ocean and a little rim of the Pacific Ocean.

But what was this? Iceland was just east of Newfoundland. Now it was southeast of Newfoundland. Iceland was drifting! It was being carried by the wind to the south, south, further and further to the south, south to Nova Scotia, south to Florida, south all the way to Cuba. I had to tell somebody about all of this! Geir had disappeared. I was lying in a bed, I did not know where. Someone was beside me. I did not know who it was. Soon I thought I was at sea again. I was on my way to see Aðalheiður. I went through the Strait of Gibraltar, into the Mediterranean Sea. That must be the way to Aðalheiður. I went through the Suez Canal, the Red Sea, through the Indian Ocean, past Ceylon, through the Straits of Malacca, past the China Sea, past Japan. Now I was gliding through the air, over the Pacific, to America, over the Rocky Mountains, over the prairies, over the Great Lakes, over forests and hills, over cities, to the Atlantic. Hurrah! I had travelled around the world. One could travel around the world in less than eighty days! What would Jules Verne think about that? I set off into the ocean to find Jules Verne. Oh, it was no trouble for me to swim. Captain Webb had only just managed to swim the English Channel. Lord Byron was almost done in when he swam the Hellespont. But I was swimming across the Atlantic Ocean so easily.

All of a sudden I saw two women coming towards me. They were walking on the ocean, holding hands. They were Lalla and Aðalheiður. I was swimming again, but now I had lost my concentration. I was having trouble. "Help!" I was drowning. "Help! Help! Help!" I was going down . . . .

Then I was in my bed again. There were people around my bed.

Someone was bending over me. Someone wiped my forehead with a soft cloth.

People were whispering. "You go to sleep. You are so tired. I will watch tonight. You go to sleep." I had heard those voices before. But where had I heard them? The voices were so soft, so soft, speaking in such loving tones, just like a mother putting her child to sleep. Oh, it was good to go to sleep, to be a little child, to be rocked and rocked, listening to a lullaby. I was a little child. My cradle was rocked and rocked, ever so gently. "Sleep, my dearest, sleep, my dearest."

"No, I would rather watch. I am not tired. Oh, I have to watch!" I loved those voices!

"No, sweetheart, you must sleep tonight. He is out of danger! You must sleep, you must sleep."

I was at home in my bed. I opened my eyes and looked around the room. Lalla sat beside my bed. She smiled at me and I smiled back.

"Oh, I slept so soundly," I said, "but what dreams I had!"

"Yes, you slept soundly tonight, dear Eiríkur," Lalla said. "Now you will be getting better." She wiped my forehead with a soft cloth and she patted my hand. "You are getting better, thank God!" she said. She looked so thin and pale.

"I know that you have watched over me tonight, dear sister," I said. "You are so good!"

"I only watched over you for half the night," she said, "Thank God, you are so much better."

"Yes, I am getting better. I could get dressed today."

"No, no, not today."

"Well, tomorrow then. I am thankful that this sickness was not as serious as I thought yesterday. It is nothing to be sick for three or four days. I hope that we can travel next week as we had planned."

Lalla looked away briefly.

"Don't talk any more just now, dear Eiríkur," she said, "you are still weak."

"No, I have never been weak. I just had a cold yesterday and the day before. Now I have slept so well and I am all better. But what dreams!"

Lalla brought a glass half-full of some liquid and she asked me to drink it. "Now try to sleep again," she said.

I felt that I had slept enough. It must be late morning by now. But I rolled over, and fell asleep again.

When I woke up again Lalla was still sitting beside me. I thought I heard someone walk out of the room.

"You are getting better," said Lalla.

"I am going to get dressed," I said.

"No, dear Eiríkur, not today."

"Surely tomorrow!" .

"We will just rest until tomorrow." Then she gave me something to drink. It tasted good. I was so thirsty. She gave me something more to drink. This time it tasted even better. I perspired so much. She was always wiping my face. She brought one cloth after another and kept wiping more and more. She read two or three short stories for me and she read a few little poems. Later in the day I fell asleep again.

The next morning when I woke up Lalla was sitting beside me and she said, "Good morning."

I said, "Good morning, Lalla. I'll get up today, because now I feel fine."

"We'll wait until later in the day," said Lalla. "Do you remember that I wrote a letter to your wife?" she asked.

"Yes, you wrote it on Monday, and now I guess it must be Friday," I said. "I hope that the letter has not gone yet because Aðalheiður will worry if she thinks that I am sick."

"So you think I wrote it last Monday?" asked Lalla. "Now I can tell you that five weeks have gone by since I wrote the letter."

I stared at Lalla. "Have I been in bed for five weeks?" I asked.

"Yes, you were at death's door for five weeks."

"And have you been watching over me all this time, dear sister?"

I asked.

"Not all the time, but some of the time."

"I know you have been watching over me. You are so pale," I said.

"I sent your letter right away," said Lalla. "Then I wrote another letter myself a little later."

"Did Aðalheiður answer?" I asked.

"The answer will come tomorrow. Will you please rest easily until then?"

"Yes . . . How I wish I could see Aðalheiður!"

"She will probably come before too long," said Lalla. "I have a feeling about that. We'll wait until tomorrow and see what the letter has to say."

"I hope that you and Aðalheiður will be good friends," I said.

"Yes, we'll be good friends," said Lalla.

For the rest of the day Lalla sat beside my bed, and we talked about Aðalheiður. In the evening I fell asleep with Lalla's words in my mind: "We will hope and wait." Next morning when I woke up Lalla was not sitting at my bedside as usual. In her place was another woman, young and beautiful, but pale. It was Aðalheiður, my wife! She had come over the ocean to look after me and be with me, never to leave me again.

We embraced each other, kissed each other, cried for joy! "Dear Eiríkur! God be praised! You are getting better!" said Aðalheiður. She held me in her arms while she wept tears of relief and thanksgiving.

"Aðalheiður! You came across the ocean, to be with me and to help me through this illness. We must never be separated again!"

"No, we must never be parted again!" said Aðalheiður. "We will be together till death do us part!"

No one could be happier than I was at that moment. My loved ones were with me! They had rescued me from the grip of death. All of a sudden I felt so well, I felt so strong and healthy. Beloved Aðalheiður! Dear Lalla! My wife and my sister! Then Lalla came into the room and I saw that she smiled at Aðalheiður and gave her a hug. I thought to myself, "All's well with the world. Dearest Aðalheiður and dear, dear Lalla are best friends!" My illness had brought them together like sisters.

CHAPTER 11

Soon the doctors agreed that I was out of danger. Then Lalla went back to her home in Sydney. Mrs. Sandford, Aðalheiður, and I went there between Christmas and New Year's. That year they did not have a white Christmas in Nova Scotia. The weather was so mild that flowers still bloomed in sheltered places until the tenth day of January. This kind of winter was unheard of at that time.

The doctors told me that I should not plan to resume my studies at Dalhousie that winter, so I decided to stay in Sydney for awhile and try to find an office job while I explored other options. I thought that the Picquarts might have some type of work that I could do on a temporary basis. Aðalheiður and I had two rooms in Mr. Picquart's house for our own use. We did not want to be separated again and Mrs. Hamilton relented on that score. "What God has joined, let no man put asunder." Mrs. Hamilton corresponded regularly with Aðalheiður, and always when she wrote she included a gift of money, maybe two pounds sterling, or four pounds, sometimes five pounds or even ten pounds.

In the spring the Picquarts gave up their business and it became clear that they had large debts to contend with. Many people found this quite surprising because old Mr. Picquart had operated a successful business for many years, and he had always been a reliable businessman. "It is all Alphonso's fault," said Uncle Jean. Many people in the area now knew that Alphonso had a serious alcohol problem and that he also had taken to gambling. Many people were saddened by this but it was especially hard for Lalla. She must have wept quietly, by herself, both at this time and later on.

I soon realized that I would not be able to continue my studies and look after my wife. I could no longer hope for any financial help from Lalla or the Picquarts because they would now have enough problems of their own. I still had $200 left from the sale of Afi's farm but that sum would not go far. I loved my studies but I loved Aðalheiður a thousand times more. I sacrificed my education so that I could be with my wife. Farewell to happy college days, farewell to my friends. Farewell to the study of Latin and Greek, farewell!

In Sydney I could not find any work that interested me. Aðalheiður and I decided to go out west, to the prairies, and take a homestead farm. I wrote to my old friend Jón, who was now studying law in Dakota. He wrote back right away and said that conditions there were promising. This was indeed true. I saw that it would be better to go than to stay.

One day in midsummer, Aðalheiður and I set out for Winnipeg with four hundred dollars. Two hundred were a gift from Mrs. Hamilton to Aðalheiður. It was very hard to leave Lalla and her mother. We promised to write Lalla regularly and we asked her to let us know if we could assist her in any way. I wrote to Hendrik Tromp and the boys from Annapolis Royal, and also to Dr. Dallas and Mr. West. I did not forget to write to Geir and his wife. I thanked them all for their friendship and their help over the years.

I wished them well and I said goodbye.

We did not go to Halifax from Sydney. Instead we went over to Antigonish and from there to Truro, and west through New Brunswick, to Levis, Montreal, Toronto and Sarnia, then over the Great Lakes to Duluth and on to Winnipeg. The trip was very good and nothing special happened to us on the way.

Still, I was a little startled just after we boarded the train in Antigonish. Aðalheiður and I had turned one of the benches around because we had two large suitcases that did not fit under the seats. We had just arranged things in this way when a very stout woman entered the railway car. She did not see another empty seat so she pushed the suitcases to one side and sat down across from us. I saw at once that this was none other than Mrs. Patrick.

"Well, well, well," said Mrs. Patrick, quite out of breath. "What terrible heat! Bless me!"

Aðalheiður admitted that it was quite warm. I rushed to open the window. "Bless me!" said Mrs. Patrick as she wiped the perspiration off her face. "Bless me! The breeze is so refreshing!"

"Move the suitcase more to the side so that the lady will be more comfortable," said Aðalheiður in Icelandic. I did that.

"Well, well," said Mrs. Patrick. "You speak a foreign language. Well, well."

"Yes," said Aðalheiður.

"But you are neither French nor German," said Mrs. Patrick.

"We are Icelandic," said Aðalheiður.

I was no longer afraid of Mrs. Patrick, but we had never been reconciled so I had no wish to let her find out who I was. Aðalheiður had never heard anything about the lady and had no idea that I did not wish to get into a conversation with her.

"Well, well, well!" said Mrs. Patrick, and she looked towards me as if she was studying me. "So you are Icelandic. And where have you come from?"

"From Sydney," said Aðalheiður.

"So you would know the Picquart family."

"We lived with that family," said Aðalheiður.

"Well, well," said Mrs Patrick. "They are friends of mine. Bless me! And I understand that Mr. Picquart's son is married to the daughter of Mr. Sandford, who was at one time a good friend of mine."

"Yes, Mr. Sandford's daughter is married to Alphonso Picquart," said Aðalheiður. I was wishing that Aðalheiður would talk about something else.

"This is beautiful weather," I said.

"Yes, lovely weather," said Mrs. Patrick, and she stared at me. "Lovely weather, but a little too hot. Bless me. But where does Mr. Sandford live now? Is he also in Sydney?"

"He died," said Aðalheiður. I wanted to tell her to say no more.

"Well, well, well," said Mrs. Patrick. "Did he die? Did Police Officer Sandford die? He was undeniably a good man."

"Yes, he was a good man," said Aðalheiður.

"So you knew him well?" asked Mrs. Patrick.

"No, I hardly knew him," said Aðalheiður, "but my husband knew him well. He was really Mr. Sandford's foster son." I wanted to jump out the window and I knew that my face turned red.

"Well, well, well!" said Mrs. Patrick. "I thought that – Mr. – Sandford – never had – a foster son." And she looked at me long and hard. She thought she recognized the face.

"And you are Icelandic?" she said after a short pause.

"Yes," said Aðalheiður.

"And you are married?"

"Yes," said Aðalheiður, smiling.

"Well, well," said Mrs. Patrick as she looked at me. "Bless me. So you are married. You are a very young couple, no doubt recently married."

"Yes, recently married," said Aðalheiður.

"Well, well!" said Mrs. Patrick, looking at me, "May I ask, what is your husband's name?"

"Hansson," said Aðalheiður.

I could not sit still any longer. "Please excuse me if I leave you for a little while," I said.

"Where are you going?" asked Aðalheiður.

"I am going into the smoking car," I said. Aðalheiður stared at me because she knew that I never smoked. I bowed and left. I was thankful that I had managed to get away.

"Well, well!" said Mrs. Patrick as I was leaving. "So your husband's name is Annsinn, and you are then Mrs. Annsinn. Well, well."

"My husband's name is Hansson, Eiríkur Hansson," said Aðalheiður.

"Well, well," said Mrs. Patrick. "Is his name Irokkur Annsinn!" I was in the next car by this time.

Aðalheiður smiled.

"I used to know an Icelandic boy named Irokkur Annsinn," said Mrs. Patrick, "but I always called him Pat. I think that he is your husband."

"I think that is impossible," said Aðalheiður.

"I am sure about that," said Mrs. Patrick. "Bless me! I know it. The face is the same. It is more mature, but it is Pat's face. Pat was a good boy, a lovable boy. You have found a good man. Be good to him, Mrs. Annsinn, always be good to him. I wanted to be good to Pat. I was going to make him my son. Kiss Pat for me, kiss Mr. Annsinn, and ask him to forgive me if I was harsh and stern with him. I will be in the next car behind when he comes back. I get off the train in Truro. Goodbye, Mrs. Annsinn, and kiss Pat for me. I was fond of Pat."

She went into the next car and Aðalheiður thought she saw tears in the lady's eyes when she left. When I returned to our seat, Aðalheiður told me what the lady had said. Then I told Aðalheiður who this woman was and I told her all about my time with her.

We stopped for a short time in Winnipeg and there I met my

friend Jón. We were very happy to meet again and we talked about bygone days, days of valour and fame.

Then we travelled farther west, on to the prairie, and there we chose land for a homestead. Friends told me later that we had chosen well. We had a little cabin built that fall. The next year we had a good harvest and an even better harvest the following year. Aðalheiður and I managed well on the farm. After three years we had a large, well-built house. By this time we had 640 acres of land instead of the 160 acres that we started with. Our neighbours said that we were prosperous. I found that it suited me to be a farmer. To me it has brought freedom, honour, and blessings of many kinds. Farm people are, on the whole, the healthiest, the best and the happiest people.

I built our house on a hill. We planted a shelter belt around it for protection from winter winds and for shade in summer. Below the hill a small river winds through our land. Only a few scattered houses are to be seen as we look across the grasslands to the west.

Nine years passed from the time that we left Nova Scotia. Every now and again Aðalheiður received letters from Mrs. Hamilton. We always kept in touch with Lalla. Her mother had died. Now Lalla herself was a widow. Alcoholism likely contributed to her husband's early death. He was not by nature a bad man. In some ways, he had not had a good upbringing.

Lalla had two children, a girl, who was eleven, and a boy who was eight years old. She was poor now and she had few relatives. Her parents-in-law were poor and elderly and they barely managed to look after their own needs. I wrote to Lalla and invited her to come west with her children to stay with Aðalheiður and me for as long as she liked. I sent her money for the journey.

So nine years after we left Nova Scotia, just when the prairie was turning green and the crops were starting to grow, we had a surprise. A wagon arrived at our front door one morning. Aðalheiður ran out because she knew who the caller must be. I waited in the sitting room. After a few minutes a little boy came in to see me.

"Uncle Eiríkur," said the boy, "here I am."

"You are welcome," I said and I took the boy in my arms and kissed him.

"My name is Eiríkur," said the boy. "Mama and Juliet are talking to Auntie. We have travelled all this long way to see you, Uncle Eiríkur."

"And I am so pleased that you came," I said.

"Do you know what?" asked the boy, "I nearly fell out of the window on the train, but Mama caught me. Mama is so clever and so good, let me tell you!"

"It is good that she caught you in time," I said, as I hugged him again.

Just then a pretty little girl came into the room. She stopped in the doorway, looked quickly at me and then looked down at the floor. She was so shy.

"You are welcome, dear Juliet," I said. "Come to me, my dear." Juliet ran into my arms, gave me a hug and leaned against me.

"Uncle Eiríkur!" said Juliet.

"God bless you, my little girl," I said as I kissed this lovable, innocent child.

Then Lalla and Aðalheiður came in. Tears came to my eyes when I saw Lalla. She was so changed. She was so thin and tired. Adversity had left its mark on her face. The trials of life can change a face in such a short time.

I got up from my chair and I walked to the doorway. I took Lalla in my arms and held her close. "Dear sister, you and your children are welcome," I said. The tears ran down my cheeks.

"My dear brother!" said Lalla and she wept as she embraced me.

"This house will be home to you and the children for as long as you wish," I said.

"Yes, as long as you wish," said Aðalheiður.

"I thank you, my brother, and my sister!" said Lalla.

This was a day of celebration for us all. It was the happiest day of our lives. Lalla and her children brought warmth and joy into our home. Our house had never seemed as beautiful in our eyes as it seemed that day. The trees around the yard seemed to have a new dignity. The fields had never seemed so wide and the prairies had never seemed so green before. The birds never sang quite so beautifully before that day. Never had we seen so many wildflowers growing all about. The spring breeze was refreshing. We were blessed with warm sunshine and a wide blue sky.

"We love this place," said Lalla, just a few days after their arrival.

Now two years have gone by since Lalla and the children came to our house. Aðalheiður and I, Lalla and the children are all happy and content.

For some years I have wanted to go back to Iceland.

I would like to see the place where I was born. I would like to see the places that I remember from my childhood and the farms I visited with Amma before we left the valley of the Lagarfljót.[30]

We would all like to go there sometime. Lalla has been reading Icelandic books and she speaks the language surprisingly well. Many Icelandic people who visit us think that she is Icelandic and that she is in fact my sister.

During the past few evenings I have been reading this story to Aðalheiður and Lalla. They say that I have told the story correctly as far as they themselves are concerned but that I have left out one important part. I have to agree.

I say that I will write about that separately. They both smile.

THE END

ENDNOTES

1   búr — pantry.

2   skyr — curdled milk.

3   baðstofa — a combination living room/bedroom.

4   fell — an isolated hill or mountain.

5   fillip — a strike with the fingernail as it is snapped quickly
     from the end of the thumb.

6   Following the eruption of the Dyngja Mountains in March,
     1875, the fall of pumice (as much as two to three inches in
     depth) covered an area of approximately 2,500 square miles.

7   Lagarfljót — *fljót* is a large river that floods periodically,
     while *á* is, simply, a river

8   Seyðisfjörð — the main port in Eastern Iceland in the nine
     teenth century.

9   an attempt to speak Danish.

10   Mozart lived 1756–1791.

11   Egilsstað — Egil's place. In Icelandic tradition the Christian
     name is commonly used, with the patronymic as an adjunct.
     Therefore, it is Egil's place, not Þorsteinsson's place.

12   The Icelandic settlement was named Markland, a name
     taken from the Vinland Sagas. Markland was the name
     given by Leif the Lucky to a forested land that he
     discovered.

13   Cracknell has sometimes been wrongly identified with Mr.
     Wilson, the teacher who actually worked at Markland.
     Cracknell is likely based on several teachers who struggled to
     find ways to teach immigrant children, Icelandic and many
     others.

14   Eiki — the short form of Eiríkur, as Tom is for Thomas.

15   Jónas Hallgrímsson — a natural scientist and a well-loved
     nineteenth-century poet.

16   Bluenose — an inhabitant of Nova Scotia.

17 In Icelandic wrestling, a move called "catch with the heel" or "backheel" [*hælkrók*].

18 Egill, a poet and one of the earliest settlers in Iceland.

19 Njáll, law speaker and hero of *Njáll's Saga*.

20 Snorri Sturluson (1179–1241), a famous writer who recorded many of the sagas, which had been preserved only in oral tradition up to that time.

21 Grettir, Gunnar, Skarphéðin — heroes from saga times.

22 Dr. Guðbrandur Vigfússon and G. F. Y. Powell published *An Icelandic Prose Reader*, Oxford University Press, 1879.

23 The Battle of Sedan was fought between Prussia and France in 1870.

24 Britain was involved in a number of disputes along the Indian border during the late nineteenth century.

25 The name Aðalheiður means noble, magnanimous, generous, bright.

26 *Snót* — a book of poetry, poems by renowned poet Bjarni Thorarensen.

27 There were many prohibition groups in the U.S., Canada and Europe in the late nineteenth century. *The Order of Good Templars,* founded in Utica, New York, in 1851, was a society of abstainers dedicated to the promotion of temperance and suppression of the liquor traffic. Lodges were formed in Iceland in 1884 and in Winnipeg, Manitoba, in 1887. In Winnipeg, the Icelandic lodges Skuld and Hekla were particularly active. (See W. Kristjanson, *The Icelandic People in Manitoba: A Manitoba Saga,* pp. 264–265.)

28 The man with the parrot nose, talking about the Icelandic language, says *stelka* for *stelpa* (girl), *drinka* for *drengur* (boy), *blessa manskja* for *blessuð manneskja* (blessed person) and *anda fjanda* for *andskotans fjandi* (a damned enemy).

29 "Andy Scott Fantor" was probably what Harry Lee thought he heard when Jonky swore *"andskotans fantur"* (*andskotin,*

Satan, and *fantur,* a heartless ruffian) i.e. "some damned brute".

30 Some of the places that Eiríkur and Amma visited before they left the valley of the Lagarfljót were Meðalnes, Miðnes and Dagverðarnes; and the rivers Rangá, Eyvindará, Jökulsá and Gilsá. Hallfreðarstöð, Hnefilsdal, Sleʔbrjót and Steinsvaði. Amma had friends or relatives in or near all of these places.

ABOUT THE AUTHOR

Jóhann Magnús Bjarnason
May 24, 1866–September 8, 1945

Jóhann Magnús Bjarnason came from Iceland to Nova Scotia in 1875. He was nine years old at the time and travelled with his parents and his young sister. They lived in the Icelandic settlement known as Markland for seven years, and then moved to Manitoba in 1882.

While in Nova Scotia Magnús attended a school provided by the provincial government. The teacher, a Mr. Wilson, encouraged Magnús to improve his English by reading English literature, generously lending him books from his own library.

Magnús served as a teacher in Icelandic communities in rural Manitoba for some thirty years. He was known as an innovative teacher, and remembered for taking a personal interest in all his students. Because of his familiarity with the English language he was frequently called upon to act as interpreter and unpaid legal adviser for newcomers from Iceland. He added a great deal to community life wherever he lived. For example, he formed drama clubs, wrote twenty plays, and was director, actor or coach as needed.

He was a prolific writer, publishing novels, short stories, articles and poems. Most of his work was written in Icelandic, directed at a particular reading audience. Many of the short pieces were donated to a literary magazine called *Tímarit*, which was published annually in Winnipeg. On his seventieth birthday the government of Iceland bestowed on Magnús their country's highest honour, membership in the Order of the Falcon, in recognition of his contribution to Icelandic literature.

Magnús believed that it was important for immigrants to learn good English, and to fit into Canadian society. He believed that each group of immigrants brought with them a unique culture, which should contribute to life in the new homeland. The members of each group should be proud of their heritage and should not allow their own values to slip away while they acquired new ideas. He was one of the earliest proponents of multiculturalism.

Two former students who became medical doctors, practising in Saskatchewan, kept up a lifelong friendship with Magnús. They were Dr. Jóhannes P. Palsson and Dr. Kristján Austmann. They encouraged their old teacher to retire in their area so that they could look after him in his senior years. Magnús and his wife, Guðrún, a devoted couple, moved to Elfros, Saskatchewan, in 1922. They both died in 1945. She died first, and he died less than one month later. In Elfros, a monument erected in his memory was unveiled in July, 1945.

OTHER WORKS BY BJARNASON

Bókaútgáfan Edda, Akureyri, Iceland published new editions of Jóhann Magnús Bjarnason's work in the collection:

RITSAFN

Ritsafn, Vol. I: Gimsteinaborgin (*City of Precious Stones*), 1977
Ritsafn, Vol. II: Í Rauðárdalnum (*In the Red River Valley*), 1976
Ritsafn, Vol. III: Brazilíu Fararnir (*Travelers in Brazil*), 1972
Ritsafn, Vol. IV: Eiríkur Hansson (*Eiríkur Hansson*), 1973
Ritsafn, Vol. V: Vornætur á Elgsheiðum (*Spring Nights in Mooseland Hills*), 1970
Ritsafn, Vol. VI: Haustkvöld Við Hafið (*Autumn Evenings at Seaside*), 1971

Volumes I, V, and VI are short stories. Vol II, III and IV are novels. Bjarnason published many poems, articles and short stories in Icelandic cultural magazines such as the annual *Tímarit*.

WORKS CITED

Beck, Richard. "Jóhann Magnús Bjarnason," a preface to Jóhann Magnús Bjarnason, *Gimsteinaborgin: Saga og ævintýri*. Akureyri: Bókaútgáfan Edda, 1977.

Bjarnason, Jóhann Magnús. *Eiríkur Hansson: Skáldsaga frá Nýja Skotlandi*. Akureyri: Bókaútgáfan Edda, 1973.

—. *The Young Icelander*, a translation of *Eiríkur Hansson*, by Borga Jakobson. Halifax: Formac Publishing Company Ltd., 2009.

—. Letter to Eyjólfur S. Guðmundsson, March 28, 1930.

—. Letter to Eyjólfur S. Guðmundsson, October 7–9, 1930.

Laxness, Halldór. *Í túninu heima,* Reykjavík: Helgafell, 1975.

Stephansson, Stephan G. Bréf og ritgerðir I. Reykjavík: 1938.

WORKS CONSULTED

Bjarnason, Jóhann Magnús. *Gimsteinaborgin: Saga og ævintýri*. Akureyri: Bókaútgáfan Edda, 1977.

—. *Ævintýri*. Reykjavík: Fjallkonuútgáfan H. F., 1946.

Kafka, Franz. *Amerika: The Man Who Disappeared*, translated by Michael Hoffmann. New York: New Directions, 2004.

Küchler, Carl. *Geschichte der Isländischen Dichtung der Neuzeit (1800–1900)*. Leipzig: Hermann Haacke, 1902.

Nejmann, Daisy. *The Icelandic Voice in Canadian Letters*. Carleton: Carleton University Press, 1997.

Ringler, Dick. *Bard of Iceland: Jónas Hallgrímsson, Poet and Scientist*. Madison: University of Wisconsin Press, 2002.